...WAYS

...ork, Ireland. She is the bestselling author of *Darkhouse*, *The Caller*, *Blood Runs Cold*, *Time of Death*, *Blood Loss* and *Harm's Reach*.

For more information about Alex Barclay and her books, please visit her website, www.alexbarclay.co.uk

Praise for Alex Barclay:

'The pace is fast; the twists never feel forced; and the denouer...

'The rising star of the hard-boiled crime fiction world, combining wild characters, surprising plots and massive backdrops with a touch of dry humour'   *Mirror*

'Tense, no-punches-pulled thriller that will have you on the edge of your deckchair'   *Woman and Home*

'Explosive'   *Company*

'*Darkhouse* is a terrific debut by an exciting new writer'
     Independent on Sunday

'Compelling'   *Glamour*

'Excellent summer reading . . . Barclay has the confidence to move her story along slowly, and deftly explores the relationships between her characters'
     Sunday Telegraph

Also by Alex Barclay

Darkhouse
The Caller
Blood Runs Cold
Time of Death
Blood Loss
Harm's Reach

ALEX BARCLAY

Killing Ways

HARPER

Harper
An imprint of HarperCollinsPublishers
1 London Bridge Street
London, SE1 9GH

www.harpercollins.co.uk

This paperback edition 2015
1

First published in Great Britain by HarperCollinsPublishers in 2015

Copyright © Alex Barclay 2015

Alex Barclay asserts the moral right to be identified as the author of this work

A catalogue record for this book is available from the British Library

ISBN: 978-0-00-813286-6

Set in Meridien 10.25/13.5 pt by
Palimpsest Book Production Limited, Falkirk, Stirlingshire
Printed and bound in Great Britain by
Clays Ltd, St Ives plc

MIX
Paper from
responsible sources
FSC **FSC® C007454**
www.fsc.org

To Moira Reilly,
Thank you for being your warm, wise, and wonderful self.
With you here, the book begins on the perfect note.

PROLOGUE

Amanda Petrie stopped dead in front of the skeletal wreck of a creature stumbling toward her on legs like knotted spindles. The woman looked to be in her sixties, bruised, wounded and terrified. She was dressed in a faded blue nightgown draped no differently than if it was on a hanger in a store, except that it was caked in filth of all kinds, and it stank like something inhuman. Her matted gray hair grew between bald patches, she was missing teeth, she was hollow-cheeked, she was a shell.

Amanda dropped her cell phone, didn't even notice how it bounced and cracked and spat out its battery, how the binder she'd been holding struck the ground, broke open, sent loose pages from magazines sliding across the concrete.

From the awful silence that followed, Amanda began to hear something – a soft pit, pit, pit. She looked down. A bright photo of a rainbow-themed garden party had floated from the binder and landed between the old woman's dirty feet. Maggots were dropping onto it – pit, pit, pit – from under her nightgown.

Amanda turned away, heaving. She pressed her hand

tightly over her mouth. Her eyes bulged and watered. Slowly, she turned back to the woman.

'I'm sorry. I'm so sorry,' she said. 'Are you OK? I mean . . . do you need help? Obviously you need help . . .'

The woman stood before her, wide-eyed, not a blink. And from this desolation, Amanda noticed eyes the most incredible shade of blue, and was suddenly struck with an image of a baby girl in a bassinet smiling up at her parents, innocent, expectant, hopeful, years from this.

'Where did you come from?' said Amanda, looking around. They were on a quiet road in an isolated part of Sedalia, sixty miles southwest of Denver, Colorado. She was there only to check out a venue for her sister's surprise fortieth. She had just crossed it off her list.

The woman didn't reply.

Amanda took a step away from her, then crouched down to gather the parts of her phone, putting them back together with a shaky hand.

Kurt Vine was driving along Crooked Trail Lane, in his 1984 cream and brown pickup with the camper shell, radio off, cigarette burning down in the ashtray, running through the events of the previous night. He was on Level 9 of *Hufuki*, a video game with a great Japanese-sounding name that all the players understood was really an abbreviation of Hunt, Fuck, Kill. You just couldn't say it out loud. Kurt had hunted down, raped and murdered forty-two victims to get to Level 9 out of 10. It was getting exciting. He had missed a few obvious traps in the last session. He should have known better. Some twelve-year-old kid in Ohio had beaten him. It was embarrassing. But Kurt was undeterred – no one had officially reached Level 10. There was a rumor that once you unlocked that world, real girls played the victims. You chased their avatar, but the screams were real, live, and you could see their faces in the right-hand corner of the screen, see their fear. Whether anything was being done to these girls to elicit these reactions was not something Kurt Vine considered. They were in a distant universe. They were the unreal real.

Every night, Kurt heard voices from all over the world in his ear, every accent imaginable, the tower of fucking Babel coming through the internet into his headset. When a player pissed him off, beat him, humiliated him, he would mimic them on the walk from the sofa to the bathroom or the bedroom or the kitchen. But only if he had ever heard their reactions when they knew it was game over, man. Loser sounds. Who wants to mimic the soundtrack to a rival's victory?

Winning was important to Kurt Vine. He had a narrow focus, a regular grip on just a few small things . . . a games console, a camera, a bottle of Diet Coke, and his dick.

The camera was for taking photos of old buildings that he uploaded to his website, ForTheForgotten.net 'To honor those who lived and worked within these walls', wherever those crumbling walls may have been.

At the bottom of the site, he had a DONATE NOW button, a low-key 'If you like my work, please consider contributing to my film, development, and print costs'. He was thinking of setting up an online store to sell some of his work, he was thinking of offering his services to corporations, or news organizations or stock photo agencies. Kurt thought about a lot of things. But mainly he thought about easy things, things that required no effort.

Kurt Vine had inherited most of his grandfather's estate – including thousands of sprawling acres in Sedalia that were dotted with brush and ruins. The land and buildings were

Kurt's outright, but the remainder of his inheritance – the cash part – was dwindling fast. The donations were his only real income, and they were typically small. Sometimes he felt guilty that a lot of his donors were visual arts students, who likely couldn't spare the money but wanted to reward him for his talent, probably in the hope that the same kindness would be offered them when they were spat out into the world after graduation.

Despite the modest student endowments, there was a new Nikon on the passenger seat beside him. Nine months earlier, an email had come into his inbox. YOU HAVE A DONATION. He clicked on it, expecting the usual ten or twenty dollars. This was different. This was $10,000. He looked at it for a while, and he mistrusted it for a while longer. And then he spent most of it. And, six months after the donation came in, he got the knock on his cabin door. The man who stood there smiled and said: 'I've come to collect my debt.'

Weird shit always happens to me, thought Kurt, as he ran through the woods of his fantasy land, chasing screaming women.

He got hard just thinking about it. Kurt was always alone when he got hard.

Amanda Petrie dialed 911, her heart pounding.

'*Nine-one-one. What is your emergency?*'

'Police, ambulance?' said Amanda. 'I'd like to report . . . a lady here, who's in a state of extreme neglect, I think. She's . . . very thin, very wasted.'

'*Ma'am, what number are you calling from?*'

'My number is 555-360-9597. That's my cell phone. My name is Amanda Petrie.'

'*And what is your location, ma'am?*'

'We're in Sedalia, Douglas County . . . um . . . I pulled

in to the side of the road to take some pictures. The last place I remember is Crooked Trail Lane? I'm about a five-minute drive from there.'

'Can you give me any more details, ma'am?'

'Can't you track my location?' said Amanda.

'We don't have that facility here, ma'am.'

'Oh,' said Amanda. 'Well, I can't really say. I'm just seeing road and trees, a couple of barns. I think I've driven about seven miles from an inn called Russell's?'

'Ma'am, is the woman you are with in need of medical attention?'

'Yes.'

'We're going to send help right away for you, ma'am, and I'm going to keep you on the line with me, get some more details from you. Are you in a position to stay with her while we send help?'

'Yes, yes, I can,' said Amanda. 'Please hurry, though. Please hurry. She's very distressed.'

'Thank you, ma'am. Can you tell me the name of the woman please?'

Amanda turned to the woman, whose eyes appeared to be growing larger in her skeletal face. Her lips were dried out, cracked, ringed with deep lines. She pressed them together.

'What's your name?' said Amanda. 'Can you tell me your name?'

The woman's lips parted. She began rocking back and forth. But instead of speaking, she quietly croaked a tuneless song, her voice flat, broken, her eyes now scrunched closed: *'Needle's pointing to your heart, now I know the way we'll part, needle's pointing to your heart, now I know the way we'll part, needle's pointing to your heart, now I know the way we'll part.'*

Her arm shot out, and she slapped the phone out of Amanda Petrie's hand.

*   *   *

Kurt Vine was busy shunting memories of bad men and bad game plays out of his mind when he saw two women standing by the roadside. He looked around, for a moment thinking he was driving through a movie set. Or a game. There was a cute girl and an old lady who looked like she had been dug up from a grave. This was some kind of a two-woman zombie apocalypse situation.

Weird shit just keeps on happening to me, he thought. He watched as the old woman suddenly slapped the girl's hand. He pulled over, parked the pickup, and climbed down.

'Ladies!' he said, moving as quickly as he could toward them, wiping the sweat that always flowed so readily. 'How can I be of assistance?' It was a line from *Hufuki*, but he figured it was appropriate.

Douglas County Undersheriff Cole Rodeal stood in the ambulance bay of the Sky Ridge Medical Center, tuning out his wife, Edie, the EMS Coordinator. As soon as she had used the expression 'me time', he was gone. Maybe that was because he didn't love Edie any more, and hated himself for it. Really, it was because he was depressed and hadn't realized it. He wanted to be home, in his den, with a box set from a time when women had never heard the expression 'me time'. He was jolted from his thoughts by the screech of tires and a small scream from the wife he really did love. He turned to where she was looking.

Oh, fuck.

Kurt Vine liked being part of this emergency that he knew, in his heart, wasn't a true emergency. He was driving like he had a siren, but he knew this crazy lady in the nightgown was going to be all right. She was starved and beaten and she smelled like shit, but she wasn't dying, as far as he could tell.

He was finally easing off the gas as they approached the ambulance bay at Sky Ridge.

'What is that smell?' he said. He looked into the back seat. 'Holy shit! She's on fire! She's on fucking fire!'

Amanda Petrie turned around at the same time and screamed. Small flames were rising from the terrified woman's chest and shoulders. Her nightgown was melting into her skin, her hair shriveling.

'Holy fucking shit!' said Kurt, slamming his foot on the accelerator instead of the brake, sending the pickup shooting toward a group of EMTs, until he yanked the steering wheel hard and plowed instead into the side wall of the hospital.

On impact, the old lady said: 'I did something real bad. Something terrible brought me here.'

'That lady died.' Special Agent Ren Bryce turned to Everett King, one of her newest colleagues, an ex-trader, financial and IT expert, and quick, firm friend. 'The one from the crash at Sky Ridge Medical Center. No one came forward to claim her, no match with any missing persons . . .' She shook her head. 'Rodeal reckons she was held captive somewhere for months at the very least: she had rope burns on her wrists, bruises on her ankles as if she'd been shackled, she was starved, beaten. But they found nothing in the neighborhood canvas. They ran her details through the system – nothing. Imagine that's your life . . . tortured and neglected to death.'

'Like your liver,' said Everett.

Ren was shaking a bottle of Fiji to help dissolve the two Alka-Seltzer she had broken into it.

'My liver is well tended to,' said Ren.

'Like a captor tends to his captee.'

'Stockholm Syndrome.' She took a drink. She had already drunk a bottle of freshly squeezed pineapple juice. Hangover Cure Supreme. The Alka-Seltzer was a rarely required second step. The previous night was a blur of bright lights, colorful drinks, and dancing on chairs and half-empty dance floors with two girls she had met at her bipolar support group two weeks earlier. They had presumed that, like them, she was unlucky enough to be a bipolar-loved-one wrangler, not the wranglee. That was often the case. Ren didn't want to lie, but she didn't want to correct them. She just wanted to party. The women were at the support group to learn how not to enable their loved one. Instead, they were fine-tuning the art of enabling a stranger. But there was no law against it. Ren smiled to herself: there should, in fact, be laws to fully support it.

Ren had been off her meds for three months.

'Did you see the video of the crash?' she said.

'No.'

'Rodeal was quite the hero – dived for his wife, totally saved her life, broke his arm in the fall. Sexism in Emergencies: it's not all bad when a man thinks women need to be saved.'

'It was his wife . . .'

'I've dealt with him, work-wise,' said Ren. 'I walk away with a twitch in my eye. Sometimes I think he expects me to be the one serving the refreshments.'

'Oh, baby girl, you *al*ways servin' up the refreshment!'

'And you keep topping up those glasses, handsome man.'

'God help this guy,' said Everett, nodding toward the glass panel of the interview room where murder suspect Jonathan Briar was perfectly framed. Briar's fiancée, twenty-three-year-old Hope Coulson, had now been missing from their Denver apartment for twenty-eight days. Briar had ignited public suspicion with the first dopey words out of his mouth when asked about her on live television: 'Aww . . . I'm sure she'll be back,' he said, smiling like an idiot, next to Hope Coulson's weeping parents.

'He doesn't yet know that he meets a lot of the criteria for the Ren Bryce Book of Wrong,' said Everett. 'Stoner – check! Skinny dreads – check! Mouth too small – check! And my second favorite: rat-colored hair – check! I mean, rats are gray. His hair is mousey.'

'Rats are creepier.'

'And my all-time-favorite,' said Everett. 'Eyes overly almond: check!'

'Because I *like* almond-shaped eyes,' said Ren. 'Too almond, though – that's a problem.' She looked at Everett. 'I'm a nightmare. I know. Judgey McJudgicles.'

'On the upside of his issues,' said Everett, 'every time he appears on screen or in print, the line of volunteer searchers grows.'

Hope Coulson had captured the public's hearts. She was a sweet, blonde, kind-hearted kindergarten teacher, a volunteer for everything from painting the ladies' nails at her local retirement home to delivering Meals on Wheels to the housebound, to being stationed at First-Aid tents at community events. At one time, Jonathan Briar looked like nothing more harmful than a guy who was batting above his weight. Now, he was looking like a killer.

Ren drank the rest of the Alka-Seltzer, then held a hand to her stomach.

Ooh. Not good. Drank too quickly, despite best efforts.

'You drank that way too fast,' said Everett.

'Ugh.' She threw the empty bottle in the garbage. 'OK. Shall we dance?'

'We always do.' He turned the door knob and let Ren go first.

Jonathan Briar almost jumped from his seat. 'Did you find her?'

So dramatic. So forced.

Ren shook her head. 'No, Jonathan. No, we did not. Not yet.' She sat down. 'Jonathan, I'm Special Agent Ren Bryce, and this is my colleague, Special Agent Everett King. How are you holding up?'

Briar shrugged. 'I'm OK . . . I guess.'

'Let me explain who we are,' said Ren. 'Agent King and I are members of the Rocky Mountain Safe Streets Task Force. Not to alarm you – we do handle all kinds of crimes – but we are technically a violent crime squad. We're multi-agency, meaning there are FBI agents like us, and there are detectives from DPD – that's Denver PD, along with members of the Jefferson County Sheriff's Department, Aurora PD, etc.

'We have to consider that Hope may have been the victim of a violent crime. Of course, we don't know that yet. I understand you've been questioned by DPD—'

'Every day!' said Jonathan. 'Every day since she left.'

'Left?' said Ren.

He shrugged. 'It's exhausting.'

Not my point. 'You said "left",' said Ren. 'Do you think Hope just left?'

Jonathan looked away, shrugging again. 'It's better than thinking anything else.'

'Back to what I was saying,' said Ren. 'We're talking to you today at the request of Detective Glenn Buddy at Denver PD, and because some new evidence has come to light.'

'What evidence?' said Jonathan.

'I want to show you a photograph of your fiancée, Hope,' said Ren, ignoring the question. She set it down on the table. 'Well, actually it's a photo of you *and* Hope. When was this taken?'

Jonathan swallowed. 'Christmas just gone. At my mom's house. Why?'

'You look really happy,' said Ren.

'We were,' he said, nodding.

Were: past tense.

Jonathan blinked, but there were no tears.

'Now, here's another photo,' said Ren. She set down an aerial photo of a landfill site.

'Do you know Fyron Industries?' said Everett, shifting forward in his seat. 'They manage this landfill site. It's off of I-70. The dumpster by your house – that's where that goes.'

Jonathan looked at Everett as if he had just crawled from a dumpster himself.

Everett took out a red Sharpie and drew a large box on the photo. 'This area here,' he said, 'is three acres square. The garbage runs twenty feet deep if we're to go back almost a month to when Hope went missing . . .'

Jonathan recoiled. 'What the hell are you showing me this for? What do you mean "go back almost a month"?'

Don't look at me for answers. That's not how this goes.

'To search this area, we're calling in all the favors we can,' said Everett. 'Law enforcement across a lot of different agencies, along with volunteer civilians. That's the effect Hope has had on people. They're coming from all over to offer to search a stinking hellhole for her, to suit up and go right in there to look for your missing fiancée. If we can in any way limit all that searching . . . or if we knew, for example, that we were wasting our time, or anyone else's time . . . or if there's somewhere else we should be looking . . .'

As Everett spoke, Ren was studying Jonathan Briar. *You are a dull-eyed dope-smoking moron. I have little time for dope-smoking morons.*

'Is there anything you'd like to tell us?' said Ren.

'No!' said Jonathan. 'No. Except that you *are* wasting your time: thinking I did this!' There was no anger, just a whining, pleading exhaustion.

'Everyone in your position tells us we're wasting our time,' said Ren, 'but, as you know, a lot of the time we're not. The odds are not in your favor. Before we go in here,' she pointed to the landfill photo, 'before we bring people into this wonderland, we'd like to know the truth.'

'I've told you the truth!' said Jonathan. 'I've told you a million times. I'm innocent! Last time I saw Hope she was alive and well. What more can I tell you? That's my story.'

'Story?' said Ren.

'You know what I mean,' said Jonathan. 'I didn't mean it that way.'

'Were you and Hope happy?' said Ren.

'Yes!' said Jonathan. 'Fucking leave me alone with the happiness bullshit! I don't think I can take this any more! I feel like I'm losing my mind, here. All you people looking at me! It's fucking driving me insane!'

Snap. Snap. Show your hand.

'Jonathan, we found traces of Hope's blood in the living room,' said Ren. 'Do you know how that got there?'

'She cut her finger, I don't know. Were they drops, smears, spatters?'

Go, CSI.

'If they were drops or smears,' he said, 'then she cut her finger a while back. If they were spatters, then, I guess, someone might have killed her at home, right? Is that your point?'

How Not to Talk to Law Enforcement 101.

Ren looked at Everett.

Jonathan started to cry. 'I love Hope. I always have. From when I was nine years old. I wouldn't lay a finger on her. All I ever want to do is protect her.' He cried harder. 'What if you find her and she's dead?'

Wow. Have you really only thought about that now?

He kept talking. 'What if she's there in all that garbage and she's dead? Then what happens? Then do you just, like, assume it's me? What evidence is going to be on that body at that stage? I'm terrified of what's going to go down. I want Hope found, but I also don't want her to be just pulled out of some garbage. I mean, I know what you're thinking, it's disgusting anyway, it's a murder, who gives a shit, but I do.' He went quiet. 'I do, because Hope would. She wouldn't want anyone seeing her that way.'

'What way?' said Ren, keeping her tone neutral.

Jonathan leapt from his seat. 'Dead on a garbage heap! What do you think I mean? Why do you people always think I mean something I don't mean?'

Because you say weird shit. Because your answers are weird. Your phraseology. Your language. Your focus.

'Sit the fuck down,' said Ren.

Jonathan sat down, but kept talking, the words speedy and tumbling. 'Dead after weeks, rotting away and all that other shit. Jesus! Who would ever want anyone to see them that way? I know I never would. But what happens then? I say nothing to you today because I know nothing and then you arrest me? Like, will I look suspicious to you because of that? I mean, I'll say anything not to come across as someone shady. I wasn't there that night at the time you're talking about. I was working! I'm not thinking about how Hope looks because I killed her in some horrible way. I'm thinking about what a fucked-up mess dead bodies are after all that time.'

2

Ren closed the door behind her and walked with Everett
into the bullpen – the open-plan office the task force worked
out of. Their boss, Supervisory Special Agent Gary Dettling,
had his own office. The admin team had theirs. There were
two interview rooms, two conference rooms, an A/V room,
two cells, rest rooms, a creaky elevator, a haunted basement
– everything brought together under the roof of one of
Denver's oldest buildings, The Livestock Exchange Building
– an icon of cowboy heritage.

'Well?' said Gary, looking up, hands on his hips. He was
a fit and handsome man of few words.

*I am tiring of you, Gary. The look that says 'impress me', 'prove
yourself to me' every time. Your smart-ass bullshit. Everything.*

'Early morning landfill search it is!' said Ren.

Gary's face said it all.

Ren looked at Everett. 'I don't know about you, but is
Briar just a dumb asshole?'

'That's in no doubt,' said Everett.

'I get that he doesn't have a face for TV,' said Ren, 'and
that indefinably weird shit falls out of his mouth, but . . .'

She shrugged. 'Does he say things that raise my suspicion because he is guilty or because he is just dumb, dumb, dumb? Because he has no filter? Because he cannot understand that in an interview with a Fed, you might want to not say some of the shit your low-flying brain fires out? I mean, even if you just imagine the physical distance between your brain and your mouth – that's time to pause, isn't it? Pause while it's at your nostrils or something. God, do you ever feel like the world is just populated with a lot of really dumb people? His face! I want to slap it.'

She drew breath.

You are all looking at me funny. Am I talking too fast again? Keep up, bitches. Jesus.

'So, here's what we know,' said Ren. 'Hope Coulson was last seen, alone, at eight thirty p.m. leaving Good Shepherd Church on East 7th Avenue where she'd gone to host a youth meeting. Everyone else had left ahead of her – a person walking by ID'd her. She was to drive right home – that's what she told Jonathan. He was out working at the pizza place, her last text to him at eight fifteen p.m. was "See you at home, kiss kiss". That's it. We have no witnesses. There are no HALO cams in the immediate vicinity.'

Denver had over one hundred HALO – High Activity Location Observation – cameras, all monitored from a central location by DPD.

'Hope Coulson's car was still in the church parking lot the next morning,' said Ren. 'Did she leave her car because she was planning on drinking? Wouldn't she need her car to get to work the next morning? Was she having an affair? In that case, again, why wouldn't she drive home if she was planning to take a guy back there? Unless she was going back to his place.' She shrugged. 'And if she was going for a drink alone, wouldn't she have chosen somewhere near

17

her apartment? She was a twenty-minute drive from there. So she either walked a route with no HALO cams, or someone drove by and picked her up. But this can't have been pre-arranged on her phone, because there were no calls or texts to indicate that. And nothing came up with friends, family, acquaintances, work, church members, etc. The neighborhood canvas came up empty. We have a list of vehicles and owners with no priors.'

'Could something have happened at the church?' said Everett. 'I don't know – someone made a pass at her. Maybe she needed to go have a drink, calm down . . . she decided to have another . . .' He paused. 'Yet, no one from the local bars ID'd her. Her face has been everywhere. At this point, we would have heard something.'

'My gut is just not liking Jonathan Briar for this,' said Ren.

'How many times has the partner killed the wife or girl-friend in the house at night, then claimed they never made it home?' said Gary.

'Many, many times,' said Ren. 'Just this is not one of them.'

As everyone dispersed, Ren sat down at her desk and dragged her keyboard toward her. She started typing up her notes, super speedy. Her phone rang.

Go away.

She kept typing.

Fuck. Off.

The phone kept ringing.

Her cell phone beeped.

Jesus Christ.

She glanced at the text. It was from Gary: **Pick up.**

She picked up. 'Hi.'

'Can you come into my office, please?'

'Sure,' said Ren. 'What's the emergency? Nothing you can say over the phone?'

Silence.

Alrighty then.

She walked into Gary's office.

'You stink,' said Gary.

'Wait 'til you smell me after the landfill search,' said Ren, sitting down.

Gary was staring at her.

'Hold on – are you serious?' said Ren. 'What do you mean stink? Literally?'

'In a way that tells me if I don't open a window, I'll have to check my own blood-alcohol level.'

Oh.

Shit.

'Please tell me,' said Gary, 'that you did not go drinking last night with some lost soul you picked up at your meeting.'

'Jesus Christ,' said Ren. 'I didn't even have a meeting last night.' *Which is the truth.*

'Just remember you're not there to make friends,' said Gary. 'Or even eye contact. The rule is you walk in there alone, you walk out alone.'

'That's me – Renegade.' She fired an imaginary gun. She paused. 'Was that your way of trying to find out if I'm going to my meetings?'

He eyeballed her. 'Lose the tone. This is about my concern that you are over the blood-alcohol level this morning.'

'I apologize for my tone,' said Ren. 'And yes, I did drink last night. As people often do after work, meeting or no meeting. Is that forbidden? Is the whole of Safe Streets fired?'

Stop. Talking.

Gary dared her to hold eye contact with him.

'I'm sorry,' said Ren.

'Go.'

Eight hours later, Ren and Everett were six drinks down in a new bar off Sixteenth Street.

'Do not let me drink tonight,' said Ren.

They laughed. Ren looked around her. 'There is nothing more unattractive to me than a group of men in their late forties in *leisure*wear on a night out,' said Ren. 'Especially the ones who were once hot, you can see the traces, and now they're just beat-down and filled with loss and white carbs.'

'Jesus, Ren.' Everett craned his neck. 'I need to see who you are savaging. "Filled with loss and white carbs" . . .'

'I know, I know,' said Ren. 'And, really, can something be filled with loss? Like, with an absence of something. But why abandon all hope at that age? You've half your life left. Go to the fucking gym.' *Like Ben. Like Gary. Like you.* 'And I say this while not actually finding super-buff bodies attractive.'

'Which makes no sense,' said Everett.

'I maintain that a lot of unhappiness in life is caused by people trying to make sense of things,' said Ren. 'Try this: for one week when someone says something strange to you, just say to yourself "interesting and senseless, goodbye". Like, goodbye to considering it any further.'

'If I did that, I don't think I could actually carry out my job,' said Everett.

'OK – maybe restrict it just to things I say.'

'The things I can do with those reclaimed hours,' said Everett. 'Go to the gym, for example.'

'Shall we dance?' said Ren. 'It's filthy rap.'

'Yes, we shall,' said Everett.

They hit the empty dance floor and immediately drew attention. Everett was clean-cut, dark-haired, side-parted kind of handsome. Ren had an exotic look of wild abandon.

'And so they danced, and the eyes of the onlookers fell upon them!' said Ren into his ear.

This is high-larious!

Everett was laughing at her, but when he really started to move, Ren was the one who had to fall away to the side she was laughing so hard. He was an excellent dancer.

They went back to the bar and slumped into their seats.

I am soooo shitfaced. 'I think I look like a whore when I dance the way I really want to dance.'

'I agree,' said Everett. 'Don't ever change.'

'And you dance like no one is looking,' said Ren. 'Pinterest gold.'

At two a.m., a cab with Ren in it pulled up outside the home of Annie Lowell, a dear Bryce family friend, who had allowed Ren to house-sit her beautiful, historic home while she was touring Europe.

'This is me!' said Ren, reaching forward and handing the driver twenty dollars.

She looked out the window. Then back at the driver.

'Oh, shit,' she said. 'I'm sorry. I don't live here any more.'

3

It was a beautiful ninety-degree morning in Denver: the landfill site sweltered under the same sun that was giving everyone else's day a glorious start. Ren was sitting in the passenger seat of her Jeep.

This cannot be my life.

Outside, the rest of Safe Streets were already dressed in white Tyvek suits, Kevlar gloves, and black half-face masks, sharing a range of looks that covered misery, repulsion, sorrow, and panic.

The panic was flickering in the eyes of Janine Hooks, Ren's closest friend, and ex-Jefferson County cold case detective. Janine had joined Safe Streets three months earlier. She was a brilliant, thorough investigator with a sharp, wise mind and a heart of gold. Ren was certain Janine had an eating disorder, but had never dared to raise it.

It breaks my heart how tiny you look inside your suit.

Janine was staring down at her feet, lining the tips of her boots up.

Terrified about wearing a mask. Or shy around Robbie.

Robbie Truax was ex-Aurora PD, with Safe Streets from

the beginning. Janine had met him first through Ren, and was comfortable liking him from afar, a little less so now that they were up-close colleagues.

Everett came into Ren's line of vision, walking her way. He pulled open the door of the Jeep.

'How's my girl?'

'Seriously,' said Ren, 'I have zero idea how I got into the apartment I did not remember I lived in.'

'Too much grammar in that sentence . . .'

'But you look fine – that's not fair,' said Ren. 'I don't think I can go through with this.'

'You can. You can always puke into the mask.'

'Jesus Christ. Thanks. My ultimate nightmare.'

Fifteen minutes and one fake urgent phone call later, Ren was suited up with the others.

I made it.

They stood in a group, still apart from the other searchers.

'OK,' said Ren. 'Let's go through the hand signals again . . .'

Everyone looked at her. She pushed her hand into the circle, low down, and raised her middle finger. 'Fuck. This.'

The others smiled.

And fuck this heat.

Ren surveyed the landscape ahead of them: rotting food, filthy diapers, decaying animals . . . *stop the inventory of this hellhole.*

'Stretched out before us,' said Ren, 'is a landscape that looks like how my mouth feels. There may be a cadaver in both. May your masks serve and protect you.'

She walked toward the rest of the searchers: Denver PD detectives, Sheriff's Office investigators, landfill site workers, and volunteers.

Volunteers, you extraordinary people. Have you no place else to be? God bless you all.

They moved in and began the search. It was as hot, foul and arduous as they expected. Two days later, they were back. Four days. Five. On day six, the body of Hope Coulson, hanging from black plastic coming undone, was hoisted from a stinking mound of life's waste and set on the ground at the feet of the Safe Streets' team. Janine Hooks' eagle eye had spotted the bag, the Duck tape wrapped around it at each end with extra at the center.

Thank you. Thank you. Thank you.

Everett, Janine and four DPD detectives stayed with the body until the coroner arrived. Ren called for Robbie and they moved quickly toward her Jeep. They stripped out of their filthy Tyvek suits, balled them into a bag in the back, and hopped in.

You have gained quite a bit of weight, Robbie Truax, which I feel mean noticing.

'So, how've you been?' he said, as he strapped himself in.

Ren looked at him. *We're together almost every day . . .*

She started the engine, and drove.

'I mean – we only see each other at work these days,' said Robbie.

'I know,' said Ren. 'It's been crazy. And you've missed some nights out. A lot of nights out. Is everything OK?'

They both understood the silence that followed. Robbie, the blond, fresh-faced, boy-scout Mormon, was in treatment for porn addiction, a problem that had been going on for months before he finally told Ren, the sole guardian of his secret.

He shrugged. 'I . . . was wondering if you were so . . . horrified by what I told you, that . . . you were trying to create distance.'

'Oh my God,' said Ren. 'Please tell me you don't mean that. Did I seem horrified to you? Jesus – I'd have no friends if I distanced myself from people with porn and promiscuity issues. And how could I distance myself from myself?'

Robbie smiled. 'I guess I just miss hanging out, you coming over, or staying around after work. Just having pizza or whatever.'

But not drinking. Which isn't seeming like fun to me right now. Sorry!

'You and Everett,' said Robbie, 'you're—'

Ren's heart sank.

And now we have hit the real problem. You think I have abandoned you for Everett.

After three months, Robbie was struggling to get along with Everett, and it was making for some awkward moments.

But, you're right. I have abandoned you. Everett is more fun. Everett drinks. He dances. I can't hurt Everett. I could hurt you, sensitive man.

Robbie had once admitted to Ren that he loved her, and she had told him that she saw him more as a brother. Their friendship was strong, they had recovered from it, but Ren couldn't help feeling that a responsibility had come with the admission: if he loves you, if he ever did, you could still hurt him.

I never want to hurt you, Robbie Truax. You mean too much to me.

'I'm sorry if you feel like I haven't been around,' said Ren. 'You're right. I've just been party, party, party. I think it's moving into the apartment, everything . . . I can't settle. I feel like I'm jumping out of my skin.'

'That's how I feel when I'm . . .' He stared out the window. 'Treatment is hard.'

'I didn't want to ask,' said Ren. 'It's so *personal*.'

He turned to her, his eyes bright with sincerity. 'But you're the only person in the world I can talk to about personal things.'

Ren reached out and squeezed his forearm. 'I love you, Robbie Truax. I'm so sorry.. Please talk to me. I know it's probably like—'

'Trying to catch a wild horse?'

'Blindfolded.'

Robbie raised a hand in mock-defiance. 'His eyes filled, nevertheless, with hope . . .'

Ren pictured the smiling face of Hope Coulson.

Jonathan Briar, here we come. And this time, we have Hope.

When Jonathan Briar heard that his fiancée's body had been found, his knees buckled, and he cried out with such force, Ren was startled. She had been standing with Robbie in the living room of the apartment Jonathan and Hope had shared for the previous two years. Ren caught Jonathan as he went down. Now she was on her knees, and he was limp and weeping in her arms.

This was not my vision.

Ren glanced up at Robbie, who had been temporarily immobilized. Eventually, he kicked into action and helped Jonathan Briar onto the sofa. Ren took a seat opposite and looked around the room. It was her first time there.

This is a beautiful place. Cozy and cute. Seems like the home of two people in love. This is . . . so strange. There is nothing cold here. No sense of death or darkness.

'How could this happen?' wailed Jonathan. 'How? I thought she was alive! She's . . . Hope isn't someone . . . just she wouldn't be murdered. By anyone! She was in the garbage, just like that? She didn't belong there. Jesus Christ! I just thought she was alive!'

'Where did you think she was?' said Ren. *Seriously. It's been almost five weeks.*

Jonathan stopped sobbing. 'I couldn't even bring myself to think about that.' His hair was standing on end. 'I just couldn't go there. Where did I think she was? I was thinking nothing. I was thinking nothing bad. I was—'

In shock. All this time. You weren't an emotionless asshole. You were resisting being forced to think of a horrific ending. It was the last thing you wanted to think of for your sweet, beautiful, caring Hope.

Jonathan Briar locked eyes with Ren.

The pain. You can't fake that. That agony cannot be faked. Can it?

4

Hope Coulson's autopsy revealed that she had been strangled, and it likely happened not long after she had gone missing. She had been raped with something green and ceramic that had broken, and left shards behind, one of which had a partial fingerprint that matched Jonathan Briar's. Her father identified her body. Jonathan Briar identified the shards as parts of a tall green ceramic sculpture – an engagement gift they had been given – that he had failed to notice was missing from their living room.

'Well, being raped with one of your engagement gifts would be a serious fuck-you if you cheated on your fiancé,' said Ren. She was sitting at the edge of her desk in the bullpen, where most of the squad was gathered. 'Yet no one in all the interviews has suggested that Briar was anything other than kind and loving toward her. But, of course, behind closed doors . . . who knows. However, if he raped her with that in the apartment and it broke, which it clearly did, there should be more blood there. And it's highly unlikely there would be no evidence of the sculpture. Unless he raped her on something that he took away and destroyed. His car was clean. Nothing was found with her in the landfill. The black plastic used has no connection to any product found in their home, which doesn't mean much. Then there's the issue – if we are to believe he was the rapist and it didn't happen in their home – he would've had to have taken her somewhere to carry it out, and he would also have had to carefully package up the sculpture and bring it with them. Would someone do that? I don't think so.'

'Who gave them the gift?' said Everett. 'That could be significant.'

'If that guy's innocent, I would be amazed,' said Gary.

'Prepare to be amazed,' said Ren.

Gary stared at her. As Gary often did.

'We also have to consider the fact that she was raped with a foreign object,' said Ren. 'That's typically carried out by a man with sexual problems, which, again, there is no evidence of in Briar's case.'

'That doesn't mean anything,' said Gary. 'He could have had a problem for months not being able to get it up. He's a young guy, too embarrassed to go to the doctor, she's too embarrassed to mention it to anyone, thinks it's her fault . . . and, maybe, she goes elsewhere to get what she's not getting at home . . .'

He has made up his mind.

'Can you really see a kindergarten teacher having that attitude?' Ren paused. 'You should go talk to Briar . . .' *Open your mind.*

They stared each other down.

'How about we go through the night of her disappearance again?' said Ren. 'And how Briar was at work for the entire evening—'

'And out making deliveries,' said Gary.

'All of which he appeared to have made in a reasonable time frame,' said Ren. 'Unless he has a cape somewhere . . .'

'That entire shift was made up of his dope-smoking, mouth-breather friends,' said Gary.

'And we have video to back up most of his comings and goings,' said Ren.

'Most,' said Gary. 'And they're in over-sized jackets and baseball caps, faces not very clear . . .'

Grrrrr.

The meeting broke up, and everyone returned to their desks through the haze of tension. Ren fired up her computer. A rubber band flew through the air and whipped her hair off her face. She looked up. Robbie was standing in the center of the room with a wooden gun. Ren laughed.

'Beautiful shot.'

'Thank you,' said Robbie, blowing imaginary smoke from the top of the barrel.

'But you do know you are now dead,' said Ren. 'There's a price on your head. Fifty per cent off.' She slid open her drawer to take her own wooden gun out.

No ammo. Shit.

Ren's email pinged. She glanced at it. Gary.

Subject: BP support
Oh, here we go . . .

Tonight. Henderson Hotel.
Control explosion.

Ren went to Gary's office. Her fist was poised to knock on the door, until she heard his rising voice.

'Nothing!' said Gary. 'Nothing is wrong, Karen! Jesus Christ, I'm going to record it on a loop.'

Gary Dettling was calm, cool, rational, in control. He could rein in any emotion . . . until it came to his wife. He loved that she was crazy, he hated that she was crazy, she *made* him crazy.

But Ren knew that in some small way, Karen Dettling was bound to have made Gary more sympathetic to Ren's own brand of crazy.

'No, good. Go ahead!' said Gary. He slammed the phone down hard.

Ren let out the breath she had been holding.

Fuckity fuck.

She knocked.

'Yes!' said Gary.

Ren opened the door and walked in. 'Do you have any rubber bands?'

Gary frowned. 'Yes.'

Ren walked over to his stash. 'Can I just say I hate these passive-aggressive emails about meetings and appointments?'

'They're active-aggressive,' said Gary. 'And I can get even more active . . .'

Ren grabbed a fistful of rubber bands and walked out.

Why do you even keep them in here? You asshole.

When Ren went back to the bullpen, Janine and Everett were huddled together. They looked up.

'Was he shouting at *you*?' said Everett.

'You could hear that out here?' said Ren. 'No – it wasn't me. For once.'

'Are you coming out tonight?' said Janine.

'No,' said Everett, 'she's checking into a facility . . .'

'You may be right,' said Ren. 'No, Janine. I was out last night, and the night before. I think even I need a break every now and then.'

'Well, I'm ready to strap on my drinking boots,' said Janine.

'As am I,' said Everett.

'Damn you both!' said Ren. 'Well, if you're going, Janine, would you like to stay in my place? Save your drinking money.'

'Even better, thank you,' said Janine.

'I will try not to be bitter,' said Ren.

'Robbie's going to come too,' said Janine.

D'oh! Everett's face . . .

Only Ren noticed. And only she could see the sparkle in Janine's eyes.

Ren sat at her desk and thought about Hope Coulson – how she hadn't driven home, how that likely meant that she had met with someone unexpectedly, that something had changed her plans.

'I think someone was watching Hope Coulson,' said Ren. 'I think she was taken from right outside the church.'

'Like she was bundled into the back of a van?' said Everett.

'I don't know,' said Ren. 'Who knew where she was going to be? Was it someone close enough to her that they knew her routine? Was it a member of the congregation? Someone who was served Meals on Wheels by her? A relative of one of the elderly people she visited? Maybe one of the fathers whose kids go to her school. Maybe someone she trusted . . .'

'Maybe some creepy guy who had a thing for her,' said Everett. 'Or maybe it was an opportunistic thing – some guy who lived near the church?'

'There are ten registered sex offenders in the area,' said Janine. 'According to DPD's notes, they were all cleared.'

'Every sex offender was, once upon a time, unregistered,' said Ren. 'And every killer had a clean record before their fairy tale ended.'

5

After work, Ren took the five-minute walk to the River North Arts District, RiNo, where her boxing gym defiantly stood – fierce and battered, like a prizefighter – between two shiny rookies: a pristine artisan coffee shop, and a crafts store/ceramics studio. The area was slowly regenerating, with warehouses being renovated and new buildings going up in what were once abandoned, overgrown lots.

The filthy man-gym was scattered with bulked-up men working on bags, sparring in the four rings. Ren went to the token lady area, and got changed into black shorts and a black tank. She put in her EarPods, cranked up her beat-the-shit-out-of-people playlist. She strapped up her hands, put on her gloves and got to work.

Jab. Jab. Hook. Hook. Uppercut. Uppercut. Jab. Jab. Hook. Hook. Uppercut. Uppercut. Rinse. Repeat.

She moved over to the speed bag, did ten minutes on that, left, hot and sweaty, and took a shower in the quiet after-work calm of a hushed Safe Streets.

*   *   *

Ren drove home, walked into the hallway of the apartment building, went over to the wall of mailboxes and took out her mail.

Bill. Bill. Bill. Store card. Bill. Bill. Store card. Bill.

A woman wheeling a mountain bike came in behind her. She looked like the type who described herself as 'wacky' in her online dating profile. Thirtyish, hair in pigtails, a tie-dyed T-shirt, full lips, blaring red lipstick, XL plaid shirt as a cover-up.

I have zero interest in meeting bikes in the hallway when I get home from work. Or wacky people. I am maladjusting to apartment living.

'Hi,' said the girl. 'I'm Lorrie, are you new?'

'Hi, Lorrie,' said Ren. 'Yes. I'm Ren. Nice to meet you.'

I have dead-body photos in a folder under my arm right now. Be on your way.

Ren had moved in two months earlier, just days before Annie Lowell returned from her travels. She had clung to the hope that Annie would extend her trip as she had done before. The move was painful, and sad, and already blocked out. Annie's house was a home. The apartment was a base. It never drew her in in the same way. Instead, mania and the night drew her out, bars and bright, shiny things. Bright shiny people.

Ren had decided not to rush into renting somewhere she didn't adore. So she sucked it up, even though it meant handing over her beloved black-and-white border collie, Misty, to her dog-walker, Devin, to look after until she found a proper place for both of them. If only she had the time to look. Devin was a smart and bubbly young student who lived across the street from Annie, and adored Misty as much as Ren and Janine did.

'If you need anything, just ring my bell,' said Lorrie. 'I'm 28A.'

'Oh,' said Ren. 'Thank you.'
Never gonna happen.

Ren took the elevator alone to the fifth floor. She unlocked the door to her apartment, and went in, hit with the smell of paint.

At least I have fresh new walls. There are positives.

She dropped her briefcase in the hallway and went to the kitchen. She took out a St Émilion red, uncorked it, poured a glass. She opened the refrigerator. There was a bag of arugula, a block of parmesan, some fillet steak.

Not hungry enough to make great effort.

She threw together a salad of arugula and parmesan, cracked some black pepper over it, soaked it in balsamic vinegar and a dash of olive oil and sat back on the sofa to eat.

Her phone beeped with a text from her boyfriend. She had been going out with Ben Rader for ten months. He was an FBI Agent in D.C., keen to make a bigger commitment than Ren was willing to. She had deflected his offer to look for a transfer to Denver so they could move in together. He hadn't even made the suggestion that she move to D.C. But she loved him, and he loved her. It was only the lying about the meds that stood between them. One giant pharmaceutical wall.

Ren ate half the salad before she set it aside. She pulled a bright red cushion onto her lap, set her laptop on it and opened Hope Coulson's Facebook account. She spent over an hour going through it. She was struck by one thing: Hope always posted photos from her nights out, throughout the night, and always commented on the event the following day: Blast in XYZ bar with m'girls! or Me&J in XYZ's. Except for one Friday night, two weeks before she went missing.

Hmm. Why the deviation?

That day, Facebook showed that Hope Coulson went for a late lunch with her girlfriends for one of their birthdays, and posted photos over the course of the afternoon. The next photo uploaded was at 7 p.m., taken in a sports bar – a loved-up selfie with Jonathan. The next photo, in a different bar, was taken at 10 p.m. and was just of Jonathan. And that was it; no comment on the night the following day. And the next post was on Monday afternoon, when she had finished work.

Something about that isn't right. She was drinking at lunch, kept going when she went to meet Jonathan, didn't appear in a photo herself. Because she was too drunk? She had a kindergarten-teacher reputation to uphold. Or maybe something happened. Did they have a fight? Maybe whatever happened that night sent her into hiding the following day. Maybe the night was not a night worth writing about for whatever reason . . .

Ren put down the glass of wine.

She texted Janine. FOMO. *Fear of Missing Out.*

She got a text right back: You know where to find me. Robbie left early on. Everett just gone . . .

Four hours later, Ren was leaning into the mirror in the ladies' room of Gaffney's, her makeup bag open on the wet tiles.

Why can't there be raised shelves away from the sinks? How hard can that be, people?

Janine arrived, passing two girls who had been taking selfies together before they left.

'I'm so old,' said Ren. 'The idea of constantly updating social media when I'm trying to get hammered is hellish. I hate even being around people who do that. Relax, everyone. And get the fuck out of my face.'

'I know,' said Janine. 'But at least it helps us do our job . . . suckers!'

'Speaking of which – Hope Coulson was out two weeks before she went missing, then thirty-six hours disappeared into a black social media hole, which was not her style. I'm just wondering, did something happen? And we know I don't like to wonder for too long. I like to go out there and find the fuck out.' She ran her finger under each eye to tidy up her mascara. 'I need to speak with Briar again.'

'You heard he's lawyered up, though . . .'

Ren turned to her.

'Oh, I know that face,' said Janine. 'Don't go there without the lawyer.'

'I just have a couple of tiny questions . . .'

'Oh, they're cool with the tiny ones . . . phew.'

'But I don't think he's a suspect,' said Ren.

'Not the point. Don't risk it. Gary will go apeshit. And speaking of risking shit, whatever you're about to do here, don't.'

'I was about to put some lip gloss on,' said Ren. She raised her eyebrows and smiled.

'You know what I mean,' said Janine. 'I don't know what's going on with you and that guy out there, but . . .'

'I'm fine,' said Ren. 'Don't worry. I have zero interest in him.'

'Hmm. I'm not sure he feels the same way.'

'That's his problem.'

Janine studied her in the mirror.

'Honestly, I'm fine,' said Ren. 'The guy's not even drinking.'

'I don't think a man needs to be drinking to make a move on you,' said Janine. She paused. 'Anyhoo, I think I'm about ready to call it a night.'

'Noooo,' said Ren.

Janine nodded. 'I'm exhausted. Do you mind?'

'No, but I'm wiiide awake – do you mind if I stay?'

'Not at all,' said Janine. 'I'll see you back at the ranch.'

She hugged Ren, and pulled back. 'I know Gary's not actually here, but you seem to be in his crosshairs. I'm not sure it's to do with all this partying, but—'

'Fuck Gary!'

6

Ren was dancing hard and fast, bright-eyed and soaring, wild of heart and intentions. The people around her were happy and free and smiling and a reflection of her. They moved together, buoyant and powerful. Two guys joined her on the dance floor – one in front, one behind.

I may be old enough to be the front guy's mother. He has no clue. Or does he?

He was smiling at her with his gorgeous, perfect teeth.

Ren smiled back.

Boom-boom-BOOM. Boom-boom-BOOM. Boom-boom-BOOOOOM.

I wonder what Ben would make of this? I mean, it's all perfectly innocent, but still. Would I like to see him in a girl sandwich? I don't know . . . Yes you do. You'd kill him.

Ren backed into the other guy, and the front guy moved forward. They all moved with instinctive rhythm.

'We're good at this!' said Ren.

'We are!' said the front guy.

She could feel the back guy's breath on her neck.

Ew. Garlic stranger breath.

She squeezed her way out from between them. 'Thank you, gentle men!'

'Don't go!' said one.

'Stay!' said the other.

'Bar!' said Ren. *I'm way too sober for these shenanigans. I've sweated out the alcohol.*

Half an hour later, Ren was back with her original group of strange men. Her phone buzzed in her purse. She took it out.

It was a text from Janine. She could barely focus on it.

I can't find the key! Stranded outside apartment . . . !

Shitttt. I don't want to leeeave. Fuck. Maybe Janine can go back to her house. Don't be an asshole.

'Excuse me, gentle men,' said Ren. 'I'm going to have to go.'

'What? Why?' said one of them.

'My friend is locked out of my apartment.'

'Is it far?' said the guy.

'Ten minutes in a cab,' said Ren.

'I can drive you,' he said. 'I haven't been drinking.'

Ren felt a small spike of sobriety. *He could be a psycho. Lots of psychos don't drink or do drugs because they don't want to lose control. Jesus. Worst-Case Scenario Girl strikes again.*

'That means I can drive you back here after,' said the guy. 'Keep the party going!'

I hate that expression. 'OK! That's an excellent idea! What's your name again?'

'JD.'

'Thank you, JD!'

They pushed through the hot, crowded bar onto the street. The night was warm. There was only a gentle breeze, but it hit her like a slap.

Whoa. My head.

She called Janine. She picked up right away.

'Are you OK?' said Ren.

'Yes,' said Janine.

'I'm on my way,' said Ren. 'One of the guys is giving me a ride.'

'What?' said Janine. 'Get a cab. Who is he? Has he been drinking?'

'Nope,' said Ren. 'He's tonight's designated driver. With a name like JD that's a bit cruel, isn't it?'

JD laughed. He unlocked the car door.

'He's going to bring me back to the bar after, too,' said Ren.

Pause. 'Really?' said Janine.

What's with that tone of voice? 'Yes. Would you like me to call one of my neighbors, see if they'll buzz you in, make sure you're safe?'

'Ren, it's almost two a.m.'

'Exactly,' said Ren. 'It's very late to be hanging around—'

'Ren? Ren, listen to me: do not call your neighbors. I'll be fine.'

'OK,' said Ren. 'See you in ten.'

Janine was waiting on the steps outside the apartment.

'There she is!' said Ren. 'Safe!' She jumped out of the car, with the key already in her hand. 'Here.'

'I'm so sorry about this,' said Janine.

'It's fine!' said Ren. 'Don't worry. Will you be OK?'

'No,' said Janine.

'What?' said Ren.

'No,' said Janine. 'Come with me. I need to talk to you about something. It's important.'

Nowww? Ren glanced over at JD. He was a blur standing

41

by his car. The streetlights were glowing, everything was glowing. Ren turned back to Janine, struggling to focus.

'OK,' said Ren. 'OK.' She ran back down the steps. 'Thank you, JD! But I'm going to stay, now that I'm here.' She kissed him on the cheek. 'Thanks for the ride.'

'Aw, that's a shame,' said JD. 'Are you sure? I just got a text from one of the guys – party at his place.'

'Sounds good,' said Ren, 'but I better not. I don't want to leave Janine.'

JD looked up at Janine with an expression that said killjoy.

Inside the apartment, Ren went looking for vodka, Janine went looking for water and Vitamin C tablets.

'Here,' she said, putting them down in front of Ren.

'What is this?' said Ren. 'The drinking is not over yet. What would you like?'

'I'm good, thank you,' said Janine.

'So,' said Ren, 'what do you need to talk about? Are you OK?'

'Yes,' said Janine. 'I . . . just wanted you to stop what you were doing.'

Um, what?

'I know you said you were fine,' said Janine, 'but I was afraid you were going to do something you would regret.'

'Like what?' said Ren.

'Come on,' said Janine. 'JD, he's a good-looking guy. You two were flirting.'

'Jesus Christ, why does everyone think I'm flirting when I'm just having fun?'

'It seemed like more than that to me,' said Janine, 'and definitely to him. Why else would he offer you a ride home? A guy wouldn't do that unless he wanted something in return.'

'Cynic!' said Ren. 'And I think you over-estimate my attractiveness.'

Janine shook her head. 'I don't. I've seen it enough times. When you focus on people you focus on them, it's so lovely, it really is, but you know men . . . they want the world to revolve around them, and you make it so.'

Oh, God, I've heard that before. 'I was just having fun!' *I don't have a dial to regulate the attention I pay.*

'I know,' said Janine, 'but I know that it wouldn't be fun at all if you cheated on Ben. You'd never forgive yourself. I wasn't sure you were in control of all that tonight, and I didn't want to wake up to an empty apartment or – worse – have you wake up to a different man to the one who loves you. The one you love.'

Damn it. 'I wouldn't have done anything.'

'Another drink might have changed all that,' said Janine. 'I had a bad vibe.'

'Well,' said Ren. 'Thanks for caring.'

Janine laughed. 'Once more with feeling.'

Ren got into bed and texted Ben. **Love you. XX**

7

Ren woke at eight thirty the next morning. *Oooh. Where am I? Oh, I'm home. Thank God. Alone. Phew. OK. Janine stayed here. How did I get here? Cab. OK. No – a guy called JD. Nice guy. Nothing happened. That's a positive. There's hope for me.*

Hope. Victims should never be called Hope. What happened to you, Hope Coulson? Did you get drunk in a bar, take a ride home with a stranger?

Ren got up and stuck her head into the living room.

No Janine. Why didn't she call me? She hates me. I'm a liability on nights out.

Ren turned on the radio and went into the bathroom. She stepped onto the scales: one hundred and nineteen pounds. *Thank you. Don't ever change.* She went to the toilet, washed her hands, dried them, then stepped on the scales again: still one hundred and nineteen pounds. *So, I didn't drink that much.*

I'm high-larious.

She looked in the mirror. *Ooh: not a good look, though a familiar one. I like the cheekbones, though.*

She jumped in the shower and used every energizing product and scrub she could find to startle her awake. She dressed in gray, high-waisted straight-leg pants, a starched white shirt, a pale gold necklace with two pendants: one shaped like a crescent moon, the other shaped like a star. She did a quick makeup job, left her hair wet, and ran.

Fifteen minutes later, she parked outside the Livestock Exchange Building. She began to jog up the steps, but her pounding head slowed her march. She walked through the doors, her footsteps echoing across the polished marble floor. She headed for the wide central staircase instead of the elevator. The staircase led onto a landing, then left or right for more steps to the next floor, and the same all the way to the top. She could hear a man above loudly announce, 'This is not safe!'

Ren looked up. He was rattling a clearly unstable guard-rail along the second floor balcony.

And who the fuck might you be?

'Is this even forty-two inches high, I have to wonder,' he was saying.

Really? Do you?

He made his way up to the fourth floor.

The Safe Streets floor.

Ren recognized the woman rushing up the stairs behind him as Valerie, the real estate agent – giving him a tour. There were four office spaces to rent in the building.

On other floors.

Oh – Valerie! She might help me and Misty find a home!

Ren continued up the stairs. 'Sir, this is not the floor with the vacant space,' Valerie was saying. She looked down at Ren, exasperated.

'That's not the point!' said the man. 'How well maintained

45

is this building is what I'm thinking.' He tried to rattle the guardrail on the fourth floor, but it held firm. He looked disappointed.

Ren smiled at him as she passed by to walk through the door into Safe Streets. He was standing about four feet to her right. She paused. 'We don't walk out around there,' said Ren, pointing down to the second floor balcony. 'No one does, so, we've never noticed the problem. That's a dummy door at the end. The elevator bank is down the other way. However, I'm sure we can get the guardrail that you will never use fixed for you in no time, so that when you never use it, it will be safe, and you won't plunge down if you never fall from a place where you will never again be going.'

She walked through the door. She could hear Valerie rambling about the fourth floor being a federal area.

'And there's no security in the building?' said the man. 'No scanners? Nothing?'

'This is not the FBI's main federal building in Denver,' Valerie was saying. 'Would you really want to have to be scanned every morning coming to work, Rodney, really? Emptying your pockets? Taking out your phone, your coins, having your bags searched?'

Ren was smiling as she walked down the hallway. *No, Rodney, you would not. I wouldn't want that myself. God bless our compact little squad in our beautiful historic home.*

Ren's cell phone rang.

Ben!

She picked up. 'Hey, baby.'

'Hey,' said Ben. 'Thought I'd catch you before work. How you doing? How was your night?'

'Great,' said Ren. 'Just let me take off my jacket, sit down. Yes, great night. We met some hilarious guys at the bar . . . one of them gave me a ride home. Janine forgot her keys—'

'Who was this guy?' said Ben.

'Just a guy called JD,' said Ren. 'Why?'

'Why? I don't know – rides home with strange guys and I can't ask who he is?'

'"Strange guys" . . . one guy. A regular guy, not strange. Janine met him.' *And tried to keep me away from him.* 'He was fine.'

'Good to know.' He paused. 'Aren't you exhausted? All these nights out?'

'No, Mom. I'm good.'

'Fine, I'll let you get back to work,' said Ben.

'Great,' said Ren. 'Talk to you later.'

'Don't call me late.'

'I won't.'

Bo. Ring.

Everett came into the bullpen with two mugs of coffee and put one on Ren's desk. 'We must stop meeting like this,' he said.

She smiled. 'God bless you and the caffeine I'll ride out on.'

Ren opened up her laptop again, and went back to Hope Coulson's Facebook page.

Something is not right here.

She filled Everett in on what she had read the previous night. 'I need to pay a visit to Jonathan Briar,' she said.

'Well,' said Everett, 'news just in: he's lawyered up.'

'No, I know,' said Ren. 'Janine told me. I just want to ask him about that one night.'

Everett shook his head. 'Not without his lawyer . . . who, by the way, is well aware of the lack of hard evidence against his client.'

'As am I,' said Ren. She leaned in. 'Has Gary mentioned to you his exact theory on what happened to Hope Coulson?'

'No,' said Everett, 'but doesn't he seem a little . . . distracted to you?'

Ren nodded. 'Yup. I don't think he's himself right now.' *Something is rotten in the state of his marriage.*

'I don't know him well enough to know what "hisself" is,' said Everett.

'I know him too well,' said Ren. 'And he's still a fucking mystery.' She looked up. 'Speaking of mysteries . . .'

'Hello, flatmate,' said Janine, walking in.

'Where did you get to this morning?' said Ren.

'I took Misty for a run.'

'Oh my God – you took *my* dog for a run. Bad mom, bad mom.'

'That's not how it works,' said Janine. 'You are hungover. I needed a run, Misty did too: win-win.'

'How *is* my baby?' *Whom I haven't seen in four days.*

'She's beautiful,' said Janine.

'How's Devin?' said Ren.

'As happy as ever. Is she not one of the cheeriest people on the planet?'

'I swear she doesn't have a bad thought in her head,' said Ren.

'Everyone has bad thoughts,' said Everett. 'Don't be idolizing.'

I do idolize, he's right. Everyone is better than me.

Robbie walked into the bullpen with a stack of files up to his chin. 'Don't ask,' he said. 'Just don't.'

'I'm sorry I missed you last night,' said Ren.

'You came out in the end?' he said.

'Yes,' said Ren. 'We're going to have to coordinate better . . .'

She sat down at her desk. Something was tugging at her. Something that had just been said.

What? Idolizing? Bad thoughts?

She opened up Google and stared at it blankly.

Win-win! That's what it is! Stephanie Wingerter.

Ren jumped up from her desk and went to the file cabinet. She pulled out the file on the rape and murder of Stephanie Wingerter, a twenty-three-year-old meth-addicted prostitute who went by the name of Win-Win. She had disappeared in late June and was found a week later in a shallow grave in Devil's Head, Douglas County. Ren laid out the photos on her desk. The first was a mug shot – Stephanie's blank eyes in a skinny, washed-out face dotted with scabs. Her mouth was half-open, showing gaps where two teeth should have been. Her thin, punky blonde hair was a mess, her eyebrows over-plucked.

The next photos were of where she was found, left to decompose in the beautiful July sunshine. Stephanie Wingerter's face and body had been ravaged by drugs before any killer had gotten near it, but when he did . . . her right eye socket was impacted, as was her nose, both left swollen and caked in blood. Her upper and lower lips were split, and there was no pale skin visible – it was all shades of blue, purple, red and black. Dried blood darkened her hair. Her throat had been cut. Much of the lower half of her body was burned down to her ankles.

Ren read the autopsy report. Cause of death was exsanguination. Accelerant had been poured on her, post-mortem, then lit.

You poor, tragic soul. Why do some people have to live such miserable lives and die such horrible deaths?

There were photos of a younger Stephanie from before she became an addict, and she was not unlike Hope Coulson: slim, pretty and bright-eyed.

Everyone in Colorado knew who Hope Coulson was. Stephanie Wingerter, visible in life only to those in her shadowy underworld, had scarcely registered in the media. She was the type to be considered a victim-in-waiting by people who could never see her as a young woman struggling to survive or desperately feeding a habit that was never on her list of life's goals, but was, instead, a marker on a gene.

Ren went through the last photos – what had remained of Stephanie Wingerter's tiny clothes, filthy, torn and bloodied.

8

After work, Ren went to visit Misty, and met with Janine for coffee afterwards in Crema on Larimer Street.

'The sooner I get a house the better,' said Ren. 'I miss my girl.'

'Did she go insane when she saw you?' said Janine.

'She did,' said Ren. 'It was adorable.' She stared down at her coffee. 'I hope she won't need therapy after me deserting her.'

'You haven't deserted her,' said Janine. 'You've made a major sacrifice, so she can stay in an area she's familiar with, with someone else who loves her. I visit her, you visit her. Misty is beloved!'

Ren smiled. 'She is.' *Sometimes, though, I can't even raise my game to see her. I'm so hungover, I just want to get back to the apartment after work. Or a bar. Or I can't face getting up early enough to see her before work.*

'Are you being neg?' said Janine.

Ren laughed. 'Maybe . . .'

'That's just the alcohol in your system.'

'Why do we do it?'

51

'Because it's fun.'

Ren let out a breath.

'Are you OK?' said Janine. She put a hand on her forearm.
Just tell her.

No.

Do.

'Thanks for looking out for me last night,' said Ren. 'God.
I was so wasted.'

Janine laughed. 'Nooo.'

'Was I an embarrassment?'

'No! Don't be ridiculous.'

'Ugh. I think you're just being nice.'

'No. Honestly.'

'Look, I just wanted to let you know something,' said
Ren. 'Not that it's got anything to do with last night. But
. . . I suppose, I just haven't told you and now it seems
weird after all this time. I'm . . . bipolar.' *Ugh, still hate it.*

'Thanks for letting me know.'

'You mean you guessed already!' said Ren.

Janine laughed. 'Not exactly. I figured . . . there was
something there.'

'Something *wrong*, you mean. When? Why didn't you say?'

'It's not exactly something I'm going to throw out there
. . .'

'True. Anyway, there it is, my sorry tale.'

'It doesn't change a thing as far as I'm concerned,' said
Janine. 'But, yes, I'm glad you told me.'

'Well, now that we're working together . . .'

Janine frowned. 'Now that we're working together?' She
paused. 'Are you trying to tell me I can't rely on you?'
She was half-smiling. 'That if we were in a gun battle you
might be across the room dancing to "Happy"?'

Ren laughed. *I love you, Janine Hooks.* 'Thanks.'

'All I will say is please talk to me if you're struggling . . . or if there's anything on your mind.'

'Of course,' said Ren. 'And you can talk to me too.'

Now, have you anything you'd like to tell me? Like about your possible eating disorder?

There was a sparkle of the onset of tears in Janine's eyes. She blinked and they were gone, swallowed up.

Just like that. Talk to me. Or do you think I'm just not the right kind of friend?

'Gary makes me go to these bullshit support groups every two weeks,' said Ren. 'In that shit-ass Henderson Hotel. It's enough to make you blow your brains out. Shit – I was supposed to be at one last night.'

'Don't the meetings help at all?' said Janine.

Not right now. At all. Ooh. You, troubled lady, need to know support groups help. 'They do help,' said Ren. 'Just sometimes they remind me that there's something wrong with me. And, like, I feel great. I could go there in the best humor ever, and someone's up at the lectern talking about killing themselves or getting injected in the ass with clozapine and I'm like "that is not my life".'

'Of course that's not your life,' said Janine. 'I mean, look at you.'

Yes. Seconds from a clozapine shot at all times. Ooh: that's a great idea. Shots called Clozapine. I'll have a round of Clozapines. Like Mind Erasers. Mind Numbers. With a silent 'b'. The pharmaceutical company probably wouldn't allow a brand name to be used. Obviously.

She let out a breath.

'And, Ren, I want you to know I can't be your friend in half-measures. Like, I don't half-care about people. I'm all in. Which I hope explains why I was the way I was last night. So if that doesn't sit well with you . . .'

'It's just . . .'

'What?' said Janine.

I hate my behavior being scrutinized. I hate being watched. I hate being stopped. I hate my fun being curtailed. I shouldn't have told her. Now I have another person in my life with a worried look on their face. Fuck that.

'Just . . . thanks,' said Ren.

Ren started the drive back to her apartment. She kept thinking of Hope Coulson's party pictures.

I am missing something. I need to talk to Jonathan Briar.

Fuck his lawyer.

You really don't want to do that.

Gary will go—

La la la la la . . .

Ren rang the buzzer outside Jonathan Briar's apartment building, waiting patiently for him to pick up.

'Hey,' he said.

'Jonathan, it's Ren Bryce here from Safe Streets . . .'

Silence.

'I was looking at Hope's Facebook page and there's something I need to ask you.'

'I have a lawyer now,' said Jonathan.

'This will take five minutes,' said Ren. 'Please. You want to find out who did this to Hope, don't you? You're not a suspect. I just have a couple of questions.'

'What about her Facebook page?' said Jonathan.

'Something doesn't add up,' said Ren. 'Please – can I come up? I'll show you.'

Silence.

Then the buzzer.

Thank you. Thank you. Thank you.

9

The apartment was a mess. Ren pushed aside cushions, a hoodie and two dirty plates to sit on the sofa. Jonathan went into the kitchen to make coffee. Ren could see him through the doorway, leaning against the countertop, gripping it, his head bowed. She got up and went in after him. There were fast-food wrappers, Styrofoam boxes, empty soda cans, empty chip packages, all across the countertops. The bin was over-flowing.

'Why don't you sit down on the sofa,' said Ren, putting a hand on Jonathan's back. 'I'll take care of this.'

He looked up, tears welling in his eyes. 'You don't have to.'

'Don't worry about it,' said Ren.

'Thank you,' said Jonathan. 'Thanks.'

Ren opened the cupboard under the sink, took out a garbage bag and started to fill it up. Then she loaded the dishwasher, washed down the countertops and put the kettle on. As she waited for it to boil, she looked around the kitchen. The side of the refrigerator still had notes signed by Hope, and a calendar that had been turned to the new month. Ren went over and flipped it up. Every Monday from the beginning to the end of the year, read: Good Shepherd, 6 p.m.

Eerie. A schedule that would never be followed through on . . .

Ren took out her cell phone and photographed all the months of the calendar.

Just in case . . .

The kettle boiled, Ren made coffee and went back in to sit with Jonathan Briar. He had made a half-assed attempt to tidy the living room, but he appeared to have stalled.

'Thank you for cleaning up,' he said.

'Not a problem,' said Ren.

'I told everyone to stay away,' he said. 'People offered to help . . .'

'It's not easy having people around when you're grieving,' said Ren. 'Sometimes you just want the whole world to go away.'

He nodded.

'I lost my older brother to suicide when I was thirteen years old,' said Ren.

'Really?' said Jonathan.

'Yes,' said Ren. 'His name was Beau. He was only seventeen.'

'Man . . .' said Jonathan. 'Do you ever get over that?'

'No. But it does get easier, and there's the cliché that I know you won't believe applies to you . . . until it does.'

'I can't imagine . . . getting past this.'

'I know,' said Ren. 'And you don't have to. Just take each day at a time.'

'Each day sucks.'

'Jonathan, I wanted to talk to you about a Friday night two weeks before Hope's disappearance.' Ren took her laptop out of her bag and opened it to Hope's Facebook page.

'Hope didn't update Facebook for thirty-six hours,' said Ren, 'which is kind of unlike her, right?'

She studied Jonathan's face. He was lost in the photos.

Shit. I should have prepared him.

He started to cry again.

Fuck.

'I'm sorry if this is upsetting,' said Ren, 'but I just wanted to find out, did anything happen that night?'

He shook his head. 'No.'

Ooh. I don't believe you.

'Are you sure?' said Ren. 'Hope was drinking all afternoon . . . she continued when you joined her. She could well have been very drunk that night . . . Did you guys have an argument?'

'No,' said Jonathan. 'But, yeah, she was really drunk. But she never got mean or anything, like some girls do. We didn't have an argument.'

'Did you come home together?' said Ren.

'Yes,' said Jonathan.

'How did you get home?' said Ren.

'Uh . . . we . . . got a cab.'

Once more with feeling.

Ren glanced down at the screen. 'From this bar? The Irish Hound?'

He nodded. 'Yes.'

'How long did that take?' said Ren.

'Five or ten minutes?'

Love that guessing tone of voice.

'OK,' said Ren. 'Thanks.' She paused. 'Are you sure there isn't anything else?'

He nodded. 'Positive.'

Positively lie-telling.

Ren got back to her apartment, changed, and went up to her second gym of choice – the top-floor glamor gym of her apartment building. Its glass windows looked out over the twinkling lights of Denver and made her feel like she was in a hotel. It was blessedly empty.

Woo-hoo. No stranger sweat.

Proud to be here: drank only coffee earlier. Albeit the ninth mug of the day. But not alcohol. That makes me a winner.

She pushed in her EarPods, hit buttons and set the treadmill speed to low. She started with a one-minute walk, then cranked it up.

Run, run, run.

Music pounded in her ears, loud and piercing, and hammering. She cranked it up again.

I am alive. I am alive. I am alive. My mind is a wide-open space. Everything is possible.

She thought of Hope Coulson. The face of Stephanie Wingerter quickly slid in beside her.

I know you are connected. You look so . . . alike. You were both brutalized, discarded. Just . . . I know you're connected. I know it.

What the fuck are you lying about, Jonathan Briar? I told you I don't think you're a suspect.

Ren ran for forty-five minutes, finally slamming her hand on the Stop button, slowing to a walk. She was hot, but barely sweating. She breathed deep.

I will find you, killer. I will run after you. I will be fitter and better and stronger than you. I will not fail.

She went back to her apartment. *I need Ben. I need to fuck him. I need to fuck. I need to fuck now.* She took a shower, then went into the bedroom, and sat on the edge of the bed. She dialed Ben's number. He picked up right away.

'Are you alone?' she said.

'Yes.'

She lay back on the bed. 'I need you to talk me through something . . .'

She lay there afterwards, staring at the ceiling, her left arm up over her head, her right hand holding the phone.

'It was fun while it lasted,' she said. 'Now we're just alone, which sucks.'

'I'm at the supermarket . . .'

Ren laughed. 'Ben . . . I'm sorry about earlier. I was hungover and cranky.'

'That's OK, baby.'

'How are you doing?'

'I'm good, busy. How about you?'

'We've got that murder case – the Hope Coulson one, and I'm thinking . . . there are similarities to another rape/murder from two months ago.'

'I thought the fiancé was looking good for the Coulson case . . .'

'Trial by media, yes. And Gary.'

'You're still having issues with him . . .'

'Has he said anything to you?'

Ben and Gary had been friends for years – Gary trained Ben in the Undercover Program, as he had trained Ren.

'No, but I doubt he would,' said Ben.

Paranoia. 'So, anyway, I got to thinking about serial killers—'

'Whoa, what? You think this is a serial killer?'

'Well . . . I think the same guy may have raped and killed two women – does that count?'

'Technically? No.'

'OK – forget that,' said Ren. 'In general, though, how do you feel about the following? A problem with the wiring of the brain results in: me. And: serial killers.'

Patient pause.

'I'm serious,' said Ren.

'What exactly are you saying?' said Ben. 'Are you trying to relate the two things? You and serial killers?'

'What I'm saying is – I have something in common with serial killers.'

'That's just nuts,' said Ben.

That's not a very nice thing to say.

'Is that what you're actually thinking?' said Ben.

'No.' *Yes.*

'Ren, I know you don't like me reading up on these things, but I know that bipolar people can sometimes think everything is their fault. Like, they see a natural disaster on the other side of the world, and can manage to feel guilt on some level about that. This sounds to me like a version of skewed thinking.'

'But . . . think about it,' said Ren; 'a serial killer goes around thinking things that no one knows about. He has these internal thoughts that he can't say out loud because people would know. They would *know*.' She paused. 'And I have thoughts like that.'

'All thoughts are internal,' said Ben.

Oh, yeah.

'And your thoughts are not about raping and murdering people . . . That makes a serial killer just that little bit different.'

'I like how your mind works.'

'It's pretty much how most people's minds work.'

Ouch.

'I didn't mean it like that, before you get weird.'

'Thanks.'

'I'm going to stop talking now.'

Ren laughed. 'I think that would be very wise.'

10

Donna Darisse reached out of the shower, grabbed a faded towel from the hook on the wall, and wrapped it around her slender body. She stepped onto the tiled floor of the tiny bathroom, grabbed a second towel and quickly dried her fine, wispy dark hair. She looked in the mirror. She sometimes expected to see her pre-chemo hair – this fragile, but fighting hair still had the power to startle her.

There was a knock on the bathroom door.

'Mommy, can I come in?'

'Just give me a moment, Cam,' said Donna. 'Is everything OK?'

'Yes! I just wanted to say hi!'

Donna smiled. 'Hi yourself,' she said. 'Now, you go back in to your movie, I'll be out in a little while.'

'I wish you weren't going to work,' said Cam as she walked away.

It was Donna's first week back since her treatment. She was high on guilt, low on options. She listened for the DVD player to kick in, and she went into her bedroom. She went straight for the drawer and the wig hidden at the back. She couldn't bear to tell Cam – she was only six years old. So Donna always wore the wig unless Cam was staying with her father. Five of Donna's friends had their heads shaved in solidarity when she lost her hair. Cam just thought they'd all gone crazy.

Donna pulled out a red dress she had often had to diet to fit into. She looked at herself in the full-length mirror, pulling at the loose fabric. She had made remarks about skinny people in the past – they needed fat on their bones, they needed a burger, a home-cooked meal. She felt a little differently since she became one of them. She had never known the stories of the people she judged.

Donna walked into the living room with a smile on her face. 'Mommy loves someone very much,' she said. 'And Mommy thinks that person is right here in this room. Do you have any idea who that could be?'

'Me!' said Cam. 'Me!' She leapt up from her cushion on the floor, ran across the room and dived into her mother's arms.

The doorbell rang, and Donna carried Cam to the door and let the babysitter in.

'Now,' said Donna, letting Cam down, 'you be good, and you enjoy your play date this afternoon. I'll see you for supper.'

'Yes!' said Cam. 'You look so beautiful, Mama. And I like your white cowboy boots!'

'You look beautiful too . . . Belle. I wish I had such a pretty yellow dress. I would dance around the room all day and all night.'

'Your dress is the prettiest dress in the whole wide world,' said Cam. 'You might meet a prince!'

He sat in the car watching the street hookers making their way up and down Colfax Avenue.

Fuck that Hope Coulson bitch. Fuck her and her kindergarten smile and her lines of volunteers.

He turned his attention back to the street.

People only line up for you pathetic whoring bitches when you're alive. Only so's you can suck their cocks.

He couldn't see anything he liked in the parade before him.

Fuck the landfill site. Fuck Denver PD. Fuck the sheriffs. Fuck the Feds. Fuck today's miserable luncheon buffet. No man could get full on that.

Just as he was about to drive away, he saw one, just the way he liked them.

Hold up, scrawny lady! You're about to be crowned winner of today's pitiful pussy pageant!

He drove alongside her.

Donna Darisse leaned down, spoke into the driver's side.

'How are you, handsome man?'

'Well, that's about the nicest thing anyone's said to me all day.'

'Oh, I'm sure you hear that all the time . . .' said Donna.

He wondered if all the conversations taking place along that strip were the same as his, loading and unloading a whole pile of bullshit every time the trick opened her mouth, every time the john did.

'Well, you're a Texan, right?' she said. 'You like to keep your boots on? I like that.' She smiled. 'How do you like my boots? Do you approve?'

'I like them very much,' he said. *I'd like to slam them over and over into your face.*

'And how do you like your women?' she said.

'Satisfied,' he said. 'Hop on in.'

'Just so you know, I don't do anal.'

Ha. Ha. Ha.

'Where are you going to take me?' said Donna.

'Right through the gates of heaven,' he said.

He glanced across at her. He could see a tiny flash of something in her eyes, and how she smiled quickly to try to bury it. His dick swelled. He closed his eyes, breathed in, loved this, loved the anticipation, had trained himself not to rush through to the end, but to savor every part of what was about to unfold.

'Tell me more,' she said.

'Show don't tell is my motto,' he said.

'Do you have a name?' she said.

'Yes, ma'am. You can call me Harris.'

'Short for Harrison?'

He shrugged. 'It's what I *long* for that matters . . .'

She laughed. 'You on business here in Denver?'

'Serious business.'

Donna reached over and slid her hand from his knee all the way up. 'Me too, sweetheart.' She smiled and he got a little softer, and all that ever brought was confusion. Confusion angered him.

He had done his research. It wasn't difficult to find a map online of the HALO cam locations. He chose a route from East Colfax that would circumvent them all. Even though he knew, without a vehicle description, the cops wouldn't have a clue what to look for. And he was making sure to take her to an area that had untouched corners. He liked violating what was untouched.

Donna turned toward him, reached out for him again.

And you – you've been touched by every motherfucker the length and breadth of Colfax, you sick-looking, dick-sucking bitch.

'Not here,' he said.

Donna followed his gaze to a wall lined with dumpsters.

'I'm sure we can pick somewhere prettier than this,' she said. 'You've got a nice car here we could get comfortable in.'

'Sweetheart, never in my life have I considered comfort in any decision I've ever made.'

And I sure as hell have never connected it with fucking.

'So, we're going to do this outside,' he said, 'then I'll drive you on back to your friends.' He smiled.

Donna relaxed a little. They got out of the car and she walked toward the wall. Harris still hadn't gotten hard when he turned her around and pushed her up against it, when he pressed himself against her. There was a moment of stillness.

'I'm kidding,' he said. 'We're not going to do it here. My office is inside.'

He could feel her reaction – confusion, relief, the desperate optimism that made her want to believe that the person her every cell was telling her was so very wrong, was really OK, that the evil she was sensing was not real. He had an office!

He unlocked the door and pushed her inside an empty, cavernous warehouse.

'Hey,' said Donna, half-turning, 'you never asked how much I charge.'

Harris laughed as he slammed the door behind them. He grabbed her by the wrist and flung her to the ground. 'Oh, honey, you're the one paying.'

'Wh—'

'With your life.' He laughed, a short crazy laugh as if this had been such an obvious thing for her to have not considered.

Donna screamed, and it echoed around the vast, black space. 'No!' she said. 'No – please.'

He was holding a knife with a long blade that was catching

the scant moonlight from the row of windows at the top of the room.

'Take off your clothes,' he said. 'All of them.'

'Please don't do this,' said Donna.

'Don't say please to me.' He walked a step closer, patient, and dead-eyed.

She did as he asked, and stood trembling, naked, trying to cover herself.

He looked her up and down, stopped with his eyes locked on hers.

'OK,' he said. 'I'll be fair, I'll be fair – I'm gonna give you a chance to get away.'

She stared at him. He nodded.

'Go ahead,' he said. 'Go ahead.'

She frowned, but within seconds, she bolted into the gloom. He gave her time, then followed her. She cried out as her feet struck glass, but she kept running, left and right, wildly panicked, thrilling him. He gained on her, with little effort, reaching out to her, grabbing her hair, but pulling the wig from her head. He recoiled, threw it to one side, but barely broke his stride. He grabbed her arm this time, yanked her toward him, flung her to the ground. He tied her wrists with cable ties behind her back.

He knelt down in front of her, pushing her limp legs open. 'I'm doing you a favor,' he hissed. 'Is this the life you want for yourself? What do you think those milked-dry titties are gonna do for a man like me? Flat little saving-up-for-fake-ones kind of titties? Your stretch marks. All of that tells me you've got kids at home and you're out streetwalking. You're nothing but a rodent bitch looking for someone to prey on her bony ass. Well, you got me. You got me. And how do you like it?'

He grabbed her thigh hard, burying his fingertips into it,

and with his other hand, pushed the blade inside her, over and over.

Donna screamed and screamed, but had no power against his weight. He pressed the side of her face hard against the damp, stinking concrete.

'You asked me how I like my women,' he said. 'Face down in the dirt and dying!'

He laughed hysterically. Donna was disoriented, struggling to breathe, trying to get her head from under his hand, which he released only to punch her jaw hard. He heard a crack. After that, it was just moaning.

Face down in the dirt and dying.

He felt something sink inside him.

Face down in the dirt and dying. Dirt: not here, not on a cold concrete floor.

It's not enough, is it? It's not enough. You need to fly again. You need to fly. Nothing else matters now. You need to fly. You need to fly.

11

Ren sat at her desk with a Danish in front of her that she had taken one bite out of.

Why did I bring this in here? It is just looking like fatness to me. How could I ever have eaten so many of these?

She opened up a document and wrote the date of the night that Jonathan Briar was lying about.

Why was he lying?

Ren looked up the Irish Hound bar on Google Maps. It was the last stop on Hope and Jonathan's night out.

His 'cab' answer was the least convincing.

Would they have gotten a cab for such a short trip if Hope Coulson was as hammered as I believe she was? Wouldn't they have gone for some fresh air in their lungs?

Ren called the Irish Hound for the video from that night. They had aready erased it.

Shit.

She went back to the map and marked out three separate routes they could have taken home . . . if they had walked. From that, she put together a list of businesses and homes that they may have passed, and who may have captured them on CCTV cameras.

Her phone rang. She looked down and saw the flashing name of Glenn Buddy, DPD.

She picked up. 'Hey, Glenn. Before you say anything, I didn't get a chance to ask you last time – how's Brenda doing?'

Glenn was close friends with Cliff and Brenda James. Cliff was Ren's adored big-bear JeffCo colleague who Janine had replaced. His wife, Brenda, was undergoing cancer treatment and had been given just months to live. Cliff had gone back to work at JeffCo Sheriff's Department to be closer to home.

'It's not good,' said Glenn. 'But they're holding up, they're holding up.'

'I haven't spoken to Cliff in weeks,' said Ren. 'I'm afraid to bother him.'

'I know, I know – time is precious, but I'm sure he'd appreciate a call. You cheer him up, Ren.'

'I don't know about that.'

'You do. Now, I'm about to not cheer you up. We've got reports of a missing prostitute. Name's Donna Darisse. We brought her in a few times. Real nice lady. She's a cancer survivor.'

The word *survivor* sounded stark when side by side with Brenda James's prognosis.

'She's got a six-year-old girl,' said Glenn. 'It was Donna's first day back on the job after treatment. The daughter's friend's mom called it in this morning – Donna never came back to pick her up after a play date at six p.m. yesterday. That was totally out of character for her. But the friend's mom figured she had to work late – she thought Donna was a waitress – and that her battery had died. She took her to school this morning, then nothing. The school hasn't heard from her either. The friend's mom knew that Donna would never do something like that.'

'Please let her have fallen asleep in some luxury hotel suite with Edward Lewis.'

Silence.

'*Pretty Woman* . . .' said Ren.

'I'll go with that,' said Glenn. 'According to some of the other girls, she was last seen on East Colfax, getting into a dark sedan. No description of the driver. We're going through the HALO cams now, see if we see anything. Her last cell phone signal was picked up in that area, then nothing.'

'Is she a user?' said Ren.

'No,' said Glenn.

'Do you have a photo of her?'

'Yup,' said Glenn. 'Emailing it through.'

'OK.' Ren got off the phone, opened the email, and saved the image. Donna Darisse had a thick head of chestnut hair that fell past her shoulders. She had a warm smile, good teeth. She looked healthy. She didn't look like a street hooker.

I'm finding comfort in that. If *the skinny blonde is his type, and not just a coincidence.*

Shit. Cancer . . . she had cancer.

Ren called Glenn back. 'Sorry, again, Glenn – had Donna Darisse dropped a lot of weight?'

'Oh – yes, according to one of the other girls.'

'And did she lose her hair?' said Ren.

'Yes,' said Glenn. 'Shit, I didn't think of that. Let me see if I can't get a more recent photo.'

Twenty minutes later, a new photo of Donna Darisse hit Ren's inbox. She was holding a little girl in her arms. Both of them were laughing. The girl had her hand in the air, having just placed a tiny gold plastic tiara on her mother's head.

Oh. Shit. Hollow cheeks, blonde hair . . . blonde wig.

Stephanie Wingerter, Hope Coulson, Donna Darisse. These women look too alike for this to be a coincidence.

Donna Darisse, I think you wore the wrong-colored wig. That is fucked up.

Ren opened a document and typed: prostitute / teacher / prostitute.

Did you return to what you knew best? Women who were easier to take? Did the media attention on Hope Coulson send you back under your rock? Well, we care about all of them, you fucking reptile.

Everett came into the bullpen. 'What's going on in your world?'

She filled him in on Donna Darisse.

'Shit,' said Everett.

'I know.'

They both turned as they heard footsteps rushing down the hallway.

'Where is she?' a woman was roaring. 'Where is she?'

No security in the building . . .

Everett and Ren both got up, drew their weapons, ran to the door. Gary rushed out of his office past them toward the woman. He had no weapon drawn.

'Don't do this,' he said. 'Don't.'

What the . . . ?

The woman almost growled, struggled to make herself seen around Gary. Ren saw a flash of blonde hair.

'Where the fuck is she, Gary?' she shouted.

That's Gary's wife! What the fuck?

Ren put her weapon back into her shoulder holster. She turned to Everett, shaking her head silently, letting him know to put his away. They started to back into the bullpen.

'Ren!' Karen was screaming. 'Ren!'

Me?!!

But Gary was wrestling Karen down the hallway toward the conference room.

Everett turned to Ren. 'What the hell is that all about?'

Ren made a face. 'That's Karen Dettling – Gary's wife. And I have no idea.'

'Is she nuts?' said Everett. 'And why was she looking for you? Are you guys friends? Was she pissed at you? Or looking for your help? What's going on with those two?'

Ren turned to him. 'Jesus, you sound like a girl.'

'What the hell, though?'

'I know.'

'Ren!' Karen was coming back toward the bullpen.

'Karen, get into the conference room,' said Gary. 'Do not say another word. Ren . . . in the conference room now.'

Me? What the fuck is this shitshow?

Ren followed Gary and Karen into the conference room. Karen turned to Ren.

'You bitch!' she said. 'How could you do this to us?'

Am I hallucinating?

Still drunk?

Starring in Punk'd*?*

'Do what?' said Ren. She looked at Gary. He was warning her with his eyes.

What IS this?

'You came to our home, you taught Claire Spanish!' said Karen. 'How long has this been going on?'

'What?' said Ren. 'Oh my God.' *She thinks—*

'Did you spend all night together or did you just fuck her and leave?' said Karen, stabbing a finger into Gary's chest. She turned to Ren. 'Did you wake up in my husband's arms?'

Oh. Jesus. Christ. Don't laugh. Don't do your nervous fucking laugh.

Ren started laughing.

Karen looked fit to explode. 'How dare you? You—'

'I'm sorry – I'm nervous – but we're not having an affair!' said Ren. She turned to Gary. 'Gary!'

'We're not,' said Gary. 'Jesus, Karen.'

So casual, while I'm getting attacked. What the fuck?

'Where are you getting this from?' said Ren. 'Gary wouldn't dream of cheating on you. Gary adores you! Everyone knows that.' *And the fact that you drive each other nuts, but still.*

Karen was stalled. She looked from Ren to Gary. Mortification started seeping into her face.

'Karen,' said Ren, 'Gary's my boss, he loves you. And I'm with Ben.' *Have you lost your mind? Gary, say something, for fuck's sake. Why am I getting all this shit?*

'Gary!' said Ren. *Wake the fuck up!*

'Karen,' said Gary, 'I'm not having an affair with Ren.'

Jesus, even I'm not sure I believe that . . .

'We're on an important case,' said Gary. 'So, please . . . just go home.'

Go home? She's distraught, you fuckwit. Go home? That's it? Get your wife out of here. Go with her. Get her help.

Karen slumped into a chair. 'I don't know what to believe,' she said. She started to cry.

'I'm going to give you some privacy,' said Ren.

'Don't go,' said Karen. 'I'm so sorry. I . . . I'm not feeling great right now.'

'I'm sorry to hear that,' said Ren. 'But, really, I don't think it's my place to be here.' She gave Karen a hug. 'Gary is not cheating on you.' *He's too fucking straight! He sees me as evidence of why not to cheat!*

Not that I haven't thought *about fucking your husband, but still . . .*

Ren looked at Gary. He gave her a nod of permission to leave. He looked worn out. Ren closed the door behind her.

What the effin' crap?

12

Ren went back into the bullpen, sat quietly at her desk, shuffled papers.

'That's it?' said Everett.

'That's it,' said Ren.

'You're killing me . . .'

'Let's just leave it at "Well, that was surreal".'

'Did you trade blows?' His eyes were sparkling.

'I'm a lover, not a fighter.' *NOT a lover, in fact.* 'What did I miss?'

'The media has gotten hold of the Donna Darisse story – they're not revealing she's a prostitute, but they are saying she was last seen on Colfax. They have already interviewed some fantastic creatures there. Some will be viral by close of business.'

'Oh, no,' said Ren.

'Oh, yes. One woman was so high . . . it was just cruel to put her in front of a camera.'

'I hate that shit.'

'That would be like filming you in Gaffney's.'

'Jesus, the idea of watching my vulnerable self . . .'

'Is vulnerable the new euphemism?' said Everett. 'Oh my God, I was so vulnerable last night. Where's my pineapple juice?' He grabbed the remote control. 'It's on again,' he said. He turned up the television. 'Check out this goddess.'

'This is a very safe area!' the woman was saying. *'Always has been! Now I'm afraid of my life.'*

'Ahm afeardamalaff too,' said Ren.

'I'm not surprised,' said Everett, nodding toward the door.

They laughed loud, then turned their attention back to the screen.

'Donna Darisse was last seen at lunchtime yesterday on Colfax Avenue. If you know anything about Ms Darisse's whereabouts, please contact Denver PD . . .'

'Fuckerooni,' said Ren.

She went back into Stephanie Wingerter's file. 'Stephanie Wingerter disappeared at night. This was lunchtime. So, does he have a nine-to-five job he has to work around? Or does he cruise whenever he feels like it?'

'You're sticking to the one killer theory,' said Everett.

'I am. I'm not afeardamalaff to do that.'

'Agent Bryce was always so brave,' said Everett. 'Even – no, no *especially* – on the dance floor.'

They looked up. Gary was in the doorway, his face set. *Not the time to bring up serial killing.*

'I have an appointment this afternoon,' he said. 'My calls will be redirected to you, Ren.'

'OK,' said Ren. 'See you tomorrow.' *I hope your life isn't imploding.*

Ren called Glenn Buddy.

'Glenn, have you got many statements from today's canvas on Colfax?'

'I'll have some tomorrow,' said Glenn. 'I don't know what

you guys are equipped with over there, but my guys have one pair of hands each to type with.'

'Fair point,' said Ren. 'Have you got any names of johns who—'

'Ren, what I got is five live homicide cases giving me a pain in my ass. Which victim will I swap for the missing hooker – the dead child or the other dead child?'

'Glenn, I think this is a serial case . . .'

'I have no doubt you do,' said Glenn. 'You're like one of those people who sees dead people.'

'Are you saying I'm imagining this?'

'No,' said Glenn. 'I believe in ghosts. I just need to see a body first. I need a pin in a map before I can make a network with my red string to the next pin.'

'You don't do that.'

'I do not. Stay safe.'

That night, Ren lined up photos of the victims on her kitchen table:

Stephanie Wingerter. Hope Coulson. Donna Darisse.

Sorry, Donna. I know we haven't found you yet. But I know we will.

Underneath, she laid down printouts of the bullet points of the cases she had made at the office earlier.

I need a beer.

Her phone rang. *Janine.*

'Hello, lovely lady,' said Ren. She went to the refrigerator and grabbed a bottle of Coors Light.

'What happened today?' said Janine. 'I believe I missed some action.'

'You don't want to know, trust me,' said Ren. 'A Dettling domestic. They've happened before. Though not quite with such dramz.' She opened the beer.

'I heard from admin that she called you a bitch. What was that about?'

Shiiiiit. It's out there. 'Ugh. She thought I was having an affair with Gary. Please don't say that to anyone.'

'I won't, don't be ridiculous, but . . . shit.' She started laughing.

'I know,' said Ren. 'But the worst part about it was that I have been really attracted to him lately even though he's a total asshole to me.'

'Oh, God – don't be that girl.'

'No, I'm not, that's the thing. I like being treated well. Anyway, I'd never act on it.'

'Neither would he,' said Janine.

'I know that,' said Ren, laughing. 'It's embarrassing, though. I hope Karen didn't get that vibe off me.'

The doorbell rang. She checked the intercom screen.

'Holy shit,' said Ren. 'That's him at my door.'

'Gary?' said Janine. 'Maybe Karen planted the idea in his head . . .'

'Stop!' said Ren. 'You brat. Call you later.'

'Behave.'

'Jesus!'

'Oh, and don't call tonight,' said Janine. 'I have serious lady pain. I'm planning to be unconscious.'

'Aw, you poor thing. Hot-water bottle. Lots of love.'

Gary rang the bell again.

Yikes. I don't think he has ever been in any of my homes. Weirdness.

Ren buzzed him in.

She poured the beer down the sink, and put the empty bottle in the cabinet underneath. She put on the kettle. She tidied away the photos and pages on the table, put a magazine on top of them.

Gary walked right past her into the apartment, and into the living room without saying a word.

This place is so tiny. You look so big.

'Nice place,' he said.

'Sit down,' said Ren.

Gary nodded. 'Ren, look, I know this is inappropriate.'

'No it's not—'

Oh, you're not talking about calling in here.

'I need you to do something for me,' said Gary. 'It's . . . just . . . Karen was obviously wrong about you and me, but . . .'

Oh, no.

He nodded.

Jesus Christ, Gary.

'And you need me to cover for you,' said Ren.

'Yes,' said Gary. 'I wouldn't ask—'

Well, fuck that. I like Karen. We get along. I like Claire. I . . . respected you. Respected. Shit, Gary, you're the moral one. Don't make me lose faith in humanity. I didn't realize how much I respected you until I stopped . . . round about two seconds ago.

'Why would she have thought it was me, though?' said Ren.

Gary gave her a patient look. 'I know you enough to know you're not a homewrecker,' he said. 'But, not all women see you that way.'

That's not very fair. Though I am, even now, thinking about fucking you. What is wrong with me? But I never would. So, yes, it is unfair.

'But I get along with Karen,' said Ren. 'I like her a lot.'

'I know,' said Gary, 'she's obviously not thinking straight right now.'

'How come you didn't cover your tracks better?' said Ren. 'What did she find out?'

'My saving grace is your love of champagne . . .' said Gary.

'It's my saving grace too,' said Ren.

Gary shot out a laugh of relief. 'A champagne cork . . . ended up in my overnight bag . . .'

La la la la la la la . . .

'Karen found it,' said Gary. 'I needed an explanation. And you were the quickest one I thought of.'

'So, I've already helped you on this . . .' said Ren.

'Yes . . .' said Gary.

'What do you need me to do?' said Ren.

'Back me up,' said Gary. 'Call her.'

This is grim.

'So – let me get this straight,' said Ren. 'You said what exactly? That we were—'

'In Breck,' said Gary. 'We had a bottle of champagne in the room, where my bag was open, but nothing happened between us. I hate champagne, she knows that. You were a safe and logical choice to be the person drinking it.'

'Me, safe, logical and champagne . . .' *How have these words come together?*

'Well, it backfired anyway,' said Gary. 'She still thought something was going on.'

'I'm kind of offended . . .'

'Don't be,' said Gary. 'She's a wife who found a champagne cork in her husband's overnight bag . . .'

'I'd have a hard time believing anything after that.'

'So, can you call her?' said Gary.

'Yes, of course,' said Ren. 'But . . . fuck.'

'I know,' said Gary.

'If I'm going to do this very wrong thing,' said Ren, 'I'm going to do it right. You need to arm me with all the facts, so I don't fuck up. There is no going back if I fuck this up. For either of us.'

Gary nodded. 'Thanks.'

The fucking pressure.

'Dates and times, please,' said Ren. 'And you'll have to tell me who this woman is. I don't *want* to know, that's your business. But I *need* to know.'

'I ended it,' said Gary. 'It's over.'

'Promise m—'

'It's over.' He pulled out a notebook and tore out a page with a list of dates.

Alrighty, then.

'Thanks, Ren. I appreciate this.' He stood up.

I don't want to do a quid pro quo, but . . .

'Before you go,' said Ren, 'I want to run something by you . . .'

She got up and gathered together the photos she had brought home from the office.

'Did you print these at Safe Streets?' said Gary. 'In color?' Ren nodded.

'Stop wasting ink and paper.'

Internal eye roll. 'On an unrelated note – here are three victims of a violent rapist and murderer . . . can you see how similar they look?'

Gary looked across the line of photos. He looked back at Ren. 'Yes.'

'Three victims . . . that makes a serial killer, official definition. I'd like to call a meeting with DPD, see if we can—'

'Who's this third one?' said Gary.

'Donna Darisse, a prostitute reported missing this morning.'

'So she's not dead.'

'Not *found*. She's been missing since yesterday afternoon. Didn't show up to collect her six-year-old from a play date. Apparently, that was totally out of character.'

Gary stared at her. 'Let me know when you have a body.'

'There will be a body,' said Ren. *Mark my words!*

'I'm not doing this unless you're one hundred per cent,' said Gary.

'OK – who . . .' *the fuck* 'could be one hundred per cent about something like this?' *Seriously.*

'At the very least, a body is a one hundred per cent guarantee of a death.'

High-larious. 'I want Donna Darisse to be safe and well,' said Ren. 'I just don't feel in my gut that she is.'

'Let me know when you have a body.'

I heard you the first time.

'There's another thing,' said Ren, 'I spoke with Jonathan Briar, and—'

'And his lawyer, I hope . . .'

Not so much. 'Well, I just had a few little—'

'Ren, for crying out loud! What were you thinking? He'll never let us talk to him again if you—'

'It was fine,' said Ren. 'We got along OK. I helped him out in his apartment. He answered my questions, but . . . he was lying about something, about a night out they had two weeks before Hope Coulson disappeared.'

'If you think he was lying,' said Gary, 'that he's got something to hide, then the next time we might need him for something, that lawyer won't let us within a mile of him. Jesus Christ, Ren. You know this. Why are we having this conversation?'

Gary's phone beeped. He checked it. He turned the screen to Ren.

'Looks like you've got your one hundred per cent guarantee,' said Ren.

13

Ren and Gary drove through the city of Arvada and ten miles along Highway 72 into the unincorporated part of Jefferson County.

And another jurisdiction joins the party.

The flashing lights of the police cruisers led them to the small collection of warehouses where Donna Darisse's body had been found by a carload of college kids looking for nothing other than an out-of-the-way place to go through a few six-packs.

Cliff James was standing sentry.

'Hey,' said Ren, hugging him.

He held her extra long.

'How's Brenda doing?' said Gary.

'We're doing good,' said Cliff. He smiled, but his eyes were sad. 'It's not a pretty sight back there.'

Donna Darisse lay beside a row of dumpsters, outside one of the warehouses.

Robbie, Everett and Janine were gathered a distance away from the body.

Poor Janine. So much for her plan to be unconscious.

Ren and Gary went straight to Donna Darisse's body. She was naked, except for her bloodstained white cowboy boots, lying on her stomach, facing away from the wall, her arms behind her back, her wrists bound with cable ties. Her face was swollen to twice its size, the flesh bursting and cut and oozing. Her red dress and tiny red lace G-string were discarded ten feet away, along with a blonde wig. Cheap glamor, transformed into something poignant and tragic when met with such boundless savagery.

Ren looked for a moment at the stars above, and breathed in and out, in and out, until she could face looking back down.

This is beyond horrific.

From her lower back, down her bare buttocks, and between Donna Darisse's legs was a terrible mess that could have been nothing other than the result of a chemical burn.

Acid.

Ren felt like her body was liquefying inside. She felt spikes of pain in the same places where Donna Darisse had been brutalized. Her stomach churned.

I have no words.

They went over to join the others. Everyone looked grim-faced and tired.

'Dr Tolman is on vacation,' said Janine. 'We have a stand-in . . .'

A hooting laugh broke out. They all looked up, knowing that it meant who that stand-in was: Dr Mark Gaston, the new Medical Examiner for the 18th Judicial District, which covered Arapahoe, Douglas, Elbert and Lincoln Counties. Gaston was forty-five, but looked early thirties. His pouting lips were his most striking feature, followed by the prince-from-an-animation hair: light brown, thick, and wavy, the type of hair that marked out generations of the same family, the type that was celebrated in portraits.

Arrogant hair. Book of Wrong.

Gaston walked toward them.

Ren leaned into the others. 'Gaston always looks like he's been called away from seducing a nineteen-year-old. "OMG – you're a Medical Examiner! *So hot!*"'

Gaston was too close for them to laugh.

'Is that a dead hooker on the ground or are you making excuses to see me?' said Gaston, smiling at Ren. He crouched down beside Donna Darisse. 'Yes, she is dead. Despite all signs to the contrary.' He stood up. 'And that's acid. That's a man who's going all out not to leave any swimmers behind. Die, boys, die!'

Swimmers . . . ugh.

'How long's she been missing?' said Gaston.

'About forty-eight hours,' said Ren.

'I'm guessing she was killed not long after that,' said Gaston. 'Not here, though. The scene is too clean. But you don't need me to tell you that. Let me do my thang and I'll let your boys in. Stand back, bitches. Dr G is here.'

Dear.

God.

'I'm going to do you a favor here,' he said, when he was finished. 'I'm going to prioritize this little lady. So, if you want to meet me at the autopsy suite at seven a.m., I'll bump her to the top of my list.'

He's a hooker with a heart.

'Appreciate it,' said Gary.

'Ren?' said Gaston. 'You up for the early-morning autopsy?' He almost winked.

'Yes,' said Gary. He turned to Ren. 'I gotta go – can I leave this with you? I need to get back.'

To whom?

'No problem,' said Ren. She looked at Gaston. 'You won't be too tired?'

'I've done a ton of coke,' said Gaston. 'I was expecting a different night.' He laughed loud.

'Everett?' said Ren. 'You up for it?'

'Yes, ma'am.'

She turned to Janine. Her face was white, her eyes narrowed in pain. 'Janine, you go home, sleep,' said Ren. 'Robbie, we'll notify the next-of-kin. Everett – here are the keys to my place. We'll join you there right after.'

'What?' said Everett.

'I don't want to waste any time,' said Ren. 'You can sleep on the sofa for a half hour. And I promise you high-end coffee on our return.'

Ren and Robbie arrived back to the apartment at four a.m. and woke Everett up.

'That was suitably grim,' said Ren.

'Your sofa, on the other hand, was not,' said Everett, stretching out his legs, standing up, and walking around the living room. 'You promised high-end coffee, remember.'

'A promise I am following through on,' Ren called from the kitchen. 'God, though, this apartment depresses me. And this micro-kitchen. I love cooking, and I don't even cook here. Most of my kitchen stuff's all packed away in boxes in Annie's attic. I've got all their crappy utensils, blunt knives, shady-looking forks. It's like the whole place is designed to guide you to the microwave so you can stand – alone – and watch your meal-for-one perform a tragic pirouette.'

'You are not alone tonight,' said Robbie.

'This *morning*,' said Everett. 'Need us to come in there and make the kitchen feel like it's hopping?'

'You just concentrate on squeezing yourselves around that table, leaving enough room for me and my expansive mind.'

She came in and set the tray down at the center of the table.

'I hate glass tables,' said Ren. 'I need a tablecloth. But I'm not a big fan of tablecloths either. Actually, that's wrong – it's the pressure of keeping them clean that bothers me. I love tablecloths.' She put a coffee mug in front of each of them.

'No cookies?' said Everett, forlorn.

'Much as I'd love to soften the blow of mutilated genitals, I have nothing,' said Ren.

'Toast even?' said Robbie.

'I have arugula,' said Ren. 'And an angry inch of parmesan.'

'Mind if I order in?' said Robbie.

Inward narrowing of eyes. You are replacing sex with food, Robbie Truax. Jesus . . . does anyone not have an issue with food?

'You order whatever you like,' said Ren. 'As I deliver an apology for the bare cupboards.'

'Ren has been following the jalapeño popper diet,' said Everett. 'You go from bar to bar—'

Robbie looked unimpressed with Everett's insider knowledge. He picked up his phone and began ordering breakfast from an all-night diner.

'And dessert is the olive at the bottom of the Dirty Martini,' said Ren, helping Everett out.

A silence fell.

Stephanie. Hope. Donna.

Rape, murder, mutilation.

'So,' said Ren, 'what the fuck is going on? These three women look remarkably similar . . . at least Donna did the day he picked her up. So, is he killing the same woman over and over – an ex-girlfriend, an ex-wife, a sister, his mother—'

'Someone who didn't return his affection,' said Robbie.

'Women in general?' said Everett. He paused. 'That happen to be blonde and skinny . . .' He laughed. 'Sorry, maybe I'm too tired for this. This will be going to Quantico for profiling, though, right?'

'Yup,' said Ren.

'That'll take weeks,' said Robbie.

'Well, it's not like we're going to sit around and wait for it to guide us,' said Everett.

'I swear to God,' said Ren, 'if I see another profile that says male, aged between twenty-two and thirty-two . . .'

Dr Gaston welcomed Ren and Everett to the autopsy suite at seven a.m.

'First off,' he said, 'as we saw, her junk was dunked – her entire body was washed down with bleach. The acid was evidence of super-caution at work, because the bleach should have done the trick. Using acid on the genital area as well seems like a pretty good indicator that she was raped, or why would he bother?'

I'm still at 'junk was dunked'. Did I hear that?

'Sorry – run through all that again?' said Ren.

Gaston raised his eyebrows, but complied.

'He may not have raped her,' said Ren. 'It might have been all about the mutilation.'

'Well, that's for your investigative minds to work out,' said Gaston. 'I was just throwing in my two cents.'

Please don't.

'Cause of death was sharp-force trauma – her femoral artery was severed. Manner of death – exsanguination, which is why we know she wasn't killed at the scene. There was no blood. I don't need to tell you this would have been bloody.'

He began examining the external surface of the body. Ren

became mesmerized by Donna Darisse's feet. They were scratched, bruised, and sparkling in the light.

'Is that glass?' said Ren.

'Yes,' said Gaston. He used his forceps to pluck out the shards – clear, green and blue – then drop them into a stainless-steel dish.

'Just in the soles of her feet, nowhere else,' said Ren. 'I'm presuming she walked on it—'

'As opposed to the killer using forceps to carefully push the pieces in . . .' He looked up and winked.

Oh, fuck off, Gaston.

'She walked across glass for him, yes,' said Gaston. 'Or ran. They're in quite deep.'

'Did you see any glass at the scene?' said Ren.

'No – not to my naked eyes.'

He managed to make that sound sleazy.

'And what caused the abrasions?' said Ren.

'Probably running on a concrete surface,' said Gaston.

'So she could have run away from him,' said Ren.

'Not far – or fast – enough,' said Gaston. 'Then the particular damage to her heels that you can see here could have happened if she was raped – if she was lying on rough ground, kicking out, trying to get purchase . . . she also has abrasions on her knees, which would be consistent with her having been raped from behind.'

'God, and he put her boots back on.' *Jesus.*

Feet. Feet. Feet.

Something is clawing at me.

14

That afternoon, Gary stood at the top of the conference room in front of the Safe Streets squad, twenty DPD detectives, Cliff James, and Douglas County Undersheriff, Cole Rodeal.

'How's the arm?' said Ren, as she walked by.

'It's healing,' said Rodeal. 'Another two weeks, the cast is gone.'

'OK,' said Gary, eyeballing Ren into silence. 'SA Ren Bryce called this and will be case agent. Everything is to go through Ren. She will be coordinating the investigation with – on the DPD side – Glenn Buddy.'

'Easy to remember cuz they rhyme – Ren and Glenn!' said one of the DPD detectives.

Larry Someone. Dimwit.

Ren was walking to the top of the room. 'Sadly not everything we need to remember on this case will rhyme, so I hope that doesn't make things too difficult for you.' She delivered it deadpan. Then smiled as she turned to face everyone.

Nervous laughter.

'OK,' said Ren, 'we have – as far as we know – three

brutally violated victims of what we believe is the same killer. In chronological order the victims are: Stephanie Wingerter, Hope Coulson, and Donna Darisse—'

'Can you explain to us why you were linking them?' said another one of the DPD detectives. Ren searched for the voice.

Unkempt, lazy-looking fuck. Sorry.

'To break this down very clearly,' said Ren, 'the victims are of a similar physical type: petite, and blonde. In Donna Darisse's case it was a wig, but the killer wasn't to know that when he saw her. All three victims were either raped with a foreign object and/or sexually mutilated. Stephanie Wingerter was bound at the wrists with rope, Donna Darisse, with cable ties. The same two victims were prostitutes. Knives were used both on Stephanie Wingerter and Donna Darisse; manner of death was exsanguination. Hope Coulson was strangled, as evidenced by the broken hyoid bone. Post-mortem, he has inflicted burns on bodies both by setting the body alight in conjunction with an accelerant, and by using acid.'

'And do we know for definite they were all raped?' said the detective.

'Because of decomposition in the case of Stephanie Wingerter, and because of the acid on Donna Darisse's genitals, no,' said Ren. 'But Hope Coulson was violently raped with a foreign object. And, like I said, all three women were clearly sexually mutilated. The UNSUB could well be in the system, so he knows we have his DNA. Therefore he doesn't want us to have any more of it. So, we have to ask the question – is the mutilation part of the thrill for our UNSUB or is it simply to destroy evidence? Also, what was the reason behind the rape with a foreign object? Did he try to rape initially, but then couldn't sustain an erection, so resorted to whatever object was closest? I don't know. And where were they killed if not where the bodies were found?'

She paused.

'Weirdly, Donna Darisse had glass embedded in the soles of her feet, and Stephanie Wingerter's feet were burned. I haven't come across feet being targeted before, but there's always a first time.'

'Maybe the killer gets a kick out of making them walk over surfaces that will cause pain?' said Rodeal.

'Maybe,' said Ren.

'Are you absolutely sure it's just one killer?' said the detective who asked the first question.

Yes!!!! 'I have a problem dealing in absolutes,' said Ren. *LOL.* 'But, yes – I believe it's one killer. And in my opinion, this UNSUB doesn't want to get caught. However, despite himself, he has clearly created a series of crimes that are linkable.'

'What's his motive?' said Rodeal.

'I think he has more than one,' said Ren. 'Yes, it's a sexual thrill, yes, it's a power thing, but I think there's more. We've sent details to our profiling unit in Quantico, and they will be back to us within two weeks with a profile.'

'It takes that long?' said another DPD detective.

Ren searched the room until she found the questioner. 'Is this your first case involving the use of a profiler?' *You little shit.*

'No, ma'am.'

'Then, I don't really need to answer that.' *Do I?*

Silence.

'I'm ready,' said Ren, 'with your help, to find this monster. I do not want him to be caught because he has a broken fucking taillight. He will not be stumbled upon because of a routine traffic stop. This is not routine: there is a psychopath out there raping, killing, and mutilating innocent women. He will not win. I will not let him win. And, I know, neither will you. We are going to find him. We will stop him.

'At the end of this briefing, I will be assigning different tasks to each of you. I want you all to do what you're assigned to do, to focus intently on the task at hand, but to also have a three-sixty view of the entire investigation. I need you all to cross-reference things, to read everything in detail, and to sharpen your ability to make connections. There is now a copy of the preliminary autopsy findings for Donna Darisse on the table by the door, along with the autopsy reports of the other two victims.

'On the subject of the media, I do not want one breach. Is that as clear as it sounds to me? This is not going public right now. We will be agreeing on what we're releasing to the media. Our UNSUB will be brought to justice. There will be no compromises. I do not want the lives of the women of Denver, our investigation, or the resulting court case to be fucked up because the wrong thing appears in the newspaper, because someone in this room, or someone they know, releases information for money or to get a fucking kick out of seeing it in print or because they have a better plan than mine to catch the killer. If misleading information enters the public domain, someone could be killed. By me.' She smiled. 'I'm not fucking kidding.'

She put her hands on her hips.

I can't believe I just put my hands on my hips.

'For those of you who don't know me,' said Ren, 'I don't like repeating myself. In fact, I hate it. And I would find it very strange to have to repeat myself to adults who have reached a certain age, made it through college, through police academy, Quantico, wherever. So if you're in a conference with me, you need to listen the fuck up to *everyone* who speaks. Please – ask all the questions in the world – I have no problem with that, but I don't want to hear the same question asked twice. I mean, go ahead, by all means, but—' She shrugged.

Gary was giving her a shut-the-fuck-up look.

'So, that's it,' said Ren. 'Good luck. Come to me with any issues, big or small.'

Gary called her into his office after the conference.

'"Come to me with any issues, big or small",' he said. 'Do you think you made that easy for them?'

'Uh: yes,' said Ren. 'Why?'

'You're coming off arrogant.'

What?! 'I'm not arrogant.'

'You're coming across that way.'

'Who says that?' said Ren.

'Me,' said Gary. 'But I doubt I'm alone.'

'I'm sorry, but I always think people are pussies if they can't handle being expected to live up to a certain standard. I don't mean standard, but fucking do your job is what I mean. Do your job, don't be stupid, don't talk to the media. Hardly traumatizing . . . this is serious shit, Gary. I'm not having people coming in here like lazy assholes, half-listening, checked out, just thinking about what time their wife is going to put supper on the table. Women are dying.'

'Yet it's OK for you to go out and party every night . . .'

Oh, fuck off, Gary. 'I'm working, minimum, fifteen hours a day on this. I haven't been late once. What I do with the remaining nine hours of my day – two of which, I'm likely to spend working out – then what can I say?'

'So, you're surviving on how many hours' sleep?'

Jesus CHRIST ALMIGHTY. 'I'm more than surviving.' *I'm fucking thriving.* 'I love how you talk like you get ten hours' sleep a night.'

'It's not the same for me.'

I want to punch you.

Gary checked his computer. 'Do you have an appoi—'

Appointment! Yay! Let's top this the fuck off with that! 'Yes, tomorrow. I do.'

'And . . . did you get a chance to call Karen?'

Even better! Let's top this the fuck off with your wife!

'Not yet, Gary. But I will.'

I can think of two stronger candidates for therapy right now.

Gary stared at his screen, then glared at Ren with barely contained rage. 'Well, here it is, as expected – an email from Briar's lawyer: stay the fuck away from my client.' He sat back in his seat. 'Ladies and gentlemen, introducing your case agent . . .'

This is a fucking AK-47 of a conversation . . .

15

That night, Ren worked her way up to calling Karen Dettling.

Breathe. Breathe. Breathe.

Karen picked up.

'Hi, it's Ren.'

Silence. 'Hi.' Terse.

Ooh. 'I'm calling to put your mind at rest about me and Gary.'

Silence. 'This isn't a conversation for the phone, Ren. I'd like to meet you face to face for this.'

Noooo. 'No problem,' said Ren, 'but I want you to know that there's nothing going on between me and Gary.'

'We'll talk,' said Karen. 'I'll come to your apartment, if that's OK. I don't want Claire to hear this.'

'Of course,' said Ren. She looked down at the list of dates and times. *Now I have to learn this off. Great.* 'Can you give me an hour? I just have to finish something off.' *Like a tall tale.*

Karen Dettling arrived beautifully made-up, carefully put together, looking far saner than when she had come to the office.

Conscious of not looking like the crazed wife. You don't need to do that for me.

Ren left her to settle on the sofa while she made tea.

'It's just, he's been so strange . . .' said Karen when Ren brought out the tray, and sat down.

'If it's any consolation,' said Ren, 'he's been strange at work, but that's because I think this is *about* work. There have been a lot of staff upheavals: Colin Grabien resigned in such murky circumstances—'

'What happened with Colin Grabien really got to Gary,' said Karen. 'You wouldn't believe how badly he took that. Colin was part of the original Safe Streets team, he was this hotshot IT genius financials guy who Gary felt very proud to have hired. Colin could do no wrong, *professionally* . . .'

She trailed off, but Ren knew what she was intimating, and what she was too discreet to say: Colin Grabien was, basically, an asshole who had a problem with the world. And in the end, with Ren in particular; she had found out he shafted the other candidate in order to get his job. She kept it from Gary, but she made sure Colin knew, and made sure he did the right thing by resigning. Gary had a hard time committing to a replacement. Until Everett came along.

'And,' said Ren, 'after Colin, Cliff requested a transfer, so Gary had to find someone to fill that spot. And, you know me – I've caused him problems. Karen, I'm well aware of my shortcomings, and I would venture Gary has spoken about me at home . . .'

Karen nodded.

'I just can't imagine him ever talking about me in a way that would suggest he has any kind of feelings toward me other than frustration . . .'

Karen started laughing.

'Personally, I think I am Gary's worst nightmare,' said Ren. 'Like, he would actively avoid me on a personal level.'

Karen was now crying and laughing at the same time.

'I understand more than anyone that a series of different things can lead to what feels like a logical, concrete conclusion,' said Ren. 'I mean, a champagne cork in a bag . . . that's not great. I'd have a hard time with that.'

'And if Ben had a hot colleague he was away with that same night . . . who is known for drinking champagne . . .' She smiled.

Ugh. You're such a nice person. You feel like a fool and I'm complicit in that. And I would be devastated if someone did that to me.

Karen sighed. 'I'm an idiot. I'm so sorry. This is not about you. I just . . . I'm at my wit's end.'

'You're not an idiot,' said Ren. *Not at all.* 'Your husband's been withdrawn, you found this random cork . . . any woman would be freaked out.'

'Thanks,' said Karen. 'I don't want this to be an issue between us. Is it too late for that? You know Claire adores you, and part of me was just so mad at the idea that you could be in our home with all that going on. I probably shouldn't be saying any of this. Claire is only seventeen . . . part of me was panicking that . . . this would be an example I'd be setting for her, that she'd think she should sit back and tolerate a cheating husband.' She let out a breath. 'I don't know what to think . . .'

'Please don't worry about this,' said Ren. 'It doesn't affect anything as far as I'm concerned.' *It really doesn't.* 'I totally understand how you could have thought what you thought.'

Karen's eyes almost narrowed. 'Can I ask you one thing?' *No. Please don't. I know where you're going.*

'Sure,' said Ren.

'Is there someone else?' said Karen. 'Do you know? Is Gary seeing someone else?'

Oh, fuck. Fuck. Fuck. He's not seeing her. The affair is over. 'No,' said Ren. 'No. He is not seeing someone.' *IS not. Not WAS not. Is not. And that is the truth.*

'Thank you,' said Karen. 'Thank God.' She stood up, and started to walk toward the door. She paused, and turned back. 'What were you celebrating?'

'Pardon?' said Ren.

'Why the champagne?' said Karen. 'What were you and Gary—'

Fuuuck. Fuuuck.

'—celebrating?' said Karen.

Ren stared at her feet. They were bare, polished in a beautiful shade of aqua.

Help me. Help. Me.

Oh. My. God. Feet! That's it! God bless you!

Ren jumped up. 'It's the case! Sorry, Karen. I just realized something. There's another victim. Oh, Jesus Christ. Please, excuse me. I need to call Everett.'

Ren ran into the kitchen, picked up her cell phone, dialed Gary's number.

'Everett!' she said.

'It's Gary—'

Duuuuuh! 'I'm calling because – do you remember Gia Larosa, the young runaway?' She lowered her voice. 'Karen is here. What were we celebrating that night – the champagne. Jesus Christ.'

'Ren, you drink champagne all the time – you don't need a reason. It's your drink.'

'Oh my God, I never thought of that,' said Ren. 'That's how fucking stressed out this is making me!'

'How's Karen?'

'Ugh. Fine. Back to Gia Larosa – do you remember her?'

'Her body was found on her eighteenth birthday – that stuck with me.'

'Yes, raped, murdered, found on Lookout Mountain at the beginning of June, torn apart by critters. I remembered the autopsy report saying that she had splinters in her foot . . . remaining foot.'

She could have run away from him.

Not far – or fast – enough.

'Maybe,' said Gary, 'but it stands to reason that if any woman was trying to run away from a killer outdoors, and she was barefoot, her feet would be damaged. Her shoes were bound to have been kicked off or removed, especially if they were heels.'

Wind out of sails. 'I'll look into it tomorrow.'

Ren ended the call.

'I'm sorry about that,' she said, walking back in to Karen.

Karen was standing in the living room with her jacket on. '*I'm* sorry,' she said. 'I've stayed here long enough. You're busy, this is an important case. Do you really have another victim?'

'I think so, yes. From back in June.'

'And what did Everett think?' said Karen.

I see the hurt in your eyes. This is vile. 'He isn't sure.'

'Well, you keep doing what you're doing,' said Karen. 'You're an excellent agent. And I'm so sorry for dragging you into all this. I'm so ashamed.'

'Oh my God, don't say that,' said Ren. 'Shame is a total waste of time.' She hugged her.

'Thanks,' said Karen. 'Thanks so much.'

Too obvious to bring up the celebration answer now.

Ren closed the door behind Karen.

Oh, Karen. You do not deserve this.

As Ren got ready for bed, she remembered the autopsy photos and the chipped aquamarine nail polish of Gia Larosa. She remembered thinking that, on the table, Gia Larosa looked no bigger than an eight-year-old. Her belongings were a denim skirt with a jagged hem, a cropped white Ramones vest, a red cotton bandeau top, a plastic charm bracelet.

Tiny, blonde, rough around the edges.

Stephanie Wingerter, Gia Larosa – lost souls, easy targets. Was Hope Coulson a move to a different league for the killer? A greater challenge? And Donna Darisse was a return to a comfort zone?

The comfort of lost souls and easy targets . . .

Jesus Christ.

16

Ren pulled Gia Larosa's file as soon as she got into work the next morning. It was JeffCo's case, but had started out with Safe Streets, because there was a last-known sighting in Denver. Gia Larosa had run away from her home in Montana, and hitch-hiked to Denver with various truckers, all of whom were cleared of any involvement in her death. Her body was found a month after she arrived in Denver – two days after she went missing.

Ren went through the photos of the crime scene. Temperatures at the end of May and early June were high, but Gia Larosa had been left partially covered by undergrowth, so the problem was not so much the heat, but the critters that had gotten to her. She was too decomposed to tell whether or not she'd been raped. But Ren honed in on one of the little yellow plastic markers at the scene, and an ax handle beside it.

Rape with a foreign object.

The lab report said that the ax handle had no prints on it. It was clean clean – bleach clean. There was evidence of sharp-force trauma to the lower spine that was likely caused by the ax, the blade of which was never found.

Gia Larosa's cause of death was undetermined.

Ren sent an email out to all the agencies working on the case that Gia Larosa should be considered a victim of the same killer.

Sorry, Gary. Can't fight another fight with you.

I have an appointment to get to . . .

Dr Leonard Lone was Ren's psychiatrist, an intelligent, kind-faced man, gray-haired, bearded, soft-spoken. Behind the air of normality was an abnormally large family fortune, and an enduring, under-the-radar commitment to share it with those less fortunate. Ren secretly called him Batman.

'How are you doing, Ren?' Lone opened the door wide in a deliberate flourish.

Greetings, Batman! 'I'm great, thank you,' said Ren, taking a seat. 'You look like you're in a good mood.'

He sat at his desk opposite. 'Don't I always?'

She laughed. 'Well, yes. But I'm liking the door-opening.'

'I'm cultivating grand entrances today,' said Lone.

'Well, how about this for a grand entrance: there's a serial killer in Denver. It's not been formally announced yet. I'm case agent.'

'Good for you,' said Lone. 'That was Gary's decision?'

'Yes.'

'How do you feel about that?'

'Confident, thank you.'

He nodded, then waited for an elaboration that didn't come.

'So, with this new responsibility . . .' said Lone.

'Comes great power!' said Ren.

Lone smiled. 'Comes the more mundane issues of longer hours, irregular hours, increased workload . . .'

There's no such thing as a long hour. An hour is an hour.

She glanced at the clock.

Then again . . .

'How has your sleep been?' said Lone.

Why are we even doing this? I'm smart enough to know the right answers. And smart enough to know never to say out loud anything that egomaniacal. Flag. 'I'm sleeping well, eating well, working well.' *Suppressing checking the time well.*

Dr Lone nodded. 'Are you happy with your meds?'

Happy I am no longer taking them, yes. Ren nodded. 'Yes.'

'The dosage is right for you?' said Lone.

'Yes, absolutely.'

'When do you take them?' said Lone.

Pause. 'At night.' She thought of her shoebox of shame – the meds box – lying under her bed, untouched.

'Are you having any adverse reaction?' said Lone.

'No, nothing – they're great. I'm feeling very . . . on an even keel.'

'Good,' said Lone. 'Is there anything in particular you think we need to address today?'

'Hmm, not really.' *Jesus, make something up.* 'Oh, there is something, actually. What am I meant to do with this information? A married colleague, who I greatly respect, had an affair. I was his unwitting alibi. I have gone along with this, lied to his wife, whom I know well. And I feel like shit.'

'I don't need to know names, but is this colleague a superior?' said Lone.

'Yes,' said Ren.

'Then that alters the dynamic,' said Lone.

'Not really,' said Ren.

'Well, do you still respect him?'

Hmm. 'Yes,' said Ren, 'totally.'

'Do you still value his judgment?' said Lone.

Ooh. 'Yes.' *But, seriously, what the fuck was he thinking?*

'Do you still feel he has your back?' said Lone.

'I guess I feel a little thrown to the wolves.'

'Is it affecting how you're interacting with him?' said Lone.

'Yes, actually,' said Ren. 'And him me . . . and to cap it all off, if I'm perfectly honest, part of me wishes that, if he was going to cheat, that I could have been someone he might have slept with.'

Lone nodded.

'I know that sounds screwed up,' said Ren.

'No,' said Lone. 'It does sound unwise, though. Has he always been faithful to his wife?'

'Well, I thought so.'

'And is that what stopped you ever pursuing anything with him?' said Lone.

'Well . . .' *He's my boss.* 'Maybe if he were single, I would have gone there in the past.'

'Do you feel now that "all bets are off"?' said Lone.

'I shouldn't,' said Ren. 'But part of me does.'

'And what about Ben?' said Lone.

Ren let out a breath. 'I don't know. I'm feeling kind of . . . bored.'

'Be wary of bored,' said Lone. 'Boredom likes to make mischief.'

'Boredom is my kryptonite.'

He nodded. 'Yes. You've just described an unhealthy environment for you, Ren. Boredom, work drama, increased workload, sleep deprivation, sexual attraction, and the perceived availability of the focus of that attraction.'

Jesus Christ, is anyone not fucking boring around here?

And are you studying me a little too closely, Batman?

Ren went home that night and put together a hot meal of cannellini beans, spinach, lemon juice, the remaining shard of parmesan, and black pepper. She ate in front of the television, with a glass of red wine, and a magazine open on the sofa beside her. Out of the corner of her eye she saw a big red blast of BREAKING NEWS.

Oh. Shit.

She grabbed the remote control and turned it up.

'Unconfirmed reports have come in that authorities are on the hunt for a violent serial killer in Denver . . .'

'Shiiiit!' said Ren. 'And unconfirmed my ass!'

The frowning reporter stared straight ahead, unflinching, earnest: *'The FBI has joined forces with Denver PD, the Douglas County and Jefferson County Sheriff's Offices in piecing together events surrounding the murder of Gia Larosa whose body was found at Lookout Mountain in June; Stephanie Wingerter, who was found in July at Devil's Head in Douglas County; kindergarten teacher, Hope Coulson, discovered last month at the Fyron Industries landfill site in Denver; and the latest victim – mother-of-one, Donna Darisse, who was last seen on Colfax Avenue, before her body was discovered off Highway 72 in Jefferson County. It is believed that some or all of the victims were brutally raped before they were murdered. Authorities have no leads.'*

'Noooooo!' shouted Ren, grabbing a cushion to throw at the television, knocking her wine glass from the coffee table onto the floor. 'Nooooo!'

17

Carrie Longman sat on a high stool at Manny's Bar on 38th and Walnut. It was Open Mic night and a tiny girl with a big guitar was filling the gloomy stage. She looked to be in her mid-twenties, a delicate thing with a cute black cowboy hat on, and her dirty blonde hair falling across one eye. There was no doubt she had once been beautiful, but was now damaged, possibly by drugs, or mental illness, Carrie guessed. This was the type of girl who rang alarm bells for Carrie Longman, the type she rescued every week. Now, she felt permanently on high alert: there was a serial killer out there. One month had gone by since the prostitute, Donna Darisse, had been found. She thought of her face, she thought of the others who had gone before her. And that girl on stage, looked, to Carrie Longman, exactly like the type this psycho was going for.

'You're not at work now, Carrie,' she said to herself. 'Your only task tonight is to get very, very drunk.'

A spotlight came on, and the singer, her rough face now clearer, leaned into the microphone.

'I'm Dainty,' she said in a smoky Texan drawl, through

barely parted bow-shaped lips. With her skinny limbs, and her body curled in on itself, dainty she was.

She shifted the guitar on her lap. 'This song is about my father . . .' she said.

A few people in the scant crowd said 'aw'.

'. . . and how he abandoned me and my sister,' said Dainty. The 'aws' turned to 'ooohs'.

'Even though,' said Dainty, 'he was right at home with us, right before our eyes. It's about how my mama broke his heart, and he broke ours, me and my sister.' She cleared her throat, shifted on the stool, adjusted the guitar, looked around the room, nodded to what looked like no one in particular. 'So this is called "Croon On, Motherfucker, Croon On".' Dainty smiled a closed-mouth smile, incongruous in her little heart-shaped face, with its slightly jutting, pointed chin.

Every fiber in Carrie Longman's being wanted to storm that stage and rescue this Dainty stranger. Instead, Carrie Longman spoke to herself sternly, inside her head, as she often did: 'Carrie, you're drunk, your boyfriend's just dumped you, the shelter is running out of money fast . . . you cannot rescue yourself and you sure as hell cannot rescue this one.'

Dainty's mouth curled up at one side before she opened it to sing. The place went as quiet as the grave. Her voice was like that of a chain-smoking woman twice her age with the sorrows of a thousand trailer parks weighing down her soul. It was ragged and beautiful, and the crowd was enthralled.

Carrie Longman took out a pen, grabbed a napkin, and started writing.

At the end of the gig, Carrie Longman headed straight for the ladies' room. She swayed back and forth, bumping against the walls in the hallway. Crazed flies were charging the electric fly-killer, buzzing and dying.

In the ladies' room, the floor was littered with balled-up paper towels, the bins were overflowing, there was no soap. There was another electric fly-killer.

'You cannot rescue the flies, Carrie,' she said to herself. She smiled into the mirror. 'Drrrunkard! But not drunk enough to use these heinous facilities. Hell, no!'

She left almost as soon as she walked in. People pushed her away as she knocked against them on her way past. She thought of her ex, pushing her away. Six years together, four hours apart. 'Croon On You Too, Motherfucker!' said Carrie, this time, out loud. She started to cry.

She stumbled out into the parking lot. She stopped dead – she hadn't driven here. She had left her car somewhere off 16th Street. She had walked away from the bar where her boyfriend had left her. Now here she was: drunk, carless, crying again, and three miles from home.

'You are a big loser, Carrie. America's Top Loser. Biggest Model. Whatever . . .'

She swayed back and forth, rummaging for her keys in her bag.

He was sitting in the dark in the borrowed truck, watching her.

You came into this bar crying, you walked out of it crying – who am I to turn off those tears? And you can't find your keys, you dumb bitch, 'cos I got them right here from when you dropped them on the floor by the bar when you pulled that sweater out of your purse. Isn't a place like this a little empty, a little off the beaten track for a girl who wears pretty sweaters with pearl buttons? But you are wasted. You don't know how wasted you are. I bet I could knock you down with two fingers, even though you're a big fat bitch, loose and lonely by the looks of you. You're not my type, now, are you? That's the problem with the news reporters, fixing their lipstick one minute, talking about someone like me the next. You can send the skinny blondes scuttling under a rock, all you like, you painted bitches, but I'm going to stomp on a big fat brunette instead.

Carrie Longman, bound at the wrists and ankles, rolled back and forth in the back of the truck. She had watched survivor episodes of crimes shows: meet the women who got away from their would-be killers! *Live to Tell!*

'You will be one of those women, Carrie,' she said to herself. 'You will be eloquent, calm, convincing, clever. You will be able to describe everything. The police will find this psycho. You will save lives. You will be a heroine to women.'

The truck came to a stop.

He dragged her out the back by her ankles, let her fall, her head making a dull cracking sound on the dry earth. He kept dragging her until they were under a tree.

He crouched down in front of her, bound her wrists with skinny, fraying rope.

'My name is—'

'No!' screamed Carrie, shaking her head wildly. 'No! Don't tell me your name. Don't. I don't want to know!'

'My name is . . . Your Killer,' he said. 'My name is Your Worst Fuckin' Nightmare. My name is Your Mama's Worst Nightmare, Your Daddy's, Everyone's Worst Fuckin' Nightmare.' He smiled. 'How. Do. You. Do?'

She screamed, and he let her, and she knew then that they were miles from help.

'Please,' she sobbed. 'Please . . .'

He remained silent and focused as he stripped her to her underwear. He slowly trailed his eyes down her body, shaking his head.

'Now, you do *not* have the body I like to take pleasure

from . . . but I'm going to do it anyway. It's just I might not be able to . . . you know . . .' He shrugged. 'Doesn't mean I won't give it my best shot, though.'

He laughed at that.

'But you do need to shut the fuck up.'

He pulled a rag from his left-hand back pocket and made a gag from it. Soon Carrie Longman's sobs were sucked into the thick, filthy fabric.

'I may have a way to solve this problem,' he said. 'The problem of you being . . .' He shuddered. 'You know what a titty fuck is, right?' He pulled a photo from his other pocket. He showed it to her. She started to convulse. Tears poured down her face. He laughed as he pushed it between her breasts.

'Now,' he said, grabbing onto the waistband of her panties, 'let's see what we've got.' He ripped them off, staring at her, opening the legs she was trying desperately to keep closed.

'Nothing you can do now, sweetheart,' he said. 'It's just you and me, this late-night romance.' He opened his belt, and started pulling at himself. 'This is your fault. I'm prepared to commit a felony for this, and I still can't get a hard-on between your wide-open legs.'

He started laughing, and as he was still laughing, he grabbed the broken branch he had set against the tree earlier that evening. He had carefully chosen it to exactly match the size of the biggest man who used to visit his mama when he was a boy.

As he thrust the branch in and out of Carrie Longman, working on her utter destruction, his eyes were on the photo stuck between her bulging breasts. It was of Hope Coulson's scrawny little ass and the two perfect stab wounds he had made above it. There would have been no real evidence of those very particular wounds when they had found her. Not after three hot weeks in plastic.

He pressed Carrie Longman's face hard into the ground. He heard a cracking sound. He could feel the blood pour through his fingers.

Face down in the dirt and dying.

THIS was it.

Face down in the dirt and dying.

He looked down at the branch. For a moment, he drifted, staring at the thickness of it. He remembered wondering at the time if the size of that man had hurt his mama as much as it had hurt him.

18

Ren had spent weeks creating a Wall of Horrors in her living room; pinned to the wall opposite the sofa were photos of faces, wounds, and dump sites. There were maps, single words, questions, answers: everything she could think of to help her catch a monster. She sat now on the sofa, with a bowl of dry Rice Krispies, staring at the block-capital bullet points of the Quantico profile that had come in the previous week.

MIXED OFFENDER: ORG/DISORG
AGED BETWEEN 30 and 45
IQ ABOVE AVERAGE
POWER ASSERTIVE / ANGER RETALIATORY RAPIST
SOCIALLY ADEQUATE
LIVES ALONE – DATES/ONE-NIGHT STANDS
ABSENT/UNSTABLE FATHER
HISTORY OF PHYSICAL AND EMOTIONAL ABUSE
MAY FOLLOW NEWS MEDIA

It had been easy to allow the apartment to become an extension of the office. She couldn't ever imagine doing this in a true home. But this grim wall felt in place here.

She finished her cereal and left the bowl beside the previous night's half-eaten pizza. She had watched the faces from the sofa for hours, wanting never to have to add another photo.

When she arrived at Safe Streets, there was a box on her desk, wrapped in pretty paper.

Severed head inside. Has to be.

'A housewarming gift,' said Robbie. 'Finally.'

'Aw, Robbie!' said Ren. 'No way! Thank you so much. Can I open it now?'

'Sure, go ahead.' He was smiling.

She started unwrapping it.

'I just thought with what you said about your kitchen giving you a pain in your behind that maybe this might encourage—'

'A block of knives!' said Ren. 'And I don't think "pain in my behind" is a phrase I'd ever use, kind, non-cursing Mormon boy.'

'Oh my God,' said Everett. 'It's bad luck to buy someone knives.'

I know this. But there was no need to say it to poor Robbie.

Robbie looked distraught. 'Is it?'

'Yes!' said Everett.

But Robbie wanted the answer from Ren.

'But I don't see why,' she said. 'I mean, if you stood behind me and planted each of the knives in my back, that, to me, would be bad luck. But in a block, like this, that I could use every night to actually prepare dinner and think of your thoughtfulness, that's very good luck.'

Robbie smiled. 'I'm returning them.'

'No, you're not,' said Ren. *Though I am finding it spooky.*

'He is,' said Everett. 'A pall has descended.'

OK, shut up, Everett. You're not helping the advancement of your relationship with Robbie.

Robbie came over to Ren and prised the box out of her hands. 'I'm sorry. I hope you're not feeling jinxed.'

Hmm. 'Of course not.'

Gary stuck his head into the bullpen. He had his jacket on.

'We have another body,' he said.

'Our guy?' said Ren, sitting up.

'Too early to tell,' said Gary. 'Different physical type for one . . .'

Carrie Longman had been left up against a tree under a pile of earth, branches, and leaves. She was naked, curled on her side, ruined.

Different body type, different hair color.

The ground was muddy underneath her.

Even though it hasn't been raining.

I can smell it. She's been washed down with bleach.

A dog had found her, wrapped his teeth around her wrist and pulled her hand out from under cover. The dog owner was sitting, shocked, on a bench to one side, being tended to by a paramedic. The dog was pressed up against her leg.

You little hero.

The contents of Carrie Longman's purse were scattered all around her: wallet, phone, keys, notebook, bus tickets, lip balm, a bag of trail mix, a card she had yet to mail, its ink bleeding, the name and address washed away. Ren followed the trail of objects to a squat row of bushes, where a damp pile of clothes had been thrown, alongside a piece of frayed rope.

Ren looked up at Glenn Buddy. 'Fuck this.'

He nodded. 'Her name is Carrie Longman. She was a social worker, thirty-three years old. No one realized she was missing for two days. She broke up with her boyfriend of six years last Friday. When work hadn't heard from her on Monday, they just assumed maybe she was sick, or he had whisked her away somewhere because it was their anniversary. Nice guy. Apparently, once the asshole dumped her, she looked up Denver's best dive bars and picked number one, Manny's, went there for Open Mic night, texted a friend that's where she was, drowning her sorrows. I've got some of our guys heading over there now. The friend she texted was away herself that weekend, so she just assumed Longman was sleeping it off. Tried her a few times, let her be.'

Ren looked up. Mark Gaston was striding up the hill toward them. The sun was shining down as if to illuminate only him, like he was the hero prince come to save the kingdom.

'Is it Kill Your Girlfriend Season in Denver?' he said, putting down his bag, taking out a pair of gloves, putting them on. He crouched down.

'She's very dead.' He glanced down at the tree branch jammed between her legs. He had no jokes for that. He looked up at Ren. 'I think he might have . . . kicked that while it was inside her.'

Ren closed her eyes.

There was all kinds of depravity in the world and she had met it in all kinds of ways. She knew there were people who Googled crime scenes, and wanted the most grotesque photos, who would never stop at the graphic contents warning. There were people who loved torture porn, who wanted to be part of it, make it, watch it, jack off to it. And there were whole other levels too, levels that she had yet to meet and hoped never to. This felt like a step closer to a world she didn't want to know, a world that these women were likely never to have imagined.

'I'm sorry, but this guy is a maniac,' said Gaston. 'What he hasn't done to this body . . . Who is he hating on? Every woman alive? Who didn't dance with him at his senior prom?'

19

Ren sent Robbie and Everett to Carrie Longman's autopsy the following day, hoping they could bond over the tragedy. She called everyone together for a briefing afterward, and directed Robbie to go through the findings. He stood at the top of the room, neat, shiny and earnest.

I love your utter faith in justice, Robbie Truax.

'Preliminary reports suggest time of death is consistent with when Carrie Longman was last seen at Manny's Bar,' said Robbie. 'The cause of death was exsanguination as a result of sharp-force injury. Her stomach was slashed three times – twice on her left side, once on her right – using a short, curved blade. The weapon was not recovered at the scene. Carrie Longman was bound at the wrists with rope, and vaginally raped with a tree branch, which was kicked further into her, or, certainly, pushed with considerable force. It's likely she was held face down during the attack. She suffered a broken nose, and had aspirated blood. The body was thoroughly cleaned in bleach to destroy trace evidence. The tree branch was also thoroughly soaked in it, as were her clothes and the rope. There was a piece of fabric, likely used as a gag, also soaked in bleach. Gaston said the lab will be lucky to find anything. Under the victim's fingernails was completely scrubbed too. There were no hairs, no fibers. The victim's blood alcohol level was 0.15. She probably wasn't in any condition to fight back.'

'So this guy had to have driven as close as he could to that location,' said Ren. 'He couldn't risk leaving her body unattended, and he wouldn't have been able to drag her and a giant bottle of bleach at the same time . . . unless he had help.' She paused. 'Why the different physical type? Especially when he knew he would be doing some of the same things he'd done before? Things that would link these victims.'

'We did get one item our killer overlooked,' said Everett. 'It was in her jeans pocket – a napkin with what looks like her writing – I checked it against the notebook that was in her purse. Here's a photocopy. It says: *"tiny fingers pointing your way, needle's pointing to your heart, sharps disposal, sharps disposal, now I know the way we'll part . . . "'*

'It's like a poem or a song,' said Ren. She Googled it. 'It's nowhere. Let's see if her ex recognizes it. Also, that napkin could have been in there from the last time she wore the jeans, if she hadn't washed them. It looks like a standard, white, cheapo napkin – it could have come from anywhere. But we'll check with the bar staff at Manny's – it was Open Mic night, so someone could have been singing their own composition—'

'Ren, she wrote some lyrics on a napkin,' said Gary. 'They're not in someone else's handwriting. This is not a note a killer's left behind: *Now I know the way we'll part*: by me raping and murdering you, my name is . . . These were words that struck a chord with a jilted woman, probably.'

Grrr. And why does 'jilted woman' always sound so demeaning? Why do we never hear of jilted men? 'What if the killer *made* her write it?' said Ren.

'We'll see if the lab comes up with anything,' said Everett.

'Janine and Everett,' said Gary, 'you go talk to the bar staff in Manny's.'

Janine and Everett?! What the fuck? Why them? Even though I love them.

Gary kept talking. 'See if anyone saw the victim write this on the night.' He turned to Ren.

And what the fuck is with that look?

'So . . .' said Gary.

I need to get out of here. I am vividly aware of my weapons. Mainly my fists.

Ren stood up, walked like a normal person into the hallway, then changed into long strides, stiff limbs, and held her breath until she exploded into the ladies' room.

Gary. Is. An. Asshole.

And WHY am I finding myself attracted to him?

Ren left the ladies' room, and went into the A/V room.

I want to hide in the darkness for the rest of the day.

One after the other, she looked through videos of each victim's last movements, up until Carrie Longman.

I am good with video. I see things.

Maybe there's nothing to see here.

There has to be.

She kept looking. She concentrated on Hope Coulson. She had asked two DPD detectives to approach local businesses for video of the mystery night two weeks before Hope disappeared. One shop owner, who had gone out of business the following week, had yet to get back to her.

Ren tried him again, left him a voicemail with a gentle reminder.

At five o'clock, everyone gathered again in the conference room.

'First off,' said Janine, 'Manny's has no cameras trained on the crowd – just on the staff behind the till to discourage thievery. Secondly, they remember Carrie Longman, said she was very drunk, but was perfectly pleasant. She sat at the bar, and was alone the entire night. She didn't really talk to anyone, though people were coming and going at both sides of her to order drinks. They're already rounding up a list of regulars for DPD, so we can take a look at that. Also, because it was Open Mic night, they had a lot of strangers in there, but really, guys, there are never that many – see, what I did there? – people in Manny's, so I don't think this is going to be some epic trawl.'

'We went to talk to Longman's ex,' said Everett, 'who we can confirm is an asshole.'

'Yup,' said Janine.

'He didn't recognize the lyrics,' said Everett, 'but he said that Carrie had spoken about writing a novel. He thinks maybe that was why she chose a bar like Manny's – to get a window into the grittier side of life, which makes no sense to me—'

'Because in her job as a social worker,' said Janine, 'she was dealing with that all the time. The ex may just be trying to assuage his own guilt so he doesn't have to feel responsible for her fleeing somewhere off the beaten track to drown her sorrows.'

'Imagine breaking up with someone a) around your anniversary and b) then they're murdered,' said Ren. 'That guy is going to be the pariah of plenty of fish. I mean piranha. There was a joke in there somewhere.'

'It should have stayed in there,' said Everett.

Ren started pacing. 'Back to what you were saying, Gary – I think the killer doesn't want to get caught and Carrie Longman was chosen because she did *not* fit the profile. He wanted to avoid being predictable or having that murder linked too.

'I want everyone all over this,' said Ren, walking to the top of the room. 'I don't want to be here giving another briefing on another autopsy. He has now returned to killing a woman who is not a sex worker, though, of course, that doesn't mean he won't target one in the future. This time around, he used bleach not only to wash down the victim, but also all her personal effects, which means he must have made contact with them, for whatever reason.'

'Robbery?' said someone.

Hmm. I don't think so. She ignored it. 'OK, everyone,' said Ren, 'I want to thank you for your great work to date, but I now need you processing information with greater speed and more efficiency than you have ever done before. Our end point is that we have this guy. I want your theories, I will have time for all of you, I will respect your gut instinct, I will respect your hunches. We are a team and we each come with different strengths. Use them, make me aware of them if you think I am not already. Everyone will benefit, all of us here, but especially the women out there who are afraid to go outside their doors.' She paused. 'We can do this.'

We are all fucking amazing.

20

Ren's cell phone rang as she was walking down the hallway to the bullpen. It was Matt, her wonderful, witty, intuitive, psychologically astute older-by-a-year brother.

Man Most Likely To Be Avoided Right Now.

Her finger hovered over the red button.

Don't be a bitch.

She picked up.

'Hey, sister, go, sister . . .'

'Matthew!' said Ren. 'How are you?'

'Good. How are you, mystery lady? I left you many, many messages.'

'I know, I'm sorry, I've been busy – the raping and murdering going on in this city.'

'Are you serving and protecting the citizens?'

'Yes, I am. How's Lauren, how's Ethan?'

'They're all good, missing you. Last I heard, you were in a bar downing shots with a bachelor party. And before that, in a bar—'

'Yes, I get it. I've been having fun.' *Which seems slightly more noticeable to you now that you're a married, settled father-of-one.*

123

'Mom says you haven't called her in a while.'

'Mom is correct.'

'Big brother Jay says the same.'

'Ah, but what does Jesus say?'

'OK,' said Matt. 'Can you hear me, Ren? I'm shuffling along here, I'm dodging branches and leaves, OK. I'm here. I'm out on a limb . . .'

Ren stopped dead.

Oh, fuck. This is about—

'Here goes,' said Matt. 'Are you taking your meds?' He said it in one go, comedy-fast for effect.

'Yes,' said Ren. *God, this business of people giving a shit what I do . . .*

'Can you promise me that?' said Matt.

She nodded. 'I can promise you that.' *But I won't. Woo-hoo! Loophole! I have the* capacity *to promise you that.*

'OK,' said Matt. 'Just looking out for you. Making sure you're feeling the rails underfoot.'

'Don't worry. I'm on the rails.' *But who says I need meds to be on the rails? Not that I would dream of saying that out loud. Especially not to someone who has no clue.* 'Matt,' she said. 'Seriously. How many people do you know who are case agent on a serial killer investigation?'

Boom!

Back in the bullpen, Ren sat at her desk and turned her attention to the case.

What am I missing in all this?

Where is the chink?

'Did you ever see the movie *The Greatest Show on Earth*?' said Ren, looking up at Everett. 'Starring the dashing Cornel Wilde.'

'No,' said Everett.

'I quote the opening in deep tones: "*A fierce, primitive*

fighting force that smashes relentlessly forward against impossible odds: that is the circus — and this is the story of the biggest of the Big Tops — and of the men and women who fight to make it — The Greatest Show on Earth!"'

'Bravo! Bravo!' said Everett, clapping high, to the right, to the left.

'"*Where Death is constantly watching for one frayed rope!*"' said Ren. '"*One weak link! Or one trace of fear!*"' She leaned back. 'It freaked me the fuck out. The guy, this dashing trapeze artist, attempts a double somersault without the net. You're watching him swing back and forth, it's actually only a short scene, but the tension! And he fucking falls! I couldn't believe it. I just couldn't believe they let him fall. And I was so furious that he was jumping without a net in the first place. Why, oh, why would you jump without a net? Whyyy? God damn.'

'Seriously – don't watch that again,' said Everett. 'Was there a point to that story?'

'Well, all I'm looking for in this case is one frayed rope,' said Ren. 'One weak link!'

'Just don't ever jump without a net,' said Everett.

Wise words . . .

And we know how I feel about them.

'God,' said Ren. 'I just thought of Carrie Longman's wrists and the rope. In the literal sense, I don't want to find any more of that.'

Janine walked into the bullpen.

'Are you around for drinks later?' said Ren.

'I'm afraid not,' said Janine. 'I've got some things to do in the house.'

'Aw, man,' said Ren. 'Put them off! Do them another night. Come out.'

'I can't,' said Janine. 'I have to clean out my kitchen cabinets before I lose my mind.'

'Oh my God – your kitchen is pristine,' said Ren. 'Are you nuts?'

'I will be if I don't do this,' said Janine. 'Anyway, I don't think I can keep up with you.'

'What?' said Ren.

'Honestly . . . your stamina,' said Janine.

Don't know how to take that. It doesn't sound good.

'You go out, you have fun,' said Janine. 'Don't think about me cleaning out cabinets.'

Hmmm.

I hope she's not pissed at me.

Ren went into the conference room where there were folders of information on each case. She called one of the admin staff in and told her she wanted everything photocopied, and stacked in a corner with her name on it.

That evening, Robbie helped Ren to fill the back seat of the Jeep with them. She unloaded them all in three trips to her apartment.

Apartment living . . . grrr! It's good for exercise. Stay positive.

She picked up her cell phone to text Everett to come out for drinks. She paused.

No. I'll surprise Janine, help her with her cabinets instead. I'm not great with cabinets, but . . . we can make it fun. Is that ever possible with housework?

Ren drove the thirty minutes to Golden, listening to a radio station she felt twenty years too old to be loving, that was playing songs she felt twenty years too old to know the lyrics to. When she got to Janine's, she bounced up the steps to her front door and rang the doorbell.

Janine opened. 'Oh . . . hey!' She looked a little startled. 'Uh . . . come in!'

Shit. She has a man in here. Robbie?! 'Um . . . I thought I'd help you with the cabinets,' said Ren. 'Use my stamina for a higher purpose!'

'I abandoned the housework,' said Janine.

'Oh,' said Ren.

Janine nodded. 'I couldn't face them in the end.' She paused. 'And . . . a friend called over . . .'

A friend?! But who? 'Do you have a man stashed in there?'

'No!' said Janine. 'It's Terri.'

Who the heck?

Janine looked embarrassed. 'Just a friend. You haven't met her yet.'

Or heard you mention her even once.

'Do you want to come in and meet her?' said Janine.

Once more with feeling. You look uncomfortable, I feel uncomfortable. 'No, thanks – I will leave you to it,' said Ren. 'I should have texted.'

'Oh my God – you don't need to text, don't be ridiculous,' said Janine. 'Come in.'

'It's OK, honestly,' said Ren. *I feel like I've caught you cheating. Weirdness.* 'I wanted to stop by and visit Cliff and Brenda anyway while I was here. Don't worry! I'll see you tomorrow.'

Ren drove a little down the road and parked.

Well, that was all rather strange.

She called Cliff.

'Cliff!' said Ren. 'How are you?'

'Getting by, little lady, getting by. Missing you.'

'You have no idea how much I miss you. Right now is the perfect time to hear your voice. How's Brenda doing? I'm in Golden. I was going to stop by.'

Silence. 'Today's not a great day.'

'Oh, sweetheart.' *I hate this. I don't know what I can possibly say.*

'She's . . . she looks so different, Ren. She . . . she even smells different. The chemo . . .' He took in a breath. 'It's a cruel disease. It's cruel and the treatment is cruel, and . . . everything's changed. It's . . . almost like she's already gone. And I hate myself for saying that. I don't want her to be gone, but it's like . . .'

'She's right there,' said Ren. 'Her heart is right there with you, Cliff. It always will be. You love each other too much.'

'We're all just . . . running on empty.'

'You poor things,' said Ren. 'Is there anything I can do?'

'Listen to my bullshit,' said Cliff.

'I'm here for all forms of bullshit,' said Ren. 'And if you want to stop by for coffee if you're in the city, or come especially, or go for a drink . . .'

'There's only so much danger a man can put himself in . . .'

They laughed together, and ended the call that way. Then Ren cried.

My wonderful friends. I don't want any of you to suffer.

Ren went back to the apartment and started to unpack the boxes from the office.

How many more rainforests can I bring into my apartment?

I miss my friends.

There was a knock on the door.

Ren looked through the peephole, saw her neighbor, Lorrie, holding a cardboard box with a bow wrapped around it.

Shit.

Ren glanced back at the living room and her wall of photos and arrows and Post-Its.

You can't not answer the door. She heard your footsteps. You can't be that asshole neighbor.

Ren opened the door.

'Hey, Ren,' said Lorrie. 'Consider this my delayed official welcome to the building.'

Aw! 'Thank you so much!'

Come view my Wall of Horrors.

Lorrie handed her the box. 'It's a giant cinnamon bun.'

You are shitting me. 'This is my favorite cake on earth!'

'I make them myself,' said Lorrie. 'Risky choice of gift, I know. But chocolate cake, I felt, was too predictable.'

'Oh my God – what a perfect risk to have taken,' said Ren.

Lorrie beamed. 'Well, that's great to hear!'

And now you're thinking, 'Why aren't you inviting me in?'

'Lorrie, I would love to invite you in right now,' said Ren. 'And it feels completely weird taking this gift *without* inviting you in, but I've got a whole work thing going on back there that I need to finish, it's all over the place and—'

'Don't worry!' said Lorrie. 'That's perfectly fine, but if you see a notice by the mailboxes about how rude the new neighbor is . . .'

Ren laughed. 'Thanks for understanding. Let me take your number and we can arrange some night, maybe you could come over for a glass of wine or several bottles . . .'

'I'm an alcoholic,' said Lorrie, deadly serious.

'Oh, I—'

'Sooo, bring it on!'

I like you, enabler neighbor. One more person to party with.

21

Ren went into the office the next morning and over to Everett's desk.

'What's going on in your tiny mind?' said Ren.

'The roll of tiny tumbleweeds,' said Everett.

'Were you out last night?'

'Of my mind,' said Everett.

'Good for you,' said Ren. 'I shall pick you up some pineapple juice.'

'I don't like pineapples.'

'Who doesn't like pineapples? Literally, who?'

'Me. I know. It's a popular fruit – what can I say?'

'How did I only find this out now?' said Ren.

'You never asked.'

'Do I never ask you about things? Is it all about me?'

'Yes, but that's OK.'

'I have a question,' said Ren, 'Are you skilled with a drill?'

'Are we on euphemisms again?'

'I need someone who can put up a curtain rail,' said Ren. 'Someone who has been forewarned that I have OCD

130

tendencies and will be hyper-aware of anything even fractionally off-level—'

'I have just the man for you.' Everett sat back. 'He is rigorous in his attention to detail. He has worked on every room of my house.'

'I must see your house some day.'

'You must.'

'OK . . . send this talented man my way.'

'You might not send him back . . .'

'What's that supposed to mean?' said Ren.

'Nothing,' said Everett.

I see the twinkle in your eye. You can't fool me! I'm guessing the guy is hot. And Everett views me as a philanderess.

Janine arrived. 'Greetings, Streetlings.'

'I like that,' said Ren.

Janine came over to her desk. 'I hope I didn't offend you last night . . .'

'No!' said Ren. 'Not at all. I was the one intruding.'

'You weren't intruding!' said Janine. 'It's just Terri.'

'Who is Terri?'

'Oh, I met her in the park in Golden – she was walking her dog. You know me – I had to stop. He's a gorgeous chocolate Lab. I've only known her a few months. She seems really nice.'

There is something a tiny bit off with this tale . . . or is it just me?

That night, Ren went to her bipolar support meeting. The main speaker of the night was in his early fifties, with neatly combed brown hair, glasses, a crisp short-sleeved shirt, pants that were tight on the hips, with a crease down the center.

Wrestled from behind the desk of a geography class.

131

'Mania is a thing of increases,' he announced.

OK – math class, then . . .

He continued. 'Increased appetites for spending, gambling, exercise, sex, alcohol, drugs, risks . . .'

Yet people come down so hard on mania . . .

'There is an increase in the number and speed of thoughts,' he said, 'in the speed of speech, in socializing, in levels of irritability, and – literally – an increase in driving speed. You'll even notice an increase in the incidents of cussing.'

Shock fucking horror: not the crime of cussing! The crime of cussing is that it exists as a word at all.

Ren looked at the guy sitting to her right. Sexy, rough-looking, edgy, shaved head, cool blue eyes, late forties.

What is my thing with the rough guys? And the handsome, older, uptight ones? And the hot younger ones? And the elderly charmers? And the . . .

The guy beside her turned and smiled at her. He had a white raised scar that was like an extension of his smile. *Don't judge.* Ren smiled back. The guy side-eyed the speaker at the top of the room. Ren nodded. *Yes. Poor us.*

She zoned back in on the speaker. 'Mania works like broad brushstrokes of black paint swept across a rainbow,' he was saying. 'But to the manic, the black is neon.' He paused. 'And neon is brighter than any rainbow.'

Ren's neighbor leaned in to her. 'We need to find a bar.' There was a hint of a drawl.

Nice. 'Yes,' said Ren. *Yes, we do.*

'Want to make a run for it?'

Totally. But . . . I'm here by Order of My Boss. There could be spies dotted around this room. 'I'm going to sit it out,' said Ren. 'But what bar are you going to?'

'Nah – I'll wait too.' He checked his watch. 'It's only ten more minutes.'

'Sounds like a plan.'

Check this shit out – the speaker eyeballing us. Stop talking in class, children! Fuck this bullshit.

They were two beers down and hadn't exchanged names. It was like a pact.

The Privacy of Lunatics Act, 1828.

'That guy at the podium,' said Ren, 'talking about mania and increases. There was something about him. I get the sense that he had reconstructed himself after a post-mania crash. Like, last week he was in Speedos, bent over a table snorting coke at a pool-party in Vegas, then he collapsed with a nosebleed, ended up in the emergency room, was resuscitated, like ten times, then medicated, cleaned up, styled as a 1980s geography or math teacher . . . Do you ever think that people restyle themselves post-mania as a form of protection? Like, if they look nerdy on the outside, it's easier not to become a party person, or attract party people, or they can look in the mirror and not see the party person they were the previous week when they slept with their wife's best friend or OD'd or ran naked through their upscale gated community. I mean—'

The guy's brusque laughter cut her off. 'When did *you* ditch your meds?' There was no mirth in his voice.

'Excuse me?' said Ren.

'Just . . . well, you're talking a mile a minute, and—' He shrugged.

And what bipolar love ripped your heart out, dickhead?

'This probably wasn't a good idea,' said Ren. She stood up.

'Man, I'm sorry,' he said. 'I don't even know you. You probably aren't even bipolar.'

'Nothing to be sorry about,' said Ren. 'And you're right – I'm not. It's my brother who's bipolar.' *Sorry, Matt. Sorry,*

Jay. And Beau, if you're looking down on me. But please don't be looking down on me. No one needs to see that shiz.

'I guess I've been burned,' said the guy. 'And I haven't quite got a handle on it.'

'I'm sorry to hear that,' said Ren. *And eager for either you or me to leave.* 'You might just need more time.' *Stop engaging.*

The guy nodded. 'It's just, I feel . . . all the things I loved about her were because she was crazy.'

'That's not really true,' said Ren. 'But I understand why you feel that way right now.' *This is all very grim. I just wanted to have some fun. I hate turns for the worse.* 'Shots?'

He shook his head. 'No, thanks. Sorry for bringing the misery.'

'That's OK,' said Ren. 'You didn't. I don't mind.'

'I guess I slotted you right on into the "beautiful and crazy" category. And that's one rodeo I don't want to sign up for.' He smiled an extra-wide smile. 'I better be on my way . . .'

You be on your way, cowboy.

'You must think I'm crazy myself,' he said.

'No,' said Ren. *Weird? Yes. If you were a different type of guy, I might have said that out loud.*

'Will you be OK here?' he said, looking around the bar.

'OK?' said Ren. *I'm in a bar! Filled with strangers! Who have no insight into any part of me! Who know nothing of madness and meds!* 'I'm perfect.' *Fucking perfect!*

22

Ren sat at her desk the next morning pulling her drawer open and closed at intervals to refill her glass from a carton of pineapple juice. Everett was slipping her cups of ice from the kitchen.

'Lord have mercy,' said Ren to no one in particular.

Her cell phone rang.

She picked up.

'Is this Special Agent Ren Bryce?' said the voice.

Male, older, efficient.

'Yes,' said Ren.

'My name is David White – I got a message from my landlord about CCTV footage from his business in relation to the Hope Coulson murder investigation. As I believe he told you, his business was closed down two weeks prior to her disappearance, so he had no video operational on the Friday night in question. However, I was renting the upstairs apartment at that time. This may not be significant, but I wanted to let you know that I was disturbed that night at about two a.m. by people walking by. I looked out the window – there were three of them – two young women and a man. One of the women had stopped to throw up in the gutter. She was very drunk. So was the guy – he seemed to be her boyfriend. The other woman didn't seem quite so drunk. When my landlord called about all this and I told him, he said to look at the Hope Coulson case online. And she was definitely the woman I saw throwing up. And the photograph of the fiancé – that was definitely the guy. The other woman – I didn't get a good look at her. She was blonde, though, thin, quite short.'

Oh. My. God. Why was Jonathan Briar hiding this?

'Did you hear them speaking?' said Ren.

'No – they were making a lot of noise, but I couldn't make out what they were saying.'

'Did they stay there for long?' said Ren.

'Ten minutes at the most.'

'OK,' said Ren. 'Thank you for your call, Mr White – if you would kindly leave me your details, that would be great.'

'Yes – please call me at any time if you have any more questions. And if I remember anything else, I'll call you.'

'Thank you.'

Ren took his details, and put the phone down. 'Looks like Jonathan Briar and Hope Coulson walked home with a mystery lady friend two weeks before Hope disappeared. The question is, was he too hammered to remember that fact? Or is this the lie I was picking up on?'

'Well, maybe his lawyer will be able to enlighten you,' said Everett.

'Is that a shot across the bow or are you just happy to . . . be like Gary?' said Ren.

'Ouch,' said Everett. 'But, behave, bad girl. Remember that safety net . . .'

Ren smiled. Everett shook his head slowly. One minute later

her phone beeped with a text. It was from Everett – no words, just the See No Evil Hear No Evil Speak No Evil monkeys.

I love emoticons!

Jonathan Briar did not take long to tell Ren what he left out of his previous endless conversations with law enforcement. He seemed happier to do it in his apartment alone, than in Safe Streets, or his lawyer's office, or with anyone else.

'So, you and Hope had a threesome two weeks before she was killed . . .' said Ren.

You total fuckwit.

'I didn't think it was important . . .' said Jonathan. 'We're, you know, respectable people, I didn't want this getting out, making it into the newspapers. It was the only time. I know how people can view people's "lifestyles" . . . I thought they might judge Hope, judge both of us, not help with the searches. I've seen crime documentaries . . .'

'Then haven't you also seen how people withholding evidence can screw things up?' said Ren.

'I know,' said Jonathan. 'I'm sorry. But Hope . . . she was the beautiful kindergarten teacher that everyone fell for. I didn't want to shatter that illusion – not because of one threesome. Hope seemed so innocent to everyone. I mean . . . Hope *was* innocent. This didn't change that. She was amazing, she was Hope, I loved her, but . . . she wasn't, like, perfect, the way everyone thought.'

'I need you to understand, Jonathan, that the media does what the media does,' said Ren. 'And we do something entirely different. We think about each victim as a person who did not deserve to die, and their killer as someone who does not deserve to be out on the streets. That's it. Whether you're a kindergarten teacher or an internet troll, we're viewing you the same way.'

'But I figured if you knew stuff about her, then she might seem like some skank to you and you wouldn't care—'

'That's absolutely not the case,' said Ren. 'I simply don't see women as skanks.' *Unless they are actively trying to steal my man.*

'I thought about telling you, but then there were prostitutes mentioned in the newspapers and I figured you'd, like, put Hope in there with them—'

'Two of the victims were prostitutes, yes,' said Ren, 'but they are two of four photos on my wall that I look at every day when I sit at my desk. Each woman is as important as the next.' She paused. 'So, how did this threesome happen?'

'We picked up a girl at a bar, we took her back to our apartment, like, I mean, invited her back . . .' He shrugged.

'This was at the Irish Hound?' said Ren.

'Yes.'

'And . . . ?' said Ren.

'Well, that's it,' said Jonathan. 'We were all pretty wasted, we smoked some pot back at the apartment, we had sex, the girl left some time in the middle of the night. I can't remember much of the details.'

'Did she give you her name?' said Ren.

'Yes,' said Jonathan. 'It was a funny name, like Day-something, Daisy maybe? But not Daisy.'

'Can you describe her for me?' said Ren.

'Kind of raggedy blonde hair, skinny, big eyes, Southern accent, she didn't tell us where she was from, she was kind of . . . quiet I guess. Kind of mellow.'

'Was she alone when you met her in the bar?' said Ren.

'I think so,' said Jonathan. 'She said she was from out of town, here on business. But she was kind of kidding, because she didn't look like a business lady.'

'What happened during the threesome?' said Ren.

He looked like he wanted to curl up in a ball.

'Like, what do you mean?' said Jonathan.

'Did anything strange happen?' said Ren.

He shrugged. 'Not really . . . I don't know. I mean, it was my first time having a threesome.'

Who paid the most attention to whom? 'Did you have sex with the woman?'

'Depends on what you mean . . .'

'Did you have penetrative sex?' said Ren.

'No. She didn't want me to.'

'Hope didn't want you to?' said Ren.

'No – the girl,' said Jonathan.

'So,' said Ren, 'was she paying more attention to Hope than you?'

'Yes,' he said.

'Was there any violence involved?' said Ren.

'No.'

'How did you get talking to the girl in the first place?' said Ren. 'Who approached whom?'

'Well, she was at the bar when Hope went up to order drinks. I was in the men's room. I met a friend of mine; I was gone a long time. I think the girl told Hope her T-shirt was cool; they started talking. When I came back, the girl definitely looked a little pissed, like I was the one intruding . . . then a while later, she came over to our table, just sat down, without really asking if she could, but we didn't mind that. We had a couple more drinks . . .'

'What did you talk about?' said Ren.

'It was drunken talk, I guess,' said Jonathan. 'Music, bands, nights we partied . . .' His eyes went wide. 'Do you think this has something to do with what happened to Hope?'

'We're taking in as much information as we can,' said Ren, 'and we're focusing on anything out of the ordinary. This girl was a stranger who came into your lives not long before Hope's disappearance, so it might be significant. We won't know right away. Is there anything else you can think of?'

'No,' said Jonathan. He paused. 'There was something about her that was a bit wild.'

'Could you define that for me?' said Ren.

'Not really, no.'

Jesus.

'Did you exchange phone numbers with her?' said Ren.

'Well, I didn't. I don't know about Hope. I doubt it. Denver PD asked me to look through her cell-phone records to see if there were names or numbers I didn't recognize. There were a few, but I don't know if any of them was her.'

'Did you know or get the sense this girl might have had a boyfriend?' said Ren.

Jonathan shrugged. 'She didn't say she did, and, like I said, she was alone in the bar.'

'OK, well if anything else comes to you about her . . .' said Ren.

Jonathan sat forward. 'Do you think she could be the killer, a tiny little thing like her? She was like five feet tall.'

Actually, she sounds like a potential victim.

Could the killer have scored a two-for-one?

23

Carly Raine stood in her back garden, dressed in a white tank and blue denim cut-offs. There was a laundry basket at her bare feet. She was hanging white bedsheets on the washing line, enjoying the cool as they lapped back against her bare arms and legs. It was the highest breeze to rise in weeks, and as soon as she felt it that morning, she thought of doing laundry. And right after that, she thought of how sad and domesticated she was. But she smiled – she loved her life. Partying and dating were behind her – and they had brought her a big handsome husband, and two beautiful children to love all day, every day. Even on Saturday nights, when all over the world people were lighting up bars and dance floors and not having to worry about getting up the next day to be mom to a three-year-old boy and nine-month-old baby girl. Carly Raine never thought she'd see the day. And love that day. Every day.

He had taken a wrong turn. He had come here for someone else, but he was hidden now at the back of this sheltered property, out of the parked pickup, drawn through the trees by the flapping white sheets. He had seen her at the washing line, her back to him, and he felt the breath being sucked from him, as if by a violent force that wanted to rob lives in one terrible inhalation.

He was taken home, decades back. And he never wanted to be taken home – not then, not now. He felt a surge of heat through his body, a powerful rage to push back – to push back on whatever was trying to destroy him.

He sucked in a huge breath, and made his way, out of sight, to the back door of the house.

I worry when it goes quiet, thought Carly Raine. But she was smiling. She was sliding a peg down onto the last corner of the last bedsheet. Something in her chest tensed. Her heart. It had gone really, really quiet. She had zoned out. Silence had fallen, and . . . where was Tyler? Isobel was asleep in her crib upstairs, she knew that. But where was Tyler? He had been running all over the garden. A shiver swept up her back.

'Ty?' she said. 'Ty, sweetheart?'

She whipped back the white sheet. The kitchen door was closed. She knew she had left it open. Her gaze was drawn to the right, where she could see Tyler, standing in the window of the dining area, his hands flat against the glass.

What's he doing in there?

Carly was slow to process the scene.

'Oh my God!' she screamed.

There was a man dressed in black, standing behind her son.

Carly ran for the kitchen door. She realized that the man was now walking through it, without Tyler, but closing the door behind him, coming toward her. She glanced at Tyler, who was screaming now, but it was silent and terrible, and this man was on top of her, knocking her back, sharply onto her back.

Carly went to scream, and as her mouth opened wide, her attacker's mouth opened just as wide, and he clamped down on hers. It was a suffocating, terrifying pressure, his tongue plunging down deep, making her gag, making the veins on her neck bulge as she tried to raise her head. He kept on, depriving her of breath, closing off her nostrils, leaving her desperate and coughing for air.

She never imagined that in a situation like this she could go limp, she always imagined herself fighting, but this was it, this was her moment, and she turned to liquid.

My babies. My babies. My babies. Help me! Someone!

He pulled his head up, smiled down at her, waited for her to catch her breath.

'Please don't do this to me,' said Carly. 'Please – my babies. I want to live. I want to live. I really want to live. I'll do anything you want. And I'll never tell anyone what you did. I swear to God. I won't even report this. Just . . . you can do whatever you want to me. I swear. You can even hurt me. I . . . just don't kill me. I don't want to die. I have my family. I love my family. My friends. I . . . I just don't want to die.'

'Well,' he said slowly, like he was giving it thought. 'I wouldn't be doing my job right if you didn't feel like dying by the end of it, now would I?'

She let out a choking gasp, and he slapped her hard across the face. She started to shake as she stared into the vast, gaping blackness of his eyes. It was like nothing she had ever seen. It was like a possession. She believed in that. Carly Raine had learned about the devil when she was in Sunday School and she remembered a line she had first

143

heard when she was seven years old: the devil wears coats. And she knew what that meant, even then. The devil can slip inside anyone and make himself one with them. Carly began to pray. She began to pray to Jesus, who she always believed was not just all around her, but inside her heart and soul. Right now, he was rising up to fight this devil off, because the devil never wins. Right? The devil never wins.

But the devil did win, and in winning, he could soar. He was above her now, above them both, looking down on this perfect scene: woman, naked, hunted, soon to be raped, soon to be lifeless. And he would be there, kneeling behind her, bending over her, filled with life, overflowing with it, as he was taking hers away.

24

Ren stood at the stove in her kitchen, preparing a supper of popcorn. The buzzer rang.

She went to the intercom.

Whoa: who is this hotness?

She picked up. 'Hello.'

'Mrs Bryce?'

Not so much. 'This is Ren, yes.'

'I'm Luke – Everett King's friend. I'm here to put up a curtain rail.'

Cue porn music. 'Come on up.'

Ren opened the door. Luke was six two, dark, frowning, dressed in tight black work gear and boots, muscles everywhere. Tool belt on, tool box in hand.

Well, hello.

'So,' he said, all business. 'You have a curtain that needs mounting.'

Curtain. 'Yes,' said Ren. 'And thank you so much for coming.'

'Pleasure.'

'Straight ahead,' said Ren.

He stepped past.

'I'm hoping it's your easiest job today,' said Ren, 'Two screws in a wall . . .' *Or up against it.*

Shit – the wall.

'Actually,' said Ren, 'could you go into the kitchen for a moment? Help yourself to whatever.'

She ran into the living room and took all the documents off the wall and brought them into her bedroom.

What a pain in the ass.

'You can come in now,' she called. *As if I'm standing here nekkid.*

Luke put down the toolbox. 'OK, tell me what I'm doing here.'

'I'd like a curtain rail across that wall,' said Ren, pointing to the wall opposite the sofa.

'Can I ask why you're putting a curtain right in front of a wall?' he said.

'Yes,' said Ren. She waited.

'Are you like this all the time?' he said.

'Yes,' said Ren. 'I'm lots of fun. To answer your question, the curtain is a decorative feature.' *Or to hide shiz.*

'You want it up to the ceiling?'

'Yes,' said Ren. 'Let me get you a chair.'

Ren watched as he worked, specifically the hollow in his lower back when his T-shirt rode up. He was like a bigger version of her ex – confidential informant, Billy Waites – who had a body made to be admired. Ren imagined these men sketched, like concept cars, by the hand of God. *Concept men. This guy, Billy Waites, Ben . . . they were concept men. Gary was too, in his own way, like some sort of intelligent design special . . .*

Luke jumped down. 'Do you have the curtain here?' He

gestured to the floor. 'Like somewhere among the hundred shopping bags?'

'I was running low on . . .'

'Every product ever made?' said Luke.

Ren grabbed the curtain from where it was hanging over the back of the sofa.

'And I took it out of the bag,' said Ren. 'I even ironed it.'

'Sounds like that's rare for you.'

'Of course it is. Jesus.'

She handed it to him. It was petrol blue with teal backing.

'Aren't these things usually a little more sheer?' said Luke.

Not if you're covering up the faces of killers and victims, wounds, dump sites . . . 'It's a little fancy,' said Ren, 'but I just wanted something pretty to look at.' *Like you, hot, practical man.*

Universe: stop, yet continue, to send concept men my way.

'That looks great,' said Ren. 'And super-speedy.'

'That will be one hundred dollars.'

Whoa.

'I'm kidding. It's on the house.'

'What do you mean on the house?'

'Any friend of Everett's . . .'

'No way – I'm paying you.'

'No, ma'am, you're absolutely not. Take this up with Everett.'

'Man, this is wrong.'

He shook his head. 'It was a pleasure. Good to meet you.'

'You too. I really appreciate this.' *And feel awkward.*

He shook her hand. 'See you again, hopefully.'

Ooh . . .

Ren closed the door after him and went back into the living room. She pinned everything back up on the wall: row after row of names and images, faces and bodies and wounds.

She used the opportunity to streamline everything. She moved things around. She made everything clearer . . . to her. After three hours, she drew the curtain across and went to bed.

The next morning in Safe Streets, she went straight for Everett.

'Well, thank you very much for Luke,' she said.

Everett laughed loud, sat back in his chair. 'I thought you might like him.'

'He wouldn't let me pay!'

'Suck it up. He's a good guy.'

'So, so hot,' said Ren. 'He's lucky he made it out in one piece. Only kidding. Don't tell him I said that. Has he got a girlfriend?'

'You're a bad girl,' said Everett. 'No, he does not have a girlfriend. But I'm sure if he wanted one, he'd pick you.'

Ren laughed. 'Oh, you guys.'

'You're a disgrace,' said Janine.

Gary walked into the bullpen.

'Were you home last night?' he said to Janine.

'Yes – why?'

'You're one lucky lady,' said Gary. 'We have a body and it's about a mile from your house.'

Janine was mute.

'No fucking way!' said Ren.

'Our guy?' Janine managed to say. 'Again? In Golden? Are you sure?'

Gary nodded. 'Her husband couldn't get hold of her this morning and called the local PD. Two patrol officers did a welfare check . . . they found her—'

'In her home?' said Ren.

Gary nodded. 'Let's go.'

'He's going into people's homes now?' said Ren. 'Fuck that.'

Gary was gone.

'Make a call,' said Ren to Janine.

'You bet your ass I will,' said Janine. She called her former colleague. 'Logan? It's Janine. I believe you have a homicide victim. I need you to station the biggest, burliest, most discreet, ominous-looking dudes at that property and tell them to let no one in. Zero. No one's name is on the list.'

She listened.

'No, no,' said Janine, 'You *can* do this. Believe. We'll be there in about forty minutes, and we want to be the next ones in the door, OK?'

She nodded. 'Thank you, thank you, thank you.'

She listened. 'Oh, God – children. No. No. OK . . . see you in a while.' She put down the phone. 'Oh, God,' she said. 'There were two kids in the house at the time. A son, three years old, and a daughter nine months old. Logan heard it is one ugly, ugly scene. The husband arrived home and was literally wrestled to the ground in the driveway. He was absolutely hysterical. He had to be sedated.'

'Are the kids OK?' said Ren.

Janine nodded. 'But their mother most certainly is not. Logan said "be prepared".'

Ren stood in the hallway of Carly Raine's house. She was waiting for the gagging to stop. She had chosen not to eat breakfast, but could feel the beginnings of weakness, the hollowness, the light head.

Popcorn dinner – not wise then, wise now.

The first thing she noticed was a trail of blood that ran toward her from the kitchen door at the end of the hallway. Before it reached her feet, it moved to the right, and up the stairs. There were smears, and every now and then tiny little red footprints. Tiny red handprints and streaks on the walls.

No.

Ren sidestepped the blood to walk to the kitchen. The refrigerator door was open. There was a carton of apple juice, open and empty, lying discarded in the corner. There were flies buzzing around it. But where the flies swarmed, that was to the left in the corner, where the brutalized body of Carly Raine lay. Ren walked over.

Holy shit.

There were three pink Cheerios stuck to her lips. There was milk, spilled and stinking, lumpy and pooled, on her chin, her bare chest, on the ground. There were Cheerios stuck into the clots, scattered around the floor.

Oh, God. Your son tried to feed you. He wanted to give you breakfast. He wanted you to wake up.

I will kill the man who did this to you. I will kill him with my bare fucking hands.

Carly Raine was lying on her back, naked, with her arms out and her right leg bent and across her left as if she was trying to block her killer. As if he could be blocked. She had been savaged. Above her, on the sideboard, was a photo of how she should have looked: bright and bubbly and beaming. Underneath, on the floor, her face was beaten to twice its size, the colors a palette of blue and purple, fading and garish. Her face was turned slightly to the left and there was a sharp slice out of her scalp above her right ear. Her lips were huge. Flies were gathering in all the dead places flies gathered, all the rich moisture of the cavities, the wounds, the secretions; workers in shifts, coming to the body of an innocent to gorge on it.

Layers upon layers of damage, decay, hurt.

Outside the window, two Jefferson County Investigators were bent over, throwing up. They weren't the first.

Ren looked down again at a body ruined.

I am walking the earth with monsters.

Mark Gaston walked into the kitchen behind her, set his bag down on a safe part of the floor.

He looked down at the body. 'Anyone for Cheerios?'

Ren turned to him. 'OK – I don't know where the fuck you worked before this, but I can't, I just can't listen to your fucked-up, disrespectful bullshit any more.'

All around them, people seemed to freeze.

'It blows my mind,' said Ren, 'that a woman gave birth to you and you can still come out with some of the shit you come out with. I don't give a fuck if it's a defense mechanism or if you're just a massive prick in all your waking hours, but if for one more second of *my* waking hours, *I* have to listen to your horrible, cruel and nasty remarks, I will beat you to within an inch of your pathetic fucking life. Do your job, Gaston. You are clearly very talented at it – otherwise how the fuck would anyone hire such a fucking asshole?'

She turned around and left.

25

The mood was altered in Safe Streets – every killing had been brutal, but there was something about the intrusion into the home, the innocence of the children, the Cheerios, even the white sheets on the washing line, that made what happened to Carly Raine all the more harrowing.

'We're bringing in Sylvie Ross to speak to the three-year-old,' said Gary.

Sylvie Ross was one of the best child forensic interviewers in the country, a member of the FBI's Child Abduction Rapid Deployment Team, based out of Quantico.

Ah, sporty, marathon-running Sylvie Ross.

One man connected Ren to Sylvie Ross: Paul Louderback, their PT instructor at the academy. For years, Ren and Paul had a deep emotional affair that, for different reasons, at different times, never really advanced. Just before she and Ben got together officially, she and Paul spent a night together, before they realized it would never work. Last she heard, he had gotten back with his ex-wife.

Did you sleep with Paul too, Sylvie?

Why are you even thinking about that now? Get a grip.

'Who flew her in?' said Ren. *Is the whole CARD team here? Will Paul Louderback be flung into my monogamously unstable path once more?*

'She was in town, and she's the best there is,' said Gary. 'Have you got a problem with that?'

'No,' said Ren. 'Why would I?'

'I don't know . . .' said Gary. 'You tell me.'

What the hell are you getting at?

'Are the autopsy results on Carly Raine back yet?' said Ren. 'It's been two days.'

Gary looked at her like she had ten heads.

'What?' said Ren.

'After your outburst at Gaston, you can hardly—'

'You *know* the guy is a dickhead—'

'Not the point!' said Gary.

'It's exactly the point!' said Ren. 'I got about fifteen text messages of congratulations from people who were there or who heard about it—'

'The point,' said Gary, 'is that if you were wrong, for example, if it was one of Ren's wild beliefs that wasn't backed up and you went off like that – you would have pissed off a brand-new Medical Examiner who you have to work with—'

'I get it!' said Ren. 'But—'

'But nothing!' said Gary. 'Yes, the guy is an asshole. But how you handled it? Was worse. You can't behave like—'

'Like what?' said Ren.

'Jesus, Ren, just zip it! For once in your life, just fucking zip it.'

That is fucking IT.

Ren left, bound for the ladies' room. She walked in, slammed one of the open locker doors shut. She opened more, slammed them, breathed deeply, wallowed in the sound of metal ringing in her ears. It was better than words.

I feel possessed.

She sat down on the bench, leaned back against the cold brick wall.

I want to feel this hardness against my spine, the discomfort. I deserve it. The fury I'm harboring.

The human body is an incredible thing. Everything I am feeling is contained within this one body, I am alone with it, I am the only one who can feel this rippling pain, this rising and falling of emotion.

I have to do something to ease this pressure.

Ren knocked on Gary's office door, but pushed in before he could finish giving her permission to enter.

'You don't get to take this out on me,' she said, slamming the door behind her. 'I'm not taking the hit for your perfectionism issues.'

Gary stared at her.

'Everywhere you look, you're seeing failure,' said Ren. 'At home with Karen, with Claire, here with me on a professional level and on a personal level. You can't load all that guilt and blame on me. It's not fair. I can see you – since you had to involve me in your "issue" – you're looking at me like you can't handle the fact that I'm aware of your fucking *humanity*. *My* flaws have become enormous to you. You're totally projecting. How can I work with you hovering around me like I'm a fucking bomb about to go off—'

'It *feels* like you're a bomb about to go off,' said Gary.

'Or,' said Ren, 'do you feel that way only because of what *you've* done? Maybe, because of all this shit, maybe, for once, Gary Dettling really does have to question his judgment. I mean, whoa, you slept around. Or is it that you got caught sleeping around . . . the fucking cliché. Maybe I'm not the only one here who is going off the rails. And how does that feel after all your judgment of me?'

'So you think you're going off the rails?' said Gary.

'That's what you got from all that?' said Ren. 'Are you fucking serious? Stop fucking deflecting! The only things you've responded to that I've said are about me. *Me* doing something wrong. That's the way it's always been—'

'That is not true,' said Gary. 'I have always praised you when—'

'Reluctantly!' said Ren. 'Reluctantly.'

'I have fought for you every step of the way,' said Gary. *He has. He always has.* 'No you haven't,' said Ren. 'And if you have, it's like some kind of extension of your own ego. "Surely I didn't spectacularly misjudge my own star UCE!"'

'Where is this coming from?' Gary threw his hands up. 'I'm not here saying I'm perfect.'

'No,' said Ren, 'but you're believing you should be, believing that you have to be, believing that everyone has to be. And that's your problem. Your wife's not perfect, that pisses you off; Claire isn't, that pisses you off; I'm not. Maybe if we were all perfect, you wouldn't have to be faced with a world of imperfection every fucking day and you could continue to believe that everything can be perfect in your tiny fucking bubble of perfection. Then you could look in the mirror and not see whatever the fuck it is you are seeing.'

Rein it in, Ren, rein it in.

They stared at each other, in the shrinking room, through the excruciating silence, their faces flush, their eyes black.

Fuck, you are sexy. I bet you are a wild fuck.

'I need to get back to work,' said Gary.

Oh, I'm not finished yet.

Do not speak, Ren. Do not speak. Shut up.

'You can't spend your whole life compensating for your cruel, cheating army father,' said Ren.

'Don't analyze me,' said Gary, in a tone like a slap across the face.

'Really?' said Ren. 'Really? Extra bang for your buck on my therapy sessions. I can pass on my wisdom for free.'

'I had no idea you were this angry.'

'Oh, fuck off, Gary, with your calming tone.' *And I am way beyond 'this angry'. This is me contained.*

'You're a different man to your father,' said Ren. 'Yes, one who screws up every now and then – screws around, as it turns out. One who is – oh my God – fallible, but you're not him. I'm sorry, but he sounds like he was not a very nice man. And you are. Regardless of any of this. You're not out to fuck up lives.'

Her heart was beating too fast. *Why am I feeling like the genie is out of the bottle and I could fuck you right now on your desk? Or murder you? I need to leave.*

26

The conference room slowly filled with members of the task force. Ren was standing at the door beside Gary, going through the newly arrived autopsy report.

He leaned in to her. 'I apologize for involving you . . .' said Gary. 'It was unprofessional.'

Ren faux-gasped. 'You?' *Admitting you're . . .* 'Unprofessional?'

He smiled.

'Good,' said Ren. 'And I'm sorry I lost it.'

Which is not true. I found it both therapeutic and thrilling.

Ren went to the top of the room.

'Our latest victim is Carly Raine, thirty-nine years old. She was found raped, murdered, and mutilated in her family home two days ago. From what we know of the crime scene, the UNSUB entered the house through the unlocked back door. She was not killed where she was found – there is evidence that she was killed in the wooded area that borders her home's property. She was raped with something – we don't know what, it wasn't at the scene. The UNSUB's consistent in his inconsistencies. There are scratches on her feet from where she tried to run away from her attacker. This leads me to believe that he, at least initially, allows his victims to get away, that he enjoys the pursuit of naked women. Her clothes were found in the garden, so we can assume they were taken off there. I just can't see how several of his petite victims managed to get away. I think he's making them run.' She looked around the room.

Hard to say who's agreeing with me here.

'There are rope burns on her wrists – the rope was not left at the scene – and there were abrasions to the face – both types of wound were found on some of the other victims. We now have six in total,' said Ren, pointing to a whiteboard where she had pinned up their photos, alongside maps marking where they lived and where their bodies had been found. 'Gia Larosa, Stephanie Wingerter, Hope Coulson, Carrie Longman, Donna Darisse, and Carly Raine,' said Ren. 'Six women, aged between eighteen and thirty-nine, all brutally raped and murdered. Six women all with friends and families, boyfriends or husbands, or ex-boyfriends or ex-husbands, colleagues, neighbors, people they've fallen out with, people they loved to see every day on their way to work. It is exponential. These women all had passions: favorite movies, books, TV shows. They had bars they liked to drink in, restaurants they liked to eat in, parks they ran in, stores they shopped in. Our victims have all made mistakes in their lives, they may have written shitty things in emails, on Facebook, on Twitter, they may have had shitty things written about them. But they've written beautiful things, loving things, kind things. They were loved. They all had reasons to live. Not one of them had a reason to die. Not one of them woke up that last morning thinking they wouldn't make it to the end of the day. Every single one of those women *deserved* to make it. And every single woman in the city deserves to make it today. And tomorrow and the next day. And every day. We have to stop this.

'The UNSUB is careful,' said Ren. 'He leaves no trace that can be connected to him. The bleach, the acid, leaving no weapons at the scene. This means, obviously, he's got a vehicle in which he can transport not only a victim, but all the other tools he uses to carry out his crimes. He could even be driving a vehicle big enough to allow him to carry out some of the killings inside of it – in the instances where the body was dumped, as opposed to being killed at the scene. Or he has access to a large and private property, where he can come and go unnoticed, and carry out his crimes undisturbed.'

She stopped, looked around the room, eyeballed as many people as she could. 'We can't be overwhelmed. I understand that this is challenging, but I don't want anyone to lose heart. Please stay motivated. He won't walk free – it's just a question of meticulously going through what we have. Always look for patterns, any thread that runs through every scene, or victim. For every one thing this guy throws at us, there is a new connection to him, a fresh opportunity to find him. He is not invincible. He will make a mistake. He doesn't appear to be on a kamikaze mission. He wants to be alive. Right now, he's getting away with his ultimate fantasy. Why would he ever want that to end?'

She paused.

'My mom fell over once,' she said. 'Tripped and fell, just on the street. I was here, she was in New York. It was nothing alarming, she wasn't badly injured, just a little sore. But the idea, just the idea that she had fallen, needed help, that none of us was there, that she was among strangers . . . that really got to me. I found the whole thing a lot more upsetting than she did. I couldn't stop thinking, "She was just there alone, I wasn't there to help her, none of us was."

'Luckily, my mom was surrounded by kind strangers. Now, can you *imagine* being a loved one of one of our victims? Knowing that there were *no* kind strangers there, just one person, a monster, someone who wanted only to hurt her, someone who was getting *excited* by hurting her, that the whole point *was* to hurt her, that she was likely screaming, crying, running for her life, *questioning* her life, her choices? From "Did I wear the wrong thing?" to "Why did I have to drink so much?"; "Did I smile the wrong way at someone?"; "Why didn't I work out more so I could be fitter so I could run faster?"; "Did I lead this guy on?"; "Why did I leave my kids to go out into the garden to hang my washing?" It's not right.

'This is affecting people like no other investigation we've ever been involved in. For the women of Denver, there is less distance, psychologically: this is not a missing child, which is utterly heartbreaking, but at a remove in most people's eyes. Like, no matter what, they don't think they could be next. Not really. They might cry, they might be empathetic, but they don't necessarily fear for their own safety. This time, people out there – *women* out there – are thinking they could be next. And they are terrified. He has crossed another boundary – their homes are now violable. He has raped and murdered while children were nearby, unattended, vulnerable.'

Ren pointed around to the whiteboard, the noticeboards, the photos, the reports, the statements, the stacks of documents.

'Somewhere in this mountain of information lies something that could lead us to our killer. Something. Anything. I will take anything.'

*　　*　　*

Ren went home that night and added Carly Raine's details to the Wall of Horrors, pinning them under the relevant categories.

She sat down on the sofa and studied the additions.

Bound by rope at the wrists. So was Carrie Longman. So was Stephanie Wingerter. So was . . . someone else.

She scanned the wall again.

Who? Why am I getting the feeling the answer is not on the wall?

She closed her eyes. *Where did I hear rope burns recently?*

She sat up. *Oh my God – the Jane Doe in Sedalia, the neglected lady in the crash into the medical center! Rope burns. And – burns to her body. Like Stephanie Wingerter! What the fuck?*

Ren Googled the Jane Doe, and the details of the crash. *Oh. My. God.*

It was the night before Stephanie Wingerter was found . . .

Ren called Gary.

'Gary – sorry for calling so late, but I have something – Stephanie Wingerter was found the morning after that Jane Doe turned up in Sedalia – the one who was in the pickup that crashed into Sky Ridge Medical Center. Stephanie Wingerter had burns – with lighter fluid as an accelerant – and so did the Jane Doe. Plus, they both had been bound with rope at the wrists.'

'Bit of a stretch,' said Gary. 'And didn't that lady set herself on fire?'

'I know, but . . .' *It's a gut thing.* 'Two women – tied with rope, burned flesh, within twenty miles of each other? I mean – could it be the case that Jane Doe escaped from the same man who killed the others?'

'That he had one old lady in the middle of all those skinny blondes?' said Gary.

'If I could understand the mind of every killer . . .'

'I need more.'

They all wanted proof; it was their job to have proof. But Gary wanted rock-solid. Everything had to be rock solid.

Goddamn it.

27

The next morning, Ren put a call into Undersheriff Cole Rodeal in Douglas County.

'Rodeal – could you cast your mind back to your heroic night in the ambulance bay?'

'Why, I've barely moved on from it, I've been so busy basking in the glory.'

'The woman who came in . . . she was burned, wasn't she?' said Ren.

'She was burn-*ing*,' said Rodeal. 'She'd just poured lighter fluid on herself, she found it on the floor of the truck, and she lit herself on fire.'

'And you found nothing else out about her – is that right?' said Ren.

'Yes, ma'am. Why are you asking?'

'Nothing other than she was found the same night Stephanie Wingerter disappeared – they both had burns.'

'Totally different burns,' said Rodeal.

'I know, I know. But lighter fluid as an accelerant . . .'

'Would it help if you spoke with my wife, Edie? She was around the whole time that lady was at the hospital.'

'Thanks,' said Ren. 'That would be great.'

Ren waited until after work to drive to the Sky Ridge Medical Center to meet with Edie Rodeal.

'Our Jane Doe,' said Edie. 'Yes – she was ninety-three pounds, a serious IV drug user, we found heroin in her system, she was malnourished, she had been beaten, she had broken bones, she had been tied by her wrists and ankles, she had wounds infected with maggots . . .'

'The stuff that doesn't make the newspapers . . .'

Edie nodded.

'Any personal effects?' said Ren.

'She came in with nothing,' said Edie. 'I mean, her night-gown was destroyed when she set herself alight. She had nothing else with her. The young woman had stumbled across her, the gentleman in the pickup stopped to help them.'

'And did the guy and girl know each other?' said Ren.

'No. It was obvious from how they were talking. Or not talking. He tried his best.'

'Do you think the woman was psychotic?' said Ren. 'Is that why she set herself on fire?'

'We ordered a psych eval, soon as she came in,' said Edie, 'but the doctor saw no evidence of psychosis. She refused to speak, so that made any specific diagnosis impossible. She was an abused and broken woman, but he did not believe she was psychotic. He believed she was choosing not to speak.'

'Why would she have set herself alight?' said Ren. 'She was being rescued. She had obviously escaped from somewhere.' She paused. 'Unless she was trying to destroy something . . . an identifying mark, maybe – a mole, a tattoo, bite marks.' She shrugged. 'But if she was the victim, why would she do that? Were the burns anywhere in particular?'

'Mainly her shoulder,' said Edie. 'She had poured most

of the lighter fluid there. They were full thickness burns. You wouldn't even be able to tell what might have been there to destroy.'

Weirdness. 'How did she even get to where she was found?'

'Like I said, she didn't speak to us, but—'

A young nurse at the counter looked up. 'Are you talking about the old lady? I heard her moaning something when I went in at night. Kind of singing in her own way. A few times. I thought she might have been hallucinating.'

'What was she singing?' said Ren.

'Something about tiny fingers pointing at her and about needles. She was distressed. We had to put a lot of lines in.'

'She was an IV drug user,' said Edie, dismissively. 'She was used to needles.'

Ren had zoned out. All she could see were the words she had been staring at for weeks on her Wall of Horrors: words that were written on the napkin taken from Carrie Longman's jeans: *"tiny fingers pointing your way, needle's pointing to your heart, sharps disposal, sharps disposal, now I know the way we'll part . . . "*

"Sharps disposal". That's quite a medical expression for a song lyric . . . usually a songwriter, that wouldn't be their world. Would it?

Was the songwriter moon-lighting: medical person by day, singer by night? This Jane Doe was singing those lyrics six weeks before Carrie Longman was at Manny's. Was the songwriter someone at the hospital who heard the Jane Doe's ramblings when she was admitted and later used it in a song? Performed it in Manny's?

Who was this Jane Doe? What has she got to do with Carrie Longman? Could she have known Carrie Longman? Or known that Carrie Longman was going to be a target?

'Do you have any amateur singers on staff?' said Ren.

'Everyone's an amateur singer these days, if you ask me,' said Edie.

'Anyone who has performed on Open Mic night in Manny's Bar in Denver?' said Ren. 'In any bars?'

'Not that I know of,' said Edie. 'I'll ask around.'

'Can you show me any photos of the Jane Doe?' said Ren.

The nurse opened the file, passed them to Ren.

Fuuuuck.

'I know,' said Edie. 'Not a pretty picture.'

'And worse than I imagined,' said Ren, 'which is impressive.'

The woman's face was ruined by drugs, hard-living, abuse and neglect. The fire added new scars, new colors and contours. Her neck was horrifically burnt, her jaw, most of her left ear. Her hair had shriveled on that side of her head.

'A merciful Lord has taken her,' said Edie.

'Was there any evidence that she was sexually assaulted?' said Ren.

'No.'

'Do you have anything else on her?'

'Nothing,' said Edie.

Ren nodded. 'OK – thank you for your time.' She paused. 'Before I go – do you have the names of the two people who came in with her? They weren't in the newspaper reports.'

'I can't imagine they were,' said the nurse. 'Neither of them was the type to want publicity: she was a sweet thing, wouldn't want any credit for an act of kindness type of girl, and he was just the loner type who'd be like a bug under a looking glass in the sun with any attention on himself. Apparently, the young woman found the lady wandering along the side of the road. And the young man was driving past and stopped to help. The ambulance got lost trying to find them, and the young man took matters into his own hands. She was a pretty girl, and he looked like he was trying to impress her. He might have thought that this was his only shot at ever being a knight in shining armor. You know – like my husband.' She smiled. 'Let me go get those names for you.' She came back and handed them to Ren on a yellow Post-It.

Kurt Vine and Amanda Petrie.

Ren ran them through the system. Kurt Vine lived close to where he picked the two women up. It was an hour from Sky Ridge.

There is nothing to stop me from dropping by. Amanda Petrie lives too far away for tonight.

Ren called Gary as she drove. She got his voicemail.

'Gary – I have your rock-solid connection. It's just not one I expected: this time it's that Jane Doe and Carrie Longman. It's a weird one: the lyrics Carrie Longman wrote on the napkin are exactly the same as the ones that lady was singing while she was in the hospital. They were the only words that came out of her mouth. Nuts! Call me.'

Ren drove on to Kurt Vine's house, thinking about tiny fingers and needles.

Creepsville.

She pulled into a clearing at the front of his house.

Griiiiiim.

Everything about it was unmaintained.

How do people live like this?

Her cell phone rang. It was Edie.

'Ren, it's me again – I forgot something. It was only when I was talking to one of the nurses on my break about you coming in. She reminded me that after the crash, when I got up after Cole jumped in to protect me, I ran over to the pickup to check on the occupants. The Jane Doe kept saying that something terrible had brought her there, that she did something bad. I told my friend on the night, but

I had completely forgotten it until she reminded me just now.'

'The woman said that *she* did something bad?' said Ren. 'The woman herself?'

'Yes,' said Edie. 'I figured it was a reference to setting herself on fire. And it's fairly clear that something terrible had brought her to the hospital. But just in case there's any other angle I'm not thinking about, I thought I'd say it to you.'

'Thanks,' said Ren.

So this lady may have been complicit in something. Or have been so psychologically damaged that she simply thought she was complicit in what happened to her. Like she'd been told enough times by her captor that she had done something bad.

Ren walked over to the timber steps up to the porch, and stopped to inspect them.

Steps through rotten wood, cuts up legs, dies of exsanguination.

She went up the steps anyway, holding the shaky railing as she did. She rang the bell.

Sweat was pouring down Kurt Vine's face, his erection was straining his track pants, hurting him. The stinging, the cramp in his hands – he was locked into it all.

The doorbell rang. Nothing good had ever come to Kurt Vine when he opened his door at night. *'I came to collect my debt.'* He shivered at the memory.

The doorbell rang again.

'Not happening,' he muttered. 'Not fucking happening.'

28

Ren wandered around the back of Kurt Vine's house. There was a battered Mitsubishi Montero parked there. She took a photo of the license plate, then went around to the front of the house again and rang the bell. No answer.

Another time, Kurt Vine.

She ran the license plate when she got back into the Jeep – it was registered to Kurt Vine.

No dramz.

That night, Ren sat on the sofa, writing the lyrics over and over.

There's something more to these.

Sharps disposal . . . getting rid of the needles . . . now I know the way we'll part . . . death? Anesthesia? Needle's pointing to your heart: that's where it hurts? Someone's heart is being pierced by pain. Or . . . maybe it's literal.

She sat up.

Heroin? Injecting heroin? Edie said that the woman was an IV drugs user.

'Tiny fingers pointing your way . . .' In accusation?

Was the song written from the perspective of a child about a heroin-addicted adult? A child who thinks they know that the needle will end their relationship?

'Sharps disposal' is not about disposing of the needles: it's about the singer. A person who feels he or she's being disposed of by a drug abuser? By Jane Doe?

Now, what the hell does that have to do with Carrie Longman?

Maybe it's nothing more than she recognized in those lyrics the lives of the people she dealt with every day. Or maybe it was sung by one of the people she dealt with.

Annnd, we're back to wondering who the Jane Doe is . . .

Ren got up to get a bottle of water from the kitchen. She had left her phone on the table.

Shit! On Silent!

Five missed calls from Gary. She called him right back.

'Where the hell were you?' he said.

'Sorry – my phone was on silent. I was checking out new—'

'Listen: I'm with you tonight.'

'The what now?'

'Can't talk. I'm with you . . . if Karen calls. I'm on my way to your apartment. I've been there all evening working on the case.'

Well, fuck you, Gary. 'OK.'

Twenty minutes later, Ren buzzed Gary in. She smelled the beer on his breath before she had the door fully open.

Oh, God, you look just-fucked. Delete image. And, Ren, pull pointy shard of envy from your chest.

'You said it was over.'

'I thought it was,' said Gary. 'I wanted it to be.' He went into the living room and sat on the sofa.

You don't look like you want it to be. Not one bit.

Ren sat down at the other end of the sofa. 'This is a disaster. I'm not judging you, I'm not in any position to, but please don't do this. Whoever she is, she's not worth it.' *WHO IS IT?*

'But . . . I think . . .'

Oh, Jesus. No. 'Do not say it,' said Ren. 'Do not say you love her. This is not a conversation to have with me. Save it for therapy.' She paused. 'And don't look at me like that. Do you think you don't need help? That it's just for the crazies? Let me tell you something – if a crazy is telling you you need help, you need help.' *I can barely look at you, you're so fucking excited by this woman.*

'You don't love her,' said Ren. 'You're just having a ball, more excited than you've been in years. I get it. I really do. But it will fuck you up, fuck Karen up, especially because of how convincingly you lied. And, I'm leaving the worst till last: this will shatter Claire. She's seventeen, Gary. This would be so bad for a seventeen-year-old. And you've only gotten close in the past two years. How do you think she's going to feel? End this now. Please. I can't watch you self-destruct. I've done it. It's not pleasant.' *And I'm probably wired to keep doing it.*

'This is different,' said Gary.

'If this was different, then why does the cliché of the mid-life crisis exist? You're smarter than that. Can I venture: your girlfriend is younger than you, has longer hair than your wife, isn't a stay-at-home mom, laughs at all your jokes, and wears killer underwear at all times?' *Which I strongly believe in, actually.*

Gary gave a one-shoulder shrug.

'Well, there you go. This is not different. I'm sorry. Just ask yourself that long list of questions. And imagine, really, really, imagine integrating your girlfriend into your life—'

'Stop calling her that,' said Gary.

'Mistress sounds alluring and mysterious,' said Ren. *'Girlfriend' sounds pathetic for a man in your circumstances.* 'There is nothing alluring and mysterious about this whole shitshow. So, I'm prompting you again to consider this woman as part of your family, your career, everything. Spend some time with that. Because no one else is going to be as enamored with her as you are. No one will see her as anything other than a homewrecker. You don't love her: you're unhappy at home. Sort home out first. *Apart* from this woman. Try treating Karen the way you're treating your girlfriend and she might look at you with sparkly eyes too . . .'

Suitably stung. Good!

'It surprises me,' said Ren, 'that you can respect a woman who has such low self-esteem that she sees herself as deserving nothing better than second place in a man's life.'

'Jesus, Ren . . .'

'My final advice is – give your marriage a proper chance. And if you still love your girlfriend, then you love her, you'll be together and everyone will embrace her with open arms . . . eventually.'

The excitement had evaporated from Gary. He looked tired and older and foolish. And then he looked like he was going to some beautiful place, in some wonderful memory with his new side piece, and the light was back in his eyes.

Gary is off the rails.

'And one more thing,' said Ren. 'Men are weirdos – after years of marriage and a child or two, they take their foot off the gas and when the car stalls, instead of reapplying that foot, the man goes out and buys a new fucking car! And – this is the best bit – he thinks that his wife is still in the original car, having the ride of her life. It's unbelievable. Does any of that make sense to you?'

What a stupid fucking analogy. Men love cars. Gary is away in killer-underwear land . . . driving a Ferrari.

She let out a breath.

Gary is off the rails.

We can't both be.

But I'm fine.

You're off the rails.

No, I'm not.

Gary is my fulcrum. He is my guardian. Without him at the helm . . . who knows what could happen? I need to get my shit together.

I'm fine.

Ren got up, went into the kitchen and made coffee.

Go, caffeine, go.

Gary followed her.

'OK,' said Ren, 'we were working on the case.'

But, fuck, I won't be able to sustain this lying for too much longer.

When he was gone, Ren abandoned work and took the elevator to the glamor-gym.

She put on her gloves and started pounding a punchbag that was so pristine she wondered if anyone else ever used it.

Right, left, hook, hook, right, left, fuck, fuck, right, left, fuck, fuck, fuck, fuck, fuck.

He didn't even ask me about the lyrics! Nothing! Does he even give a shit?

She finished thirty minutes later, hot, sweaty, more wired.

How does that even work? This is not the plan.

She went back to the apartment, stripped off, threw the clothes in the laundry basket and ran the shower. When it was hot enough, she got in.

Too hot. Too hot.

Breathe.

She turned down the temperature.

Gary, in the shower, soaping my . . . stop. Ben. That's better. That's way better.

When she was done, she put on navy blue shorts, a white tank.

She went into her bedroom.

Screw you, Gary. I cannot believe you're making me do this.

She knelt down on the floor and slid out her shoebox of shame. She opened it. She took out her box of mood stabilizers. She slid out a pack. The information leaflet came with it.

Ain't nobody got time for that.

She was about to throw it loose into the shoebox, when she realized it wasn't an information leaflet. It was a hand-written note. She unfolded it.

I knew you'd do it. x

Ben's handwriting. Ren stared at the words. Tears welled in her eyes. She slumped back against the side of the bed.

Ben, you angel. You know. You said nothing. You have faith.

She put the lid back on the box and slid it under the bed.

But it's misplaced.

I'm sorry.

I can't afford to be numb. I need a sharp mind, I need to solve things, make connections, have clarity. I need to find a killer.

She went downstairs.

Gary is off the fucking rails.

She opened a bottle of champagne.

This will soothe me, though. And bring me enlightenment.

She pulled back the curtain, sat down on the sofa, and stared at the wall. Over the next hour and a half, she finished the bottle. Then she had two glasses of white wine. She woke up with a start on the sofa at five a.m.

Gary is so off the rails.

29

Ren was at her desk the next morning when a call came through from reception. She picked up.

'Hello?' It was a woman, tentative, her voice trembling.

'Yes? This is Special Agent Ren Bryce – how can I help you?'

'Are you working on the serial killer case?'

'Yes, ma'am.'

'I saw this . . . this man in the woods out near where Stephanie Wingerter was found,' said the woman.

'OK . . .' said Ren.

'A male, five eleven, I guess. Hairless.'

Hairless: the earnestness in her delivery.

Ren wrestled the smile out of her voice. 'And when did you see him, ma'am?'

'It would have been about three months back – I'm only calling now because of all the recent appeals to the public in the media on account of the investigation going nowhere . . .'

Thanks.

'So I did a few internet searches,' said the caller, 'and I saw that Stephanie Wingerter was found at Devil's Head. I can't remember the exact date I was there, but it was around that time.'

'Could you describe the man you saw, please?' said Ren.

'Well, I say man, but, really, it was a creature I saw.'

Here we go.

'Looked like an alien,' said the woman.

'An alien . . .' Ren nodded. She drew an alien with antennae like *My Favorite Martian*, standing beside a mountain. She drew some trees. She wrote: 'They. Are. Among. Us.' then turned the page around to Janine. Janine smiled.

'Honestly, that would be an accurate description if you saw him,' said the caller. 'I mean, maybe it was because I was driving toward him, and he was in the headlights, so he was just this black silhouette. It scared the hell out of me. I slammed on the brakes. He was kind of startled. I saw him a little better when my eyes adjusted. He was completely naked, wiry and muscular, but he seemed very pale . . . or maybe he was just bleached out in the lights. He had no hair on his body. Not one hair.'

Because you went right up there with your microscope. 'How did he react to you?' said Ren.

'After he got himself together, after he'd been startled, he started moving toward me, real angry,' she said. 'I totally freaked, slammed my foot on the accelerator, but my truck wasn't in reverse, so it looked to him like I was shooting forward to run him over. He dived sideways, disappeared into the dark. I drove up a little ways toward him, I rolled down the window to see if he was OK, and he jumped up, pounced toward me again, like an animal. I was terrified. His face, everything. He was like an alien. No hair. Not one bit.'

'Nowhere . . .' said Ren.

'No, not down below,' said the woman. 'He was like this bald alien.'

Alien. I get it.

'He smelled real bad,' she said. 'Like, real bad.'

'What kind of smell?' *Mars bars?*

'Like mothballs.'

'What was he doing when you arrived?' said Ren.

'He was taking something out of the trunk of his car,' she said. 'I'm not sure what – a piece of wood, maybe? A stick? I'm not sure.'

'What size was it?' said Ren.

Silence. 'His—'

'The stick!' said Ren. *Jesus Christ.*

'Oh, my. It was about two-foot long.'

Glad we clarified. Or I'd be heading for the woods . . .

'Was he alone?' said Ren.

'I think so,' said the woman. 'I mean, I don't know. I didn't see anyone, I didn't hear anything.'

'Did you get his license plate number?' said Ren.

'What I got was the hell out of there.'

Ren smiled. 'Do you think you could show me on a map where that was? Could you email me something?'

The woman groaned. 'You're asking pretty much the worst person in the world. I have the worst sense of direction. But I'll go to Google Maps and put something together for you.'

'Thank you so much for your help.' *Nutjobs of the world unite.* Ren gave her her email address, hung up and slumped back in the chair. 'Can someone please not send me the fucking lunatics?'

'Your brethren,' said Everett.

'Seriously, though . . .'

Ren looked in the direction of the door, where Gary was now hovering.

Oh, how you suck the life out of the room.

'What's going on here?' said Gary.

'Well, I just got a call from a woman who saw an alien at Devil's Head, near where Stephanie Wingerter was found,' said Ren, her fingers paused over the keyboard. She began to type in time with the words: 'Pale-skinned, scarred face, hairless – down there.'

'Give the woman a break,' said Gary.

Ren stopped breathing for several seconds. *Annnd release.* 'As it is his jurisdiction, I will be letting Rodeal know – don't worry. Yes, this woman may have stumbled on a couple of mating aliens or a single masturbatory one, maybe woodland grass provides the perfect environment for alien babies to grow . . . like Cabbage Patch Kids. But, still, there's always the possibility she was seeing somebody pulling a shovel out of a trunk, about to dig a shallow grave.'

'She might have been drinking,' said Gary.

'Might have been . . .'

Ren turned to Everett when Gary was gone. 'And haven't I got a Crazy Bitch bitch? Don't I have a DPD guy taking the weird calls? I mean – not that he knows that's what he's doing. But reception does – and that's the main thing. They have the power.'

'The loons are the most fun,' said Everett.

Ren turned to Robbie. 'Can you look into two people for me without drawing Gary's attention to it? Their names are Kurt Vine and Amanda Petrie.'

'Sure – what are you looking at?' said Robbie.

'That Sedalia lady – the Jane Doe,' said Ren. 'I found out that she was singing the exact lyrics that Carrie Longman had written on the napkin in Manny's. And she was on fire – the same night Stephanie Wingerter went missing, and she was found with burns too.'

'What?' said Everett. 'That is so . . . random.'

'I know,' said Ren. 'And I'd like it to be less so.' She turned to Janine. 'Janine, could you speak with the staff who worked with Carrie Longman, see who at the shelter has a history of IV drug use, either themselves or in the family? See if there are any lyricists among them or if they know any?'

'Yes, ma'am,' said Janine.

'On to more important things,' said Everett, pointing to Ren. 'Do you want to light up a dance floor with me tonight?'

'Ben is flying in,' said Ren. 'But, yes, I think he needs to see our moves.'

Gary came into the office. 'Just to let you know – Sylvie Ross will be coming in at eight a.m. tomorrow to talk about what she got from Carly Raine's little boy.'

Ren looked at Everett. They smiled.

This early start development will not stop our moves. Nothing stops our moves.

30

Ren went to Devin's house on the way home to reintroduce herself to Misty. She and Devin took her for a walk in the park, and stopped in a café for hot chocolate on the way back.

Ben was in the apartment when Ren got home.

'Hey there, pretty lady,' he said. There was a bunch of flowers in a vase on the table.

Ren threw her arms around him. 'I love them!' They kissed. 'I love you!'

'Well, I love you too.' He paused. 'Your Wall of Horrors? Not so much.'

'Bedroom,' said Ren. 'Now.'

Ren got up off the bedroom floor afterwards, and headed for the shower.

Ben was watching her as she left. 'You might not want to lose any more weight . . .'

She stopped and turned toward him. 'Or I might want to lose lots more. Who knows?'

'You're getting a little too thin . . .'

'What – for your liking?'

180

Ren looked at herself in the mirror. *I look way better skinny. And I've muscles, anyway. I don't want to lose weight. I just want to work out as much as I feel like working out. Not my fault if that makes me thinner, buddy. Suck it up.*

'I'm just saying you're working out a lot,' said Ben.

'Well then, just say "you're working out a lot" instead of "you're repelling me with your boniness".'

'Which I did not say,' said Ben.

'Not maybe in those words . . .' said Ren.

'Literal Studies with Ren Bryce.' Ben grabbed a magazine from the nightstand.

'What did you say?'

'Nothing.'

'You can use my hip bones for purchase,' she shouted.

Ben laughed.

'I don't want to live in a place where we can hear each other so easily,' said Ren.

'I don't know how to take that . . .'

'From behind . . . as you slice your finger open on my hip bone.'

'It's just wall-to-wall sexual images tonight . . .'

'OK, let's start again,' said Ren. 'Come into the shower, close your eyes and pretend I'm someone huge . . . like Kate Moss.'

'Can we stay in tonight?' said Ben.

Aw, maan. 'No.'

'We're always going out,' said Ben.

'No – *I'm* always going out.'

'Can't we just watch a movie?'

'No. Let's have a life.'

They got back at two a.m. Ben caught Ren by the elbow as she stumbled in the door, tried to hold her steady. She shrugged away from him.

'Ren, what the hell was that about, earlier?' he said.

'What do you mean?' said Ren. *Ooh, my head is spinning.*

'The bar!' said Ben.

'Don't raise your voice,' said Ren.

'I'm not raising my voice,' said Ben. 'You disappeared for nearly half an hour, three separate times, then I go check you're all right, and you're talking to a group of guys . . .'

'Why would you even be checking if I'm all right?' said Ren. 'That's ridiculous.'

'No, it isn't,' said Ben. 'You were gone so long.'

'Jesus,' said Ren.

'It's not like I'm here all the time,' said Ben. 'And, I'm sorry, but you looked like you were flirting.'

'Oh, please,' said Ren. 'I was not flirting. There's a difference between being friendly and flirting.'

'I know that,' said Ben. 'I'm telling you this bearing that in mind.'

Ugh. 'This is bullshit,' said Ren. 'Where is this going to lead? Is there some conclusion? Let's just agree to disagree. I'm here with you. I haven't disappeared with one of those guys. Nobody died.'

'Nice, Ren. Real nice.'

'Jesus, Ben.' *Why does everyone want to suck the life out of the room?* 'I'm going to bed. You can have the sofa if you want.'

Slam.

Ben was sitting in the living room when she came down the next morning. The duvet was folded up beside him, the pillow on top of it. He looked pale.

Shit.

'Hey,' said Ren.

'Hey.'

'What time is it?'

'Six thirty.'

Jesus, why do I do this to myself?

She walked over to him and sat down beside him. 'I'm sorry about last night.' *I was so drunk. I'm off meds. I was so, so drunk.* 'I don't know what to say.'

Ben slumped back, stretched his hands above his head. 'Neither do I.' He pointed to her phone. 'You left your phone on the table. It beeped in the middle of the night. I picked it up to turn it to Silent . . .'

Uh-oh. Did you see anything else? Scan memory. Scan memory . . . FUUUUCK.

'I know I shouldn't have read anything . . .' said Ben. 'So I want to apologize for that first.'

'I can't believe you did that,' said Ren.

'I'm sorry – it began as an accident, but then I figured I might get some answers as to why you've been behaving strangely.'

'What?' *Maintain eye contact.* 'What do you mean strangely?'

'You have not been . . . yourself. I read your texts to Janine . . .'

Oh, noooo.

'I quote,' said Ben. '"Why can't I stop thinking about fucking YKW?" Ben looked up at Ren. 'I'm going to presume that YKW – You Know Who – is not me, because it would be OK to think about fucking your boyfriend. Who is YKW?'

This is pretty fucking shit. 'No one.'

'Seriously . . .' said Ben.

'No one important,' said Ren. 'I mean . . . it's not real. It's not like I'm actually going to do it.'

'Well then,' said Ben. 'I'm going to guess it's Gary.'

Whoa . . . ly shit. 'Gary?' said Ren. 'Why Gary?'

'Because I know you like Gary and respect him, I know you've referred to him as handsome in the past, and I get that women like him. Plus, there's the Paul Louderback tradition of older males.'

'This is so embarrassing,' said Ren. 'I was drunk when I texted that.'

'At seven p.m.?' said Ben.

'Well, yes,' said Ren. 'That was the Saturday night we had that fight over the phone. It was after that long lunch . . .'

'And what would have happened if that long lunch was with Gary?' said Ben.

I may indeed have slept with him if the opportunity arose. 'Nothing.'

'And what am I supposed to do with that information?' said Ben.

'I don't know. I really don't. Forget it! It's embarrassing. It's not how I feel. I don't even know why I sent it. It's like . . . I don't know . . . a weird celebrity crush thing . . . I mean, read Janine's reaction: This is not real.'

'You should hear yourself,' said Ben.

'I *can* hear myself,' said Ren. 'It's embarrassing.'

'I get it,' said Ben. 'But think about how I feel. Do you still keep thinking about fucking him?'

Only when I'm alone with him. And myself. 'No. No. I don't know what that was all about. I don't get it.'

'I heard a rumor that he's been sleeping around,' said Ben.

Ooh.

'I'm guessing by your face that's true,' said Ben.

Damn you, traitor face. 'Yes. But please don't say that—'

'Was it with you?'

'What? No,' said Ren. 'I can assure you of that.'

'Do you wish it was?' said Ben.

Part of me does, yes, which I can barely understand myself. 'No.'

Now: blow-job time! Look down here! Look down here!

'Ren, stop – I'm not in the mood.'

What guy is ever *not in the mood for a blow job? That's not normal.*

She sat up beside him on the sofa.

I'm such a loser.

She started to cry. 'I'm sorry.'

'Don't cry,' said Ben. 'It's definitely not worth crying about.' He studied her face. 'But, are you OK?'

She nodded. 'Yes. Just . . . a little stressed.'

'You don't seem yourself.'

Which self?

'Come here,' said Ben, drawing her onto his lap, stroking her damp hair.

Oh, God. What am I doing to this sweet man?

The same thing I always do.

31

Ren was in Safe Streets by seven thirty, applying makeup in the alarming light of the locker room.

Minimal improvement.

At seven forty-five, child forensic interviewer Sylvie Ross appeared in the doorway of the bullpen, bright-eyed and eager, a clipboard pressed to her chest. She was dressed in a razor-sharp gray pencil skirt, and a white sleeveless blouse. Her shiny brown hair was twisted and piled up at the back of her head. She was wearing thick-rimmed glasses and red lipstick.

Well, you are not sartorially aiming at children today, that's for sure.

'You all remember Sylvie,' said Gary.

Sylvie, who is currently dressed to stand over a naked man for cash, call him names, and bury her stiletto into his—

'Ren,' said Sylvie, walking over, shaking her hand. 'Lovely to see you again.'

God, I hate sleeveless blouses. 'You too,' said Ren.

'Right,' said Gary, before he left them, abruptly, to go back to his office.

Nice, Gary. Smooth.

'How have you been?' said Sylvie. Her smile was warm. 'You look great.'

'I look like a piece of shit.'

Sylvie's eyes widened.

Alcohol is evil. 'I had a bad night's sleep.'

'Well, it's not showing.'

'How did the interview with Tyler Raine go?' said Ren. 'The whole thing is beyond horrific.'

Sylvie wandered over to the noticeboards, flashing a whole lot of her muscular, marathon-running legs with a slit in her skirt that went halfway up her thigh.

You wear it well, Sylvie Ross. And I'm not sure if that's a compliment.

Everett caught Ren looking and smiled at her. Ren smiled back. He shook his head and mouthed 'Bad girl'. Ren mouthed back, and pointed. 'Me or her?'

Sylvie turned around. 'This guy is some piece of work.'

'Oh, he is,' said Ren.

Sylvie walked around the room, jotting notes with a stylish pencil – sharp, black with gold lettering.

'How was the little boy?' said Ren.

'That kind of trauma has profound effects on a brain that age,' said Sylvie. 'It was some tough work. The father . . . that was possibly one of the most difficult moments of my career. He had to sit in with Tyler, and to see the man trying to hold it together was . . .' She shook her head. 'I spoke with him alone first – the little guy was with his grandmother. I have never seen a man so utterly devastated in my life.' She walked over to Ren's desk, holding her clipboard to her chest.

Ren read the gold lettering on the pencil.

Take your mind away from the horror. Hay-Adams Hotel, Washington D.C. Swish.

'Will he be able to block out that memory?' said Ren. 'Or is it with him for life?'

'Well, blocking out is not the healthy way to deal with anything, really,' said Sylvie.

Ren sat back in her chair. 'Now, that's where I've been going wrong all these years.' She turned to Everett. 'Who are you, again?'

They laughed. Sylvie tried to.

'So,' said Ren, 'are you ready to do your thing?'

'Yes,' said Sylvie. 'Thanks, Ren.'

There is something different in your attitude toward me, Miss Ross. What could it possibly be?

The conference room slowly filled with the task force. When everyone had gathered, Ren introduced Sylvie, and dissolved into the crowd.

'OK,' said Sylvie. 'Here's what I've put together based on my interviews with Carly Raine's three-year-old son. So I'm talking you through this from how I see it going down, not in his words. If you want to read how I came to these conclusions based on a combination of the evidence and what Tyler Raine told me, please read the report.' She laid a manicured hand on top of the document.

'OK,' she said, 'Carly Raine was in the back garden hanging washing on the line. The UNSUB came into the house, unbe-knownst to her. The back of the house contains the kitchen – which has a window and door onto the garden – and the living/dining area – which has a wall-to-wall, floor-to-ceiling glass window. The kitchen can be closed off from the living/dining area by a partition, which the UNSUB closed when he arrived, leaving Tyler in the living/dining room, looking out the window. Then, Carly Raine was naked, the UNSUB was with her, and then they were both gone.

'I think what happened after the attack was that the UNSUB came back into the house alone, took Tyler and locked him in the downstairs bathroom under the stairs. He then carried Carly Raine from where he left her in that wooded area, through her back yard and into the dining area where we found her.'

Ren felt empty inside, listening to this.

Sylvie continued. 'The Raines' bathroom door is one of those that locks on one side, but has a safety lock on the other that you can open with a coin or anything that fits in the slot. The father had mounted it the opposite way, so that the kids couldn't lock the bathroom while they were in there, but that adults could if they were using the bathroom. The father said the little guy had seen him unlock it before, so he must have known where the coin was and how to use it.

The terror he must have felt, the desperation.

'As you've seen from the crime scene,' said Sylvie, 'when he got himself out of the bathroom, Tyler found his mother in a devastating state, and made every attempt to awaken her. It looks like he may have been alone with her for several hours. He said that the baby was upstairs asleep in her crib. The little guy went to check she was OK, eventually, and it was only then that she woke up. Tyler was unable to give me any description of the UNSUB, just that he was taller than his mom. But his mom was only five four, so that doesn't give us a lot.'

Afterwards, when Sylvie was gone, Ren and Janine were in the ladies' room together.

'So, how's Ben?' said Janine.

'I don't know – it's really claustrophobic when he's here,' said Ren. 'There is one bedroom. There is nowhere to go. When he is here, he is here.'

'Just a question,' said Janine, 'but when he used to come to Annie's, didn't you spend most of your time in the same room together, regardless of how many rooms were in the house?'

'Yes, but . . . it's . . .'

'Psychological maybe?'

'Maybe . . .' She paused. 'But, it's like I feel he's just watching me the whole time.'

'Looking at you adoringly, you mean.'

'Hmm, I'm not sure.'

'Really? Why?' said Janine.

'I don't know – just a feeling.' *That I can't shake.*

They went back into the bullpen. Gary was standing in the center, his hands on his hips.

'I think Sylvie's going to talk to the kid again, see if she can get some more information from him,' he said.

'Hmm,' said Ren. 'It's not likely, is it?'

'Why?' said Gary. *Terse.*

'He was locked into a room, the attack happened mainly out of his line of vision – thank God – and he's three years old – what else can he know?' said Ren.

'What you heard from Sylvie is what she's been able to report *for now*—'

'Give the poor family a break,' said Ren. 'Sylvie said that the husband is distraught, and really had to get his shit together not to fall apart during—'

'I know that,' said Gary. 'But—'

'Look, it's not likely Tyler will have heard "Hey, Mrs Raine, my name is XYZ and I'm going to—"'

Gary glared at her. 'Ren, can I see you in my office, please?'

Sweet. Jesus.

32

Gary and Ren sat down in Gary's office.

'I'd like you to listen to something,' said Gary. 'This is a voice recording of a call to a law enforcement agency called . . . Safe Streets.' He hit play.

'Hello, Rodney Viezel here. Is that Special Agent Bryce?'

Ren shifted in her seat. *Oh, fuck. Rodney.* 'That's that idiot who's been looking at the office space with Valerie, rattling the guardrails—'

'Ren – listen,' said Gary.

'Hello, Rodney . . . again. Yes, it's Special Agent Ren Bryce here . . . again.'

Rodney laughs. *'Well, what are the chances?'*

'Pretty high, Rodney, pretty fucking high. One in eleven. My boss doesn't lower himself to take these kind of calls.'

'What kind of calls?' says Rodney.

'Crank calls!' said Ren. 'Come on, Gary. Give me a break. Ever since he came to view this place, and I – foolishly, I admit – engaged with him, he's been calling for some bullshit reason or another.'

Gary glared at her. 'Keep listening.'

'*I just wanted to follow up on an electrical concern,*' says Rodney. '*Your building doesn't seem to have a backup generator . . .*'

'*As a courtesy, Rodney, I'll respond to that, even though it's not my job,*' Ren says. '*This is a very old building. Building code states that because we are under six stories high, we're not required to have a backup generator. However, yes, we could have one retrofitted, but that requires many other factors to be taken into consideration – like the space needed to house it, noise levels, etc. This is a matter for the building owner. Or, at the very least, it's something Valerie can help you with.*'

'*And,*' says Rodney, '*that light switch that was loose in the lobby, the socket . . .*'

Ren laughs, not unkindly. '*You're like a superhero with your supersonic vision.*' Wrong, but who cares?

'*Supersonic relates to sound,*' says Rodney.

'*Anal eyesight, then,*' says Ren.

Gary hit Stop. 'There's more along those lines, as you know.' He looked at Ren. 'If he didn't have a crush on you, this would have been posted online for the world to hear. Instead, I got it, so I could have a word with you. What were you thinking?'

'But you know none of this has anything to do with me!' said Ren. 'I don't own the building, I'm not a realtor, I'm not an electrician. The closest thing I can come up with is I have a lot of energy. None of which I want to spend on calls with Rodney fucking Viezel. After that last woman and the aliens . . .'

'Ren, you can't control who ends up on the other end of a phoneline – none of us can. Consider this how not to take a call.' He paused. 'You don't know whether someone is nuts or not. We can't afford to alienate people.'

'Aliens – see what you did there?' said Ren.

'Go.'

After work, Ren got in the Jeep and dialed Valerie's number as she pulled out of the parking lot.

Thanks for the reminder, Rodney!

Ren left a voicemail for Valerie.

'Valerie, it's Ren Bryce here from Safe Streets. I was just wondering if you could help me find a home. There's only so long I can handle the apartment! Please call me whenever you get a chance. Thanks so much!'

Ren started to drive home. Her mind wandered to Amanda Petrie, the girl who stumbled across the Jane Doe.

I never visited her. She might tell me more about the woman and the lyrics that are haunting me.

Ren arrived at Amanda Petrie's house at seven p.m. She got no answer when she rang the bell. She went to the neighboring house, where a woman in her early fifties, in paint-spattered clothes, answered.

'Hello,' said Ren, flashing her credentials. 'I'm Special Agent Ren Bryce with the FBI. I'm wondering if you know Amanda Petrie.'

'Yes, yes, I do,' she said. 'Is everything OK?'

'Absolutely,' said Ren. 'I'm just following up on an incident that happened last month. Amanda wasn't home just now. Her car is in the drive. I was wondering if you'd seen her today.'

'As a matter of fact, I did,' she said. 'Coming back from the beauty salon. It's her sister's fortieth birthday party tonight.'

'Is it on right now?' said Ren.

'I guess so,' said the neighbor. 'She was home from the salon at four o'clock, looked like she just needed to throw on her dress. She probably had to go early to make sure everything was OK at the venue.'

'You didn't see her leave . . .' said Ren.

'I just got back from the store an hour ago,' said the neighbor. 'Do you want me to give you her cell phone number?'

'No, no,' said Ren. 'I won't bother her tonight.'

'Well, Amanda's a sensible girl – she won't be out too late, so you could probably get hold of her first thing in the morning. She's not the type to need to sleep off a hangover.'

Ren glanced at Amanda's car in the driveway. 'And she didn't drive?'

'No, I guess she took a ride with family or got a cab. She was probably planning at least to have a cocktail or two.' She smiled.

'OK, well, I can try her tomorrow,' said Ren.

I don't want to burst her party bubble by reminding her of a maggot-riddled lady and a car accident. Not tonight.

Ren's cell phone rang when she got into the car.

She picked up. 'You can be my hero, baby.'

'Well, that might just be the case,' said Rodeal.

'I like the sound of that.'

'I've got something,' he said. 'A connection of sorts – goes back to what you were saying about Jane Doe – the people who brought her in.'

Ren felt a shiver up her spine. 'I'm listening.'

'We'll need your help on the other end of things, but what we've got is – we picked up a license plate on video close to two of the scenes: it was a rental car, registered to Kurt Vine – he's the young man who was driving the pickup that crashed into Sky Ridge. It was totaled: his insurance gave him a replacement. It was caught driving west on I-72 the night of Hope Coulson's murder. And on the night Carrie Longman was last seen.'

'Jesus Christ,' said Ren.

'Now, we did some digging on this guy – he lives in Sedalia.'

I knowww! I was there! Which I can't say out loud. Because Gary will kill me for going alone.

'It's about five minutes from where he picked up the Jane Doe, and the young woman helping her,' said Rodeal. 'We just didn't have the resources to search that entire property at the time she was picked up – it's easily over four hundred acres. A couple of our detectives called to the house, got no answer, took a look around. They didn't find anything hinky. Anyway, I looked the guy up today – he doesn't really register anywhere. He doesn't seem to have a job, a life, a membership to a club, nothing. No priors. He has a website – ForTheForgotten. net – a whole bunch of photos of abandoned buildings. Anyway, I get the impression this is a guy who lives online. And we don't have the kind of resources to get any further into that.'

'Well,' said Ren, 'luckily we have the resource that is Everett King! He could be *our* hero. He mightn't break his arm in the process, but he will definitely do some damage to a keyboard.'

The next morning, Ren watched Everett get to work, marveling at how his fine fingers struck the keys so lightly, how his eyes scanned the screen so swiftly.

'Oh, how huge your tiny mind is,' she said, smiling.

Everett winked, without looking up. 'Takes one to know one.'

Ren laughed. She brought him coffee, glancing up at him every now and then to admire his talents.

Eventually, he stopped.

'Are you ready for this?' he said. 'There's an underground online game that Kurt Vine plays called *Hufuki*. A game created by losers, played by losers—'

'Lost by . . . losers!' said Ren. 'What kind of game?'

'A hunting game is all I know. But I can't just rock up and ask to play without drawing suspicion. This is a delicate maneuver. I will use my wiles to join the forum now, then request to play tonight.'

'I wonder,' said Ren, 'if I could get some spa treatments as part of the investigation . . .'

'This will be neither relaxing nor sleep-inducing . . .' said Everett.

'You haven't met my masseuse,' said Ren. 'Someone's going to file an assault charge on her . . .'

Ren's phone rang. She picked up.

'Ren, it's Rodeal – I just wanted to let you know – a Missing Persons report came in last night on Amanda Petrie: apparently she was a no-show at her sister's birthday party.' *The one she organized.*

Oh. Fuck. 'Oh my God – I was at her house.'

'Yeah – the neighbor said she spoke with you. Why were you there?'

'I was following up on the Jane Doe after I spoke with Edie.'

'You didn't see anything suspicious . . .'

'No,' said Ren. 'But I just rang the doorbell – that was it. I didn't look in the windows, go around back or anything. I mean, I was just there to ask about the Jane Doe. I wasn't thinking Amanda Petrie could be in some kind of danger. Shit.'

'Did you get anything on that Kurt Vine guy?' said Rodeal.

'He's a gamer. Everett's going online to play tonight, find out more, maybe make a connection.'

'OK,' said Rodeal. 'Keep me posted.'

Ren put down the phone. Her stomach tightened.

Did my presence at the house bring something bad to bear on Amanda Petrie? Was she in there while I was outside? Was she in trouble?

Ren filled Everett in on Amanda Petrie.

'No Amanda Petrie, no Kurt Vine – it might be a coincidence,' said Ren, 'but it might not. Get playing as soon as you can, see if we can get a window into his world.'

The next morning, Everett arrived into Safe Streets, white-faced.

'It turns out that *Hufuki* stands for – wait for it – Hunt, Fuck, Kill.'

'What the—'

'I've been up all night playing. I'm scarred. It's not good. Or it is – depending on your angle. It's basically about chasing women through woods, and you can work out the rest . . .'

'What is wrong with people?' said Janine.

'And,' said Everett, 'it appears its most successful player is one "twistedvine".'

'Oh, God,' said Ren. 'Amanda Petrie . . .'

Everett pinned up an aerial map of Kurt Vine's property, with all the buildings marked in, and a floor plan of the main house.

Kurt Vine was at the end of Level 9. He had been playing for sixteen hours straight. He couldn't stop. He was chasing this hot bitch through the woods. She was dressed like one of those Seventies chicks, tiny red shorts, white knee-high socks with the red stripes, red sneakers, tight white top, pointy tits, about to die. Sweat stung Kurt's eyes. This was incredible. His heart was pounding. He was about to reach LEVEL 10. LEVEL FUCKING 10.

It all became insignificant as two strangers, dressed in black, appeared in his doorway.

Kurt dropped the console, scrambled back in the sofa, grabbed a cushion to cover his erection.

Weird shit just keeps on happening to me, he thought.

The room erupted in crazed laughter from the television screen. It lit up with: *YOU'RE* THE BITCH WHO DIES! BURN, BITCH, BURN!'

He turned to the two strangers. 'Who the FUCK are you?'

33

Kurt Vine's blacked-out living room smelled of nachos, cheese dip, salsa, and cigarettes. There were discarded chip packages around the floor, shards of nachos on every surface, ashtrays overflowing with cigarette butts and balled-up tissues. The screen glowed. It was frozen on *YOU'RE* THE BITCH WHO DIES! BURN!

'What are you playing?' said Ren, following the trail of wires across the floor to the sofa.

Kurt Vine's eyes darted left and right. 'Uh . . .'

'Just to save me the trouble of having to eject the cartridge,' said Ren. 'I've got a sore back.' She smiled.

'Uh . . . well,' said Kurt, 'it's a Japanese game called *Hufuki*.'

'Oh!' said Ren. 'Hunt Fuck Kill!'

Vine hung his head.

'What level are you at?' said Ren.

'It's just a game,' said Kurt.

'We know that,' said Ren, laughing. 'Just, I'm a competitive person. And a former *Mario Bros.* addict.'

Kurt sucked in a breath. 'Level 10.'

'Impressive,' said Ren. 'That's where the real girls come in.'

'Who are you?' he said.

Ren and Robbie flashed their credentials like *Men in Black*. 'We're the FBI,' said Ren.

'What the—'

Ren sat down on the edge of the coffee table in front of him. 'This game,' said Ren. 'It's fairly violent, would you agree?'

'Extremely violent, I would say,' said Kurt. 'I know it doesn't look good, but it's only a game. I'm not that kind of guy. That's like saying people who watch *Game of Thrones* want to go around chopping people's heads off and raping women and – they don't, it's fantasy, it's what people do.'

You're not the brightest man in the world.

'Mr Vine, do you know this woman?' said Ren, setting down a photo of Amanda Petrie.

His eyes widened. 'No.'

'Are you sure?' said Ren. 'Take another look.'

'I swear to God,' he said, 'I have never seen this woman in my life.' He paused. 'I will admit, though, that there is something familiar about her. Who is she?'

'Keep looking, Kurt,' said Ren. 'I think you do know this woman.'

'Oh, you're right, yes!' he said. 'I can definitely help you there. Her name was Amanda, she had bumped into this crazy lady and I bumped into them. You must have seen it in the news – we crashed into the medical center. It was a whole nightmare.'

'Kurt – Amanda Petrie is missing,' said Robbie, stepping in, sitting down beside Ren. 'She hasn't been seen since yesterday evening, which normally wouldn't bother anyone, except for the fact that she's missing a very special family occasion that she organized.'

'That was her sister's birthday party! She told me about that. Aw, maaan—'

'Do you know where Amanda is?' said Ren.

'What? No. How would I know that? I only met her, like, once. We didn't even exchange details or anything. I don't even know where she lives. I don't know anything about her, apart from the party.'

'Did she tell you where the party was going to be at last night?' said Ren.

'Uh . . . no! Because she didn't know at that time. We barely spoke . . . she just said she'd been looking at a venue, hadn't even pinned down a date.'

'Kurt, where have you been for the past twenty-four hours?' said Ren.

'At the store, like for an hour yesterday, and back here then, playing this. You can check – I've been playing almost seventeen hours straight.'

What a life.

Robbie set his black rucksack down, unzipped it and took out a Quick Capture kit. He hooked it up to his laptop with a USB cable. Kurt Vine looked at it, panicked.

'Hey, what's that?' he said.

Relax, tinfoil boy.

'It's for taking your fingerprints,' said Ren. 'In twenty seconds, they're captured, then uploaded to Detective Truax's computer.'

'Then what?' said Kurt.

'Then we create these amazing collages that we exhibit in the Robischon Gallery,' said Ren. 'We run them through AFIS. Which I'm sure you know is a national database of fingerprints.'

'Fine,' said Kurt, holding out his hands. 'Go ahead. I've got nothing to hide.'

'Well, then, that's great . . .' said Ren. 'You'll be able to make the opening night of the exhibition.'

Kurt wiped the back of his hand across his sweaty brow.

'OK,' said Robbie, 'put two fingers at a time on the glass.'

As I stand idly by, contemplating the glorious world of the round-the-clock gamer.

Robbie glanced up at Ren. She moved around to the screen.

What the fuck?

Ren turned to him. 'Kurt, this is not good news for you.'

His eyes widened. 'What? What do you mean? Why not?'

'Your prints have been found at the scene of a serious crime.'

'What? No way. That's bullshit. That can't be right. Show me that.'

Really?

'This is a set-up, man,' said Kurt.

'Do you have alibis for the six dates listed here?' said Ren.

'Six dates?' said Kurt. 'Oh my God – do you think I'm that serial killer? No way! I know absolutely nothing about these women. I am not a rapist or murderer. I'm just a regular loser, playing a fucked-up video game.' Kurt looked from Ren to Robbie. 'I don't even have to look at those dates,' he said. 'Home, home, home, home, home, home: alone.'

'Who do you think would set you up?' said Ren. 'Who would have reason to do that?'

'Set me up? I'm not . . . this is, like, a nightmare. I'm not . . . who would set me up? This is the greatest ever mind-fuck. I need to wake up from this. I need to wake up.'

'Level 10 of *Hufuki* has real women,' said Ren.

'Yes, but not *real* real,' said Kurt. 'They're women who like to *pretend* they're being hurt. It turns them on. That's not my problem. They're not actually hurt. I'm not actually hunting them. This is all fantasy. Don't you people get fantasies?'

'Kurt, we've taken a look at a map of your property.' Ren unfolded it and handed it to him.

'Let's take a little drive,' said Ren. 'Down to here.' She pointed to a row of barns.

'Mm, I don't know . . . do we have to?'

'Do I look like someone who does things I don't have to?' said Ren.

Kurt shook his head. 'No, ma'am.'

'Well, let's go, then.' She looked at Robbie. 'Can you please take him via his wardrobe?'

This is not a pants-optional trip.

When they had driven a mile through Vine's property, they began to see smoke rising up through the trees.

What the fuck?

'Where's that coming from?' said Ren.

'Oh my God!' said Kurt. 'I don't know! Near the barns?'

As they got into the clearing, they could see flames. They screeched to a stop.

Fuuuuck!

Robbie put a call in to the fire department.

'They won't be here for at least half an hour,' said Ren. She turned to Kurt. 'What's going on here?'

He was wide-eyed. 'I don't know! I don't know! I was in the house. You saw me. I couldn't have done this.'

'This has been burning quite some time,' said Ren to Robbie.

Ren jumped out of the Jeep. Robbie jumped out after her. 'Ren! Don't! It's not safe.'

'It's fine!'

She was hit with a wall of heat.

'Don't be crazy!' said Robbie.

She kept running. 'Don't leave Vine!' she said. 'Stay where you are!'

I'm in the middle of a fire . . . what the fuck?

She ran toward the barn and could see, through the smoke, it was filled with chopped timber. In front of it was a wooden box, about six feet long, twenty inches wide and with KEEP OUT! and DANGER DO NOT ENTER! written on it in child-like cursive.

What's in there?

She ran closer. She was coughing, her eyes started streaming.

'Ren!' roared Robbie. 'Get back!'

She stopped. It looked like the box was moving.

It's my eyes watering.

She blinked.

That box is definitely rocking.

The flames were moving closer to it.

The box rocked again.

What the fuck is in there?

'Shit!' she roared, glancing back at Robbie. 'There's some-body in there!'

She held her arm in front of her face, and ran into the barn. The flames were intense, the smoke rising.

Even if I can reach that, I won't be able to move it.

It's too hot. I can't . . .

She ran back out of the barn, and over to the Jeep.

'What are you doing?' said Robbie, panicked and wild-eyed. 'Are you insane? Get in the Jeep, and we're driving out of here.'

'No, no, no,' said Ren. 'There's someone in there. There's a box in there, and I saw it move.' She got into the back of the Jeep and grabbed Kurt Vine by the throat. She slammed his head up against the window. 'What the fuck is in that box?' she said. 'Is there someone in that box?'

Vine was white-faced. 'What box? I don't know what you're talking about!' he said.

'There's a box in there – about the size of a coffin, and—' She released her grip for a moment. 'Oh my God! It's Amanda Petrie. Is Amanda Petrie in there?' She tightened her grip and struck Vine's head off the glass again.

She didn't even hear Robbie shouting her name.

'Get the fuck out of this Jeep, Vine, and we're going to go in there before that thing goes up in flames, and—'

'Ren!' roared Robbie. 'We're not going in anywhere! The fire department will be here in minutes. Whatever is happening in there, there is nothing we can safely do until they arrive.'

'There's a woman in there who could be about to be burned alive!' said Ren.

'That structure could collapse at any moment!' said Robbie. 'Ren – don't make me cuff you to this Jeep.'

'Are you nuts?' said Ren.

They heard a loud bang as a section of the roof of the barn collapsed. As Robbie was distracted, Ren jumped out of the Jeep and ran for it.

Jesus Christ. The smell. The heat.

She heard the Jeep door open behind her. 'Ren!' Robbie called. 'Ren, get back here now.'

The flames were rising, crackling, sparks were shooting into the sky. Ren turned back to Robbie, and heard another crack as a bullet exploded into the glass beside his head.

Oh my God! No!

Robbie crouched down, withdrew his sidearm, fired in the direction of the shooter.

Ren did the same.

What the FUCK?

She veered right, diving for cover in the trees.

Shots rang out again, coming from the trees opposite her. Crouching down, she made her way back toward Robbie.

The Jeep was standing between him and the shooter.

'What the fuck?' said Ren.

Robbie turned to Kurt Vine. 'Get out,' he shouted. 'We need to take cov—'

The back window shattered with the next round of shots. Ren and Robbie returned fire. For a brief moment, it went quiet. The only sound was the growing fire, the crackle of burning timber.

Nothing from Kurt Vine.

Ren pulled open the back door of the Jeep.

Oh, Jesus.

Kurt Vine was slumped, lifeless, on the floor, a bullet through the back of his head. More shots rang out, striking the trees behind Robbie.

Motherfucker!

The shooter fired, again peppering the trees at either side of Robbie and Ren, sending up an explosion of splinters. Ren and Robbie returned fire.

Oh, fuck. This guy is good. This guy is good. Fuck.

'We need to get out of here now,' said Robbie. 'Get in.'

I'm a better, faster driver. A vehicle is a bullet trap. 'Only if you're fucking fast,' said Ren.

'Get in,' said Robbie, his eyes bright with fury. He crawled into the driver's seat of the Jeep, crouching low. Ren slid in beside him.

Robbie started the engine.

The Jeep exploded with gunfire again.

'Go, go, go,' said Ren. 'Right for him!'

The windscreen shattered as more shots were fired. The front of the Jeep was hit, over and over.

Keep going, keep going. Drive on. We have to get this guy.

But Robbie swung a sharp left, and the Jeep rocked back and forth along the bumpy ground to where they came from.

'Robbie!' said Ren. 'For fuck's sake!'

'Are you nuts?'

The next shots hit the two back tires, and the Jeep lurched.

Nooo!

Then, from ahead of them in the trees, came the sound of sirens.

Oh, thank God, thank God, thank God.

The gunman fired one more time.

Ren went to get out of the Jeep.

Robbie reached over and grabbed her arm, yanking her back into the Jeep hard. 'Don't even think about it. Don't.'

34

It was two days before Ren and Robbie could return to work – two days of the Shooting Incident Review team poring over the scene of the shooting, analyzing the trajectory of the bullets, the results of Kurt Vine's autopsy, interviewing Ren and Robbie to determine whether or not they followed procedure. The report would come back describing events from the moment they arrived at Kurt Vine's house to when emergency services arrived at the scene.

The body in the box was that of Amanda Petrie. Whether she had been alive when Ren arrived was impossible to tell, but she had certainly been alive when she was cuffed inside it at the wrists and ankles. The box had been rescued by fire-fighters before the flames had reached it, preserving the cold facts of the brutality Amanda Petrie had suffered before she died. She had been beaten, raped, and stabbed, then locked away in a box that had been tailor-made to take a captive, a box that appeared to be a much-used, years-old prison.

Ren walked down the hallway into Safe Streets.

'My girl is back!' said Everett, coming toward her. He hugged her.

Ren pulled away, grabbing his arm. 'I wouldn't if I were you—'

'Ooh – nice perfume,' said Everett at the same time. 'Very nice. Fresh like laundry and—'

Ren was shaking her head. 'Are you serious? This is not about the perfume. It's what the perfume is covering up. The shower in the filthy man-gym was broken. I boxed for one hour before I knew that. And the water is cold here. Some fuck-up with the heating.'

Everett rolled his eyes. 'You're hardly a sweaty lumberjack.'

She released his arm. 'Do I not absolutely stink? I won't go as far as to smell my armpit. I can barely even say the word.'

'So, seriously – you were taking me aside to tell me about the shower . . .'

Ren nodded. 'I didn't want you to think this was a new direction I was going in.'

'In your absence, I've been going through a list I compiled of all the other freaks who play Hufuki. Three thousand, nine hundred and seventy-seven of them across the country. Forty-nine of them were twelve years old. Can you believe that?'

'I think the world is too much for me,' said Ren. *I need comfort. I want to hide away.*

She left him and went into the bullpen. There were boxes and books and other random objects stacked on top of Everett's desk. She glanced across the room, where Everett's laptop was now on a perpendicular desk by the window, facing away from her.

Oh my God. Everett has requested to be moved away from me.
He hates me.
Be cool.

Everett came back from the kitchen with coffee for both of them.

Ren gestured to his new desk. 'What's all this?'

'Gary told me to move.'

'For good?' *Panic. Panic.*

'I hope not – I won't be able to see your purty face.'

'Nor I yours. Farewell, sweet prince.'

Ren went to the kitchen to make coffee. Robbie was sitting at the table drinking hot chocolate.

You're like a little boy sometimes.

He glanced up at her.

No smile. No warmth.

Shit.

She sat down with her coffee beside him.

'I'm sorry,' she said. 'I really am.'

He still looked livid. 'That was officially the most terrifying thing I've ever gone through.'

'I know that—'

'No,' he said. 'I really don't think you do. You couldn't. You wouldn't have done what you did if you had a clue what the reality of that situation was.'

'What? I didn't—'

'Ren, I covered your ass in that interview with the Shooting Review team. I watered down some of your actions. And I'm sitting here thinking, was that the right thing to do? Like, was that actually a dangerous thing to do? What if I had thrown caution to the wind too and I had run after you into that burning building, and we were both out in the open? We could have gotten killed. You're my friend, Ren. If you had gone in there for any longer, or made it back in there the second time, I think I might have gone in after you. I would have taken that risk. And I shouldn't have to. It was so unpredictable, and you made it more so.'

'I'm sorry,' said Ren. 'But . . . we're fine. We made it. It's OK.'

He just looked at her, stood up, shook his head, and walked out.

Gary came in as she was still sitting there.

'Hi,' said Gary.

'Hi,' said Ren. 'I was wondering why you moved Everett . . .'

'Is it bothering you?' said Gary.

You and your penetrating gaze. You know it's fucking bothering me. 'No – I just thought he fit in so well where he was. I think we work well together. I just don't get why you moved him. I'd just like to understand the thinking behind it.' *Because I feel like you are testing me, that you're rearranging the pieces on the board to see how I'll react. Because I don't feel like I can handle change right now. And I think you know that. And you're manipulating it. You're screwing with me to see if I'll break.*

'There's a problem with the wiring at his desk,' said Gary. 'There's an electrician coming in to look at the sockets. I'd rather he was not electrocuted before then.'

Oh. 'When is the electrician coming?'

Gary's tone was patient. 'Next week. Don't look so traumatized.'

'I'm not.' *Leave me alone. Are you trying to provoke me? A whole week, though?*

'And at least your buddy, Rodney Viezel, will have his concerns addressed.'

'No more calls to me!' said Ren.

Everett knocked on the open door.

'Can I have a word?' he said.

'Go ahead,' said Gary.

'So, I've been looking into Kurt Vine's financials,' said Everett, 'and eleven months ago, someone wired ten thousand dollars into his bank account, via his website donation facility. I haven't been able to trace where it came from.'

'A one-off payment?' said Gary.

'Yes,' said Everett.

'What's on this guy's web pages?' said Gary.

'He was a photographer,' said Everett. 'Took arty photos of abandoned buildings . . . including one where a series of rapes happened . . .'

'If I wanted an accomplice in my dastardly acts, I think trolling for one in a fucked-up underground gaming site might be a plan,' said Ren. 'Or targeting the creator of a website about abandonment and places where women were raped.'

'Was he being paid up front for services to be delivered at a later date?' said Gary.

'My gut is telling me there's more to this guy,' said Ren. 'He was chosen very specifically by the killer to either facilitate or enhance the rape/killing experience. Everett, did Kurt Vine look like a rapist to you?'

Everett opened his mouth to answer, but didn't get a chance.

'Until we know more, we don't know what Vine's involvement was,' said Gary.

'Unknown unknowns?' said Ren.

Gary did not crack a smile.

'The key is,' said Ren, 'what did Kurt Vine have that his accomplice slash overlord does not?' She paused. 'I think it's more than just a remote property.' She paused. 'Oh my God. What if it's Colin Grabien? He never had any respect for women. He always treated them like shit. And he would happily kill me if he got a chance. Like, I firmly believe that deep down, he hates women. And right up at the surface, he hates me.'

Everett glanced at Gary, his face registering a flicker of a frown at the same time.

What the hell is that look about?

'It's not Colin Grabien, Ren,' said Gary. His voice was flat.

How can you be so sure?

Gary left, and as he was walking out the door, turned back to Ren.

'Can you please meet me in my office when you're done?'

'Sure,' said Ren. 'No problem.'

Everett looked at her and made a face.

Ren rolled her eyes. 'It's a thing we do . . .'

'Robbie doesn't seem very happy with you,' said Everett.

'About the shooting?' said Ren.

'I presume so.'

'Did he say something?'

'No, but he wouldn't. You know that.'

'Do you think he said something to Gary?'

'No, no. Not his style either.'

'I didn't mean to freak him out,' said Ren. 'I thought I was doing the right thing.'

Ren knocked on Gary's door.

'Come in,' he said. 'Take a seat, Ren.'

Ominous.

'Are you taking your meds?' he said. His eyes were cold, straight, narrow.

'What?' *Do not drop eye contact with this man.* 'Are you serious? Yes, I am taking my meds. Of course I am . . .'

'And just so we're real clear here,' said Gary. 'I will never ask you that question again.'

Ren nodded. 'Thank you.' *And thank God.*

'And you're happy with your answer,' said Gary. 'That's your answer.'

'Yes! Of course.' Her heart was beginning to thump. 'Is this because of my Colin Grabien theory? I was kidding!' *To a degree.*

Gary stared at her. 'You've a great imagination, Ren, right?'

Shit. Where's this going . . .

'So,' said Gary, 'we're in this beautiful building, it's historic, it's Olde Denver, so it will make this task a little easier. There's no sign over the door, no *sign* sign. But I need you to picture one—'

What the . . .

'Every time you walk up the steps of this building,' said Gary, 'where you work, where you uphold the law, where you uphold my laws, where you honor victims, where you honor your colleagues, where you are responsible for their safety and the safety of others, where you work hard to get justice for victims of violent crimes, I don't want you to picture Federal Bureau of Investigation spoiling our original late-1800s timber doors. I need you to picture this sign: Last Chance Saloon.'

Fuck. Fuck. Fuck. Fuck. Fuck.

'The Last Chance Saloon,' said Gary, 'is a dry bar.' He paused. 'And it's an honesty bar.'

Oh, God.

'And,' said Gary. 'I'm done serving mavericks.'

He slid a piece of paper across the desk. Dr Lone, today, 1 p.m.

Ren left the office without saying a word. She walked down the hallway, upright and composed.

How he had the balls to talk to me about honesty bars.

Seriously.

If I was a different person, with the information I have, I could hang him.

In the town square.

Right outside his fucking saloon.

35

Ren sat in the office of Dr Leonard Lone.

'Can I just say, not to be flippant about it,' said Ren, 'but this was no big drama. Everyone is over-reacting.'

'You and your partner were fired at,' said Lone. 'A man died. That's a serious matter.'

'But it's what we're trained for,' said Ren. 'It's something we have to expect. I believe a killer was twenty feet from me, and I couldn't pursue him? That, to me, is dangerous. He's still out there.'

'But surely protocol says that you wouldn't pursue a suspect alone in the woods, in unfamiliar territory. Or run into a burning building.'

'How did you know that's what happened?' said Ren.

'I spoke with Gary.'

'Jesus Christ! He's like a fucking . . . I don't know. It's like he always has to get to you first. It wasn't . . . dangerous. I wasn't in danger. I'm not traumatized in any way. My most extreme emotion is fury at Robbie. Not active fury – just internal fury.'

Dr Lone studied her. 'Ren, could you talk me through a typical day for you at the moment . . .'

What? Um . . . well. Hmm. Wake. Work. Work out. Home. Drink. Work. Work out. Drink. Work. Sleep. Work out. Repeat.

'There is no typical day, I guess,' said Ren.

'Are you taking your medication at night or in the morning?' said Lone.

You asked me this already. 'Oh, at night.' *Nod.*

'Are you feeling anxious?' said Lone.

By questions re untaken meds, yes.

'No,' said Ren.

'This is a high-profile case that seems to have cast a real shadow over the city,' said Lone.

'Your female patients are probably all having meltdowns . . .'

Lone didn't reply.

'Sorry – you asked me about anxiety,' said Ren. 'I'm not anxious, no.'

'Are you fearful for your own safety?' said Lone.

'No way,' said Ren. 'No. I'd like to see him try.' *I really would.*

Dr Lone was watching her.

What are you thinking?

'It's important that this case doesn't take you away from your appointments here,' said Lone. 'Gary, as you know, is adamant about that.'

'Gary . . .' *should be concentrating on himself, not on me, and not on banging his side piece.*

Back at Safe Streets, Ren went into the conference room with a large artists' pad, opened it on the first page and wrote in a pink Sharpie:

KURT VINE WAS AN ACCOMPLICE FROM ALL THE
WAY BACK TO GIA LAROSA?

REGRETTED LETTING AMANDA PETRIE GO FIRST
TIME, CAME BACK TO HER?

HAD BEEN WATCHING HER BEFORE SHE EVER
MET JANE DOE?

K.V. HAD BEEN TOLD TO WATCH AMANDA PETRIE?

K.V. BETRAYED OTHER KILLER BY LETTING AMANDA
PETRIE GO?

BURNING LADY IN SEDALIA – VINE'S CAPTIVE / OR
OTHER KILLER'S?

AMANDA PETRIE SPECIFICALLY CHOSEN AS A
VICTIM TO MAKE FRAMING K.V. EASIER BECAUSE
OF HIS EARLIER CONNECTION TO HER?

OR K.V. CHOSEN AS A COVER AFTER THE FACT?

K.V. AND ACCOMPLICE – MEET ONLINE? GAMING
WORLD?

WHO *IS* ACCOMPLICE?

She turned to her computer, and opened up the file on
the victims' wounds. She added Amanda Petrie's as described
in the autopsy.

She rubbed her jaw, got a waft of perfume.

It is nice. Everett was right.

217

Something is gnawing at me. Like a rat at something random on a landfill site. Too tired to come up with something. Dead body?

Oh. That's it. Perfume.

It's not about the perfume. It's what the perfume is covering up.

Oh. Fuck.

'We've been focusing on the wrong injuries!' said Ren.

Everyone looked up.

'It's not about the burning, or the mutilation, or the chopping away of body parts – it's what doing that is covering up,' said Ren. 'Amanda Petrie didn't burn! It's all here, laid out, every step of the killer's M.O. Too much evidence was left behind: she was raped with a foreign object, had two stab wounds to the lower back, three slash marks on each side of her ribs, injuries to the soles of her feet.'

Shit! That's it.

Ren stood up. 'The UNSUB did what he wanted with Amanda Petrie, because he didn't fear revealing his entire M.O. He thought she would be incinerated in the barn. But, more importantly, he believed he had successfully framed Kurt Vine. He killed the way he truly wanted to kill, because he knew that we would no longer be inputting his data into ViCAP. We would believe that Kurt Vine was our UNSUB. And if our killer stopped killing, or moved state, then he was free. He just didn't bank on us visiting Vine so soon – he probably didn't think of the *Hufuki* link. Which also means that he did not meet Vine playing that game – otherwise he would have been aware of that possibility.'

Ren opened up ViCAP again, input the exact details of Amanda Petrie's injuries. She read through what came back.

Oh. My. God. This is not good. This is not good.

Ren picked up her phone and called Gary. 'I'm sending you an article you need to read: a horrific serial murder case that kicked off all the way back in 1987. It has disturbing echoes of this. The killer hunted his naked victims first, then he brutally raped them, then he murdered them. He started out with prostitutes, and moved on to other women. They were mainly skinny blondes. There was less sexual mutilation of the bodies, but I think that, over the years, he has escalated. It's beyond fucked-up, Gary. I hope I'm wrong. See what you think. There's an old photo – he has the deadest look in his eyes: you can see that he could be capable of this kind of depravity.'

Ren stared at the photo. There's something familiar about him. I'm wondering did I read about this case at the time? And block it out . . .

'Anyway,' said Ren, 'there's one former detective who was heavily involved in it – personally involved in it. I think we need to talk to him.'

Within ten minutes, Gary walked into the bullpen. 'Your ex-detective is flying in tonight, eleven thirty p.m. You can pick him up at the airport.'

'Jesus – speedy response,' said Ren. 'I didn't want to be right. Does he think I'm right?'

'We both do,' said Gary. 'This is bad news. If we've got the right guy . . .' His face was ashen. 'He's a monster.'

Ren nodded. 'And he's mutating.'

It was midnight in Denver International Airport. Ren stood at Arrivals, running through theories, sifting, discarding, re-evaluating. The killer had a face now. She thought of being alone with him in a tiny, claustrophobic room, punching him in that face. She thought of splitting open the skin under his eye, watching it bleed. She thought of burying her Glock into his jaw. *Boom!* She thought of forcing him to stare at what she had stared at for months, the Wall of Horrors, the fallout from his fucked-up fantasies. She thought of the frustration of him feeling absolutely nothing at the end . . . so she would have to beat him all over again.

Jesus Christ, what is wrong with me?

She focused on the people ahead, and guessed from the landing time, the accents, and the clothes, when the New York flight was filtering through. There were very few passengers left. Ren checked her phone for a message that he had missed his flight. Nothing. She checked her email. Nothing new. She glanced up at the last stragglers.

A slender man in an immaculate blue tailored suit walked through arrivals, pulling a vintage peacock blue suitcase with leather trim.

Not him. And why can't I look that good coming off a flight? I always look like I've been in a sauna drinking liquor and having relations.

Another man walked through with a sleeping little girl in his muscular arm, her head tucked against his neck. *Too adorable.*

He looked like he was in his late forties, tan, dark hair, flecked with gray.

Have you been working out?

Stop staring.

But is there such a thing as a FILF?

She turned her attention to the rest of the passengers coming through.

The FILF was coming her way.

Ooh – what's going on here?

He kept coming her way.

Shit. It's him. He looks different from his photo. More ex-Marine than ex-NYPD. He has been working out.

He stopped in front of her. 'Agent Bryce?'

'Yes. But, please – call me Ren.'

He shook her hand. 'Good to meet you. I'm Joe Lucchesi.'

A shiver ran up Ren's spine: Joe Lucchesi's expression was preternaturally calm, eerily intense.

Your name is Joe Lucchesi. You're here to kill a man. That man is Duke Rawlins.

36

Ren smiled. *Lucchesi? For Duke Rawlins, you can stand in line.*

The little girl stirred in her father's arms.

'This is my daughter, Grace,' said Joe.

Grace Lucchesi had beautiful long hair, that, unlike her dad's, was light brown with strands of blonde running through it. She had long, fair eyelashes, a pretty pouting mouth. She was a skinny thing, dressed in a cute pink sundress with a white cardigan over it.

You will break hearts, little lady.

Grace opened one eye, looked at Ren, then closed it.

'She's beautiful,' whispered Ren. *But why the heck did you bring her here?*

A flushed young woman, petite, with shiny black hair to her shoulders, jogged up behind the Lucchesis. She had a booster seat under her arm. 'I'm so sorry, Joe.'

French. 'But I found it!' She was holding up a tiny gray bear. She unzipped the backpack Joe was wearing and put it in.

Joe smiled. 'Agent Bryce, this is Camille, Grace's nanny.'

'Hi,' said Ren. 'And please call me Ren. Nice to meet you, Camille.'

I wonder, are you and Joe a thing?

'You must be wondering why we're all here,' said Joe

Not exactly what I was wondering.

'My son, Shaun, is graduating. He did a Masters in Forensic Psychology here – in Denver University. We were coming to visit him anyway. Once I spoke with your boss, I brought my flight forward. I was tempted to leave Grace behind, but I couldn't. She was too excited to see her big brother graduate.'

Bomb in auditorium.

Why do I think this shit?

They began to walk toward the exit. Camille was walking a respectful distance behind.

'I hope you don't mind we're a whole posse,' said Joe.

'Not at all,' said Ren. *But I think you're insane.*

They settled into the Jeep. Grace was still asleep. Camille put on Bose noise cancellation headphones.

'I spent the last few hours reading everything I could online about Duke Rawlins,' said Ren. *And about you: forty-nine years old, ex-Manhattan North Homicide detective, current holder of P.I. license, born in Bensonhurst, Brooklyn, was married to Anna Lucchesi, one son – Shaun, twenty-six, no mention anywhere of Grace.*

'Tell me what you've got,' said Joe. He seemed tense, ruffled.

Ren glanced in the rear-view mirror.

'Grace won't wake up,' said Joe. 'And Camille knows the drill.'

'You're a scary boss,' said Ren.

His face was set.

Alrighty, then.

Ren began with the crimes, the M.O. and the victims.

'That's his M.O.,' said Joe, nodding. 'It came from Rawlins' obsession with Harris hawks: one of the only birds of prey to hunt collaboratively. That never made it into

223

the media. The obvious wounds you've described on the most recent victim mimic those made by the hawk and its talons. Rawlins and his accomplice – Donald Riggs – killed as a team. They started out in Stinger's Creek, Texas when they were teens. Donald Riggs would 'flush out' the victim, he and Rawlins would strip her naked, then hunt her through the woods. Most of the time Rawlins used an arrow shot from a bow to bring the victim to the ground, but when he was forced to improvise, he did – using a knife. When the victim was down, either or both men raped her before killing her, then left the bodies out or made some kind of bullshit attempt to cover them. Obviously, Rawlins is no longer using a bow and arrow, which could simply be a convenience thing or that he's come to prefer the closer contact of using only the knife.

As you know – Rawlins is a mixed offender. From what you told me about the woman who was killed in her back garden, I think he stumbled upon that – I don't think she was someone he planned to kill. It was risky. Especially with children there. Something must have made him snap. He killed a woman in similar circumstances in his original spree. Maybe anything that seems like a happy home to him is something he wants to destroy. Son of a junkie prostitute doesn't make for a happy home.'

'When you put it like that . . .'

'Tell me about this guy, Vine, that Gary mentioned.'

Ren talked him through it.

'And has Rawlins approached you?' said Joe. She could see his jaw twitch.

'No,' said Ren. 'Why do you ask?'

'Well, he has a major problem with law enforcement.'

Did you ever think maybe Rawlins just has a major problem with you?

'You killed his partner in crime,' said Ren. 'Is that not reason enough for him to have targeted you?'

'It's more than that,' said Joe. 'Haven't you spoken to your boss?'

Wow – loving the disdain.

'Gary?' said Ren. 'About Duke Rawlins' problem with law enforcement?' *What the hell? Does he know something? Why hasn't he told me whatever it is already?*

'I'll let him tell you,' said Joe.

Grace Lucchesi woke up only when Ren parked the Jeep outside the hotel.

Very fancy.

'Daddy?' said Grace.

'I'm here, sweetheart,' said Joe, turning around to her. 'We're in Denver. We're at the hotel.'

'Where's—'

Camille pulled off her headphones and handed Grace the gray bear. Her face lit up.

'Grace, say hi to Ren,' said Joe. 'She'll be working with Daddy.'

'Nice to meet you, Grace,' said Ren.

Grace reached forward and shook her hand. 'You too, ma'am.'

Ren looked at Joe. 'Adorable.'

'How old are you?' said Ren.

'Six!' said Grace, holding up her five fingers, eventually adding the thumb on her other hand. 'I'm nearly seven!'

'Good for you,' said Ren.

What else can I say to that? I'm not great with child small talk. 'I like your dress.'

'Daddy got it for me,' said Grace.

Bless his heart.

He looked uncomfortable with the release of this small personal detail.

'I don't have a mommy,' said Grace.

I knowww. But I hoped we wouldn't go there so soon! Rescue me, someone!

Joe's head snapped around, but his voice was gentle. 'You do have a mommy, sure you do—'

'She's in heaven!' said Grace, cheerily. 'It's a really beautiful place.'

'It is, you're right,' said Ren. She turned to Joe. He looked stricken.

'Why don't you guys hold on here,' said Ren. 'Your daddy and I will get the bags from the back.'

'Thanks for the ride,' said Joe when they were at the back of the Jeep. 'I know it's late. I appreciate it.' He took the bags and put them on the sidewalk.

'I'll swing by in the morning,' said Ren, 'pick you up at eight thirty – is that OK?'

'There's no need,' said Joe. 'I can—'

'It's not a problem.'

He nodded toward Grace, who was happily chatting with Camille. 'She's never said that about her mother before.'

'It's probably one of those things, someone said something in school or . . .' *What the hell do I know?*

Joe let out a breath. 'She hasn't a mommy because Duke Rawlins injured her mommy so badly, her body couldn't cope with giving birth.'

Jesus Christ. I had no idea that was the reason.

'Duke Rawlins once said it to me himself: "I'm the gift that keeps on giving."'

Joe was staring at Ren, but his thoughts were clearly drifting.

Oh, no. You're not here for regular justice. You're here to kill a man with your bare hands.

*　　*　　*

Ren drove away, watching them all shrink in her rear-view mirror. There was something so tragic about them.

She dialed Gary's number. He picked up.

'It's me,' said Ren. 'What have you not told me about Duke Rawlins?'

'What do you mean?' said Gary.

'Is he watching me?' said Ren. 'Do you know something? Joe Lucchesi asked me had Duke Rawlins approached me and—'

'Whoa, whoa, whoa,' said Gary. 'This is not about you.'

'Really?' said Ren.

'Believe it or not, no,' said Gary. 'I'll explain tomorrow. It's late—'

'Who is it about, then?'

Patient sigh. 'Go to bed. We'll talk tomorrow. What's Lucchesi like?'

Hmmm. 'He's all right.'

'Renspeak for you don't like him.'

'So far,' said Ren. 'He had a weird reaction to me, like I unsettled him. Maybe he doesn't like women or can't take them seriously as case agents.'

'I doubt that,' said Gary. 'Don't make rash judgments.'

'I don't, but . . . we're not exactly . . .' *Stop talking or Gary will take you off this.* 'It's late, we're tired, he's been traveling, there's a serial killer out there, he knows how bad that is, so do we.'

'Get some rest,' said Gary. 'And thanks for picking him up.'

As Ren drove toward home, her phone beeped with a text.

Denver bars are empty without you.
Mauser! My drinking buddy from Breckenridge!

Another text came in.

Or have you erased us from your mind? There's a Little Dick here
waiting for you.
Little Dick! My other drinking buddy from Breck!
Work tomorrow. Important day. Visiting detective.
Ren drove home, and parked the Jeep. She ran into the
apartment, changed into pale gray evening trousers, a silver
vest top, a chunky cuff, dark gray metallic heels, and a short
gray jacket. She came down, ran onto the street, and hopped
into the cab she had called on her way. It was one thirty
a.m. But she was home by six.

37

The next morning, Ren pulled up in a cab outside Joe Lucchesi's hotel at eight thirty. He got in, smelling of cologne and coffee.

Sexy.

Hungover and horny.

'The Jeep wouldn't start . . .' said Ren, gesturing around the cab.

Joe looked at her. She looked at him. Something passed between them.

The knowledge that I may just have stepped out of or drunk the contents of a bar?

Joe nodded.

Tense.

'I've been up all night doing a lot of thinking about . . . this,' he said. He had noticed the cab driver's attention on them.

We both know that thinking about 'this' is not what I've been up all night doing.

'This is serious,' said Joe, without looking at her. 'We need to be at the top of our game.'

Shot. Across. Bow.

He opened the window.

I am serious, asshole. Seriousness and drinking are not mutually exclusive. Any serious drinker will tell you that.

They got out at Safe Streets. Joe had paid the cab driver before Ren got the chance.

Oh, blessed solid ground. Ugh. My stomach.

Ren gave Joe the talk on the historical significance of the building as they walked up. He was interested. He told her about the old lighthouse he had lived in with his family in Ireland.

Where your wife was left for dead. Are you over any of this? Are you safe on this case? Are you too personally emotionally invested? Are any of us safe with you around? Before I picked you up last night, I read every article there is to read on you and your family, from here to Ireland and back again. Will you be an overbearing nightmare to work with?

They walked into the bullpen. There were three rows of boxes stacked five-high beside Ren's desk.

'What the fuck is this, people?' she said. 'Hoarders: Denver.' *My head! Pound. Pound. Pound. Pound. Pound. Throb. Throb. Throb.*

'They're from me,' said Joe. 'I FedExed them ahead. The Duke Rawlins files.'

Suitably embarrassed. 'Oh.' She walked over. 'Thank you.' *Overbearing nightmare it is.*

She introduced Joe to the half-squad that was there.

Gary walked into the bullpen, shook Joe's hand. 'Good to meet you,' he said. 'Thanks for coming.'

'Not a problem,' said Joe. 'Sorry about all the files.'

'The more we have, the better,' said Gary. 'Ren, can you please divide this up later?'

But I want to read it all myself! I'm not sure anyone else has my eagle eye! 'No problem.'

'Joe, if you'd like to come into my office,' said Gary.

'Sure,' said Joe.

Gary turned to Ren. 'Ren, maybe you could take the lunch order later—'

Food? Noooo! Nooooo!

'Then we'll come together at two p.m.,' said Gary. 'The other agencies will be here by then.'

Crowded room? Heat? The breathing of others? Their existence? Noooo! I need pineapple juice.

Robbie and Everett carried all the boxes from beside Ren's desk into the conference room, lining them up against the back wall. Ren directed them from flat on her back on one of the tables. She turned her cheek to the cold surface. Her arm was stretched out, limp.

'Is that door closed?' she said. 'Don't let him see me like this.'

'Him Joe Lucchesi?' said Everett. 'Don't worry – we like to shut the door on your shame.'

Robbie laughed.

Progress.

'What was I thinking?' said Ren. 'Anyone?'

'You should probably sit up,' said Robbie. 'You'll fall asleep. You'll feel worse.'

'Says the man who has had one hangover in his entire life,' said Ren.

'Which you *caused*,' said Robbie. 'I'm an expert in hangovers because of observing *yours*.'

'Depressing,' said Ren. 'I will be silent for a short while.' *I need to sleep. I can't bear the thought I won't be able to.*

'Do you want pineapple juice?' said Everett.

'It's become my red flag to Gary,' said Ren. 'You know something, I'm going to lay down on the bench in the ladies' room, just in case. Bang on the door if I'm not back by one fifty.'

'Just so we're clear: a.m. or p.m.?' said Everett.

The briefing began at ten after two. Joe Lucchesi stood at the top of the conference room, solid, confident, but with eyes that showed he hadn't slept much. Ren had taken the position as far from him and Gary as she could. She was clutching a bottle of water.

'Duke Rawlins . . .' said Joe, 'is a brutal rapist, a serial killer, an animal. He is a psychopath in its truest form.'

38

'In 1988, at seventeen years old, Rawlins carried out his first rape/murder with his accomplice, his childhood friend, Donald Riggs,' said Joe. 'Riggs was weaker, less intelligent, pliable, and impressionable. Together, they went on to rape and murder nine women – that we know of – all along I-35 in Texas, up until the late 1990s. No one realized that they were dealing with more than one killer; it was called the Crosscut Killer investigation, singular. Rawlins and Riggs stopped raping and murdering only because Rawlins was jailed for a different crime – stabbing a guy in a parking lot.

'In 2004, Donald Riggs, working alone, branched off from their traditional targets and crimes, and kidnapped an eight-year-old girl for ransom in New York City. I was on that case. I shot Donald Riggs dead, and from that moment on Duke Rawlins had me in his sights. When he got out of prison, he tracked me and my family down, followed us to Ireland.

'He raped and murdered a woman the day he arrived, a complete stranger – a crime of opportunity. He might have done the same with some of your victims. He can switch from organized to impulsive just like that. He went on to find himself a new accomplice, a young woman this time – a heavy girl, vulnerable, insecure and, like Donald Riggs, inferior to him intellectually. He used her to lure me into a trap: he stabbed her, I came across her on the roadside, drove her to get help, but it was a ruse. Rawlins ambushed us before I got her to the hospital. He took her away and killed her, but he didn't rape her. Nor did he rape the second woman who was there that night. He did, however, go on to violently assault her.'

The second woman being your wife.

'And he is now raping only with a foreign object,' said Ren. 'Whether that is a physical or psychological issue . . .'

'Rawlins may be working alone now,' said Joe, 'or he may have another accomplice.'

'Other than Kurt Vine?' said Glenn Buddy.

Joe nodded. 'It's possible. And that person could be either male or female. Obviously, using a female accomplice would make it a whole lot easier to lure a female target. That's *if* Rawlins' approach is to engage with his victims first, rather than just bundling them into the back of a vehicle.'

A brief silence descended.

'Duke Rawlins is,' said Joe, 'without doubt, the most dangerous and disturbed man I have ever met.' He paused. 'Do not engage with him.'

Why are you looking at me? You sexist . . . I knew it.

'You're going to believe that you can handle Duke Rawlins,' said Joe. 'He's just one man, right?'

Still looking at me.

'But he's more than that,' said Joe. 'If you're unfortunate enough to be sucked in by him, he will manipulate you in ways you won't predict, no matter how smart you are.'

Joe started to pace.

Finally, looking away.

He stopped dead, facing them all. 'It is important to note that Duke Rawlins will follow through on his threats. Almost immediately. He will barely give you time to act. If he gives you a choice, it's not really a choice: its purpose is to torture you in whatever way he wants to. Beneath the surface evil of Duke Rawlins, there's a well that's always ready to pump up a fresh supply. It goes straight to hell.'

Jesus Christ. 'I can't *wait* to get close to him.'

Joe Lucchesi looked at Ren.

I said that out loud.

Gary cut in, a look of scarcely buried fury on his face. 'You don't want to meet him. Trust me.'

Everyone turned to Gary now. 'I worked on the original Crosscut Killer investigation.'

What the what now?

Ren looked between Joe and Gary. 'Hold on,' she said, without thinking. 'Joe – so, you came to Denver not just for this, but because your son lives here. And that's why your daughter traveled with you . . .'

Joe looked like she had betrayed a confidentiality. Gary looked a little surprised by the revelation.

'Yes – we were coming to visit my son,' said Joe.

Stiffly.

'Then I got Gary's call . . .'

'Duke Rawlins targeted you and your family before,' said Ren. 'You don't think he'd do that again? Also considering that now, in this one city, he's got you, who shot his best friend, and Gary, who worked his original case? Both law enforcement officers under one roof?' *Boom!*

'You think all this is about us?' said Joe. 'About me and Gary?'

Ooh, scornful tone. Nice. 'He followed you before,' said Ren. *Hello?*

'Then why didn't he just come to New York after me again?' said Joe.

'Because you were probably hyper-vigilant there,' said Ren. 'When was the last time you heard from Duke Rawlins?'

'Seven years ago,' said Joe.

'Do you think there might be anything significant in that passing of years?' said Ren.

'This is not about my family,' said Joe.

Beyond dismissive.

'And he's never come after mine,' said Gary.

'I wouldn't have brought my daughter here if I thought we were targets,' said Joe. 'There has to be another reason Duke Rawlins is in Denver.'

Ren turned to Gary with a pleading look in her eye. *Is this guy for real?* Gary returned her look with a warning glare.

After the briefing, Gary called Ren to his office.

Ren sat down.

This already does not look good.

'Ren, I'm going to have to take you off as case agent on this.'

I may not have heard that correctly.

Gary gave her his steadying look. 'I don't believe it's safe, under these new circumstances, for any woman to be on this case – and specifically not for you. I'm concerned you're going to take risks.'

'Can I just point out that Rawlins has never touched a female law enforcement officer . . .' said Ren.

'A female law enforcement officer has never been on the case,' said Gary. 'Ren, you're an attrac—'

'I'm not his type,' said Ren. 'And you know it. He likes scrawny blondes. And anyway, I have moves.' She raised her hands, straight, karate-style.

Gary looked at her patiently. 'Law enforcement officers, by their nature, are people he clearly has a problem with. So, male or female, that makes you his type.'

'Thereby negating your point: anyone who leads this is under threat.'

'I'm trying to protect you,' said Gary. 'You look . . . excited by this.'

I fucking AM! 'It's not excitement – it's focus. I believe . . .' *that I will succeed where those who have gone before me have failed.*

Gary leaned forward. 'You believe . . .' He paused. 'Ren. Don't believe you are invincible. Please.'

Not this again. 'I'm focused. That's it. That's a positive. Don't take me off this.'

Gary sat back. 'If you take one risk, go off alone, try and lure this guy somewhere . . .'

Foiled again! 'I won't take risks.'

Gary studied her face. Something in his expression changed. 'Don't die on me, Ren.'

'Not a chance.' *I'm invincible.*

Gary leaned in, his face set. 'Ren, let me tell you about Duke Rawlins and law enforcement. When I was in Stinger's Creek working on the Crosscut Killer investigation, I was with a rookie, a nice kid, fresh out of the academy. We went to Bill Rawlins' house – Duke Rawlins' uncle. He had died in jail not long into a prison term for killing a woman called Rachel Wade. At this point, I had no clue that Duke Rawlins was the killer. He wasn't on our radar – on anyone's radar. I didn't know he existed. I was going to Bill Rawlins' house because I was thinking that Rachel Wade may have been connected to the other missing women – I just didn't know how. Bill Rawlins had kept Harris hawks – and it turned out that Duke had been back, intermittently, on Bill's land, raising the hawks, breeding them with the help of some low-life junkies who got to sleep in the house in return.'

You look as unsettled as I've ever seen you.

'So I'm walking through the woods,' said Gary. 'I'm alone. It's early morning, not long after sunrise. I stood on a steel-jawed trap.' He raised his pant leg and showed Ren a small white scar about four inches above his ankle.

'Holy fuck.'

'So that snaps shut, but I don't make a sound. But when the trap closes, it cuts the rope attached to a net above that's filled with freshly killed animals, small ones: rabbits and rats and weasels.'

'What the *fuck*?'

'Down it comes, I'm laying there in the stink of all this crap around me, rats and weasels and shit sliced open. And then I hear flapping wings. Someone had released a dozen hawks and down they came. I just lay back and closed my eyes,' said Gary. 'I could hear laughter, this almost hysterical laughter coming from somewhere in the trees. Eventually, I passed out from the pain – those birds weren't just poking about the rodents. When I woke, up, my leg was freed. I managed to limp through the most obvious clearing back toward where I thought the car was. I went the wrong way. I'm guessing whoever released me turned me around so I was facing the opposite way. So I was going the wrong way for quite some time. I came across a hunter, regular guy, he smiled, he didn't have two horns coming out the top of his head.'

'Duke Rawlins . . .'

Gary nodded. 'He showed me where to go, pointed me in the right direction. He was real nice, real personable. When I got back to the car, the agent I was with was lying there on the ground, naked from the waist down. It was bad. Rawlins had raped him, done so much damage, he wound up needing

238

surgery. He was never the same after that. He lasted another five months, then he killed himself.'

'Jesus Christ.'

'I couldn't help thinking of the last thing Rawlins said to me as I walked away . . .'

A cell phone started to ring. Gary stood up. 'Sorry – I need to take this.'

Ren stood up. 'What was the last thing he said to you?'

'Boo-hoo.'

Ren left Gary's office and went into the bullpen. Joe was sitting on her desk, talking to the group.

Rebel briefing. Not arrogant at all.

Joe looked up. 'Ren, maybe you could listen to this too . . .'

Breathe deeply.

'You saw Rawlins' photo,' said Joe. 'He was once a hand-some man, he possibly still is, but what you don't see in the old mug shots is that he now has a scar that might make a woman think twice about helping him or accompanying him somewhere. This scar comes from the corner of his mouth and stretches upwards, like it's the continuation of his smile.'

Oh. Oh. Oh. FUCK.

Ren could feel something plunge down through her chest.

Scar. Texas. Shaven-headed. Now I know why he was familiar. He's the guy from the bipolar support group.

Oh. My. God. I have already engaged with Duke Rawlins.

39

In a flawlessly casual move, Ren raised a finger. 'Could you please excuse me for one moment? Thank you.'

She moved quickly to the ladies' room, retching as she pushed through the outer door, making it into a stall just before she threw up.

Oh dear God. He knows who I am. I had no clue. He didn't seem that fucked up to me. Why not? I have a good radar. What's going on? Jesus Christ.

She gathered herself, went over to the sink, washed her face, washed her hands, over and over. She brushed her teeth, reapplied foundation.

Duke Rawlins. I met Duke Rawlins. I can't tell anyone this. They don't know about bipolar support. Oh, I could tell Janine now. But she would worry. Gary . . . is never going to hear this. "The rule is you walk in there alone, you walk out alone."

Oh, God. I am on Duke Rawlins' radar.

Ren took a deep breath and walked back into the room where Joe Lucchesi was plotting Rawlins' downfall. He frowned, went back to talking.

'If Duke Rawlins is the killer,' said Joe, 'then it's likely the woman he's been killing over and over is his mama: skinny, blonde Wanda Rawlins, a former prostitute and junkie.'

'Well, that's not going to fuck him up one bit,' said Ren. 'And where's Wanda Rawlins now? Why doesn't he just go and kill her?'

'He may already have,' said Joe. 'Wanda Rawlins disappeared six years ago. Her husband, Vincent Farraday – who married her after she became a born-again Christian – was hauled in about the disappearance, questioned relentlessly, but nothing came of it. It caused quite a stir at the time – he was a pretty famous local country singer.'

'Do you think Farraday was guilty?' said Ren.

'No,' said Joe. 'He loved that woman for God-knows-what reason. He was a broken man after that, his whole family came apart. I wouldn't be surprised if Rawlins framed him. Years back, the DA in Stinger's Creek reckoned that Rawlins framed his own uncle Bill for one of the murders. So I can't see him having a problem framing his mama's husband who he despised.'

'You say "family" – does Wanda have any more children?'

'Twin girls,' said Joe. 'Robin and Chloe Farraday. They would be about twenty-six years old now.'

'Do you know where they live?' said Ren.

'Denison, Texas, last I heard,' said Joe.

'Do they have any relationship with Duke Rawlins?' said Ren.

'Highly unlikely,' said Joe.

Disdain! I love it!

'And he had a wife, I read,' said Ren. 'Samantha "Sammi" Rawlins.'

'Nah – he's done with her,' said Joe.

Disdain again! I love it even more!

241

He paused. 'Right, well, I'm sure I've talked enough. I'd like to see what you've got, if that's OK with you.'

Greaaaat.

Ren's cell phone started to ring.

She looked at the screen.

Annie Lowell.

Why am I sensing bad news?

'Excuse me for one second,' said Ren. 'I better take this.'

She picked up.

'Oh, Ren, sweetheart – Devin's been hurt. She got hit by a car. She was taking Misty for a walk . . . the driver didn't stop.'

'Oh my God – is she all right?'

'She's conscious, she's talking, she's got a broken leg,' said Annie. 'It happened just this afternoon. I've been on the phone with her mother, the whole family is at the hospital.'

'I don't believe it,' said Ren. 'And the driver didn't stop?'

'No!' said Annie.

'And is Misty all right?' said Ren.

'I've got Misty, don't worry – not a scratch on her. She ran to the nearest house, barked her heart out. And the driver just drove away! Can you imagine?'

'That's terrible!' said Ren. 'How are you doing?'

'Well, I'm very upset,' said Annie. 'Devin's like a grand-daughter to me.'

'Oh, Annie. What can I do to help? Should I go to the hospital?'

'No, no – not today. They know you're busy, Ren. I think they'd prefer if you were working on that terrible case of yours, to be honest. They're very selfless people. They knew you'd be worried – they said wait until you have an hour off some evening, then maybe stop by if she's still at the hospital, or stop by the house. I'm OK to look after Misty here, but I can't walk her for any length, obviously.'

'No, no – don't worry about that,' said Ren. 'Janine or I will swing by to do that. Thank you so much, Annie. That's such awful news. I'll make sure I talk to Denver PD about what we can do to find out who did this.'

'You take care of yourself, sweetheart, and I'll see you soon.'

'You too, Annie. I'll text Devin, but send my love if you're talking to her.'

Ren went into the bullpen and let Janine know about the accident. 'We'll stop by after work.'

'Might be a bit soon,' said Janine.

'No,' said Ren. 'She'll be happy to have visitors.'

'She could be in pain.'

'We'll cheer her up!'

'OK,' said Janine. 'You go ahead and see Joe Lucchesi – he's in the kitchen – I think he's getting antsy. I can call Glenn Buddy about Devin.'

'Thank you.'

40

Ren found Joe Lucchesi in the kitchen with Everett.

'OK,' said Ren. 'Are you ready?'

Joe nodded. 'Sure. I'll take this with me.'

That's my coffee mug.

'But, I don't really need you to go through everything with me,' said Joe.

Of course not. Why would you? 'If you're sure . . .' said Ren.

'Why don't you leave everything with me, I can go through it at my own pace, take a look around the conference room at what you've got up there on the walls.'

'Well, how about you start off in the interview room for round one? Would that be weird? We're tight on space. The only other option is one of two cells.' She smiled. He didn't. 'Anyway, when you're done, do join me in the conference room.'

'OK.'

Ren left Joe in the interview room with a stack of files.

She bumped into Everett in the hallway on her way back.

'I had to put him in one of the interview rooms,' said Ren. 'He probably thinks it's some kind of FBI mind-fuck.'

'I would too,' said Everett.

'It's a desk, a chair, four walls,' said Ren. 'Yes, teeny window, but teeny windows are better than none. I want the conference room. Or at least the freedom to wander freely in and out of it.' She leaned in. 'He's very intense. I need some space.'

'I like him,' said Everett.

'Hey, I'm not saying I don't.' She paused. 'As an aside, Gary could be losing it. We're in his office, this cell phone rings, and he says, totally spaced out, "I need to take this." His phone was on the desk. The phone ringing was clearly next door or somewhere. Could he have Alzheimer's, do you think?'

'No. Goodbye.'

Ren went to her desk and looked at her notebook where she'd been taking notes when Joe was talking. She Googled Wanda Rawlins' disappearance. She saw photos of her husband, Vincent Farraday. He had once been a very handsome, plump, well-groomed man. He had warm blue eyes, a thick head of gray hair, and a thick moustache.

Ren called the agent who had interviewed Farraday at the time of his wife's disappearance. She got him to email the video, and went into the A/V room to watch it.

Sorry, Joe – you could have had the conference room after all . . .

Ren hit Play, and got the inside of an interview room in an FBI field office in Sherman, Texas. The camera was clearly mounted in the corner of the ceiling, giving an aerial view of Vincent Farraday, who looked like he had all but disintegrated since his wife's disappearance . . . or maybe since he had the misfortune of marrying her.

'These things happen,' Agent Richmond was saying. *'You marry one woman, she turns into a whole 'nother one. You married a reformed woman, Mr Farraday. Wanda Rawlins had cleaned up her act – for you. You had sixteen good years with her, she gave*

*you two beautiful daughters. So when she was back using, you must
have figured "She doesn't care any more, she mustn't love us any
more if she can start shooting up again"?'*

'No, sir,' said Vincent. '*I understand that addiction can take a
powerful hold on a person. Doesn't make them weak, and it doesn't
make me weak to get frustrated by that, or the girls for getting hurt
and angry about it.*'

'*What about your daughters?*' said Richmond. '*Should we be
worried about them?*'

Vincent Farraday shifted forward in his seat, created a
forty-five-degree angle between himself and Richmond. '*Now,
what do you mean by that, Agent?*'

'*Your daughter, Chloe . . .*' said Richmond. '*She's been in some
trouble.*'

'*That's a low blow,*' said Vincent. '*She was just sixteen years
old.*'

'*We've spoken with the school, and with some of the parents . . .
she does appear to have anger-management problems.*'

'*That was a whole lot of nothing,*' said Vincent.

'*That's not the conclusion Denison PD came to,*' said Richmond.

'*Well, with respect, that's their business,*' said Vincent. '*I believe
Chloe and my other daughter, Robin.*'

'*Were you involved in the disappearance of your wife?*' said
Richmond.

'No, sir, no I was not,' said Vincent.

'*Do you have any knowledge of your wife's whereabouts?*' said
Richmond.

'No, sir, no I do not,' said Vincent.

'*We have a statement here from one of your neighbors who said
that you told him, quote, "I'm about at breaking point. We're living
in a kind of hell. I think we'd all be better off if Wanda was gone.
There's nothing more I can do for her."*'

Vincent nodded. '*And that's the God's honest truth. I said exactly those words, and I understand that they don't sound too good. I'd tell the police the same thing, if it was my neighbor said them. There wasn't a word of a lie in what I said. Didn't mean I thought that killing her was an option. Hell, I can't even kill a spider. My daughters will tell you that.'* His eyes welled up. *'I understand you have to do this, but can you please consider what it's doing to my girls? Their mother's gone. She's been gone years. Please don't take their father away from them too.'*

'Isn't it true that you haven't spoken to either of your daughters in six years?' said Richmond.

Low blow again.

Farraday nodded, wiped away tears. *'They blamed me for their mama going off the rails, and they blamed me for falling apart afterwards, for abandoning them. But I know one thing – they know I would never have hurt a hair on that woman's head. We can't choose who we love. I've written enough songs about it to know that.'*

Songs? Songs!

Holy shit.

41

Ren Googled Vincent Farraday's songs, looking for tiny needles and sharps disposal.

Nothing.

Children, though. Children. It could be one of his daughters, Robin or Chloe.

Ren called Richmond from the Sherman field office.

'Richmond, it's Ren Bryce here from Safe Streets in Denver. I watched the tapes – thank you. What can you tell me about Robin and Chloe Farraday?'

'Robin Farraday emigrated to London four years ago, got married over there, has a three-year-old daughter. She calls me up every now and then to see if I have any update on her mother. She seems like a real honorable young lady. She was heartbroken about what happened to her mother, even though she was treated badly by her, but she's still her mother – that's the way she looks at it.'

'And Chloe Farraday?' said Ren. 'I saw in the video that she was the wild one.'

'She was,' said Richmond, 'and that's pretty much my last

update on her. I've no idea. She was back in Denison last year, put a call into Denison PD about some stolen property she wanted to get back from her father. A whole lot of nothing. I don't know where she came from or where she went back to. Let me put a call in to my buddy in Denison PD. I'll get back to you.'

'Thanks,' said Ren. 'I appreciate it.'

Ren stuck her head back into the interview room to Joe two hours later.

'Do you want to come into the conference room?' she said.

'Sure,' he said, standing up, stretching his legs.

'It's not very comfortable, I know,' said Ren. 'I'm really sorry about that. It's not normally like this.'

'Nah, I get it,' said Joe.

Hmm.

They sat at the conference-room table. Joe Lucchesi seemed to fill every space he entered.

He put down the photo of Kurt Vine. 'I'm not buying this loser as Rawlins' accomplice, first of all.'

'Why not?' said Ren.

'Are you?' said Joe.

Not so much. 'I'm keeping an open mind on it for now.'

'I can't see how a fat gamer sitting on his fat ass half the time could be of any use to a guy like Rawlins.'

'You mentioned a girl he used in Ireland – she was heavy-set, vulnerable, insecure,' said Ren. 'Is this just more of the same?'

Joe paused. 'Well . . . she was willing to go out, be active on his behalf . . .'

'Kurt Vine went out too – he brought that lady to the hospital—'

'But he stumbled across that scene,' said Joe. 'And what was in it for him? Nothing.'

'We don't know that.'

'Then he was just doing a kindness, meaning he's hardly the type to be out raping and murdering women.'

'Maybe he was targeting Amanda Petrie. And remember, Rawlins has been changing his approach here to fuck with us.'

Joe's face was set.

'Did you read about the ten thousand dollars wired into Vine's account?' said Ren.

Joe nodded. 'Yeah . . . I can't make a call on that until I know more.'

'I understand that.' She paused. 'I'm not saying Vine was his accomplice for the commission of the rapes and murders, but for another reason. And not just as a fall-guy. See, I don't think Duke Rawlins thought he would *need* a fall guy when he started out. I think that was part of an evolving plan. I think it goes beyond Vine having that remote property. There are other remote properties in Colorado. Rawlins could have broken into one, he could have rented one anonymously or gotten his accomplice – if he has one – to rent one. Kurt Vine's photographs are about abandonment. Duke Rawlins' life is about abandonment. It could just be that. Or something else that made Kurt Vine his target?'

'Well, even if this loser, Vine, was his accomplice, he's dead now, and he will be replaced. I don't think it makes much of a difference. Duke Rawlins will always have an accomplice.'

Pcccchhhhh! Shot down.

Joe checked the time. 'I'm running late,' he said.

'I'll take you where you need to be,' said Ren. 'That's not a problem.'

'Really? That would be great. Would you mind swinging by the hotel? My kids will be waiting. The nanny has the night off – Shaun is taking care of Grace.'

He wouldn't call her the nanny if he was sleeping with her.

'Sure,' said Ren.

Why am I thinking about who he's sleeping with?

They drove through the evening traffic.

'Duke Rawlins saw it as a mistake not to have killed Anna when he had the chance,' said Joe.

Whoa – what have you been thinking?

'He wanted me to feel the pain of being responsible for her death. She didn't die, but she was attacked, she was trauma-tized. I'm still responsible. I didn't protect her from him.'

'That's not true,' said Ren. 'From what I read, it was complicated.' She turned to him. 'Why did you think that he was able to . . . leave that behind, leave things unfinished . . . that he didn't come back after Ireland?'

'He would have had a hard time getting close to her,' said Joe. 'You were right before. We were all hyper-vigilant. Anna was depressed. She barely went outside the door, she just about managed to work from home. She became a recluse, almost. If she went outside, she risked having panic attacks . . .'

Hmm. Depressed does not equal hyper-vigilant in my experience.

'But you still went to work,' said Ren. 'She was alone . . .'

'He just wouldn't have had the balls,' said Joe. 'He's a sick fuck, but he wanted to be a free sick fuck.'

'Maybe something else stopped him from coming back to kill Anna,' said Ren.

'Like what?' said Joe.

Stop talking, stop talking.

'Grace,' said Ren. 'Maybe Anna's pregnancy changed something.'

'Like, he didn't want to kill a pregnant woman?' said Joe.

'Maybe pregnancy repels a man who hates his mama.' *Or maybe he wanted her to carry her baby to term, so he could wait, wait to take them both away? Your wife and your child. Then, when Anna died, he needed you to develop that bond with Grace, and take her from you when she was older? He just wants to keep causing you more pain? Take away your little girl. Your little Anna. The only physical link left.*

'What are you thinking?' said Joe.

'Nothing,' said Ren.

'You need to tell me if you have a theory,' said Joe.

'I don't. I'm . . . processing. I presume you've taken steps to keep your family safe.'

Joe had drifted somewhere deep and dark. He zoned back in. 'Camille is not just a nanny. She's . . . trained.'

Jesus Christ.

'And Shaun's big enough and bold enough,' said Joe. 'He boxes.'

'Oh, so do I,' said Ren. 'Maybe we could spar some time.'

Joe raised his eyebrows.

'What?' said Ren. 'He'd be too embarrassed to fight an old lady? I'd beat the shit out of him without thinking twice.'

Joe laughed.

Wow. He laughs.

'Shaun's a good kid,' said Joe. 'He turned out well. It was touch and go for a while. He's been through a lot. He went off the rails in his teens when we came back from Ireland. He was drinking, in with the wrong crowd, we were arguing all the time. Then he just got his shit together. When we lost Anna . . . it was like a switch went on in his brain. Something changed in him. And Grace was a big part of that. He was crazy about her, this little baby who only had us, and he saw life in a different way, I guess.'

'I'm sure you were a big part of him getting his shit together too,' said Ren.

'I don't know,' said Joe. 'Do you have kids?'

'I love kids, but no,' said Ren. 'I just get to observe.' *And make judgments.*

Shaun Lucchesi stood up when he saw Ren and Joe coming. He was dark-haired, broad, handsome, all-American, like his dad.

'Shaun, this is Ren Bryce from the FBI,' said Joe.

Shaun shot a glance at his dad, then back at Ren. 'Hi,' he said, shaking her hand firmly, sullen and abrupt.

Could use manners.

'Hi, Ren!' said Grace.

'Hello there, Grace,' said Ren. 'Are you having fun in Denver?'

She nodded. 'Yes! Camille and me've been to lots of places. Shaun's taking me to the movies tonight.'

'Good for you,' said Ren. *How adorable: twenty-six-year-old taking his little sister out.*

Shaun picked Grace up and hugged her.

Oh, I think your big brother adores you.

'OK, let's go get something to eat,' said Joe. 'Ren would you like to—'

'We're going to eat by the movie theater,' said Shaun, setting Grace down gently.

'I thought maybe we could all eat together,' said Joe.

'Nah – you two go ahead,' said Shaun.

You two. What the heck is he getting at?

Joe looked embarrassed. He bent down and kissed Grace on the head. 'Love you, sweetheart. You have fun. Popcorn only for her, Shaun. No candy. Sorry, sweetheart.'

She flung her arms around his legs. 'Love you, love you, love you, Daddy.'

Joe beamed. 'Love you way more.'

'I'd love to stay for dinner,' said Ren, 'but I'm going to have to get back home. You guys eat together, I'll see you tomorrow at the office.'

'Are you sure?' said Joe.

'Absolutely.'

She had a sudden flash of Grace Lucchesi. Camille. And the black shadow of Duke Rawlins behind them. Why did Joe take them along? It's nuts.

Ren left them, tired and drained. Janine had sent her a text.

Think we'll give Devin some time to rest . . .

Ren texted back: OK. I'll go see Annie and Wonderdog Misty instead. ☺

Annie was thrilled to see her, and Ren quickly felt at home, and cozy, and loved. Misty nearly passed out with the excitement. Ren sat with Annie, drinking tea and chatting about her travels.

The doorbell rang.

'Let me get that,' said Ren. 'You stay where you are.'

It was Devin's ten-year-old brother holding a squishy package wrapped in white plastic.

Ren opened the door. 'Hey, there, Jack. Come in. How's Devin doing?'

'Hey, Ren. Mom saw your car, told me to come over. She says she's sorry she's too tired. Devin's doing just fine, thank you!' He beamed the family smile – wide, and extra curled up at the edges.

'That's good to hear,' said Ren.

He held out the package. 'Mom said to give you this, and that she's really sorry.'

Ren frowned. 'About what?'

'Thanks!' said Jack. 'Bye!' He turned and ran.

'Thanks, Jack!' said Ren. 'Tell your mom thanks.'

She opened the package. She recognized her black Marmot rain jacket. It was folded up with an envelope on top. She put the envelope aside, and shook out the jacket. It was shredded in three places.

What happened here?

She opened the envelope. It was a $100 store voucher for REI.

What the what?

Ren called Devin's mom. 'It's Ren, Liz – what's this voucher about?'

'Oh, hi, Ren. Did Jack not explain? Devin was wearing your jacket the day of the accident – the one she borrowed a while back. That's a good jacket, Ren. I hope you can replace it.'

'Liz, you shouldn't have. Poor Dev. I hope she wasn't worrying about my jacket in the middle of all this. I can't accept this.'

'I'm afraid you have no choice,' said Liz. 'Do you have any word on the driver?'

'No,' said Ren. 'Nothing. Unfortunately, there are a lot of kids joyriding, and fleeing the scenes of accidents . . .'

'It's terrible,' said Liz. She paused. 'I just want to say thank you for everything you do for Devin. She loves you. You're the big sister she never had.'

Ren laughed. 'Well, we have been mistaken for sisters at the park a few times, which I take as a huge compliment. Really, it's just the long dark hair . . .'

A shiver ran down Ren's spine. Oh. My. God. This wasn't an accident at all. This was deliberate. She was wearing my jacket. Someone thought Devin was me.

42

He was a hunter. He understood camouflage. When he stepped out of the car, he looked like all the other regular men who parked here, got out of their cars, and went through their stretches. It was a very nice neighborhood, and he made sure that he looked like a very nice man.

He watched as she set out on her run. She was fit-mom pretty. It was clear she looked after herself. She wouldn't be doing this at eight a.m. if she didn't. High, blonde ponytail swishing back and forth, swimmer's shoulders, tanned skin, sweet tight ass.

He bet her husband slammed that every night. Most men would love a chance at that ass.

He began to run behind her. Though she was fit, he could tell that her heart wasn't in it. Her shoulders were a little too low, she wasn't raising her knees very high. She could trip if she wasn't careful.

Just as he said it, she fell. He was amazed. He felt a surge of power. He heard her say to herself out loud, 'Seriously? Seriously? You have got to be kidding me.'

He looked around. There was no one in sight. Not one person.

He crouched down beside her. 'Are you OK?' He reached out a gloved hand.

She looked up, tears in her eyes. She grabbed his hand and let him pull her up.

'Ugh,' she said. 'I don't think the gods are smiling down on me at the moment.' She wiped her tears away. 'Thank you, thanks.'

'Is anything broken?' he said.

'No,' she said. 'Just a little sprain, and a grazed knee. I'll live to fight another day. Thanks, again.'

She was nodding her dismissal.

He just stared at her. There was a tiny flicker on her face.

'Karen?' he said.

She tried to withdraw her hand. He wouldn't let her.

'Karen Dettling?' he said. He reached into his pocket. 'Your husband and I go back a long way . . .'

43

Ren went into Safe Streets at eight a.m. and called Glenn Buddy.

'It's Ren – did you get anything on that hit-and-run driver?'

'Nada,' said Glenn. 'Not yet.'

'She was wearing my jacket at the time, Glenn – she has the same dark shoulder-length hair. She was walking Misty on the street where I used to live. You heard Joe Lucchesi – Rawlins is targeting law enforcement. I'm worried, this was meant for me. If Rawlins was working on old information on where I live . . .'

'Sounds to me like Rawlins is not the type to leave a job unfinished,' said Glenn.

'That's my concern,' said Ren. 'What if he comes back again? Devin is only—'

'Ren, my dear, if he comes back again, it'll be you he targets. And he won't miss. So, relax.'

'Thanks, Glenn. Thanks for that.'

Joe Lucchesi appeared in the bullpen.

'Morning,' he said.

'Hey,' said Ren. 'Did you enjoy your evening?'

'Yes,' said Joe. 'I went to the movie in the end, took my mind off everything for a couple hours.'

'I bet it didn't take your mind off anything,' said Ren.

Joe paused. Then nodded. 'No. You're right.' He walked out of the room.

Ren looked at Everett. 'He's a cheery fellow.'

She went to the kitchen to make coffee. Gary was standing at the machine. She told him about Devin.

'That's not Rawlins' style. You know it isn't.'

'I hope it isn't,' said Ren. 'But what if he's targeting people who mean something to people? I don't have kids or close family in Denver.'

'This is a hit-and-run,' said Gary. 'Nothing more exciting than that.' He poured her coffee. 'So,' he said, 'what do you make of Joe Lucchesi?'

'He's intense,' said Ren. 'Abrupt. But very good. He's cold, though.'

'He's had a hard time of it,' said Gary. 'I'm guessing he had a very different pre-Duke Rawlins' life.'

'It's so depressing.'

'And it's exactly why you cannot, under any circumstances, personally engage Duke Rawlins if you don't have to . . .'

Of course I have to. It's irrefuckingsistible not to. It's Duke Rawlins, for fuck's sake. It's the Greatest Psycho on Earth.

Gary's cell phone started to ring.

'It's Claire,' he said. 'I better take it.'

Ren went into the bullpen. By the time she sat down at her desk, Gary was calling her to come to his office. When she walked in, he was ghostly.

'Karen didn't come back from her run this morning,' he said.

Oh. Fuck.

'I've no way of contacting her, because she doesn't carry her cell when she runs – she lost her armband.'

'I'm sure it's nothing,' said Ren. 'She probably met a friend, got stuck into a conversation, lost track of time – it happens.'

He looked at her like he wanted to believe her. They stared at each other. Ren wondered if they were thinking the same thing.

Duke Rawlins.

Then Ren wondered if they shared the same follow-up thought.

What if Karen's found out about the affair? Because if we put out a BOLO for Karen Dettling and it turns out she's running away from her cheating FBI agent husband in the middle of a serial killer investigation, well . . .

'Where does she normally go running?' said Ren. 'Can we go check wherever that is?'

'I'll call around her friends,' said Gary.

When Cheating Attacks.

Fifteen minutes later, Gary called Ren and Joe into his office.

'That was her,' he said. 'I got hold of her. She's OK. She's fine.' His voice cracked.

'Oh, thank God,' said Ren.

Joe was perplexed. Gary explained what had happened.

Safe to explain to him now you know it wasn't your cheating that caused this.

'It's not good, guys. It's . . . Duke Rawlins.'

'What?' said Joe.

What?

Gary let out a breath, struggled to compose himself.

'Take your time,' said Ren.

'Karen was running in the park,' said Gary. 'She fell and this guy who had been running behind her stopped and helped her up. She said he seemed like a regular guy. But then he called her Karen, said he and "her husband" went a long way back. Then he gave her an envelope, and ran back to wherever he came from. When he was gone, she looked at it, and it had your name on it.' He pointed to Joe.

'My name?' said Joe.

'What the fuck?' said Ren. 'Where is it?'

'I'm going home now to get it,' said Gary. 'I told her to put it into a paper bag.'

Joe was stunned. 'Is your wife OK?'

'She's very shaken,' said Gary. 'But she'll be fine. She's made of strong stuff.'

Not from what I saw.

'He didn't hurt her . . .' said Joe.

'No,' said Gary.

There was a short silence.

Are we all thinking how Anna Lucchesi was not so fortunate?

'Is there anything I can do?' said Ren.

'Yeah . . .' said Joe.

'No,' said Gary. 'Thank you both. I'll check on things at home, bring you back the letter.'

44

Gary arrived back within the hour, and handed Joe the envelope from Duke Rawlins. Joe opened it with a gloved hand and looked inside. There was a second envelope with a single sheet of paper in it. He pulled it out. He looked up, confused.

What is it?

'Well, that's my wife's signature,' said Joe. 'It's a FedEx shipment slip, dated, like, seven years ago. Why is Duke Rawlins sending me this?'

Ren handed him two evidence bags – he put the slip inside one and the envelope inside the other.

'Does it say what she was signing for?' said Ren.

'No,' said Joe. 'It was after we came back from Ireland – Anna was working from home most of the time, she was always getting deliveries to the house of interiors things. I don't know why this one matters.'

Ren read the slip. 'I would venture this is just his way of fucking with you, just his way of letting you know he went through your garbage once . . . or got into your house.'

Joe shook his head. 'There is no way he could have gotten

into my house. Anna was on high alert. She knew what he looked like, obviously. She wouldn't have opened the door to him.'

'If he was in a FedEx uniform with a baseball cap pulled down over his eyes?' said Ren.

'That would have looked weird to her,' said Joe. 'She wouldn't have fallen for that.'

Ren handed the slip to Everett. 'I'll see if I can get anything else on this,' he said.

Oh. Fuck. 'Is it . . . could it be his way of letting you know if he got that close before, he could do it again?' *Like now? With Grace?*

'I'd like to see him try,' said Joe.

'What's security like at your hotel?' said Everett.

'Tight,' said Joe. 'But it's a hotel. There are ways and means. But, like I said, I'm not so worried about him coming after me there.'

Really?!

'There are three options,' said Ren. 'We track Duke Rawlins down, Duke Rawlins comes our way, or . . .'

Ren locked eyes with Joe. *Or we draw him our way. I know you know what I'm thinking.*

'There is just one option,' said Gary. 'We track the mother-fucker down.'

'We need to work out where his head is at,' said Ren. 'Who are the people who might still be significant in his life, for better or worse? We have his mother's husband, Vincent Farraday, who he no doubt despises. I'm sure he feels the same way about the Farraday twins – Chloe and Robin. We have Rawlins' ex-wife Samantha "Sammi" Rawlins, we have Geoff Riggs, father of Donald Riggs.'

'The Riggs family is hugely significant to Duke Rawlins' life,' said Joe. 'They were very close. The Riggs house was a refuge for Rawlins in many ways, which, when you consider that Geoff Riggs was a hard core alcoholic, is quite something. I don't know if Rawlins would still consider it a safe place to go if he was in trouble, but I do know that he has gone back to visit Geoff Riggs in the past.'

Ren went into the bullpen. Janine was sitting at her desk, doing her frowny staring at the screen. Ren filled her in on Karen and the letter for Joe Lucchesi.

'That is bizarre,' said Janine.

'I know.'

'I'm scheduling a few things for tomorrow,' said Ren. 'Am I right in saying you have a day off?'

'Yes,' said Janine. 'A most welcome one.'

'Have you plans?'

'I do. I'm meeting Terri for lunch, we might do a little shopping, nothing crazy.'

Nothing crazy . . .

Ren's cell phone rang. She picked up.

'Agent Bryce – it's Agent Richmond here in Sherman, Texas. What I can tell you about Chloe Farraday is that her last-known job was as a nurse – that was two years ago. Apparently, she has also worked, in an informal capacity, as a carer. And that's it – I'm not picking her up anywhere in the past two years. You might want to talk to Vincent Farraday – he could know more.'

Oh. My. God.

Nurse. Sharps disposal.

'OK,' said Ren. 'Thank you for the call.'

Ren went back into Gary's office. Joe was still there. 'Joe – how would you feel about a trip to Texas?'

45

Vincent Farraday's home was a disintegrating cabin in the woods outside Denison, Texas. Within its walls, his body was doing the same thing – and within that, his mind. Ren and Joe sat across from him, waiting, waiting for sense. There was a half-empty bottle of whiskey and a smeared glass on a table beside him. He knocked back what was left in it.

Ren took the time to look around the room. There were photos of Wanda still on the sideboard, looking respectable and happy, and many photos of their twin girls, only up until they were about sixteen years old.

All three – skinny, blonde; the girls – identical.

'It came from nowhere,' said Vincent, suddenly. He poured himself another glass. 'Wanda had turned her life around, found me, found God, had the girls, our beautiful twins. She was a different woman. Then I came home one day, and there she was, a needle in her arm. It went on like that for a little while – I tried to hide it from the girls, but I couldn't. She turned into an absolute wreck, became so mean and nasty, I didn't know who she was. Then, one day, I came home, she was gone . . . no warning . . .'

'And you didn't report her missing at that time,' said Ren.

'No, ma'am,' said Vincent, 'because it would have been a waste of police time. She could have been anywhere. I told our friends, my family that she was in rehab. I told the girls the same thing. Everyone had seen Wanda, they knew what was going on. At that stage, though, the girls hated her. It was so sad. Their whole lives, they thought the sun shone from their mama . . .' He drifted off. 'And so did I. I began drinking. We all have our painkillers, I guess.' He shifted in his seat. 'And then the police show up a few years ago. Some DA who was looking for glory decides to try and arrest me for murdering my wife, even though they hadn't even got a body!

'My life's been hell these last few years,' said Vincent. 'Absolute hell.' He drained his glass. 'I was interviewed for hours and hours – over twenty times by Denison PD, then by the FBI in Sherman. Imagine constantly being hauled in to go through the same questions over and over. It's enough to drive you insane. You know the truth, you know your wife just upped and left. You're thinking – did she die, did she kill herself, did she drown by accident, was she hit by a car somewhere, is she lying in a ditch, did she walk into the path of a killer? It's been a nightmare from the moment she stuck that needle in her vein. I've been a performer all my life, but then, people started looking at me to see if I was still performing, covering up a crime.'

Ren and Joe hovered, without a word, in Vincent Farraday's anguish.

Vincent shook his head, poured himself another whiskey.

'I've had kids egg my house, spray-paint "murderer" on my wall,' said Vincent. 'I've had people knock on my door under all kinds of pretenses – oh, they're studying justice or law or forensic something-or-other. One of them was all the

way from New York by the sound of him, looking for information about Duke Rawlins, about what kind of childhood
he might have had, what kind of mother Wanda was to him.
I told him I didn't know that Wanda Rawlins. And I sure
don't want to hear another thing about that animal Rawlins.'
He paused. 'You know Wanda had a tattoo of that boy's face
on her shoulder, must have gotten it in one of her guiltier,
drunker moments, way before we met. She always wanted
to get it taken off, but was afraid it would hurt.' His gaze
drifted away, then he returned to his story. 'So, I answered
what I could for the young man – he seemed well-inten-
tioned, like he wanted to set a record set straight. He seemed
to me to be invested in the truth, unlike most people.'

He paused. 'And I know what you're thinking – you
could say to me "Don't open your door", but the truth is
I think to myself "What if it's Wanda coming home?"'

Love is the mystery to end all mysteries.

'So, there you have it,' said Vincent.

His eyes were filled with pain, with sadness, with resig-
nation.

Yet no anger.

'We know that your daughter, Robin, is living in London
now,' said Ren. 'But we can't seem to find Chloe . . .'

He looked up at her, vacant-eyed. He took another drink.

'Do you have any idea where your daughter Chloe is now,
Mr Farraday?' said Joe.

He shook his head. 'I don't, I do not.' He narrowed his
eyes. 'Have I met you before, Detective?' His words were
getting slurred.

Ren looked at Joe.

'No, sir,' said Joe.

'Something about you is familiar . . .' said Vincent.

Joe shook his head. 'I can't help you there.'

'Have you seen Chloe in the past while, Mr Farraday?' said Ren, guiding him back while he could still at least partially function.

He nodded. 'She came around here looking for her guitar about twelve months back, arrived with the police, said I stole it, which I hadn't.'

'I couldn't bear to look at it,' said Vincent. 'I'd put it in the attic. I told her she could go on up and get it, told her she could stay if she liked. What she replied to that wasn't very nice at all.'

God love this man.

'Is Chloe a singer?' said Ren.

'Yes,' said Vincent. 'A very good one.'

'Does she write songs?' said Ren.

'Oh, yes,' said Vincent. 'She was writing songs from when she was eight years old.'

'Do you or your family, or Wanda's family, have any connections in Denver?' said Joe.

'Not that I know of,' said Vincent. 'Denver . . . Denver . . .' He let out a breath. 'Got an old roadie buddy there, guy by the name of Benny Jakes. Good guy, Benny.'

Ren texted Everett: Everything you got on Benny Jakes, roadie, based in Denver.

'I want you to know Wanda loved those girls very, very much,' said Vincent. 'I can't for the life of me see how it could have gone so wrong.'

They all descended into silence and before long, Vincent Farraday was snoring in his chair.

'Do you mind if we take a look around?' said Ren.

'Don't mind if we do,' said Joe. He raised his eyebrows.

Ren and Joe weaved in and out of the rooms in the house. Vincent Farraday had clearly downsized. Two of the rooms were filled with packing boxes, packed by a removals company: LIVING ROOM, KITCHEN, CHLOE'S ROOM, ROBIN'S ROOM.

Ren went into the kitchen, opened the drawers, got a knife, came back in, sliced open some of the boxes.

One of them was filled with bubble-wrapped posters behind glass and framed in black. She opened the first few. They were advertising appearances by VINCENT FARRADAY: COUNTRY STAR! in different venues across Texas. There were three photo albums wrapped in brown paper. Ren opened one of them and flicked through photos of a very handsome Vincent Farraday on stage, with his fans, at radio interviews, at press appearances. He had a big friendly smile, radiated warmth and happiness. She went through all the albums: the last one was a personal one, the most recent, and featured a clean and shiny Wanda Rawlins, their marriage, and soon afterwards, Chloe and Robin. They were pretty girls. And now they were gone.

Ren opened another box. It was filled with girly notebooks. *Journals?*

Ren picked one up and flicked through it. On the inside cover it said: *This Belongs to Chloe Farraday.*

She took all the notebooks that had Chloe Farraday's name inside.

Ren met with Joe in the kitchen.

'Could Duke Rawlins be looking for Wanda?' said Ren. 'Could he use Chloe Farraday for that? Like bait?'

'I don't know,' said Joe. 'I can't get a handle on this.'

'What we've got is this song that sounds like Chloe Farraday's life,' said Ren, 'and links her to Jane Doe and Carrie Longman.'

Vincent stirred in the chair as Ren and Joe came back in and sat down.

Joe leaned into him, spoke gently. 'Mr Farraday, have your daughters ever met Duke Rawlins?'

'Hell, no,' said Vincent. 'They don't even know he exists, they never knew Wanda's maiden name, none of that.'

Wanda Rawlins had the type of slate anyone would want to wipe clean: junkie hooker mom of a serial killer son.

46

Ren called Gary on the drive to the airport and filled him in.

'So,' said Ren, 'depending on the relationship – if there is any – between Duke Rawlins and Chloe Farraday, he could have access to an apartment in Denver owned by a man called Benny Jakes. Everett is checking that out.'

When Ren and Joe arrived at Dallas airport, they found out their flight was delayed. They sat in the airport lounge and ordered a round, and then another.

After another round, Joe was getting a little drunker than Ren.

You're on something else. Painkillers. Something.

Meds, meds, everywhere.

'I won't lie,' said Joe, leaning forward, 'but if I lay eyes on Duke Rawlins, I will kill him.'

Finally, he admits it. 'You won't,' said Ren.

Joe raised his eyebrows.

'You've a six-year-old daughter,' said Ren. 'You won't.'

Joe looked away, pressed his fingers into his jaw, like a doctor checking for pain.

'You know that if you kill him, you lose,' said Ren. 'I know you know that. However, you will win if he is jailed.' She paused. 'And ass-raped on a loop.'

Joe was momentarily quiet, then burst out laughing. 'I thought you were going to say something honorable. But "ass-raped on a loop" . . .' He nodded. 'I can get on board with that.'

Ren took her chance. 'Joe . . . could you please take Grace away from Denver, totally away, somewhere no one knows about, only you and Camille? I . . . didn't tell Gary, but I think Duke has targeted me. Someone close to me was in an accident and I think I was the intended target. Then how close he got to Karen Dettling. For you, I just don't think it's a risk worth taking.'

He didn't reply.

As they got steadily drunker, he got more maudlin.

'Anna dying in childbirth,' said Joe, 'which I didn't think was even possible these days . . . it was just so . . . shocking. Duke Rawlins had physically damaged her so badly, her body couldn't hold up . . . she had wounds to the kidney, the bowel. Scar tissue. I can't tell you the hell I would like to see that man go to. Grace saved my life. She saved my life. I was right there when she was born. As soon as I held her in my arms, I fell in love with the most perfect little human being I had ever seen.'

As your wife lay dying . . . Jesus Christ.

Joe laughed. 'Don't get me wrong, I love my son, but he's a young man now, he doesn't need me, and I screwed him up along the way. He's been through a lot. Everyone who comes near me goes through a lot.'

'You're carrying around way too much guilt,' said Ren. *Though I would be no different.*

'It's like on that one day, ten years ago, boom, shots fired,

Donald Riggs goes down and the course of my entire life was changed,' said Joe. He stared into her eyes. She could feel her heart rate accelerate.

Uh-oh.

'I've been watching you,' said Joe.

Uh-oh.

'I don't want you to be me.'

Phew. I won't be. Not a chance.

'You're thinking you won't be,' said Joe. 'I used to think the same when I looked around at the guys at work. I wouldn't be the divorced one, the drinking one, the lonely one, the bitter one, the cheating one, the damaged one. So . . . I didn't cheat, I didn't divorce. Where does that leave me? One of the lucky ones?' He paused. 'Do you have a good life?'

Um . . . 'Yes.'

'Do you have a good man in your life?' said Joe.

Pause. 'Yes.' *Why the pause?*

'Treasure it,' said Joe. 'Look after yourselves. It might not always be there.' He stood up. 'That's our flight.'

Ren watched him leave the bar.

Oh, God, I do not want to be you.

Joe slept through the entire flight. By the time they reached Denver, Ren wrote a text to Ben: This NYPD guy has sucked the lifeblood out of me.

She re-read it. *That's pretty shitty.* She deleted it. She sent a new one: I love you. We are lucky. XX

Now, let's not fuck it up.

And when I say 'us', I mean me.

Ben replied with a photo.

It was him sitting on her sofa with a beer. And: Surprise!

No waaay!

She replied: Can't make you out. Too many clothes in way.

47

Ben welcomed her straight to bed when she got home.

'You are too good,' she said afterwards. 'I almost can't handle it.'

It's overwhelming.

Ben laughed. 'I'm not sure you're old or obese enough to have a heart attack.'

'I'm not so sure.' *Why do I feel so overwhelmed?*

She rolled over on her side, out from under his arm and got up.

'Aren't you staying in bed?'

'Killers gonna kill . . .'

'A few hours won't make a difference . . .'

'You know lots of things, Ben Rader, but that, you do not.' She leaned down and kissed him. 'Grabbing my tits is only going to make this harder for both of us.' She paused. 'Don't even say it. Don't show that to me.'

Goddamn it.

Ren sat on the sofa with Chloe Farraday's notebooks open around her. They seemed to span her high school years, sophomore to senior, and one more after that. They were part-journal, part creative writing, part music manuscript. There were unsurprising threads of darkness through all of it, along with drawings of pretty girls, and pretty things.

I can relate.

Chloe was fervently anti-drugs, had been a leader in the Say No campaign, designed posters for it, given speeches.

'Hey,' said Ben, walking into the living room.

Ren glanced at the clock: *4 a.m.*

'You need to get some rest,' said Ben.

'I can't. I'm in the middle of this.' She paused, her hands resting on the open notebook.

'You won't be able to think straight if you don't rest,' said Ben.

'That's bullshit,' said Ren. 'You know that. And I'm thinking very straight.'

'Your sleep is all over the place—'

'It's not!'

'I'm not trying to interfere—'

'Yet, here you are . . .'

'Come on . . .' said Ben.

'OK, look, if I can just keep working here, then I'll be able to come to bed quicker—'

'It's four a.m.—'

'Who gives a fuck?'

'You need to look after your . . . health . . .'

She narrowed her eyes. '"Health"? I'm sitting here with eight notebooks to get through, trying to fucking absorb all this shit, trying to . . . to . . . I mean, fuck! This woman –' she stabbed the photo of Hope Coulson – 'delivered food to lonely fucking old people! And she gets raped and murdered! This woman was in her garden in the sunshine hanging out her fucking washing . . . No, fuck this, Ben. The world has gone to shit. It has gone to shit. And I'm trying to play my part in shoveling it off the side of the fucking earth, down into the burning center of hell, I don't care, where *ever*. The *idea* that the city is filled with potential victims is traumatizing me.'

'Ren, Ren, calm down,' said Ben. 'Calm down.'

I want to hurt you.

'You are not my shrink!' said Ren.

'Well, where *is* your shrink is what I want to know?' said Ben.

'Asleep – where else would he be? Or in a psychiatric unit helping people who *really* need help.' She paused. 'Why are you looking at me like that? What's your point?'

Ben sat down.

Why are you sitting down? Why are you breathing?

Ben looked pale. 'Ren . . .' he said, his tone gentle, '. . . do I have your permission to call Dr Lone?'

What the FUCK? 'Are you high? Are you out of your mind? Do you know what you'd sound like to him if you called him up about me? You'd sound like dictionary-definition first-world problem. You'd sound like a spoilt brat whose girlfriend is giving him a pain in his ass. Dr Lone would be like "I'm dealing with suicidal, psychotic, violent, sexually deviant crazy people and you're calling me about your FBI agent girlfriend? And you're an FBI agent yourself?" He'd be like: "Get a fucking grip!"'

'Ren . . .'

'I'm not having this conversation. I have work to do. And if you stand in the way of that—'

Ben walked quietly out of the room. Ren got up and walked after him.

'I can't stand this,' she said.

'I just want to go to bed,' said Ben.

'Well, I want to talk to you,' said Ren.

'I thought you wanted to work.'

'Well, you've ruined that now.'

'Ren, go back to work.'

'No! I want to talk about this.'

'It's late, I'm exhausted, so are you—'

'I can't deal with this,' said Ren. 'You monitoring me like this.'

'Well, go, then,' said Ben. 'Just go.'

'You don't think I'll leave?' said Ren. 'You never do! Men never think you're going to leave . . . until you do. And do you know what?' *Do not finish that sentence or you can never come back from it.*

'What?' said Ben.

I always do. I always leave.

'What?' said Ben. 'Finish that sentence.'

No way. 'Nothing,' said Ren. 'Nothing. I just want to work.'

'Yeah, go ahead. Stay healthy.'

'What the fuck is that supposed to mean?'

'Nothing. Nothing.'

'Grow the fuck up,' said Ren.

'I leave in the morning – I'd rather not leave like this.'

'OK, I'll come in and we can fuck, then I can get back to this.'

He hovered in the doorway. She turned around to him, waiting for an answer.

'How does that sound?' she said.

'I'm tired, I'm just going to go back to sleep. Maybe we can have breakfast together.'

'OK,' said Ren. *I'm an asshole.* 'Come here, give me a kiss before you go.'

The next morning, Ren made French toast, bacon, fruit salad, fresh juice and coffee. Ben arrived in the kitchen at seven a.m. Ren was flicking through another of Chloe's notebooks.

Don't mention sleep.

'Wow,' he said. 'This looks great.'

'So do you. And so did my refrigerator when I opened it.'

'Well, I know how it can get around here . . .' He kissed her. 'Did you get everything you wanted done?'

'Yes. I'm on the verge of something. It's like I have everything I need, I just need to put it all together. The answer is there.'

'The answer as to where you will find Duke Rawlins?'

'Why, *exactly*, is he here? Why now – at this point in time? He has his sights on Joe Lucchesi who's here for his son's graduation. But I don't think that's all there is to it.'

'You're sexy when you're thinking.' He smiled. 'See what I did there?'

'I'm always sexy! I like that. If it was true, then I'd be exactly like you.'

'Ha! Which one of us is going to throw up first?'

'Sorry about being cranky last night.' *You have no idea how much energy it takes for me not to explode.*

'You were just tired.'

I wasn't in the least bit tired. Jesus. Which part of not tired . . .
'Come on, let's go back to bed so we can send you home on a high.'

48

Ren sat in the Jeep at a red light with another of Chloe Farraday's notebooks open on the passenger seat beside her. She was flicking through it, and stopped when she came to a poster similar in style to one of Vincent Farraday's concert posters, but hand-drawn by Chloe – it was a crude self-portrait, framed with lights, but instead of the name Chloe Farraday on the bottom, she had signed it 'Dainty' in fancy, teenage cursive. Dainty – just one word.

Jonathan Briar . . . the girl . . . the threesome . . . her name was Day Something – not Daisy, but . . . Dainty.

Ren's cell phone rang. *My dear Everett.* 'Hey, there, Renaldino. How was TX?'

'It was XXL fun.'

'That was an L at the end, right?'

'Why, of course.'

'So, I was calling you to give you a lil sum-sum . . .'

'I think that's a euphemism for sex, but go ahead.'

'I followed up on your text on the roadie guy, and I have an address in Denver. I'm emailing it now.'

'Anything on him?'

'No priors, nothing shady. Respectable man, retired, sixty-eight years old, seems to spend his time in libraries and at readings, cultural stuff, music stuff, nothing weird.'

Ren checked Everett's email and drove to Benny Jakes' apartment building. She parked across the street, sat low in the seat watching people come and go. Every movement in her peripheral vision was making her twitch.

Not good.

She checked her watch. It was nine a.m. Not a good time to be watching for a girl who might sing in bars. She likely wouldn't surface until midday. Unless she had another job. Unless she was working as a nurse or a carer. Fifteen minutes later, the door to the apartment building opened.

Ren sat up. 'Yes.' She took a photo on her phone.

She got out of the Jeep, let Chloe walk down the street a short distance, and crossed to meet her.

'Chloe Farraday?' said Ren. 'Could I talk to you for a minute, please?'

'It's Dainty,' she said.

Nasty. Mean. Like yo' mama.

'And who are you?' said Dainty.

'I'm a friend of your father's,' said Ren. 'I'm sorry to be the one to tell you, but he's not a well man. He's got some money he'd like to pass along to you before he dies, before the lawyers get at it.'

Dainty looked left and right. She shrugged. 'What do I have to do?'

'First, I want you to know that there is someone else who is showing an interest in that money, and might like a piece of it. I'm wondering has he already approached you in any capacity? His name is Duke Rawlins.'

She showed Dainty the photo of Duke.

Dainty's face lit up. She started laughing. 'You're all confused. That's my boyfriend.'

The what now?

'Your boyfriend?' said Ren. 'Since when?'

'Like, two years.'

Oh. Fuck.

'And what has he told you his name is?' said Ren.

'Told me?' said Dainty. 'No. His name just is. It's Harris Riggs.'

Harris Hawks. Donald Riggs.

Jesus Christ.

49

What does this woman know about what Duke Rawlins has been doing? Or has she been operating as his accomplice in some way?

Fuck. I need backup.

'Dainty – is there somewhere we can sit down and have a chat?' said Ren. She looked around.

'There's a coffee shop on the corner?' said Dainty.

What about somewhere nice and out in the open? 'Why don't we go into that park over there, sit down at that picnic bench. It's a nice day.' *To tell someone they're sleeping with their half-brother.*

'Sure,' said Dainty, running her hand through her hair.

Little red dots in her elbow crease. Bruises on her arms.

Ren sat down opposite Dainty on the bench, and rested her forearms on the table.

'How did you meet . . . Harris?' said Ren.

'In a bar,' said Dainty. 'I was having a hard time. I wasn't in a good place, I guess. I liked to disappear into my music. I was singing one night, he came in, we got to talking.' She shrugged. 'We had a connection.'

'Dainty,' said Ren, 'I'm sorry to have to tell you that this man's real name is Duke Rawlins. His mother is Wanda Rawlins. His mother is your mother: Wanda.'

Dainty shook her head. 'What? You're saying Harris is what – my half-brother?' She laughed loud. 'No, he is not. Mama didn't have any other kids. Me and Robin were the only ones. You're talking shit. And I have no idea why.'

'This man's name is *not* Harris Riggs,' said Ren. 'It's Duke Rawlins. Does the name mean anything to you?'

Dainty shook her head again. 'No. How do you know my father?'

'He hired me to find you and Robin,' said Ren. 'I'm going to show you something to prove to you who Harris really is.' She took out her phone and called up the articles on Donnie Riggs from 2004. She turned the screen around to show Dainty.

'This is Donald Riggs,' said Ren. 'He came from Stinger's Creek, Texas. Your mother came from Stinger's Creek, Texas. You can ask your father. You can ask your father about Duke Rawlins.'

She found photos of Duke and showed them to Dainty. She watched her scan his face, add and remove the parts that were familiar to her.

Dainty Farraday started to shake. The color drained from her face. 'No,' she said. 'No. You got this all wrong. You got this all wrong. You are a crazy bitch.'

Dainty bent down, resting her forearms on her knees. She looked like she was trying to compose herself . . . or preparing to throw up. In a toss of blonde hair, she straightened up. With a knife in her hand. She jumped up and was suddenly beside Ren.

What the fuck?

Ren slid away from her and stood up.

Dainty lunged for her, swiping down hard.

Well, fuck you!

Ren deflected, throwing Dainty's arm back, sending the knife skittering across the grass.

Fuuuuck. Ren shook out her arm. *Fuck, that hurt.*

Dainty ran. Ren ran after her.

You bitch. You will not outrun me.

Ren ran.

Oh, the beautiful pain. The beautiful pain.

She was gaining on Dainty.

'Stop,' shouted Ren. 'Federal agent. Put your hands over your head—'

'Fuck you, lady,' said Dainty, still running. 'Fuck you.'

'Fuck YOU!' said Ren. *Don't take me on, bitch. Do not take me on.*

Ren accelerated. She could feel the pain searing in her calves, her hamstrings, her glutes.

She was within feet. She dived. She caught Dainty's legs, brought her down hard. Ren rolled, took the fall well, gripped the bony frame of Dainty Farraday.

But Dainty bucked, kicked her leg up, pulled another knife from her filthy white cowboy boot. She brought the blade down, aiming for Ren's forearm. Ren turned away and the knife went into the grass.

Two knives?! You psycho bitch!

She punched Dainty in the face. She punched her again.

Dainty kicked out, caught Ren's jaw. Ren grabbed her ankle, spun her away. She reached for her sidearm.

Oh, shit.

She looked up. She was looking at her sidearm. And Dainty Farraday was on the other side of it.

'You fucked-up bitch,' said Dainty. 'You haven't a clue what you're talking about.'

Ren nodded. 'You need to lower the weapon, Dainty. You need to drop it right now.'

Dainty stared at her.

What is going on in your junk-addled, brother-fucking mind?

'You haven't a clue, lady,' said Dainty.

Ren's heart was pounding.

'And that makes you lucky,' said Dainty. 'Wanna know why? Because I want to come back and look you in the eye, I want to come back, so I can tell you how you've got it all wrong. So I can make sure myself that you know that. I can look you right in the eye.'

Ren struggled to get up.

Dainty threw the gun at her and ran.

Ren went over and sat on the bench.

That family is like a brand: Rawlins Killings, Est. 19what-ever. Wanda Rawlins, face of the operation—

Oh. My. God.

Wanda Rawlins.

'I did a terrible thing. Something terrible brought me here.'

Vincent Farraday said Wanda Rawlins had a tattoo of Duke on her shoulder.

The Jane Doe . . . was Wanda Rawlins.

That night, when she was being brought to the hospital, she tried to burn her son's face off her shoulder because she knew it would connect them.

Duke Rawlins kept his own mother chained up, tortured and beaten.

50

Ren called the Douglas County Sheriff's Office on the drive to Safe Streets.

'Could I speak with Undersheriff Rodeal?' she said. 'It's Ren Bryce, Safe Streets.'

Rodeal came on the line. 'Hey, Ren.'

'Sorry, Cole – but what the FUCK?'

'Ren? Excuse me? I could say the same to you.'

'You were handling that Jane Doe in Sedalia,' said Ren. 'And you didn't run her DNA?'

'What?'

'She wasn't entered into the system, because if she was, she would have come up as a familial match with her son, Duke Fucking Rawlins. That was his mama, Rodeal. We could have had that connection.'

'Ren, you wouldn't have got the results back by now, even if I had run it.'

'I might have!' said Ren.

'Well, not judging by our current backlogs, no you would not.'

'Still! That's a pretty big thing to overlook.'

'Are you calling me to give me a talk on how to carry out my job, Agent?'

'No! I'm just mad.'

'Well, go be mad to someone else about it.'

'Thanks for taking my call.'

'Any time.'

Ren called Janine to tell her about what had happened with Dainty Farraday. She got her voicemail.

'Call me . . . I have crazy news about Chloe Farraday. She nearly killed me.'

Her phone rang. Gary.

Deep breath.

'Ren, just to let you know, I'm taking Karen to an appointment this morning. I'll be back in the afternoon.'

'No problem,' said Ren.

'Just tell everyone I'm—'

'No need to say another word,' said Ren. 'See you this afternoon.'

I hope Karen is OK.

When she got into Safe Streets, she held a briefing and, with Joe, went through everything they had found out in Texas, and the events of the morning with Dainty Farraday. Ren left out the part about Dainty taking her gun.

'We're issuing a BOLO for Chloe "Dainty" Farraday,' said Ren. 'She should be considered armed and dangerous. She is twenty-six years old, Caucasian, blonde hair, green eyes, one hundred pounds soaking wet. She speaks with a strong Texas accent. We have no recent photo of her. She is a screwed-up, lost-and-crazy-looking mess. I have no idea how she will react to what happened today . . . run *to* her man or run from him: love him more or strangle him with her bare hands. There is something feral about Dainty Farraday. She was once the privileged child of a successful father and born-again-Christian mother, whose life went to shit in a spectacular way when her mother got hooked on heroin again. And she's just found out she's been sleeping with her half-brother. She looked unhinged when I told her, but I'm not sure she looked particularly hinged from the get-go.

'She's been living in an apartment owned by a man called Benny Jakes, who apparently has no idea what's going on. We don't know exactly what Dainty Farraday knew about what Duke Rawlins has been doing – if she operated as his accomplice in some way. But when we showed Jonathan Briar her photo, he confirmed that she was the girl he and Hope Coulson had a threesome with. Everett emailed the photo to Manny's bar, and they've confirmed Dainty as one of the singers who had performed on the night that Carrie Longman was there. She sang that song; those are her lyrics. And, apparently, the song title was "Croon On, Motherfucker", and was about her father, so no love lost there. That poor man.

'We also need to be aware that, if she is Rawlins' accomplice, and she's drawn us her way, he is likely to dump her . . . i.e. kill her. She, however, probably has no clue that this is what lies ahead for her.'

Gary arrived in after lunch and called Ren into his office.

'I'm setting a world record here,' he said.

Oh, Jesus. Blind fury.

He slammed his hands onto the desk.

'Where do I start? This morning, heading to an apartment building alone . . .'

'But—'

'And, not only that, but ripping Rodeal a new one? Are you out of your mind?'

'So, let me get this straight,' said Ren. 'You called me in here to shout at me . . . for shouting at someone else because it's unprofessional.'

'I'm not shouting—'

'Yes, you are. Maybe I didn't think I was shouting either . . .'

'Ren, so help me God, if you turn one more admonishment around to make you the victim, I swear I will fire you right there and then.'

'Gary – Douglas County fucked up! They didn't run Wanda Rawlins' DNA through the system—'

'It wouldn't have mattered! You know that! Let it go. The lab wouldn't have processed it in time.'

'But still—'

He sat back in his chair, flung his pen across the room. 'Just . . . just . . .'

'Sorry, but that was unprofessional of *Rodeal* . . .'

Gary was struggling to maintain his composure.

'From the woman who had a knife pulled on her today?' said Gary. 'Jesus Christ.' He stood up. 'Do you know something? Do you know what's happened here? I've taken my eye off the ball and I have found myself riding the Ren Bryce rollercoaster again. It's a fucking nightmare ride! Get *out* of my office.'

Ren walked down the hallway, tears stinging her eyes. Everett walked toward her. They stopped.

'The shouting that time?' she said. 'That was for me.'

'Yikes,' said Everett. 'I couldn't hear what he said, but . . . I think I got the gist. You're up for Employee of the Month?'

Ren laughed and cried at the same time.

Everett squeezed her arm. 'Hang in there. Do what he wants. And don't go chasing skanks or serial killers or water-falls on your own, girlfriend. What has gotten into you?'

'Oh, you don't know me long enough – that's all.'

Ren went into the bullpen. 'Where's Janine?'

'Doesn't she have a day off?' said Everett.

'No – that was yesterday,' said Ren. 'She was going to hang out with her friend, Terri. Has Terri been on any nights out you were on?'

'No,' said Everett. 'Why?'

'She's just a little . . . like a secret friend. I don't know – it's weird.'

'It's probably just different friends from different worlds,' said Everett.

But what if it's something sinister? 'You know there's a killer out there . . .' She tried to laugh.

'Yes, and Janine has befriended her, of course . . .' said Everett.

Ren's heart started to pound. *Janine is tiny and breakable and Duke Rawlins' type. Without the blonde hair. But Carrie Longman was a brunette . . . Stop.*

She went into the conference room, called Janine, and got her voicemail again. 'Hey, now Gary is trying to kill me too. Call me.'

Ren went back in to Gary. 'Sorry to bother you again,' she said, 'but do you know the whereabouts of one Detective Janine Hooks?'

'No,' said Gary.

'But—'

'Text her,' said Gary.

'I have, and I've left her voicemails.'

'How long have you been trying to get a hold of her?'

'A few times . . .'

Gary looked up. 'I'm sorry, I don't have any more information for you.'

I have a really bad feeling about this. You will sound nuts if you say that out loud.

'Thanks!' said Ren. *Bright and breezy.*

Ren sat at her desk, and went through all the case files again. She started picturing the autopsy photos. And then Janine's face on her Wall of Horrors.

Her stomach turned.

Stop.

Janine's personal effects.

She tried Janine again, left a voicemail.

Do. Not. Panic.

Dainty Farraday's knife. Knives. Plural.

Stop.

Janine's memorial service.

Duke Rawlins' accomplices. He will have more. Multiple accomplices. Terri? Could she really be someone else? Dainty? The sister, Robin, back from London?

That's nuts.

But . . . what if it's not?

Work, go home, make dinner, relax. Jesus.

Janine – where are you?

Her heart started to pound.

51

Ren got back to the apartment after work, and went to the refrigerator. It was empty of food.

Shit. But who did I think would have filled it? I need a house-keeper. Or Ben to come back.

Where is Janine?

Her heart started to race again.

The cupboard: noodles, coconut milk, Thai green curry spice mix, vegetable stock cubes. Freezer: peas. Refrigerator door: lime juice from a bottle. I can work with that.

Janine! Why haven't you called me back?

Wall of Horrors.

Beer.

She opened a bottle of Coors Light, turned on the radio and started to cook.

She threw the dinner together.

It's missing about five ingredients.

I am so not hungry.

Where is Janine?

She turned on the television and watched an episode of *Friends*.

Where is MY friend?

She opened another beer.

I've tried her ten times now. No response. There is something very wrong.

I'll just call over. What's the worst that can happen? The embarrassment of the last time.

Ren jumped into the Jeep. She drove down I-70, listening to pounding music at full-volume, slowly increasing her speed to eighty-five miles an hour. Her back window filled with flashing blue lights.

Oh no you don't.

She hit the accelerator harder. The sirens struck up.

Fuck. Fuck. Fuck.

Ren pulled in. She rolled down the window. She took out her creds. As the cop walked toward her, she held it out the window.

'Officer, I'm SA Ren Bryce from Safe Streets. I'm on an urgent—'

The cop leaned in to the window. 'Ma'am, have been drinking?'

What the? 'No!'

'Ma'am, could you please step out of the vehicle.'

'Officer, this is a life-or-death situation here. I have to—'

'Ma'am—'

'No fucking way!' said Ren. 'My friend . . . my colleague is in very real danger. We're working on the serial killer investigation. I'm not fucking around here—'

'Ma'am, I can smell alcohol on your breath.'

'But I—' *Oh shit. Oh shit.* Her heart started to pound. 'Oh my God,' she said. 'I apologize, Officer. I had one and a half bottles of beer. I . . . I . . . forgot.' *How could I forget that?*

'One and a half,' said the officer.

'Yes, I swear to God,' said Ren. 'I was preparing dinner. I . . . I completely forgot. I don't usually do that. I . . .'

'If you're promising me that's all you had, I'm going to let you go. And I'm going to forget the attitude.'

'I really am sorry,' said Ren. Her hand was on the key in the ignition. 'My friend . . .'

The officer slapped the roof of the Jeep. 'Go ahead.'

'Thank you, thank you so much.' *I'm a fucking idiot.*

She put her foot to the floor.

She kept trying Janine's cell phone on the drive. It kept being off. Ren sped into the parking lot of Janine's building, punched in the code, ran up the stairs. She rang Janine's doorbell.

Please be here. Please be taking a nap. Or watching a box set. Or anything at all. Because nothing else matters as long as you're here.

Ren rang the doorbell.

Or somewhere safe. Anywhere. Don't be dead.

Ren rang the doorbell again.

OK. You're asleep.

Ren put her spare key in the door, opened it, walked in, listened, called out Janine's name, walked further in, called out Janine's name. She saw her cell phone on the table. She saw her wallet.

Oh. God. She's dead.

Jesus . . . she's gone for a walk.

Ren could feel her legs shaking. She sat down on Janine's beautiful cozy sofa.

This is not good. I know this is not good. But I often think things are not good when they're perfectly fine. I hate this. What am I supposed to think?

She stood up.

Janine is in danger. I just know she is. I can feel it in my heart.

She went into Janine's bedroom, pristine as always, smelling of beautiful smells. She went into the bathroom, the same. She went into the kitchen, she opened the fridge.

Salad, apples, salad, apples. Why don't you look after yourself? Eat! Be strong! Be able to fight back more! Where are you?

Ren went back into the living room and sat down. She called Robbie.

'Robbie, have you heard from Janine?'

'No,' said Robbie. 'Should I have?'

'I wish you had,' said Ren. 'She's not here . . . I'm at her apartment. Her cell phone's here, her wallet . . .'

'Are you worried?' said Robbie.

She could hear him shifting in his chair.

You'll sound like a lunatic. Who cares? It's Robbie. 'Yes. I'm really worried. I have a bad feeling.'

'Why?'

'I just do,' said Ren.

Silence. 'She's probably gone for a walk,' said Robbie. 'Maybe she's gone to Woody's for pizza, just didn't want to be disturbed.'

They shared a small silence at the unlikelihood Janine would leave her phone behind.

'Maybe,' said Ren. 'I'll go check. Thanks.'

'I mean, is there something else going on?' said Robbie. 'Are you worried about her state of mind? She's looking a little gaunt.'

Now he notices! 'No, no – she's fine. Just let me know if she calls.' Ren stood up. She looked at Janine's phone.

Ooh, last dialed calls.

She turned on the phone. The caller list was cleared.

Hmmm.

Ren scrolled through her contacts.

I feel dirty.

Terri! She might know. Ren dialed the number. It beeped like a discontinued number.

No! Terri! Something is wrong. She's not who Janine thinks she is.

52

Ren left Janine's apartment and locked the door behind her. She drove to Woody's and parked outside.

Why am I even doing this? I know she's not here.

She sucked in a breath, suddenly overwhelmed by Janine's cell phone in her hand, a rock-solid reminder that she was unable to do anything to locate her. Cell phones were strange objects – turned off, left behind, diverted . . . they stripped people of power in a way a regular phone never had. Everyone had their cell phone with them.

Didn't they?

Where are you?

Ren sat at a table in Woody's.

What am I supposed to do now? Maybe I'm losing it. She's probably fine.

A cheery server came over to Ren.

'Hey, there. What can I get you?' she said.

I might as well eat. I'm here now. 'Just an order of Jalapeño poppers and a Coke. Thank you.'

'You bet.'

Ren scrolled again through Janine's phone.

I'm not reading the texts – that's wrong. But, then . . . they could explain a sudden absence, the fleeing, the leaving shit behind.

There were epic text exchanges between Ren and Janine . . . they were the bulk of the texts. There were more to different people. But none to Terri.

Weird. Unless Janine was protecting her privacy. Unless she was just deleting sensitive exchanges. But then, she hadn't wiped the sensitive exchanges with me. And we're closer.

Maybe Terri was having some kind of problems.

Privacy! The Privacy of Lunatics Act. Eating disorder! Maybe she met Terri at a support group. That's why it seemed so covert.

Ren looked at her contact details. Terri's address was there – under her first name only – ten minutes away.

Oh, thank God. I'll do a drive-by, if I see Janine there, I'll keep going.

Ren got up to leave and met the server walking towards her with her orders. She slapped fifteen dollars on the tray, took the Coke, said thank you and left.

Ren pulled into Terri's street. It was quiet, lined with ranch houses in various states of disrepair. Terri's was one of the better ones, nothing dazzling, nothing shabby. There was no car outside. Ren went up the path. She rang the doorbell.

What the hell do I say if she comes to the door?

There was no answer. She looked in the small window. Her stomach sank.

This house does not look lived in. Nothing on the walls. Nothing under the stairs. She could see down the hallway that there was nothing on the kitchen counter.

Ren ran to the living-room window.

Oh shit. Oh fuck.

It was entirely empty. There was absolutely nothing in the room.

Terri no longer lives at this address. She may never have.

She's Duke Rawlins' accomplice. She's Dainty Farraday. Or her sister. Or someone else entirely. Oh. My. God. Janine doesn't know I found Dainty today. Janine has never seen the Farraday twins' photos. Not the recent ones.

Ren ran to the neighbor's house. She hammered on the screen door, held up her creds. A woman in her thirties came to the door, tentatively. She studied the badge. She opened up.

'Yes,' she said.

'I'm Special Agent Ren Bryce from Denver Safe Streets. I want to ask you about the woman next door . . . Terri . . .' She paused. 'I don't know her last name.' *I have no fucking idea. Jesus Christ.*

The woman looked surprised. 'No one lives next door. Not for at least two years.'

Everything in Ren's body felt like it was plunging, melting, breaking, shattering.

'Terri . . . ?' said Ren. 'There's definitely not a Terri next door. Are you sure?'

'Yes,' said the woman. 'They've been trying to rent it for a while, though the sign's been down for the past three months, so maybe someone was planning to move in. I don't know.'

Ren's heart was pounding.

The targets are Gary. And me. The fallout is Karen Dettling for him . . . and Janine for me. Ben is too far away.

No. No. No. No. No. No.

Oh, God. Carly Raine – Golden. Maybe Rawlins was really there for Janine.

She called Gary. His phone was diverted.

What is wrong with everyone? Where are you all?

Think, Ren. Where could Janine be? At the store. At a bar. Being killed. Support group! At a support group! Tonight is Wednesday! That was the night I called to the house when Terri was there!

Ren Googled eating disorder support groups in the area and found only one that met on Wednesdays in a community hall in Evergreen, a twenty-five-minute drive from Golden.

But wouldn't Janine have brought her phone?

And is it ridiculous for me to drive all that way?

The meeting was ending as Ren arrived.

Have I missed Janine? Did she go with Terri, get a ride back with her?

Ren waited until everyone left before going into the room. A woman was tidying up some pamphlets on the table at the back. Ren knew from the web page that she was Megan Knight, the support group supervisor.

'Megan Knight?' said Ren.

'Yes,' she said. 'I'm afraid you're a little late for the meeting.'

Stop eyeing me that way.

Ren held up her badge. 'Actually, I'm here about another matter.'

'Oh,' said Megan, her eyes wide.

'Don't worry – I understand you have to protect people's privacy, but I'm trying to find this woman.' She showed Megan the photo of Janine.

'Yes – I've seen her,' said Megan. 'She's been coming over the last – I want to say – three months?'

Good for you, Janine. But I'm stung you didn't tell me.

'She never speaks,' said Megan, 'but we don't like to put

300

people under pressure. They've shown up, that's a positive step we don't want to undo.'

'She's a very private person,' said Ren. 'Megan, I believe she made a friend there – a woman called Terri?'

Megan nodded. 'Yes, there's a Terri who comes here. She often talks about her dogs, how much she loves her dogs.'

Shit . . . that would totally suck Janine in. 'Did she ever mention where she lived?' said Ren. 'She told Janine that she lived in Golden, but I don't think that's true.'

'Really?' said Megan. 'Why would she lie?'

Because she's a killer. Or a killer's accomplice. 'I don't know,' said Ren. 'Is there anything you can think of that might help?'

'The nature of what we do allows for so much secrecy,' said Megan, 'I'm not sure how useful I can be. Let me rack my brains . . .'

'Were they here tonight?' said Ren.

'No,' said Megan, 'which was a little strange, because Terri was planning to speak again tonight.'

Oh, shit . . . why would she not show?

'What does she look like?' said Ren.

Oh! The Farraday girls' photo!

Ren showed Megan the photo of Robin Farraday. 'Is that her?' said Ren. 'Or if you could maybe imagine that face thinner, with different hair?'

Megan shook her head. 'No – Terri looks nothing like that. She's a little heavier . . . she would have auburn hair, smaller eyes, and a wider nose. Definitely not this lady.'

Thank God.

But I know this is temporary relief. Because Duke Rawlins has all kinds of accomplices.

I feel so sick.

* * *

Ren drove back toward Golden. She tried Gary's phones three times. Eventually, she left a message.

'Gary, answer my fucking calls! I'm not fucking around here. Where the fuck are you? This is serious shit. Janine has dropped off the face of the earth. I'm worried about her. Call me!'

I need to fucking talk to people! Where are my people?

Ren drove back to the address Terri had given Janine. Maybe she could check the mailbox, take a walk around the back this time, see was there anything there that would reveal anything.

Ren's mobile started to ring. She looked down.

Robbie.

'Did you find her?' said Ren.

'No,' said Robbie. 'I was just calling to see, did you?'

'No!' said Ren. 'I'm really worried. I—'

'You sound it,' said Robbie.

'I'm concerned her new friend is someone Duke Rawlins sucked in,' said Ren. 'I think . . .' She started crying. 'Her name is Terri . . .'

'Ren, Ren, calm down,' said Robbie. 'I'm sure it's all very innocent.'

'Are you?' said Ren, wiping her eyes. 'Are you? I can't handle this.' *I can't breathe.* 'What if this is Colin Grabien and he knows—'

'What is this Colin Grabien thing?' said Robbie. His tone was gentle. 'Colin Grabien is right now being an idiot in Vegas. Someone emailed me a screen grab of one of his Facebook posts. OK? Does that help?'

Jesus. Thanks, Robbie. 'Yes, yes, it does.'

I am losing my mind.

'Oh my God!' said Ren. 'There's a car pulling up! I gotta go—'

'Pulling up where?' said Robbie. 'Where are you?'

'I'm outside . . . I'm . . .' *Don't tell him.* 'I'm—' *I can't breathe.* 'Oh my God! It's Janine! She's fine. She's alive!'

'Well, good to know. Are you OK now?'

'Yes!' said Ren. 'Yes!' She ended the call. She slid down in the seat and watched as Janine and Terri got out of Terri's car and took out bags from Bed, Bath & Beyond, and carried them up to the front door.

Of Terri's new rental, obviously. Stupid fucking neighbor not knowing that. Scaring the shit out of me.

Ren collapsed into tears.

I'm so tired.

When Janine and Terri had gone inside, Ren drove away, went back to Janine's apartment and returned her phone.

Jesus Christ.

How can the pieces add up so perfectly to create the wrong answer?

53

Dainty Farraday was lying naked on the messed-up mattress. It was a raw nakedness, rough and careless, with nothing sensual about it, no attempt to be sensual. She had just taken a hit and was limp and dozy. Lights streamed through the high windows above her, making bright squares on her flesh and across the mattress.

Duke walked in and lay on the next mattress along, on his back, arms behind his head, legs crossed at the ankles.

He didn't like it when she stayed here. But the Feds had descended on Benny's apartment. There would be no going back there. Duke knew there was nothing of him in that place – he had never been there. But Dainty . . . Dainty was a powerful link.

'Dainty, get on over here,' said Duke.

She smiled her junkie smile. He knew that smile. He'd seen it a hundred times before. She was the daughter of an addict; he was the son of an addict. He went one way – drank in moderation, she went the other – down her mama's junkie path. That suited him, though, that suited him down to the dirty ground. He was the one who guided her along it.

'Dainty,' he called. 'Dainty lady. I'm waiting for you.' He didn't tell her about the pills he took to get him hard, she could be real mocking, like her bitch mama. 'This is your fault,' he called, pointing to his crotch. 'You need to take care of a man. Look at what you're doing to me. I'm waiting.' He took off his jeans. He took everything off.

Dainty turned toward him. Her smile was mocking. He looked down at his erection, back up at her.

She blinked a few times.

Fuck you, you junkie bitch.

She reached out her arm, rolled to the edge of the bed and picked up her guitar. She slid it toward herself, sat up against the wall and began to play, began to sing.

You have a beautiful voice. Such a beautiful voice.

He closed his eyes. *Nothing like your mama's.*

'That's real beautiful, Dainty,' he said. 'But I need you to take care of this!' he said.

Or I'm gonna come over and stuff it in your face. I'm gonna pry open your jaws and choke you with it.

Instead, she started a new song. A four-chord song. 'It's a new one,' she said. 'Here goes: found his pills inside his pants, pops them so he's got a chance, swore he'd never love another, he ain't Harry, he's my brother.'

She ended on a flourish, broke out in a cackling laugh. 'Harris – Harry! That was funny. You gotta admit that was funny.'

Oh, you dumb bitch. You dumb, dumb bitch.

Then she broke down and cried, and her guitar fell to the floor with a bang and the dull sound of tuneless strings.

Hours later, Dainty drifted out of her terrible sleep. She could feel water pouring down on her.

It wasn't water. He was standing over her.

'What are you doing?' she said. 'Oh my God!'

She tried to roll out from under the flow, and it was then her body erupted in pain. She screamed. All the realizations happened at once: she was naked, she was cold, she was wet, terribly wounded, she was bleeding.

'No,' she moaned, 'no, no, no, no.'

And there are no drugs to numb you now.

She started shivering violently.

He was laughing as he zipped up his fly. He raised his foot and kicked her hard.

She howled in pain, howled again.

'Get up,' he said.

'What are you doing?' she said. Her words were slurred, but edging into hysteria. 'Why are you doing this to me? What have I ever done to you? I'm going to be one of your victims now? We're family . . .'

'Run, rabbit, run,' he said.

She whimpered. 'I can't. I'm—'

He grabbed her by the arm and yanked her up off the ground. Her legs buckled underneath her. He tried to steady her. They buckled again.

'No!' she sobbed. 'No. Just look at me. Look at me. No.' She tried to control her sobs. 'Please don't, please. I love you. You know I do. I love you, Harris! I love you.'

Duke stared at her. 'People like us . . . we don't know what love is.'

54

Ren called in sick the next day. She had barely slept, and spent most of the day laying on the sofa, staring at the Wall of Horrors. She tried to stop, tried to watch a box set, tried to do anything to take her mind off her mind.

I am jumping out of my skin.

Her cell phone rang. Janine.

Can't face her. It's the phone – no faces. Still.

She let it go to voicemail, then listened to the message.

'Hey, there – heard you're sick. Hope you're feeling better. If you need anything, let me know. Oh, and you're invited to dinner at Terri's – she's just moved into a new place. She'd love to meet you! OK . . . call me. Hope you're cozy.'

She put down the phone and it rang immediately.

Glenn Buddy.

I can't face him.

Don't want to talk to anyone.

I can't imagine speaking, having that energy.

The world is fucked up.

The world is fucking me up.

She let the call go to voicemail.

I don't even have the energy to listen.

Curiosity killed the cat.

She checked the message.

'Ren, I'm calling with some good news. We got the guy – the hit-and-run of your friend on Mardyke Street: two young kids on a joy ride: not the Big Bad Wolf. So, no one is out to get you.' He ended with his big laugh.

I'm crazier than the alien Sedalia lady.

Ren ignored food and calls for the rest of the day, then wandered into her bedroom, sat on the bed, and picked up a novel she had started four times before. It was great, but it all felt too trivial. Bigger things were happening out there. There were bigger things to think of. She stared at her toenails – perfectly manicured in blood red. And she thought about female victims on autopsy tables, their lives cut short in all states of grooming and how one could be preserved forever, toenails in need of a pedicure, bikini line needing a wax.

There's a shitty motivation not to let yourself go.

The intercom buzzer rang. Ren went over, checked the screen.

Joe Lucchesi. What the what now?

'Ren? Hi – sorry to call over like this – I know you're sick. I just wanted to go through a few things. I hope I'm not crossing a line.'

Of course you're crossing a fucking line.

'Not at all,' said Ren. 'Come on up.' *Draw me to sane considerations.*

She went over and pulled the curtain across the Wall of Horrors.

I need to keep him contained in the micro-kitchen.

* * *

Joe Lucchesi looked ridiculous in the kitchen. Ren had no choice but to bring him into the living room, so they could both breathe and not look like they were in *Gulliver's Travels*.

They talked through the case, but something about the conversation felt forced; the lapses into silence, the awkward pauses, the strands they struggled to politely disagree on.

He has an agenda. I'm going to leave him so he can work himself up to getting to the point.

'Can I get you more coffee?' said Ren.

'That would be great, thanks.'

She went into the kitchen, made coffee, and came back in five minutes later. Joe was standing, with the curtain pulled all the way back, looking at the wall. He turned around.

Whoa. Barely restrained fury.

You heard about the Wall of Horrors! That's why you're here! Violation!

'Why haven't you told me some of this shit?' said Joe. His eyes were ablaze.

'This is my home,' said Ren. 'That was private.' *Fuck you, asshole.*

'This is my life!' said Joe. 'This is a picture of my . . . wife, for God's sake.'

'I know,' said Ren. 'You have to understand this is . . . not for anyone else but me. That's why it's at home. I'm respecting your privacy, and my own. I'm putting stuff together; I'm not sure how some of these elements are connected or even if they are.'

'There's stuff up here that isn't at Safe Streets,' said Joe.

Yes. My crazier ideas.

'Why is Grace's name up here?' said Joe.

'Because . . .' *I'm worried. I think she's part of this. She's a target . . . I don't know. I can't alarm you.*

'And Shaun's!' said Joe.

'Their names are there because your family has been targeted before,' said Ren. 'And, obviously, Gary's wife has been. Karen is up there too. This is not just about you. I'm up there myself, minus a photo. It's about so many people. Victims . . .'

'Why is there a question mark beside Grace's name?'

'A question mark – exactly. Because I don't have enough information. I don't know. I didn't want to come to you with something I don't know.'

'Is there something you want to tell me?' said Joe. 'Something I don't know? Is Grace safe?'

'Tell me again,' said Ren, 'Grace is seven or eight on her next birthday?'

'Seven.'

Ren nodded. 'That's good to hear. I had been wondering if her age was significant in terms of Rawlins wanting to hurt her, maybe, at the same age of that girl that Donald Riggs kidnapped the day you shot her – but she was eight years old.'

Joe sat down.

Exhausted and wired, just like me.

They sat in silence for a while.

'Is there anything else?' said Joe. He was studying the wall. 'Who's Devin?'

'She's my dog walker, a student from across the street from where I used to live. She's been taking care of my dog, Misty. Devin was victim of a hit-and-run . . . she was dressed in my jacket. I was worried it was a case of mistaken identity. But I just got a call from DPD . . . they got the two kids involved – it was a regular hit-and-run. And yes, they're a regular occurrence around here.'

'Anything else about all this you want to talk to me about, any ideas you want to bounce off me?' said Joe, calming somewhat.

'To be honest, I'm tired looking at it,' said Ren. 'It's all I think about.'

Joe stood up. He looked at his watch. 'In that case, come on . . . let me buy you a drink. It's the least I could do for intruding. There's a great bar around the corner from my hotel. Smallest bar I've ever been in.'

'As long as the measures are big.'

The bar was minuscule, styled like a gentleman's club, august, austere, its atmosphere ruffled by Joe Lucchesi and Ren Bryce drinking and laughing for four hours' straight. They ordered a final drink.

'OK,' said Joe. 'It's time for me to 'fess up.'

I am now nervous. And having a slight spike of sobriety. Annnd it's gone.

'I probably should have said this sooner,' said Joe, 'but I didn't want to make you uncomfortable.'

'Is there a reason why you want to make me uncomfortable now?'

He laughed. 'Well, I think you'll handle it. I don't think there are a lot of things you can't handle.'

LOL.

His face went a little serious. 'Just . . . there's something about you that reminds me of my wife . . .'

Did NOT see that coming. And I have been looking at her photo for days.

'Oh,' said Ren. *Annnd now it all makes sense.* 'Wow. I don't know what to say to that.' *Dead-wife stuff is a minefield.*

'I'm sorry if that made me treat you any differently,' said Joe. 'It kind of freaked me out. And I think Shaun had the same reaction when he saw you – he came off as a bit rude. I'm sure you saw that. He's not. Anna was slim like you, a little shorter maybe, but similar coloring, she had that . . .

311

edge . . .' He laughed. 'But it was more "French" – fiery in a moody way. You – there's something dangerous about you. Like, it's what you're looking out for. Anna wasn't. But she got it – the world at its worst. Because of me.'

'You can't keep blaming yourself . . .' said Ren.

Joe shrugged.

But you don't know any other way to live.

'Have you been to therapy?' said Ren. 'I ask with zero expectation of a positive response.'

Joe laughed. 'Correct. No, I have not.'

'Don't underestimate it,' said Ren. *Look how amazing I've turned out!*

'It's not going to happen,' said Joe. 'Not now. I'm good. I've got the kids. Grace saved my life.'

I know. You told me. We all have stories. This is your 'story'. But I'm guessing you don't get a chance to tell it all that often. And you probably need to.

'I literally don't know what I would have done without her,' said Joe. 'But I would bet that I wouldn't have made it. I will never forget when she was born and she was whisked off to one side, and Anna was in such distress, and Grace wasn't breathing, and I was there and it was fucking terrifying. It was like . . . I can't describe it. Next thing, I hear Grace crying, and the relief, I can't express it. But then, Anna . . . Anna was gone, just like that. The alarms were going off, left and right, I was pushed out of the room, and they were working on Anna. It was like . . . like her last breaths . . . went to Grace. That's what the timing was like. It fucked with my head for a long time. I couldn't get it out of my mind. But when they handed me Grace . . . I . . . I was blown away. She was this perfect, beautiful little thing. And, that was that, she got my heart. Right there. I was gone. She was mine, I was hers.'

My mascara. More details this time.

They descended into silence.

'I don't think I've ever told a woman that story before,' said Joe.

Ren wiped away tears. 'Jesus . . . maybe don't. I mean . . .' *if I was on a date with you, I'd be so outta there.*

'I know, heavy stuff,' said Joe. 'You're easy to talk to, I guess.' He took a breath. 'The graduation . . . isn't the only reason I brought Grace; we have a doctor's appointment. For test results. Well, he's a pediatric gastroenterologist, the best in the country. Grace hadn't been gaining weight for the past few months. We're not sure why. I . . . I can't bear to imagine . . .'

Jesus Christ. 'Don't imagine,' said Ren. 'I know that's probably impossible, but wait and see. Worrying won't help anyone. Grace looks like a very healthy little girl – this could be a temporary thing, a food allergy, I don't know.'

Joe nodded. 'That's what I keep telling myself.'

She put her hand on his arm.

Possibly inappropriate.

'Sorry I was an asshole to you . . .' said Joe.

'You were fine.'

He laughed. 'You thought I was an asshole.'

'Maybe. But I don't any more.' *Which is a total disaster. Because now I'm back to finding you as attractive as when I first saw you at the airport.*

Go home, Ren. Go home. This would be a good time to go home.

55

Duke Rawlins sat at the bar of the Maker Hotel, in the final flat and yellowing stages of a pint of Guinness. He rubbed his jaw – the side without the scar, which he had covered with hair sprayed from a can of tiny fake hairs. They wouldn't last long, but from a reasonable distance you could never tell. He still had the shaved head – that was a good look, that wasn't in the picture that was released to the public. He had walked by his face on newsstands everywhere. It was an old face. No one had done a double take yet.

Duke watched as Joe Lucchesi walked into the lobby, loose-limbed, unsteady on his feet, searching his pockets for his key card. There was a woman behind him, dressed in black, slim, laughing. She turned toward the darkness of the bar. Duke felt his heart pound wildly – it was like the first time he saw her run down the steps to her Jeep outside Safe Streets, how it was like seeing a ghost. Or close enough. She was a little taller than Anna Lucchesi, but if he got her on all fours that wouldn't matter. And if it was from behind, with her dark hair yanked back, balled into his fist, she could easily pass for Anna Lucchesi. Anna Lucchesi had had a powerful effect on him.

Ren Bryce! Bipolar support drinking buddy!

Right now, this special agent was leaning in to Joe Lucchesi, he was leaning into her. *Two birds, one stone!*

Joe was guiding her to the elevators, his hand on her lower back. Something was going on with these two. They were close. And this one was wild. He'd seen her drink. He'd seen her run into that burning barn. He'd seen her discharge her weapon, over and over. She was something different.

He laughed. There were so many ways to hurt Joe Lucchesi.

This time, he would make him watch.

56

Joe opened the door of the hotel room, slid the key card into the wall slot. Ren followed him in.

'Drink?' said Joe.

'Yes, please.' *Go home now.*

Joe crouched down and opened the mini-bar. 'What do you like?'

'Champagne. It's love more than like.' *But champagne's not very appropriate, is it? Jesus, relax. It's a drink. What's the worst that can happen? Ben finds a cork in my bag. That's not the worst. You know that. Stop. Leave now. This is dangerous. Don't be ridiculous. You'd never cheat on Ben. Again. That doesn't count. What does count? You'd kill Ben if he did this. I would. Go. No. It's just a drink.*

Joe had already popped the cork. 'Champagne it is!' he said. He poured them both a glass. They raised them, clinked them.

'It's a beautiful room,' said Ren.

'Well, let's just say I have a very wealthy father who insisted, because of the shitshow that is my life, on giving me a huge chunk of my inheritance so I wouldn't have to be "hanging around, waiting for him to die". That's his sense of humor. I fought against his money for years, and then, I just gave in. More for Grace than me. I make sure she appreciates every bit of it, that's for sure.'

'And just so we're clear, I'm appreciating this room a lot. And I think I used your father's approach on Dainty Farraday . . .'

She sat against the dressing table, then slid up on top of it. Joe was sitting on the table opposite her, a little to the right. The bed was a vast, ignored space, ahead of her.

They finished the bottle, swapping war stories, laughing. Joe went to the mini-bar and pulled out two vodkas and tonics.

Don't come near me.

He walked over to her, stood in front of her, but instead of handing her the drink, he didn't move. His thighs were touching against her legs. He looked into her eyes. She could barely focus on them.

You are a sexy man's man. I am weakened by sexy men's men. Man's men? Men. All men.

Joe put the drinks onto the dressing table. With his right hand, he reached out, sliding it behind her neck, lifting up her hair, leaning down to kiss her neck all the way up to her mouth.

Neck first, nice move. Very nice. I want you. But I may not mean it.

Joe pulled her toward him.

'OK . . . wait,' said Ren. 'This . . . isn't right. We shouldn't be doing this.'

'Come on,' said Joe, 'Why not?'

Where do I start? 'I have a boyfriend. I—'

Joe looked at her.

Ren laughed. 'You need a better reason, obviously.' *How about: I remind you of your dead wife?*

Joe retreated, sat on the bed. 'Well, I guess telling you that you reminded me of Anna wasn't a smooth move.'

'I'm guessing at that point neither of us thought we'd wind up back here.' She sat down beside him.

'True,' said Joe.

'So let's just keep drinking,' said Ren. She raised her glass, and stood back up again.

FUCK, my head is spinning.

Five hours later, Ren woke up on her back, her jaw tight, her fists clenched. The room was in darkness. A crack of sunlight shone through the curtains, slicing down across the floor.

Where the effin' crap . . .

She raised her head. *Oh dear God, never do that again. Never be part of such a miserable cliché.*

I am topless.

Who the fuck is beside me now?

It was Ben the last time. Let it be Ben.

I am only naked on top. Which tells me nothing. What did I do? Topless equals already a cheater.

It's surfacing. The night is surfacing. Noooooo! You loser. HOW can you do this? AGAIN! Jesus Christ. You need help.

Beside her, Joe Lucchesi slept soundly.

What the fuck happened to his mouth?

His hands on my . . . his mouth. Did I bite him? Jesus.

Oh, oh. No. She reached her fingers to her head. Ouch. Shit.

I need water. I need to check my wound. How come I have a wound? Run. Run for the bathroom. Warning: you will meet your own shabby face. And blood.

She checked her face in the mirror. *You are frightening.*

The cut was small, but quite deep, crescent-shaped, above her right eyebrow.

Errant tweezers it is . . .

She went to the toilet like she was playing the silence game. She washed her hands, dipped a facecloth in water and dabbed at the mascara under her eyes, then rubbed, then just abandoned the whole ridiculous enterprise.

She was about to walk out of the bathroom, when she heard the buzz of Joe's phone on the nightstand.

He's awake. Great. Go out, have a conversation: you, him, nothing to stand between you but your tits.

She walked out. 'Hey.'

'Morning,' said Joe. He smiled wide. 'Ow.' He touched his fingers to his mouth.

Ren smiled back. *Does any man give a shit if a woman has a boyfriend? Do they all just go for it at all times?*

I remember! We didn't have sex! We didn't even kiss! I am not a cheater! Woo-hoo!

'Can I ask,' said Ren, 'what the fuck happened to your lip and my head?'

Joe laughed, then held his mouth again. 'Ow. It was my fault. We were fooling about, I threw you down on the bed, I was getting down there beside you, but you're so light, you bounced back up and your forehead caught me in the mouth.'

They both burst out laughing. 'How old are we exactly?' said Ren.

Oh, God. More is coming back. I told him I loved my boyfriend. To be filed under: Things You Say To Widowed Colleagues While You Are Near-Naked. Widowered?

'Sorry about last night,' said Ren, bending down to pick her bra up off the floor, putting it on as Joe kindly looked the other way. 'Staying in your room and everything. I should have gone home.'

'I'm the one who should apologize,' he said.

'No reason to.' *Let's end this conversation.* Ren went around the room, picking up her clothes, getting dressed.

For ONCE can I just discard my clothing in one tidy, less demeaning pile? Or maybe I could stay CLOTHED.

57

Ren got a text from Ben as she sat down at her desk: **Morning, baby. Miss that hot body. XX**

Hot: no. Ice-cold. And in another man's bed. Jesus. Christ. If the tables were turned.

'Get in a fight last night?' said Everett.

'No,' said Ren, looking up. *Alarmed.*

Everett laughed. 'Not you – you,' he said, gesturing to Joe.

'No,' said Joe.

End of snapped explanation.

'Ren, you must have stayed out late,' said Everett. 'I see pineapple juice.'

'Aren't you the observant one?' said Joe.

Leave my Everett alone. Are you in a bad humor because of me, Joe Lucchesi?

Ren's phone rang.

'It's Gary – come into my office.'

This has *to be some kind of joke.* 'Now?' said Ren.

Gary put the phone down.

She went into his office and sat down.

'Ren, I don't believe you are taking your meds.'

Oh. Shit. But why do you think that?

'Well, I am.'

He stared her down. 'You're showing signs of—'

'With the greatest respect, you have had a lot going on,' said Ren at the same time.

That did not go down well.

'All I can say to that is remember what I take are mood *stabilizers*,' said Ren. 'They *stabilize* my mood, they don't strip me of all vitality.'

'I'm not saying you're showing signs of vitality,' said Gary. 'I'm saying you're showing signs of mania.'

'I am not manic.'

He studied her face. 'I'm sorry, Ren. I don't believe you.'

I want to hurt you. It's an extreme and terrifying urge. But I mean it. If you want to strap me down and medicate me, you go ahead. But you'll be saying goodbye to a serial killer if you do. You need me like this. You need me focused.

'I need you focused,' said Gary. 'And I don't think you are. You are case agent on a huge case – a position of trust that I put you in when . . .'

'When what?'

'Don't fuck up.'

'I won't. Please, Gary, stop asking me about meds. Let me do my job. Have I fucked up on this yet? No. And I promise, if I come riding through the office naked on a white horse, waving a bottle of vodka in the air, feel free to shoot me with a tranq gun. Just mind the horse.'

Gary stared at her.

Unreadable.

By one o'clock, Ren was sitting in Dr Lone's office.

'I'm sorry for being sprung on you like this,' she said. 'I . . . Gary just called me in again, told me "Boom, you're going to see Dr Lone at one p.m." Just like that – no warning.'

'He must be concerned for you,' said Lone. 'Do you have any idea why?'

No meds talk. You don't have the energy to lie convincingly.

'No,' said Ren, 'in that there is no problem, but Gary, *I would venture*, thinks I'm a little paranoid.'

Lone nodded. 'Why do you think that?'

EVERYONE IS ASKING ME WHY EVERYTHING. 'Because I guess I've jumped . . . come to a conclusion or two that was . . . incorrect and, I guess . . . worst-case-scenario.'

'That can happen,' said Lone.

'I know!' said Ren. 'That's what I think!'

'Can you go through the incidents he's talking about it?'

Ren talked him through Devin and Janine. *Does Grace Lucchesi count?*

'So,' said Lone, 'there were several times when you thought you were being targeted, and those closest to you, personally or professionally or both, were being targeted too.'

'Yes,' said Ren. 'The evidence pointed to that.'

'Sometimes, things can come together to create a picture that, combined with our personal perspective, our filter—'

Yeah, yeah, yeah, I get it. 'But there was compelling evidence . . .' *Wasn't there?*

'I understand,' said Dr Lone. 'But we should also look at the possibility that your angle on that evidence created an extra dimension.'

Grrr. 'What am I meant to do? My job is to protect people who are in danger. Do I have to run everything by people before I act on anything? That's not practical in life-or-death situations.'

'But some of these situations were not life-or-death,' said Lone. 'And, yes, it would be wise to run these things by at least one other colleague. You have to operate as a team. You are part of a team.'

Teamwork . . .

Lone smiled. 'That may not appeal to you at times, but there's a reason why that infrastructure is there.'

'I like to be able to make quick decisions,' said Ren. 'I mean, what if someone was trying to kill Janine? And I hung around waiting to run my theories by someone? She could be dead.'

'Let's talk about loss for a moment,' said Lone.

Loss? What?

'Would I be right in saying that you care very much for Janine?'

'Yes, of course.'

'And Ben?'

'Yes.'

'And Gary?'

'Yes.'

'Perhaps you are worried about losing all three of them,' said Lone.

What? No, I'm not. Not at all. I'm never going to lose them.

'It might not be at the forefront of your mind,' said Dr Lone, 'but you might want to consider it.'

No, thanks. Why would I want to sit around considering my worst possible nightmare?

'There's something else too,' said Ren. She told him about the previous night.

'So, what I was wondering was, do you think I should tell Ben?' she said.

'Only you can decide that,' said Lone.

Really? 'Really? Aren't you going to tell me that the truth is the only way forward?'

'No,' said Lone.

'But I need you to tell me!' said Ren. *I am a child.*

323

Lone smiled kindly. 'I know,' he said. 'But you also know that the decision has to come from your heart.'

'I can't tell him,' said Ren. 'My heart won't allow me to.' She paused. 'I don't even know if that's selfish. I don't know what the right thing to do is. He loves me, and I don't deserve him, and—'

'You have to stop thinking that way,' said Lone. 'You didn't take it any further last night, which you've told me is the first time that's ever happened under those circumstances.'

'Yes!' said Ren. 'It's a miracle!'

'As for telling Ben, you don't need to make a decision on that right now. If it's causing you distress, don't do something just as a quick fix to alleviate that.'

Ren nodded. 'OK.'

'Call me if you need me,' said Lone. He handed her a card. 'This has my cell phone number.'

'Don't tell me: is it fifty-one fifty?'

Lone laughed. Fifty-one fifty was the code in California for an involuntary psychiatric hold; urban slang for completely nuts.

'Do I seem that bad?' said Ren.

Dr Lone smiled. 'It's a cell phone number, not a straitjacket.'

Ren looked at him. 'If you know that even good people can hurt people, then how can you ever trust?'

Lone opened his palms, did an illustrative flourish with his elegant fingers. 'All you can do is accept that hurt is part of life.'

Ren took a deep breath. 'I don't want to hurt anyone. And I don't want to be hurt. I don't think I can ever accept hurt as a part of life . . .'

'Hurt is a *part* of life,' said Lone. 'It is not, however, the *whole* of life or the *end* of life.'

'I like that.'

Still terrified.

58

Ren sat in the Jeep outside Dr Lone's office. Her hands were gripping the steering wheel, her forehead leaning against them.

I can't go back to work.

I feel weird.

I have to go back to work.

She sucked in a huge breath that felt like it wasn't enough, that she needed more.

I have to go to work.

I might have a meltdown. No I won't. I will.

She started the engine and, instead of taking the turn that would take her to Safe Streets, she took the turn to take her home.

She sat at the edge of the stiff sofa in the cramped apartment.

I hate this place.

I need to be at work.

I feel weird. I'm jumping out of my skin. I'm always jumping out of my skin.

She studied the wall for two hours, getting up and down every fifteen minutes.

This is aggravating. Too many pictures. Too many documents and words and faces.

She went into the kitchen and got a cardboard box. She came back into the living room and started to take everything down. She organized them into neat piles on the coffee table, on the sofa, on the floor. The top page on one of the piles had two words: Grace Lucchesi.

You are a beautiful little girl, and, I hope, a one hundred per cent healthy girl. And you're a heroine to have rescued your damaged father. He's a good man.

And, hey, aren't we all damaged?

The doorbell rang, several times. Ren went over to the intercom. She saw Janine's worried face on the screen.

She picked up. 'Janine!'

'Are you OK?' said Janine. 'I tried your phone a hundred times.'

Role reversal.

'Come up,' said Ren.

Ren stood, almost suspended in the apartment doorway. Janine pushed gently past. 'Where did you go this afternoon? I covered for you with Gary, but he was not happy.'

She hovered in front of Ren.

'Are you OK?' said Janine.

No. I feel a little insane.

Ren shook her head. She started to cry.

Janine moved to her, hugging her, guiding her into the living room. She took the stacks of paper and put them down carefully on the floor. They didn't speak, Janine just let her cry.

'What time is it?' said Ren.

'Five thirty.'

'Shit.'

'Can I get you anything? Tea, coffee, beer, wine?'

Ren laughed. 'Wine, wine, wine.' She let out a breath. 'Thank you for coming over.'

'Of course I was going to come over,' said Janine. 'What's up?'

'Ugh . . . I . . . spent the night with Joe Lucchesi.'

'What?'

Ren nodded. 'I know. We went out, we got hammered, I went back to his room. We . . . didn't have sex. But . . . you know, I woke up in his bed.'

'Oh . . .' She paused. 'Are you sure nothing happened?'

'Oh my God – totally. He told me. And I remembered . . . eventually. He was really nice. He's a really nice guy.'

Janine's eyes widened.

'He's screwed-up, though,' said Ren. 'Duke Rawlins screwed him up bad.'

'I'm not surprised . . .'

'At either,' said Ren.

'Well . . .'

'I know you've tried to save me from this kind of shit before,' said Ren.

'That's not the point, though. I just don't want you to end up like this.'

Tears welled in Ren's eyes. 'I know. I love you for that.'

'Are you going to tell Ben?'

Ren shook her head. 'I don't think so. Should I? It was a mistake. I don't want to throw away everything we have because of drunken bullshit.'

The tears started to fall.

'We need tea immediately.' Janine stood up.

I want to be like you, Janine Hooks. You're sane. You're reliable. You're wonderful. You do not screw up. I am a perpetual disappointment.

Janine paused. 'You took down your Wall of Horrors, I now realize.'

It was freaking me out.

Ren curled into the sofa, watching the peaceful wall.

This has helped.

Janine came back in with a tray of tea and biscuits.

'And the whole world was set to rights,' said Janine.

I just love you.

I feel so guilty. I can't even tell you the crazy thoughts I had about your poor friend, Terri. And what Duke Rawlins might have done to you. There's crazy and there's crazy: the scary, genuine, can't-even-make-a-joke-about-it kind.

'Oh, Jesus,' said Ren. 'I just remembered what I did last night. When Joe went to the bathroom . . . I got Camille's number from his phone – the nanny.' Ren checked her Contacts. 'Look!'

'Why?' said Janine.

'I was so worried,' said Ren. 'Worried that his family's not safe. It was for reassurance. I have it, in case I need it. But I couldn't ask Joe for it because he'd think I was nuts.'

Janine's look told her she agreed. 'Now,' said Janine, 'To take us away from all things drunken and personal, why don't we talk about the case?'

'That,' said Ren, 'would be perfect.'

Her phone rang. *Joe Lucchesi.*

'It's him!' said Ren.

'Answer it!' said Janine.

'I feel about fourteen!' Ren picked up.

'Hey,' said Joe.

'Hello, there.'

'I'm calling with some very good news,' said Joe. 'Grace

and I were at the doctor this afternoon, and she's all good. Test results were clear. She is fighting fit.'

'Oh, thank God,' said Ren. 'Thank God. That's wonderful to hear.'

'It is, it is,' said Joe. 'And I wanted to say thank you for last night, I had fun, it was what I needed. The hangover this morning – not so much.'

'Oh, I know that feeling,' said Ren. 'And thank you too. It was hilarious.'

'I won't see you tomorrow at the office – it's Shaun's graduation.'

'What are you doing after?' *Which sounds like a come-on.*

Janine was rolling her eyes in agreement.

'Shaun's got a wild night planned,' said Joe. 'I'm going to go ahead up to Breck – we've got two nights there – he'll follow me up the next day if his head is still working.'

'Be careful out there,' said Ren.

'I'm always careful.'

You're so serious.

Bomb explodes in auditorium. Jesus, Worst-Case Scenario again.

'I think we're all safe at a graduation,' said Joe. 'We're lucky Duke Rawlins doesn't like the grand public gestures.'

Yet.

Monster . . . mutating.

Stop.

'Have fun,' said Ren. 'Tell Shaun I said congratulations.'

'I will. See you in a couple of days.'

'Looking forward to it,' said Ren.

Janine looked at her when she hung up. 'Looking forward to what?'

'Nothing,' said Ren, 'it's just an expression. Seeing him in work – that's all.'

'Back to the case,' said Janine.

'I can't get the Kurt Vine thing out of my head,' said Ren. 'The real connection. And it's still freaking me out that Joe hasn't made Grace safe.'

'How do you know that?' said Janine.

'Well, he didn't say he was going to Breck alone . . .'

'Probably because it would have sounded like he was inviting you.'

'True . . .' Ren sighed. 'It's all rather exhausting.'

'Let's check out Vine's website,' said Ren. 'If that was his first point of contact with Duke Rawlins – if that's how Rawlins found him, I'd like to know what it was that drew him in.'

They opened up ForTheForgotten.net.

They scrolled through the images.

'He wasn't a bad photographer . . .' said Janine.

'Oh,' said Ren, pointing to the screen. 'These ones were in the *Denver Post* after that retrospective series on asylums. And then . . . the rapes happened. It's Kennington – that was the building Everett was talking about.'

Ren could feel Janine tense beside her. They both knew that the Kennington rapist, now in prison, had attempted to rape Ren. Janine simply squeezed Ren's forearm, and stuck with the task at hand.

God bless you.

'And look at all the eerie woodland shots,' said Janine.

'This kind of shit fascinates me too, though,' said Ren. 'But I'm still going to decide he's a psycho and I'm not.'

'Look at this place – the Ostler Building – it's an old toy factory,' said Janine, pointing. '"Creepsville" as you would say.'

'Don't touch my screen,' said Ren.

'Sorry,' said Janine.

'Where is this place?' said Ren. 'Oh . . . it's in RiNo by the railroad, near my filthy man-gym. Yikes. I think you can see that from Safe Streets. I always thought that part was just a chimney.'

'These external shots are old, though,' said Janine. 'They're vintage. Sixties looking.'

'Yes, because I think we may have noticed if there was a giant cut-out doll's head towering over RiNo. Vine must have found the building, bought the vintage shots of it online somewhere. Or found the photos, then tracked down the building. I mean, you can't get more abandoned than that.'

'And yes,' said Janine, 'look at the inside – there's the head propped up against the wall.'

'Jesus – a flat, timber doll's head,' said Ren, 'beside a plastic bucket filled with regular dolls' heads . . . terror overload.'

'Why are dolls heads so sinister?' said Janine.

'Because they rotate three-sixty, their dead eyes blink twice, and, at night, they push nightmares – via your tear ducts – into the back of your eyeballs.'

'Did someone actually tell you that?'

'My brother, Jay,' said Ren. 'No wonder I'm screwed up. And he said they block up your tear ducts so you can't cry, so no one can *hear* you cry.' She looked at Janine. 'I think you need to stay over tonight . . .'

59

Ren spent the next morning at Safe Streets studying everything that was pinned to the noticeboards. She was briefed by the investigators present on their progress. She went for a late lunch with a paperback so she could breathe, have space, detach. Instead, she was drawn to thoughts of Duke Rawlins. She switched to thinking about Ben. And that led her to Joe.

Grr. Get out of my head.

Shaun's graduation!

She texted Joe.

Good luck to Shaun! Forensic Psychology – we may employ him in the future. To the great horror of his NYPD dad . . .

Joe replied: **Promise me, son, not to do the things she's done . . .**

'Coward of the County'! Kenny Rogers!

Ren replied: **LMFAO!**

She could see Shaun Lucchesi as an FBI profiler. A sullen one. Serious. Dedicated.

Oh. Jesus.

She looked through her contacts for Vincent Farraday and

dialed his number. It rang over and over, until he picked up as she was about to abandon hope.

'Mr Farraday, it's Special Agent Ren Bryce,' she said. 'I met with you and—'

'Yes, yes,' he said.

'Could I ask you a question?'

'Go ahead.'

'You mentioned a young man from New York calling to your home to ask you questions about Duke Rawlins. You said he seemed like he was interested in the truth, so you spoke with him. Was he one of the "forensics" people you mentioned who called on you?'

The silence stretched.

Please, please, please remember this.

'Yes,' said Vincent, 'yes he was.'

'Forensic Psychology?' said Ren.

'That was it,' said Vincent.

'When was that?' said Ren.

'That would have been oh, last year, definitely.'

'Did he give you his name?' said Ren.

'Erm . . . Banner,' said Vincent.

'Banner?' said Ren.

'Shaun Banner,' said Vincent.

Banner, my ass. And no wonder Joe Lucchesi looked familiar to you, Mr Farraday.

Ren called Denver University's Admissions Office. They had no Shaun Lucchesi, but they did have a Masters student called Shaun Banner, with an address on the Auraria Campus. Ren got there in ten minutes, and ran to his room.

There were groups of frightened-looking students gathered down the hallway, and a voice raised to an alarming level inside Shaun's room.

That is Joe Lucchesi.

'What have you done?' he was roaring. 'What the hell have you done?'

Ren held up her creds to the students. 'Please, move along, everyone. This is under control.'

'Nothing to see here!' said one of the kids, and everyone laughed.

She waited for them to start moving.

There was the sound of a crash, and broken glass from inside the room.

Jesus Christ.

Ren hammered on the door with her fist. 'It's Ren. Open up.'

There was silence.

'Joe!' said Ren. 'Open up. Now.'

Silence.

'Don't make me kick the door in,' said Ren.

The door unlocked. The first person she saw was Shaun Lucchesi, sitting in the chair by his desk, but facing the door. He was ghostly, his eyes rimmed in red. There was a smashed lamp at his feet. There were books around the floor, on the bed.

Joe was standing there, red-faced, sweating, wild-eyed.

A force.

Ren closed the door behind her. She moved the books along the bed up toward the desk, cleared a space.

'Joe – sit down,' said Ren.

'I'm good,' he said.

'You need to sit down,' said Ren.

Whatever was in her tone, he did as she said. She leaned against the wall opposite him.

'What's going on here?' she said.

Neither man spoke.

'I'm going to get the ball rolling, then,' said Ren. 'I spoke with Vincent Farraday this morning—'

Joe stood up. 'We need to talk in private for a moment.'

Ren glanced over at Shaun.

'I'm fine,' he said. 'You can go into the hallway. I'm not going to do anything.'

'Are you sure you're OK?' said Ren.

He nodded.

She stepped into the hallway with Joe, but left the door open.

'He was registered here as Shaun Banner,' said Joe. 'For obvious reasons. But before you talk to him, you need to know that he doesn't know we're looking at Duke Rawlins for this case. I made up some other bullshit as to why I was working with you. And you guys didn't release enough details to the media for him to come to that conclusion. Either way, he's been all about getting an internship and his graduation over the past few months. I'll let him tell you what he's been doing. You obviously know some of it already. But, yes, as you can see, I just fucking lost it with him, Ren. I lost my fucking mind. I hope you can understand why. I didn't lay a finger on him, but—'

'I know that,' said Ren. 'Of course.' *Jesus.* 'Take a moment, OK?'

Joe nodded. He rubbed his hand through his hair, took some deep breaths.

'I heard he was asking questions around Stinger's Creek . . .' said Ren.

'It'll blow your fucking mind what he's been doing,' said Joe.

They went back inside, and Joe took his seat on the bed. Ren stood where she had been.

'I'm sorry, Dad,' said Shaun, looking hopefully in his direction.

Well, your father is clearly not ready to accept that apology.

'Tell her,' said Joe. 'Tell her what you did.'

Shaun looked reduced, stripped of his twenty-six years, back to sixteen, back to infuriating his father.

'My dissertation for my Masters was on serial killers, and I included in that Duke Rawlins and Donald Riggs.'

Holy. Shit.

'He only told me this now,' said Joe.

'I'm not surprised your father lost it,' said Ren.

'I cannot believe that he kept that from me all this time,' said Joe.

'I guess your professors couldn't have stopped you doing this, if they didn't know your real name,' said Ren.

Shaun nodded. He turned to Joe. 'I thought you'd be proud.'

Joe erupted. 'Proud? Are you out of your mind? Proud that you threw yourself in the path of the man who has already done his best to destroy us and who will finish the job, given half the chance?'

Didn't you say you believed that Duke Rawlins wasn't after you? Oh, you lied, Joe Lucchesi. You want him to be after you. It's your only way of getting your chance to kill him.

'I cannot believe,' said Joe, standing again, stabbing a finger at Shaun, 'the risk you took, after everything I've done to protect you: the name, the move from New York, your little sister, for crying out loud – didn't you consider Grace? Wouldn't you want to protect her from even a fraction of what you've been through? You selfish, selfish, brat. I thought you'd grown up, Shaun. I thought you'd fucking grown up. But you're still a self-indulgent little shit.'

Oh, Jesus. Rein it in, Joe.

Shaun stood up to face him. 'I *do* want to protect Grace!'

he said. 'I love her more than anything in the world. How fucking dare you? That's the whole point! I wanted to find a way of getting Duke Rawlins that was peaceful, sensible, non-violent: by analyzing his psychology, predicting possible future behavior, thoughtfully studying him, not by firing a fucking gun in his direction! Which is your approach to everything!'

'My approach to everything?' said Joe. 'Jesus Christ! That's what you think?'

'Well, look where it got us the last time!' said Shaun. 'Your solution to Donnie Riggs – shoot the fucker! And here we are. This is what that gets you.'

Oh, no. Worst possible thing to say to Joe Lucchesi.

I can't even bear to see that pain in his face.

Shaun looked horrified himself.

'Please, guys,' said Ren. 'Everyone is angry—'

'Of course I'm angry!' said Joe. 'He has jeopardized his entire family. And all I've ever done is try to protect you . . .' He looked deflated.

'Sit down, both of you,' said Ren. 'This has gotten too . . . this is too much.'

They sat down, fuming, staring at the floor.

You look so alike.

'Shaun, do you want to talk to me about what you found out about Duke Rawlins?' said Ren.

'I believe that Duke Rawlins was systematically physically and sexually abused from when he was a very young child. And that his mother, Wanda Rawlins, pimped him out to pedophiles in return for drugs.'

Oh, God.

60

'How did you work that out about Rawlins' childhood?' said Ren.

'I thought of us . . .' said Shaun, gesturing toward Joe.

Joe and Ren looked at him.

'Yourself?' said Joe.

He nodded. 'I thought about how people leave places that bring them bad memories. We left New York to go to Ireland, we left Ireland to come back to the US, I left New York again to come here . . .' He shrugged. 'People leave the places that hold memories they would rather forget.'

He's right. Where is he going with this?

'I looked at all the people who moved away from Stinger's Creek,' said Shaun. 'People who were there around the time that Rawlins and Riggs committed these crimes, people who were in school with them, people connected in any way to the crimes. I spoke with everyone I could get a hold of. I researched the ones I couldn't. I found a woman called Dorothy Parnum. Her husband, Ogden, was the Police Chief at the time of the Crosscut Killer investigation. When he killed himself, she relocated to Wichita Falls—'

'Jesus Christ!' said Joe. 'The summer camp at Wichita Falls – you didn't work there at all!'

'No, I did,' said Shaun. 'Just not as much as you thought . . .'

Joe looked at Ren. 'Can you believe this shit?'

'Keep going,' said Ren.

'I tracked Dorothy Parnum down to a meeting for child sex-abuse victims,' said Shaun. 'I joined the group. She spoke. She said she had discovered that her husband had been abusing children. She found photos after he died . . .'

Joe nodded. 'I spoke with the DA, Marcy Winbaum, back in the day,' he said. 'She told me that Duke Rawlins visited Ogden Parnum at the police department when the investigation was at its height. Parnum gave Rawlins and Riggs an alibi for the night of one of the murders. Marcy Winbaum guessed he was blackmailed into it – she just didn't know why.'

'I spoke with her too,' said Shaun. 'She said the same thing to me. When I put it together with what I knew about Dorothy Parnum, it made sense. I also cross-referenced a whole lot of things that I don't think law enforcement did. I researched every single kid who went to school with Duke Rawlins or Donnie Riggs – I interviewed some of them, I interviewed their teachers. I looked at all the information I gathered from a psychological angle, with a view to building up a profile of Duke Rawlins and a full picture of his childhood.

'I found a girl who had moved away from Stinger's Creek – a girl called Ashley Ames. In school, she gave Duke Rawlins the nickname that apparently tormented him – Pukey Dukey. She told me that Duke Rawlins and Donald Riggs raped her when she was sixteen. She believed this happened because she was the one to have given him this nickname. I thought that seemed extreme, even for Duke Rawlins. Then I discovered that Ashley Ames' father was arrested five years ago on a child pornography charge. I think he also abused Duke Rawlins, and that was why Ashley Ames was raped – revenge. I was able to connect her father, Westley Ames, to Ogden Parnum – they went hunting together. And there were more men who went hunting with them . . . I'm waiting to hear back from a source who promised to give me more names. I haven't put these details in my dissertation, because I would need the legalities to be perfect, but they're part of my research.'

Ren nodded.

'I worked up a profile on Rawlins,' said Shaun. He went over to the pile of papers and books on the bed. He pulled out a slim file, passing it right in front of Joe's face to hand it to Ren.

Ouch.

Ren started to read the profile. 'This is great, Shaun. You've picked up on a lot of points from the FBI's profile.'

Nothing new, nothing new, nothing new.

Oh.

There were two things at the end:

Duke Rawlins has a deep hatred and mistrust of law enforcement, or anyone in a position of trust. This is likely due to the abuse he may have suffered at their hands as a child. It culminated in his particular hatred of NYPD Detective Joe Lucchesi, whose family he targeted in a sustained campaign following the shooting dead of Rawlins' accomplice, Donald Riggs.

'What is it?' said Joe.

'Let me keep reading,' said Ren.

She read on about the rapes and murders. But it was the final comment that sent a shiver up her spine.

Combining the background, experience, modus operandi, behavior, interests, and obsessions that come together to make up Duke Rawlins, I believe that his deep mistrust of law enforcement will lead him to pursue any law enforcement officer who has engaged with him in the past on any level. Duke Rawlins is a psychopath, and as such, suffers from all forms of cognitive distortion; his thought patterns are entirely weighted toward the negative in all aspects of his life. He is consumed by what he sees as his righteous entitlement to vengeance following the death of his closest ally, his accomplice, Donald Riggs. For Rawlins to achieve his goals, having perceived any original failures in that regard as catastrophic, he will stalk, study, and watch his targets closely before he attacks. He will leave nothing to chance.

Ren could feel a rush of realization.

The glass in Donna Darisse's feet: clear, blue, green . . . the color of dolls' eyes.

Duke Rawlins. Law enforcement. Watch them.

Like a hawk.

This was what Duke Rawlins wanted from Kurt Vine: access to the tower of the toy factory in RiNo . . . whose windows overlook Safe Streets.

Ren closed the file and handed it back to Shaun.

Jesus Christ. Duke Rawlins has been watching us all this time.

61

Ren moved toward the door, looked from Shaun to Joe.

'OK,' she said, her face impassive. She checked her watch. 'The graduation is in what – forty minutes? I'm going to leave you gentlemen to it. You can make up . . . hopefully? And go in peace?' She smiled. 'And Joe, I'll see you when you get back from Breckenridge. Congratulations, Shaun.' She handed him her card. 'If your source comes through on the names of Rawlins' abusers, could you please forward them to me?'

'Yes,' said Shaun. 'I'll do that. Thank you. I'm sorry for any trouble I've caused.'

'You didn't cause me any trouble,' said Ren. 'And – to reassure you,' she said to Joe, 'I'm going to have Everett King and Robbie Truax stationed at the auditorium for the ceremony.'

Joe's eyes widened.

Ren shrugged. 'Peace is good.'

Joe smiled. 'Thank you.'

Ren got in the Jeep and called Everett.

'Everett, have you got your magic fingers to hand? Fingers, hand – see what I did there?'

'I do,' said Everett. 'What do you need?'

'There's an old toy factory called the Ostler Building, off Brighton Boulevard. It's in some way connected with Kurt Vine; he's posted photos of it on his site. Can you find out who owns it? Vine obviously doesn't or you would have found out, but he has definitely been inside it, so he had to have keys or know someone who did . . . unless it's not locked up, of course. Didn't think of that.'

'OK – I'll check that out and call you back. Did you talk to Gary?'

'Gary – no, why?'

'Apparently you, Robbie and Janine are staying after work for a meeting. Everyone else, including me, is to go home at five on the button. He said that was a strict order.'

'Really?' said Ren. 'What the heck is that about?' She glanced at her phone. 'Oh there's a text here from him: My office, 5.30 p.m. Urgent. Woo.'

'I have no idea,' said Everett. 'I'm clearly not one of The Chosen. I presume you added that "woo" yourself.'

'Also,' said Ren, 'before you flee at five on the button, I need you and Robbie to go right away to the auditorium in Denver University – it turns out that Shaun Lucchesi has been doing some very good amateur detective work . . . that could have put him unwittingly in Duke Rawlins' sights. Joe went ballistic.'

'Shit,' said Everett.

'Well, we don't know anything yet – it's precautionary,' said Ren. 'I really don't believe he's in danger.'

On the drive, Ren thought about Duke Rawlins watching her, knowing she was on the investigation, following her to her car, finding her and sitting next to her in bipolar support.

A shiver ran up her spine. She was lucky. He had her right there. He could have done anything. She was lucky.

For now . . .

Ren pulled into RiNo and parked outside the man-gym. She crossed the street and walked the two blocks to the Ostler Building. The building was constructed on different levels, all painted in the same palette of cream with bottle-green trim. All the original signage had been removed from the exterior. The only signs left were Keep Out and Private Property. To the east side was the tallest part of the building – what Ren always thought was a chimney when she caught sight of it from the office. Up close, it looked like a small tower, albeit an adjoined one, twenty feet higher than the rest of the building. In the Sixties, it had the timber doll's head mounted on the front. Without the head it was clear that the line of small dark windows at the top had played the role of the teeth in the doll's smile.

Not one bit creepy.

There must be some kind of room up there.

Ren walked around to the north side of the building, where there were eight shuttered loading bays.

Give me a way in, here, people.

She Googled the building. It wasn't up for sale or for lease, so there was no information or floor plans to be found.

Shit.

Her cell phone rang and she jumped.

'Everett!' she said, answering. 'My heart.'

'You need to set that thing to vibrate,' said Everett.

'I hate vibration,' said Ren.

Pause.

'And yes,' said Ren. '*All* vibrations.'

'OK, I'm on my way to the university – don't worry,' he said. 'You were right about the building. I won't bore you with the details, but, basically, when Kurt Vine inherited the land from his grandfather, his cousin inherited that factory/warehouse. So it's not a big leap to say that Vine borrowed the keys to take the photos.'

'That would explain how there were vintage photos on Vine's site too – they were family photos. Where's the cousin?'

'Germany,' said Everett.

'Which means, unless Kurt Vine mailed the keys back, they're in his house in Sedalia.'

'What's the significance of this building?' said Everett.

'I'll fill you in when you get back,' said Ren.

'Okaaay,' said Everett. 'Are you up to badness?'

'Nevah,' said Ren. 'I'm going to call Douglas County, see if someone can go look for those keys at Vine's house.'

But realistically, we both know that is a giant lie and I'm going to break in myself . . .

62

Ren went around the side of the building and found a doorway with a glass upper half and a window beside it. She looked through into a narrow hallway tiled in pale green. She noticed a small crack in the pane. She looked left and right, saw no one, then struck the crack with her elbow. The glass was old, and shattered easily. Ren covered her hand with her jacket, reached inside and unlocked the door. She turned on her flashlight and went in. To the right, the door into the tower was padlocked. Ahead, an open door led into the main factory, and to the left was a long hallway and an old-fashioned sign over the architrave that read ADMINISTRATION. Ren started with the padlocked door, yanking on it hard.

Shit.

She turned and went down the hallway. The air smelled of damp, and paper and age. There were offices on both sides, all the way to the end.

May find tools in offices. May break padlock. May be delusional.

She pulled out a pair of gloves and put them on.

As she walked, she moved her flashlight along the ground

ahead, picking up the thin, threadbare carpet, stained for reasons she didn't want to consider. She directed the beam up and down the bare walls. She went through the first door on the left: half-open file cabinet in the corner, single broken chair, missing desk, one poster, and marks on the wall from four missing ones.

Why leave one? I never get that.

What was so amazing about the other four?

She went over to the file cabinet, pulled each drawer open wide. There were loose file tabs, an eraser, an orange ticket stub. In the bottom drawer, she found a lonely romance novel with an illustration of a handsome couple clutching each other as if the end of the world was just over the cover.

That writer is dead now.

She walked on, imagining the men and women who worked there and she understood Kurt Vine and how he could want to honor people this way. Real people with lives and loves and families spent their days there with real hopes and dreams and problems and ambition.

And then they died.

Great.

Imagine people coming into an abandoned Safe Streets.

They'd find weird shit in my drawers. They'd question the whole operation . . .

In the last office, Ren sat down at one of the desks and slid out the top drawer. There was a stack of Seventies-looking brochures – the top one from a furniture company. She started flicking through it, then went to the next one – stationery supplier, then the next one—

Why am I so distracted? Jesus.

She thought about the past and the present and how tenuous everything felt, and how strange futures were, how they could turn from something bright into one big shitshow, based on something as simple as an ordering or reordering of thoughts and the decisions that followed.

Or the words of a horoscope.

She left the admin offices and went into the warehouse. It was at least fifty thousand square feet contained under high ceilings, hung with fluorescent lights. Long narrow tables were pushed back against the walls. Light filtered in dimly from the rows of window at the top of the wall. The floor was concrete, mainly dust-covered, but with trails where it had been disturbed.

So someone was walking here recently. Running. She looked around. *Several someones.*

There was no sign that toys were ever made there – the bins from Kurt Vine's photos weren't here; neither was the wooden doll's head.

They may be about to put the building on the market.

Ren's boot crunched over something. She looked down and saw broken glass in blue, green, clear – all the colors that were taken out of Donna Darisse's feet.

Yes – this is where Donna Darisse was killed. The fucking horror of being hunted through this place.

The flashlight picked up a dark stain on the concrete close by. There were more stains as they walked in further. She could smell bleach and urine. But it was a newer smell, not from as far back as Donna Darisse's murder.

Ren's heart started to beat a little faster.

Relax. Relax.

She heard a sound behind her.

Oh.

Fuck.

She looked around. A man stood in silhouette in the doorway holding a tire iron.

Joe.

Thank. Fuck.

'What are you doing here?' said Ren, walking over to him. 'Didn't you wait for the graduation?'

'I guess I'm not a great peacemaker.'

'Jesus – it's his graduation.'

Joe shook his head. 'I couldn't stand by his side after what he did. I must sound like an asshole, and maybe I am. But I'd feel like a hypocrite. I'm even more anxious now to nail this son-of-a-bitch while Shaun is safe.'

'Did you follow me?' said Ren.

'Of course I did. I saw your eyes . . . you had something. You should have told me.'

'I wanted you to go to with Shaun. Whatever this is can wait.'

'And you believe that . . .' said Joe. 'Have you spoken to Gary about this?'

'Gary . . . no.'

'Why not?'

'Well, here I am breaking and entering . . .'

She looked down. Joe was holding bolt cutters. Ren smiled. 'I thought that was a tire iron that I was about to be beaten to death with.'

'Duke Rawlins is not getting near you,' said Joe.

Ren went very still. *I'm your do-over. You couldn't save Anna. You think you can save me.* 'I'm not worried about Duke Rawlins.'

'You should be.'

But I'm fucking invincible. 'Now, are you done trying to scare the shit out of me in a darkened and abandoned warehouse? Because it's not working.' *Because I'm fucking invincible.*

63

Joe pointed over to the row of doors on the opposite wall. 'Where do they go?'

'They lead into the loading bays.'

Joe counted them: one, two, three, four, five, six, seven, eight, nine.

'There are nine of them,' said Joe, 'and there are only eight loading bays outside. So that room on the right over there has no external access. Let's start with that.'

They went over to the door. Joe broke the lock with the bolt cutters. Inside, a huge plastic lidded bin on wheels stood at the center of the room. With a gloved hand, Ren reached up to the handle on the lid and pushed it up. As soon as it opened a crack, they were hit with two smells: cleaning fluid and death.

Suppress the gagging.

'Give me a leg up,' said Ren.

'Seriously?' said Joe.

'Yes.'

He did.

The liquid was murky, gray-green, stinking. And rising to the top, floating tips of blonde hair.

'That would be Dainty Farraday,' said Ren, sliding back down.

'And on and on it goes,' said Joe.

'We should check the other doors too, just in case,' said Ren.

They went through them, one to eight, and they were all cleared out.

Ren's phone went off. She jumped. Joe laughed.

It was a text from Janine. **Where are u? Gary going apeshit.**

Ren checked the time.

Five thirty-eight! Holy shit! Where has the time gone?

Ren texted Janine. **Cover for me? In the middle of something. Will be there in ten. It will be worth it.**

Janine replied: **Call Gary first. Seriously. Please.**

Grrr.

Ren called Gary.

'Ren, where the hell are you?' he said.

'I'm on my way,' said Ren. 'You're not going to believe this shit—'

The phone went dead.

Oh my God. He hung up on me!

That's bad.

Really bad.

But do not go back to him without proof. He will think you are insane. Again.

She felt a surge of frustration, a rush of violent impulses she struggled to leash. They were terrifying. And they were powerful. And they were not meant for people like Gary.

'Shall we enter the tower?' said Ren.

'After you, then . . .' Joe smiled, gestured forward.

Ren pointed to the tower door.

'He's been watching us from up there.'

'What do you think he could really see?' said Joe.

'Honestly?' said Ren. 'Not a lot. I think it's psychological. I think it's a one-up thing, a fuck-you. I don't think he's learned anything – how could he have?'

Joe used the bolt cutters on the padlock. He set it down.

They both took out their flashlights, drew their weapons. Ren walked through, the concrete floor illuminated by the beams.

Ugh.

It stank of garbage.

There were two empty bottles of bleach on the floor.

'This is it,' said Ren. 'We've found the monster's lair.'

She moved her flashlight and they struck the metal steps of a spiral staircase.

Oh, God. The lighthouse.

Ren could feel Joe pause behind her. She checked her phone, then turned to him.

'I've lost my signal,' said Ren. 'Could you call Gary, let him know, send everyone in?'

'I'm coming up,' said Joe.

'Please don't,' said Ren, setting her foot on the rock-solid bottom step. 'This staircase does not feel stable. It won't take both of us.'

She kept walking up. 'Call Gary. He won't take a call from me.'

Ren got to the top of the stairs. There were two mattresses on the ground, empty food cartons – the same kind of detritus that people everywhere collect just by going about their lives. She walked over to the window. She looked over at Safe Streets. She had a clear view. The bullpen was in darkness.

Because they're all in Gary's office at an urgent meeting.

Where I should be.

But I scored! He can't be mad.

She looked around: suitcases, clothes, girls', guys', Dainty Farraday's guitar, makeup, syringes, Band Aid, magazines, newspapers, razors; objects that echoed through so many lives, but took on a filthy and sinister quality, strewn around the lair of a killer.

Ren ran down the stairs. 'Did you get him?'

'No,' said Joe. 'It rang out.'

'Everything's up there,' said Ren. 'It's Rawlins.'

Joe started to walk past her through the doorway.

It's safe. Go ahead.

'I'll go,' said Ren. 'I'll get everyone.'

She could hear Joe's footsteps clanging on the metal behind her, then fading as she ran from them.

Ren got back into the Jeep and drove the two minutes to the Livestock Exchange Building. There were five cars in the parking lot: Gary's, Robbie's, Janine's, Everett's, and a fancy black sporty one.

That car's familiar. Hmm . . .

And why is Everett still here?

She ran up the steps and paused. It was an overcast day, but the lobby seemed unnaturally dark. She pushed open the door into the lobby. She was hit with a smell.

Oh, God. Someone is dead in here.

Oh, Jesus Christ.

64

Ren's heart pounded. She drew her weapon and walked toward the stairs. In the gloom, she could see feet sticking out from under the stairwell.

Oh, no.

She walked over, hearing nothing but her own footsteps.

The realtor, Valerie, dressed in her beautiful pink suit, was lying by the wall. There was a loose plug socket in her hand, its wires connecting it limply to the hole in the baseboard. She looked pristine, but she was clearly dead.

Oh my God. The electricity. The fault. Rodney Viezel was right. What the fuck?

Ren crouched down, put her fingers to Valerie's throat. No pulse. Ren stood up, looked up, saw nothing.

No lights on. The system has shorted. Gary didn't hang up. But why isn't everyone down here? Surely they would have come down to investigate?

She took out her cell phone, started to dial 911.

'Ren!'

She looked up. 'Janine! Oh my God – what happened?' Ren ran up toward her.

'I know. It's terrible,' said Janine. 'We've already called 911. They're on their way.'

Ren ended the call, put her phone away, slid her sidearm into its holster. 'Are you OK? Is everyone else?'

'We have our flashlights – Gary's insisting on finishing this meeting.'

What?! 'Jesus – am I dead woman walking?' said Ren.

'No, no,' said Janine. She turned and ran up ahead.

This is weird. She isn't making eye contact with me. Her tone is off.

Ren made it up to the top floor and walked into the Safe Streets hallway. It was eerily quiet.

Gary sent everyone home.

Gary's office was at the end of the hallway, the door wide open.

Empty.

'We're in here!' said Janine. 'By the cells.'

Shivers were rolling down Ren's spine.

Why aren't you all in Gary's office?

Something's not right here. Janine sounds off. Why is she not looking at me?

Ren took the right through the admin offices, and the left into where the cells were.

Oh, God.

Duke Rawlins had dragged a table into the center of the small space and was sitting on it, his arm hooked around Janine, who was now half-leaning, half-sitting on his right leg like a ventriloquist's dummy. There was an ethereal look of calm on her face. And a knife pressed against her neck, right to her carotid artery.

I can't risk a shot.

Janine. You look so tiny.

Rawlins gave Janine a squeeze. 'You did good, you did good. Your colleagues here lived.'

Ren glanced to her left. To the cells. Inside the one closest to the wall were Robbie and Everett. Inside the other, closest to her, was Gary, all of them with their wrists tied behind their backs with cable ties or handcuffs.

Ren laid her weapon on the file cabinet beside her, and raised her hands.

'I'll do whatever you want me to.' *I really fucking will.*

Everyone was looking at her.

'What do you want me to do?' said Ren.

'I want you to shut the fuck up,' said Duke. 'I need to think.'

Ren looked around the room. *What can I do? What is open to me? That won't get someone harmed.*

Nothing . . . yet.

There was a small cardboard box on the table beside Duke. 'I got a box of ringing cell phones here,' he said. 'People beginning to wonder where your asses are at! Unfortunately, y'all are always letting your people down, aren't you? Got called away on a case, found a suspect, chased a robber, got held hostage . . .' He looked around, laughed a crazy laugh. 'Being "unavailable" doesn't really set off any alarm bells in your people's lives.' He paused. 'Ms Ren Bryce, I'm going to have you come my way slowly, place your keys, and *both* your weapons in this box at my feet, and your cell phone right here in this box. Then you stand by the wall there, to my left, where I can see you. No false moves, no true ones.' He picked up her phone right away. 'Now, let me have a look at this . . .'

Janine shifted on her feet. Duke yanked her close to him.

Ren locked eyes with her.

Stay as strong as you always are. You can do this.

Ren looked over at Gary, Robbie and Everett. They looked at her with unreadable expressions.

How do we get out of this?

Ren started looking around the room again.

What is at my disposal?

'Agent Bryce!' said Duke, 'you've got mail! Neiman Marcus wants to introduce you to a sneak preview of spring's new line.' He paused. 'Dear Misters Neiman and Marcus, thank you for your kind email, but I'm not going to even make it through fall, and even if I did, there'll be no spring in my step.' He laughed. 'Agent Dettling,' he said, 'we hoped you enjoyed your stay at the Hay-Adams Hotel in Washington, D.C., Detective Truax – this is from your personal account – "CJ" whoever that is, had a great night Saturday, has been thinking about you ever since. Agent King, you need to renew your subscription to the *New Yorker*.' He paused. 'Jesus, how much time do you people spend reading this bullshit every day? Beep, beep, beep, you got mail! You got a whole pile of bullshit is what you got. Aren't you supposed to be fighting crime?'

The Hay-Adams Hotel . . . where have I come across that recently? Where? Written down somewhere. Gold letters. Sylvie Ross! Child forensic interviewer! Her sleek, stylish pencil with the gold writing. Hay-Adams Hotel, D.C. Gary being stand-offish, abandoning her abruptly in the bullpen. Oh God. Gary is having an affair with Sylvie Ross. Sylvie fucking Ross.

She looked at him, unable to hide her flinch.

Of course, you have no idea what I just realized. In the middle of all this . . .

She looked back at Duke Rawlins.

Why are you here?

There was another beep.

'Janine Hooks,' said Joe. 'Thank you for your donation! To some beat-up dogs!'

He turned to Ren, his voice ice-cold. 'Now – here's a

question for you: where the hell is Joe Lucchesi? I'm not fucking around.'

Joe Lucchesi has clearly gone off your radar. Thank God.

'I don't think you're fucking around,' said Ren. 'But Joe Lucchesi has left Denver.'

'You lying bitch.'

'I'm not lying,' said Ren. 'You can sit here looking for information I don't have or you can go out and try to find him yourself.'

'Oh, if Joe thinks his little lady is in trouble, he'll come looking for her,' said Duke.

'He's a cop, I'm an agent,' said Ren. 'He doesn't see me as a lil lady who needs to be rescued.'

'He might want to keep you alive to fuck you again, though,' said Duke.

Fuck. Fuck. Fuck. Fuck. FUCK.

'I did not—' She trailed off. 'Right now, Joe Lucchesi is non-contactable. Check my phone. See his Automatic Reply: he will not be answering his emails. It's there, black and white. His phone is diverted. You know all this. You are here because of this. You've lost him. You want to draw him back.'

Duke was barely hiding his rage.

'And Joe Lucchesi's priority is not me,' said Ren. 'His priority is his family.'

Duke laughed. 'Well, I can at least reassure him that *one* member of his family is safe.'

What the fuck is that supposed to mean?

Ren's heart plunged. She saw Grace's little face.

But as long as I can keep you here, Duke Rawlins, in the same room as me, Grace Lucchesi is absolutely safe.

Then she thought of Joe Lucchesi's own words: Duke Rawlins will always have an accomplice.

65

Duke Rawlins, his arm still around Janine's narrow waist, was now pulling her tight to him, her back against his stomach, the back of her head against his chest.

'She's the sweetest one here, isn't she?' said Duke. 'I knew you'd run to her.' He turned to Janine. 'She must think you're a little fragile.' He picked up her skinny wrist, let it drop.

Janine was staring ahead, jaw clenched, rock solid, no reaction.

Go ahead, Rawlins, underestimate her, see what happens.

'Let the women go,' said Everett. 'Show some mercy.'

Duke looked at him. 'Mercy? There was no mercy for me! My whole life.' He reached out his arm. 'No mercy for me, and that makes me? Merciless. Mercy. Less.'

'You don't need to—'

'Just shut the fuck up or I'll kill both these women. I like doing that, remember? Why would I let the females go? They're what I love to do.

'You!' he said, stabbing the gun into Janine's ribs. 'You take all these phones apart, you take out the SIM cards, batteries, everything. I'm watching you – don't do anything

359

stupid. I'm going to keep yours, Ren Bryce, so your savior can come get you. Text him,' he said, handing her the phone, 'write very simply in your regular way – nothing fancy, nothing weird – to come to Safe Streets. Then show me.'

Ren wrote: **Come to Safe Streets.**

She handed it to Duke.

'Add something else,' said Duke. 'You really think that's enough? You dumb bitch. Write: "important development".'

She did as he asked. He hit Send.

'I'll wait as long as that takes,' he said. 'Of course, he might be more anxious to respond this time round, seeing that he fucked up with his wife. Or maybe he won't show at all . . . seeing that he fucked up with his wife.'

Janine did as Rawlins asked, dismantling the phones, filling the box with their parts.

'Thank you kindly,' said Duke. 'See, I can do things kindly. I can. *How many women have you raped and murdered?*' he said, mimicking a whining female voice. 'Answer: I have lost track.' He ran his forearm under his nose, wiped away sweat. '*Why have you lost track? Why? How could that possibly be?*' He raised his arm and looked around the room. 'I have lost track in the same way I lost track of . . .'

Ren looked at him. *I know what you're thinking: lost track of the number of times* you *were violated.*

I need to provoke you. I need you to come for me, and let Janine go. She'll know what to do. If you lunge, she drops, the weapons are within her reach.

'You are no different to your mother,' said Ren. 'An addict who hurts other people to soothe their own pain.'

He didn't move an inch. 'That's bullshit. That is bull shit.'

'At least your mother was just addicted to disappearing into her own little screwed-up world. You're addicted to raping and killing your way out of it. What do you think your mother went through as a child that her pain went so deep?'

'What that bitch went through?' said Duke, his pitch rising. 'I don't care, as long as it was as close to hell as it could possibly be.'

I know why. And I understand how you could think that way.

Duke was sweating.

The temperature was stifling.

Six people in a small space. No AC.

'I took her away, Mama Rawlins,' said Duke. He laughed. 'Mama! Fuck. Me. I took her and I put her in a box: DANGER! KEEP OUT! There was a hole in it I made her watch through, so she could see the effect she had on me. I used to sing her Dainty's song. Dainty never even knew I'd disappear off to where I kept Mama.' He held out his arms. 'I raped that hooker right in front of her face, saw her beady eyes looking out, killed her there too, burned her flesh to hide her wounds. Win-Win was her name. And I swear to God, no truer name for what I was doing. Win fucking win. Oh, Mama knew what she'd done; she knew what she'd done to me. I left that night to get rid of that buy-by-the-hour hooker corpse, and Wanda Rawlins got away. Bye-bye! I'd been doing so well. I was very angry that Kurt found her. Very angry with him. But he didn't know who the fuck she was. He was thinking about boning that blonde. Got there first!' He laughed.

'Positions of trust, that's what it's called, right? That was what my mama was in, right? That's what you guys are in . . .'

A shiver went up Ren's spine. The profile. The obsession with positions of trust. This is his red-hot danger zone.

'Where was the trust in my life?' said Duke. 'Who could I trust if I couldn't trust my own mama?'

He turned to Gary. 'I see you, "supervising" all this, making streets safe, I see all of you, and I'm thinking "When was I ever safe?"' He raised his gun. 'Where were the safe streets for me to walk?' He laughed. 'You're not *safe*. You are not safe.'

He fired twice. The first bullet hit Robbie, a clean shot to the head. The second hit Everett. Ren could see his hair lift into the air, then blood spraying, then he was slumped behind Robbie.

Robbie's lifeless eyes stared ahead. The side of his head was destroyed.

Next in line, spattered with his colleagues' blood, staring down a barrel, was Gary Dettling.

66

*No!!!!!!!!!!!!!!!!!!!!!!!!!!!!! Robbie, Everett . . . no, no, no, no, no. That's
not how it works! You give chances! You give people chances. You
. . . wait. You fucking wait. You let us save people! You fucking
psycho! You fucking psychopath.*

No. No. No. No. No. NO.

*Agent down. Agent down. Agent down. Agents down. Agents
down.*

Janine was ghostly, her lip quivering, her body limp, but
her eyes were set, dark, glued to the opposite wall.

Duke was now pointing the gun at Gary, staring him
down. Gary was staring right back, unmoving, waiting, calm,
accepting.

'I thought you were merciless!' said Ren, drawing Duke
on herself.

Gary has a wife. Gary has a daughter.

'You just shot two men,' said Ren. 'Dead in an instant,
no suffering. Don't you want people to suffer? Where's the
suffering in an instant death?'

Duke blinked. Seconds passed.

He lowered the gun a fraction, moved it to the right, fired, ripping a chunk from Gary's left triceps. The blood spattered up against Ren's right side; she could feel the warm spray on her face.

Jesus Christ.

Gary cried out in pain, only briefly, then buried it.

Ren's fingers shook as she wiped Gary's blood from her face.

I'm next. Jesus Christ. No. Don't. Please don't. Don't.

Duke, instead, had pulled Janine back tight against him, and his gun was pressed into her ribs.

Oh, no. No.

Ren was immediately seeing row after row of crime scene photos and everyone was dead, and this time they had the faces of her friends.

No! No! No!

Imagine an abandoned Safe Streets . . .

Jesus Christ. What hell are we in? Stop. Stop. Stop.

Think. Think. Think.

Think. Think. Think.

Get out of this room. We need to get out of this room.

Duke Rawlins' nickname as a child was Pukey Dukey. It tormented him. That's what Shaun Lucchesi said. Throw up. It will rattle him.

'Please!' said Ren. 'Please can we move into another room? I can't . . . I . . . don't feel well. The smell of . . . everything . . . I think I'm going to be—'

'You shut the fuck up,' said Duke. 'Just shut the fuck up.'

'I'm going to be—'

'—raped in front of your boss is what you're going to be.'

Ren fell to her knees in front of Duke, and threw up, splashing his boots. Silver spots danced in front of her eyes.

Ugh.

'You fucking disgusting piece of shit,' said Duke. He jumped out of the way, staggered back, kicking out, catching her in the jaw. Ren cried out, fell onto her side, curled into a ball.

'Get the fuck up,' he said.

She stood up, slowly.

My jaw. The pain . . .

Duke was now pressing the gun into Janine's temple.

'You,' he said to Ren, 'walk, carefully, slowly toward the door. I've got your friend, don't be dumb.'

Ren moved toward the door, glancing back at Gary.

Oh fuck. No.

His face was gray, his arm soaked with blood, his head limp on his neck.

When Duke Rawlins saw Gary's face, he lit up. 'I'm gonna leave you here, leave you to go slowly.'

Ren stopped. 'Please let me help him,' she said. 'You will need him if you want to get away from here. He's in charge. He'll get—'

'Who says I want to get away from here?' said Duke. 'Who says this is not my blaze of fucking glory?'

'You do want to get away,' said Ren. *You have to want to get away.* 'You do need someone. You've always needed someone. Gary will get you whatever you want.'

'Now, why would he do that?' said Duke. 'Do you think I'm stupid?'

'In exchange for his life, Gary would do anything,' said Ren.

Gary managed a weak nod.

Jesus, please don't die. Jesus. This is not happening. Someone tell me this is not fucking real.

'And what about you?' said Duke, turning to Ren. 'What would you do?' His eyes glowed in the darkest, deadest way.

Ren's heart pounded. *Me? What* would *I do?*

His hand was on his belt buckle.

Her stomach turned.

I'd like to see you try.

'Move,' he said. 'Move.'

Ren walked through the offices out into the hallway, Duke behind her, gripping Janine.

'In there,' said Duke, pointing into the conference room.

Ren opened the door into a room that was filled with everything there was to know about Duke Rawlins and his life, and his victims, and theirs.

His eyes widened. 'This is pretty obsessive,' he said.

That's what he says . . .

He cuffed Janine to the radiator. Ren expected to be next.

'You're coming with me,' he said. 'Via the ladies' room.'

What? Why?'

She glanced down at Janine. They locked eyes. It was too much.

At least if he's with me, Janine is safe.

'Move,' said Rawlins. 'Now.' He rattled his belt buckle.

He shoved Ren down the hallway ahead of him. As she walked, she did a mental inventory of every room in Safe Streets, scanning their contents from memory, wondering what a man like Duke Rawlins would use to rape her: he always used whatever was to hand.

I am deciding what object I will be raped with.

Her stomach tightened.

Choose the source of your wildest pain. This is all so wrong.

Duke pushed the door open and shoved her into the ladies' room.

He planted her at the sink in front of the mirror, stood behind her. She could smell his skin, shower gel, laundry detergent, mouthwash, nothing as filthy or stinking as it should be. She gripped the edges of the sink. She stared, not at him in the mirror, but at herself.

How many times have I looked at this face? And hated who I saw? And was disappointed, and was guilty, and felt ruined, nothing, useless, a failure?

She felt a surge of strength.

Bring it on, psycho. Bring it on. I will fucking kill you. I am more than you think I am. I am more than I think I am.

She got a flashback to the previous year, to the teenage boy, the rapist who had fought her, brought her to the ground until Denver PD detectives had burst in.

Not this time. I'm stronger. Fitter. Murderous.

'You have all the power,' said Ren.

Duke tilted his head.

'You don't need to rape me to prove that,' said Ren.

'Maybe that's not why I want to rape you . . .' he said, running his hand up her stomach.

What the fuck?

'You think I'm a monster, don't you?' he said. 'You think I'm a monster.'

Ren didn't reply.

'Little Miss Perfect's never sinned,' he said. He grabbed a thick fistful of her hair, pulled it taut, brought fresh tears to her eyes, then slammed her head into the mirror, cracking it, yanking her back again, slamming her head in again.

'So, you can face yourself, no shame – right?' he said.

The skin was split above Ren's eyebrow. She watched the blood stream down the left side of her face.

Seven years' bad luck. One night down . . .

'Can *you*?' said Ren. 'Can *you* face yourself?'

Duke looked up at his distorted reflection in the broken glass. For a wild moment, uprooted from reality, Ren was expecting humanity. All she saw were eyes that were black, blank, terrifying. Dead in one way, alive in another.

She felt a slow shiver roll from the base of her spine to the top of her head.

This man is the devil incarnate.

I'm not going to make it out of here.

67

Ren's heart was pounding.

Where are you, Joe? Did you get my text? You had to have realized it wouldn't take us this long to get back. Maybe the tower, the steps, the lighthouse – it was all too much. It was another lifetime, a bigger nightmare, an overwhelming one.

Duke started unbuttoning her shirt.

No, no, no.

She squirmed under his hands. 'No. Don't.'

He laughed, opened the buttons even slower. When he was down to the third one, her cell phone beeped.

Thank God, thank God, please, please let him look. Please.

He took the phone, stared at the screen.

'An email,' he said. 'Shaun Banner. Copied to Joe Lucchesi?'

Shaun Lucchesi? No! It's the names of Duke's abusers! No! Oh, no!

'Don't read that email,' said Ren 'Don't read it. Please don't. It is not in your interest to—'

She watched in the shattered mirror as Duke started to read. He blinked, twice. And Ren thought of the broken dolls' eyes and the nightmares. And the pale blue glass. He blinked again. He was scrolling down. He was still scrolling.

Oh, God. How many names are on that list?

His whole body started to tremble. He kept swallowing, over and over.

'We can get justice for you,' said Ren.

Duke turned to her, squinted. 'Justice? For me?'

'Westley Ames . . .' said Ren.

Duke was struggling to keep control of his facial muscles.

'I know Police Chief Ogden Parnum is dead,' said Ren. 'But we can bring the others to justice. All those men. We can make sure that they rot in jail for what they did.'

Duke was looking around the room.

I have no idea what you are thinking right now.

'So you know all my dirty little secrets,' said Duke.

'That's not what this is,' said Ren. 'It wasn't your fault. Don't you want to—'

'No!' he roared. 'No!' He yanked her toward him, she could feel his breath on her ear. 'Which one's your locker?' he said. 'Which one?'

Oh, shit. What's even in there?

Ren pointed to her locker, and he dragged her to it, opened it, and pulled out her wash bag.

What the?

They were back at the sink. He dropped the wash bag into it. He unzipped it, and frantically searched through it.

What are you looking for? I don't want to think.

He pulled out her toothbrush.

What is he doing?

He pulled out the toothpaste.

He took the bag and threw it across the floor.

He released her waist, but grabbed her hair again, pulled it tight, held her head over the sink. He squeezed toothpaste onto the brush. He turned on the cold faucet, with a shaking hand.

'Open your fucking mouth,' he said. 'Open your mouth. Open your mouth.'

He pulled up her hair.

'Open. Your. Mouth.'

She did as he asked. He shoved the toothbrush under the water, then shoved it into her mouth and started scrubbing hard.

I am gone. I am gone. I am gone.

'I always had a filthy mouth,' he said. 'Always had to scrub at it, always. And if I couldn't? If I couldn't get to brush my teeth, if I was in school, or the toothpaste was all gone, and I had no money to buy any more, you know what? I preferred the taste of puke.'

Jesus Christ.

He scrubbed and scrubbed and scrubbed Ren's teeth until her gums bled. She was choking on the toothbrush, gagging, and he kept brushing.

'You know what I did with my few cents?' he said. 'When all the other kids were buying candy? I was buying toothpaste.'

Ren coughed, over and over, until eventually he stopped. He shoved her head under the cold faucet, and the water poured over her mouth, and she sucked it in, and it burned like acid, and she spat it out, and he pulled her head up again. Her gums were throbbing, her scalp on fire.

He threw her down on the bench by the wall, where she sat slumped back.

And then something happened that she could never have imagined. Duke Rawlins dissolved into tears.

'Did I stand a chance?' he said, wiping his eyes. 'Did I? Did I? If you have a mother as fucked up as mine and a father who's what – a whore-fucking vanishing act? What kind of blood's going to be running through your veins? How did I stand a chance?'

371

'You didn't,' said Ren. 'You really didn't.'

'Do you know my mother allowed men into my bedroom?' said Duke. 'Knocked on their behalf – a weak and shameful, pussy's knock. Knocking! As if there was an option! There was no safe place for me. Like every other kid, I'd make those homemade signs saying KEEP OUT! and DANGER DO NOT ENTER!'

'What your mother did to you was—' *sick, unconscionable* . . .

'Do you know . . .' he roared over her.

'I'm sorry . . .'

His voice returned to normal. '. . . that my mother allowed groups of men to take me away to their cabins in the woods? They'd tell their wives or whoever the hell they had back home that they were going hunting. And they were hunting me. Through the woods. And I had to show up in school Monday like nothing had happened, like no one had handed me over to a pack of wild animals Friday night for a gram of coke.' He stuck his neck forward, opened his eyes wide, like a threat, like a challenge. ''Course, it didn't matter who caught me – they all got a piece of me in the end.' He looked at Ren. 'Thing is – there weren't really any pieces. Someone like you might think I'm a broken man, but I'm not. You can't be broken if all of you has been gone since you were about seven years old. That's the fact of the matter. I didn't know until I was seven years old that what was happening to me didn't happen to most other kids.'

Oh. God. This is just so heartbreakingly, terrifyingly, chillingly fucked up. 'Do you think I trust law enforcement after what a sheriff did to me? Came to me in his pristine uniform, came *on* me in his pristine uniform. Used his baton. Anything. Everything. No, sir. And he wasn't the only man in uniform to come to my door. So you can all go fuck yourselves.

'Bet you had birthday parties and . . . comfort! Comfort in your life. I had nothing. For the first four years of my life, I could *feel*: happiness, joy. And after that . . . I could feel only pain. And after that, nothing until my one friend. I had one friend . . . that Joe Lucchesi killed! And lied to me about – told me he was cheating with my ex-wife, lying son-of-a-bitch. I almost believed him, but it was just another load that someone expected me to swallow. And it was almost the worst part. Almost worse than him killing Donnie was him trying to shit on Donnie's memory. Do you know what's so terrible? If you're like me, and you know nothing good in your life and you're numb to all pain, but then something happens that makes you feel good? Or someone comes along that makes you feel good? Well, that's a fucking miracle! That's what that is. It's the most precious thing in the world. And Joe Lucchesi took all that away. And I have made him pay, and I will make him pay some more.'

Shit on the memory of a rapist/murderer?! 'You and Donnie Riggs killed women together!' said Ren.

'Which also makes me feel good!' said Duke. 'Don't you fucking get that by now?'

Jesus. Christ.

'But it's not the same without him – it just isn't,' said Duke. 'I fuck up without him, always have. I don't get the same one hundred per cent joy I did from when he was with me. That was taken from me. The last bit of good.'

He slammed his fist into the mirror, and the phone dropped to the floor. 'Where the fuck is Joe Lucchesi? Where is he?'

He pulled back, blood streaming down his knuckles.

'I told you, he's not in Denver,' said Ren.

'I don't believe you,' said Duke. 'I don't believe you.'

She glanced down at the phone, still open on the email from Shaun, and there were just so many names.

Duke bent down, picked it up, held it right up to her face, and scrolled through it. They were numbered.

Her heart lurched.

Sixty-three names.

68

Duke looked down at Ren. 'Have you ever met someone like me before?'

Ren shook her head. 'No.'

'And what do you make of me?'

Ren looked into his eyes.

I have no words.

'You know, I wonder if you pity me,' said Duke. 'And I can't say that that's not what I want, because I think somewhere inside me, there's a little boy who wants it. He has to still be there, doesn't he? Because who else can still feel the thrill of seeing a hawk in flight or the smooth surface of a creek waiting to be dived into, or . . . because it's not me . . .' He looked away. 'I get different thrills.' He paused. 'But maybe it's not the calm of the creek water, it's the need to shatter it. It's the need to break that perfect surface. Maybe that's what that is.'

What do I make of you? What do I make of you? You make me want to kill every person on earth who has ever harmed a child.

And after what you've done, which I have to keep thinking about, after what you've done, you make me want to kill you.

He looked at her as if he was reading her mind.

'Never be too comfortable in your skin,' he said. 'Never. Never think you're better than everyone else, never look at other people and judge. Because, you know the fucking tragedy of humanity? A lot of us give in to the things we hate, don't we? Dainty did. She was disgusted by our mama . . . and I watched her become our mama. Dainty might not have been a hooker, but she was a mean, junkie bitch. Wrote a song about mama, ended up making it her own fucking anthem, ended up dancing to it, ended up dying to it. Be careful what you choose to dance to.'

All Ren could think about was Everett.

My darling dancing Everett.

'Let me help you with this,' said Ren, 'with what happened to you.'

He didn't even look up. 'You don't want to help me. Shut the fuck up. You can't manipulate me. I'm not stupid. I'm here, I've got your boss in a cell, your friend chained to a radiator. I told you how you can help me: get Joe Lucchesi here.'

'I can't do that,' said Ren. 'If I could, I would.'

Her phone beeped again. Another email.

He opened it. He looked alarmed.

Not like the last time – this is different.

What the fuck is going on here?

Two emails. Relevant to him?

'How does this work?' said Duke. 'I want to reply to this one.'

He sat down beside her.

The email address was LuckyNYPD67@gmail.com and the subject: Geoff Riggs.

What the hell is this? Donald Riggs' father, the subject of an email to me?

OK, Joe was NYPD. '67 is his birth year. Lucky short for Lucchesi. His personal email address? What has he sent me? What about Geoff Riggs?

She looked down. It was a two-line email:

We found something: Geoff Riggs is Duke Rawlins' biological father. Only problem is, he's dying. We're going to question him before it's too late. And frankly, I don't give a fuck if he has a heart attack right there in the bed . . . Joe.

Holy. Shit. What the?

This is off. Even for Joe, that last line sounds extreme.

She hit Reply, and nodded toward the box. 'You type in there . . .'

Duke grabbed it back from her and slowly input his response. Then he sat against the wall, wiped his hand across his brow, let out a breath. He was holding Ren's cell phone in his hands. He didn't take his eyes off the screen.

Where is he? What has Duke replied? Will Joe get it? Why am I still alive?

Ren touched her hand to her face.

Still bleeding.

'It's a waiting game now,' said Duke, more to himself than to anyone else.

Geoff Riggs is Duke Rawlins' father? That means Joe Lucchesi has been upgraded to the killer not just of Rawlins' friend, but of his only brother. And he's saying they're sending people to question a dying man?

This will not end well.

69

There was a sudden, rattling groan from downstairs, a creaking sound, more rattling.

Sounds like the elevator. But it's not working.

Who is about to walk into this nightmare?

Jesus Christ. The haunted elevator – maybe that's all it is.

Duke grabbed Ren. He took her flashlight from his back pocket, hustled her out the door, and used it to light their way out onto the landing.

Duke shouted, his voice echoing around the stairwell: 'If someone is down there trying to fuck with me, it ain't gonna work. I'm gonna fire into this lil lady's face if I see even a flicker of movement out of the corner of my eye.'

Who's here? Please be Joe.

There was a banging sound, loud and hollow.

That's the basement door. The basement door is open.

A cell phone started to ring in the foyer, echoing on the marble, its screen glowing. Ren listened, looked all around her, studied everything as Rawlins moved the flashlight's beam all across the stairs, up and down.

All at once, pieces started to fall into place. A plan.

'That phone will have to be answered,' said Ren, 'so as not to cause suspicion. That lady you killed – Valerie, the realtor—'

'You weren't buying the electrical fault then,' said Duke, laughing out loud. He sighed. 'That was a good one, though. I saw the electrical contractor's van last week. I figured it was a nice trap. Arranged to meet Valerie here, arranged a little water on the outlet, got her to check it out, told her I heard there was a problem in the building . . .'

You are insane.

'Valerie has a jumpy boss,' said Ren. 'If she hasn't checked in for hours, he will send someone here if she doesn't pick up. He will call one of us. And if none of us answers, and her last appointment was here . . .'

Duke shrugged, but he started to move her forward.

The phone kept ringing.

'If you don't let me answer that, this will fuck everything up for you. We just walk down there. I pick up, say she's in the ladies' room, no big deal . . . we're done.'

I need you on the second floor.

Duke switched off the flashlight, gripped Ren in front of him, fully protecting his body.

They made it down two flights, but instead of going down, Duke moved them around to the left, by the guardrail, so they could look down to where Valerie lay.

The phone stopped ringing. The sound that replaced it was the slow approach of footsteps.

From under the stairs, a figure emerged.

Joe Lucchesi.

He walked up the stairs with his hands in the air.

'Well, here he comes,' said Duke. 'To rescue his lil lady.'

'He's not here for me,' said Ren, 'and we both know that.'

Joe kept walking up. Duke didn't stop him.

'We need to talk,' said Joe.

'We sure do,' said Duke.

Joe kept walking up, hands in the air, unarmed.

Apparently.

He walked halfway up the second flight.

Why has Rawlins not shot him already?

Joe made it up to the top. He moved around. There were only six feet between them.

Duke squeezed Ren tightly, stepping back a few feet.

'Go back further,' said Ren. 'Get out of his reach. Go toward that door at the end. It leads outside onto the back of the building. You can take my car. Joe doesn't give a fuck about me or my colleagues. He wants you. He will kill you. I want you to leave. I just want Gary and Janine to be safe. If you leave now, you'll get to see your father. Before they get to him. If you stay, Joe will kill you—'

'What the fuck are you saying, Ren?' said Joe.

'That's why he's here!' said Ren. 'It's the only reason. Rawlins – you came here not knowing who your father is. Now you know – everything's changed. You need to get out of here alive. You need to see your father.' Duke moved down the hallway. 'Is there a key to that door?' he said, glancing back.

'No,' said Ren. 'It's open. You can just go.'

Joe started moving toward them. 'Fuck you, Ren.'

'Stay back!' said Ren. 'Stay the fuck away from us.'

Ren took in the scene. Joe Lucchesi was three feet from her. Duke Rawlins was behind her with his arm around her, his hip up against the guardrail. Ren thought of boxing, one of the best defensive moves: bob and weave. She thought of Paul Louderback and the focus mitts, how he swiped them over her head, how she had to come up quickly to punch them again.

380

Straight jab, bob, weave. Jab, bob, weave.

There was an eerie silence.

Joe lunged toward them. Duke wasn't holding Ren tightly enough. She was no longer useful. He didn't see her as a threat. He didn't see any woman as a threat.

Ren did it. She dropped so quickly, compressed her body, came out from under Duke's arm and spun around so she was facing him again, Joe beside her. Duke lost his balance, slammed hard into the guardrail. They heard the sound of wood cracking. Everything felt suspended. Then the guardrail broke. Duke started to teeter. He dropped the gun, reached out. Ren's arm shot out to pull him back. Joe's arm shot out.

There is something wrong here.

In a fraction of a second, Duke gripped Ren's arm, as she tried to lean backwards to pull him in, but he was heavy and she was light, and Joe seemed to be doing none of the work.

What the fuck are you doing? Jesus Christ! If Duke goes, I go too!

'Joe!' screamed Ren, yanking him out of whatever dark place he had gone to. 'Joe!'

She was sliding toward the edge of the broken balcony.

NO! Noooo! Fuck! No!

Joe lunged for her, grabbed her waist, brought his forearm down hard to break the grip Duke had on her, pulled her backwards and they both crashed onto the floor. There was a bare second of silence before Duke Rawlins hit the first-floor landing, then rolled down onto the marble floor below.

70

Joe and Ren quickly jumped up from the floor and ran down the stairs to where Duke Rawlins lay on his back, his arms splayed out to the side, his head facing away from the glass entry doors. There was a small pool of blood under his head.

Joe and Ren locked eyes.

He's still alive.

Duke managed to turn his head to look at Joe. 'Would you have told me about Geoff Riggs? Did it kill you that Donnie Riggs was my brother? Turns out I had a good family, Joe. I had a good family. So fuck you.'

Drunkard father. Serial killer brother. So much goodness.

'I have no *idea* who your father is,' said Joe. He shook his head – a lazy, taunting movement. Then he smiled.

Duke frowned. 'But . . .'

'That email Ren was sent?' said Joe. 'It was bullshit. It wasn't from me. It was copied to me, but it was sent from one of the agents right inside this building to stop you wanting to die, to stop your suicide mission. He knew you wouldn't want to leave this world without saying goodbye to your father, would you? Geoff Riggs was a kind man to you. But that's all he was. He wasn't your father. Who knows who your father could have been? Your mother had quite the list. We lost count of the possibilities. Everyone knew someone who knew someone who fucked yo' mama.'

Ease up, Joe.

Ren watched Duke Rawlins. He was smiling. His head lolled away again.

Why are you still smiling?

'So, you can die with that mystery,' said Joe. 'Who's. Yo'. Daddy.'

Ren looked at Joe. There was a chilling menace in his face.

Duke used all the strength he had to turn back toward them.

'Did you get my gift?' said Duke. He was talking to Joe. 'The one I gave to The Widow Dettling?'

No, Gary will not die. He will not die, you fucking psychopath.

'The FedEx slip?' said Joe. 'What was I supposed to do with that?'

'Read it.'

'I did read it.'

'What does it say to you?' said Duke.

'Nothing,' said Joe. 'What's it meant to say to me? You went through my garbage and stored up that information for years . . . for what?'

Duke laughed weakly. 'No, sir. It's the kind of shit that could give a man nightmares for the rest of his life.'

'I'm so tired of his bullshit,' said Joe. 'It's over. It's over now.'

Duke Rawlins was weakening. His eyes were closing. Still, he was smiling.

'You don't get it,' said Duke, staring up at Joe. 'You still don't get it.'

'Get what?' said Joe.

'Grace . . .' said Duke.

'She's gone away,' said Joe. 'Grace is safe.' He looked at Ren, almost rolled his eyes.

'Safe like Hayley Gray was?' said Duke. Hayley Gray was the little girl that Donald Riggs killed. 'Safe like Hayley Gray with a bomb strapped around her waist and a detonator?'

'There's no bomb strapped to my daughter – that, I know for sure,' said Joe. 'She is thousands of miles away and only I know where.'

Your confidence is so complete. You know Grace is safe. You know it. Why is the energy in the room unchanged? Why do I still think Duke Rawlins is holding all the cards?

'I'm the bomb!' said Duke. 'You don't get it! I'm the bomb!' With the last of his strength, his head was now rocking from side to side, smiling wider, blood smeared across his teeth and gums.

This guy is absolutely unhinged.

'I'm the bomb!' said Duke. 'And I am right there with Grace wherever she goes. I'm the bomb! I'm the bomb!'

Ren and Joe locked eyes, confused, disturbed.

'You still don't get it!' said Duke. 'I got Grace, Grace got me. Got me running through her veins!' He stopped his crazy rocking, stopped dead. His eyes burned into Joe Lucchesi.

'I'm the daddy,' said Duke. 'I'm the daddy! I fucked your wife! Lucky number seven years ago. I drugged her. I fucked her. I cleaned her up. I lay her down gently on the sofa where she spent most of her time anyway. I drugged her. I fucked her. And I gave her a baby. What are the fucking chances of that? I gave her Grace. I gave your wife Grace. Now, isn't that something?'

Oh.

Dear.

God.

71

Joe Lucchesi's face had transformed in such a powerful way, it cut short even Duke Rawlins' laughter.

This is beyond thinking about. This is beyond all levels of depravity.

Ren and Joe locked eyes.

What are you thinking? How are you thinking?

Ren's heart pounded.

You want to kill this man. I want to see him rot in jail.

Joe's face was desolate, his eyes empty. A nothing-to-lose air radiated from him.

Duke Rawlins is ready to die now. He wants to die.

You want to kill him. I want to see him rot in jail.

Ren looked at Duke. His shaven head was slick with sweat.

WantED. WantED to see him rot in jail.

Now? Now I want to kill this man.

She stared at Joe.

I want to kill this man for the lifelong pain he has caused you. You were a good man. You are a good man. What justice brought Duke Rawlins into your life?

Duke Rawlins was looking around, he was smiling wide, but he couldn't hide the fear that was sparking in his eyes.

385

He kept smiling, though, and the smile broadened. He began laughing again, harder, louder, with depthless cruelty.

That was not fear in your eyes; it was relish. You are getting an even better reaction than you expected. You have run this moment through your head a million times. And the moment is here. This is everything to you. There was no fear. Of course there wasn't. There was, simply, joy.

There was a palpable change in the air, a thickening, a dense, choking, smoking hell.

'In my own way,' said Duke, drawing out the words, 'I guess I killed your wife. I did it. In my own way, I finished her off with all that scar tissue I left her. Guess I really am the gift that keeps on giving. The gift I always promised you I would be.' He rolled his head to the side and spat out blood.

Ren looked up at Joe.

What are you going to do? What are you going to say?

Joe muttered something. Ren waited. He muttered again. She strained to hear.

'Liar,' said Joe a little louder. 'Liar. You're a fucking liar!'

Duke Rawlins shook his head slowly. 'I'm not! I mean, I couldn't have planned for the baby, that was a . . . happy accident! Soon as I saw Grace walking, though, I knew. She couldn't have been more than two years old, in that park near your house. I saw it – she had the same skinny bow legs I had, got passed down by my mama. Didn't you even wonder about her hair? I mean—'

'You fucking liar!' said Joe. 'You liar.'

'No!' said Duke. 'No! I caught it all on video. There's a date on it and everything. Like the FedEx slip I took while I was there. You'll see – that'll about match up to nine months before Grace was born. And yes. There's video evidence.' He checked his watch. 'The matinee should be starting right about now.'

*   *   *

Shaun Lucchesi was staring at his laptop. He had pressed play on the emailed video, but the screen was still black. He waited. He recognized the steps up to their old house in Bay Ridge. The door was green like it used to be. This looked like an old video. Was this some kind of joke from one of his friends? Was someone about to egg the house or something? He could see the camera move onto the front door of the house, then slide across to the front-room window. He could see the shadow of his mom moving about behind the gauzy curtains. His heart lurched at the sight of his mother. He missed her.

Then he was watching the side of the house, the air vent that went into the living room. He could see a hand doing something there, holding something up, letting it waft in through the vent. The camera was back on the window. Shaun could see the blurred form of his mother slump to the floor. He could hear footsteps as the person holding the camera walked up to the front door. He could hear keys jangling. Whoever was filming took the keys and shook them in front of the screen. It was a man's hand. Shaun recognized his own key ring, remembered losing his keys and his fake ID on a night out in a bar. The man unlocked the front door. Shaun's heart pounded as the man made his way into the living room. He crouched down beside his mother. He rolled her over onto her back. She was passed out, looked almost lifeless, there was no effort required to move her. The man started to push up her skirt. Shaun slammed the laptop shut.

Joe Lucchesi's cell phone rang. He pulled it out of his jacket pocket.

Shaun's name was flashing like an alarm on the screen.

Duke was staring up at the ceiling. Without even turning his head, he said, 'That's got to be Shaun. I'm sure he's in a real panic right about now after what he's just watched.'

Jesus Christ.

Joe was speechless, unmoving.

'Joe,' said Ren. 'Joe.' She reached out for his forearm.

Look at me. Please look at me. Look at me.

Duke was half-laughing, half-whining. 'Ignoring your only biological child?'

Joe fell to his knees, grabbing Duke Rawlins by the neck.

'No!' said Ren, diving after him. 'NO! Don't do this. He fell. He fell. You were not responsible. This . . . you will be responsible. He's not worth it.' *I can't even say, think of Grace. Jesus Christ. Shaun? Everything is so wrong.*

Joe had a white-knuckle grip on Duke's neck. 'I am going to fucking kill you! I will fucking kill you, you sick fuck. You fuck. You—'

Duke's eyeballs were bulging, his face bright with compressed blood, the heels of his boots scrambling on the marble floor. The pool of blood under his head was spreading.

Ren tried to grab Joe's shoulders. It was like grabbing rock. His muscles were rigid, boring every ounce of strength into choking the life from Duke Rawlins.

'Don't,' said Ren. 'He's dying, Joe. He's dying. Let him die. Let him die. We'll walk out of here. We'll let him die alone. Let's leave him here to die. He can't win. Don't let him win.'

Joe stopped moving. Arms still rigid, he looked up at Ren, his eyes crazed, desperate, questioning, sweat pouring down his face, his eyes stinging with it. His look said, 'Please tell me this is not the nightmare I believe it to be.'

There is a monster dying at your feet and living on inside your beautiful daughter. This is *the nightmare you believe it to be.*

There was a flash of movement outside the building. Joe pulled his bloodied hands from Duke Rawlins' neck, and fell back onto his heels. Duke sucked in as big a breath as his failing body would allow. Ren grabbed Joe's arm as he stood up to his full height. Side by side, they watched, dazed, as the doors burst open and the SWAT team plowed in. Ren looked down. Duke Rawlins looked delirious, his head moving again from side to side. He was drawing his final breaths, his face set into one final shit-eating grin.

72

Ren sat in the car outside Joe Lucchesi's hotel, her forehead pressed against the steering wheel. Gary was at the hospital, in no position to tell her to go home, not to carry out the courtesy of seeing Joe off at the airport after some of the most horrific moments of his life.

Fifteen hours had passed. Everyone focuses on the shooting, never the aftermath, never the ordinary stuff like people need to eat dinner, sleep, catch a flight somewhere.

Ren checked her cell phone. There were four missed calls from Matt. She didn't listen to his voicemails, but she guessed he had read about the shooting online. All she managed to do was text him back: I'm fine – don't worry!

She tried Ben's phone. She had left three voicemails. Surely he had heard. She'd never wanted to see him as much as she wanted to see him now.

Maybe he found out about the night in the hotel with Joe. But he couldn't have. How could he have? Maybe he's on his way. Maybe he's going to be at the apartment when I get back. Surprise!

She thought about Robbie.

Robbie will never get married, or have kids, or love or be loved the way he always wanted to be, the way he deserved. One last girl emailed him. Maybe she was going to be The One. Maybe Janine was. We won't ever know.

Everett's widowed father will never know that Luke, Everett's handsome, beautiful, carpenter friend, who fell apart when he came to the hospital, was really the man Everett had loved for fifteen years and planned to spend the rest of his life with.

What is to be done with all this grief? I can't bear this. I can't. I just can't. There is no cure. I don't believe in time. What can time do for me, Everett? You're the numbers guy. What will it take before I can dance again? Will time make me laugh, or carry me double vodka cranberries, or find me miracles in spreadsheets, and laughs on Monday mornings? And ice for my pineapple juice?

She started crying. *I can't live this way; the horror outside, the horror inside. The thoughts, all the thoughts, over and over. I want silence. I want to be the person who has one thought a day, an unchallenging thought. I want a mind where avenues are really dead ends. No forked thoughts, no networks, no links.*

But is that what I want? Is it? Who would I be then?

She dialed Ben's number again. 'Ben . . . it's me. I'm not sure if you've heard anything, but please just call me first, before you speak with anyone else. I love you so much.' She hung up.

My gut was right about some things. And my gut was wrong. This is so exhausting. Everyone has a gut they can go on and I don't. Mine is broken. What am I supposed to do? What am I supposed to do about anything? Who can even answer that?

Ren called Janine. 'Hey,' she said. 'How are you doing?'

'Numb,' she said. 'Numb.'

'Tell me what happened . . . the email everything.'

'Don't cuff me to something in a room full of documents for one,' said Janine. 'I just kicked over every pile I could and eventually a paper clip slid my way. I uncuffed myself, ran in to check on Gary. He was unconscious. I thought he was dead. Everett . . . Everett was still alive, Ren. He was still alive. He told me Gary had a second phone – for Sylvie Ross! I went to find Gary's phone in his office, somewhere in a drawer. I got it, I ran back to Everett. He told me to write an email pretending I was Joe, told me about Geoff Riggs. He knew it would change things.' She started crying. 'When I got back to him, he . . . he asked me to call his parents and hold the phone up. Then Luke . . . and . . . Ren, it was the worst . . . it was beyond heartbreaking. And Robbie was dead . . . and Everett was dying. And I was right there, and . . .' She started bawling crying.

Ren sobbed along with her.

Everett – in your dying moments, that's what you did. Made sure Duke Rawlins would want to live, would be more likely not to want to die in a hail of bullets and take everyone with him.

Everett, Janine: you saved my life, you saved Gary's.

And, Gary, your affair helped!

Jesus Christ.

'Where are you?' said Ren. 'Are you home safe?'

'Yes. Terri's on her way over. Will you come when you're ready?'

'Of course I will, of course.'

Never in my wildest dreams did I think I would be meeting Terri under these circumstances.

Ren looked up to see Joe Lucchesi walking down the steps. She pushed open the driver's door and started to get out of the Jeep. 'Hey,' she said.

'Hey,' said Joe. 'Stay where you are. Let me just throw this in the back seat.'

Where I looked back at your sleeping daughter not that long ago.

The drive to the airport was mostly in silence, two ghostly, grieving people with black memories, shared secrets, deep sufferings, uncertain paths, scars upon scars.

I don't want any more war stories. I don't want any more war.

She could see only Duke Rawlins, Robbie, Everett, Gary.

Where the fuck am I?

She was struck with an image of Dr. Gaston holding a putty knife, she heard his brutal words from an old crime scene: 'dries like concrete'.

What was he talking about?

Where the fuck am I?

Rawlins. Robbie. Everett. Gary. Rawlins. Robbie. Everett. Gary. Gun. Blast. Holes. Blood. Gray matter. Gray matter. Gray matter dries like concrete. Dries like concrete. Dries like concrete.

'I need to pull over,' said Ren. *I'm going to be sick.*

Oh, God. Oh, God. Oh, God.

The car was parked for twenty minutes. Ren lay, weakened, slumped in the seat. Joe gave her space and silence.

I'm so tired. I'm so, so tired.

I can't do this. I'm cracking. I'm going to break.

She started up the engine, continued on toward the airport.

She thought about the Cheerios on Carly Raine's lips, the torn black plastic around Hope Coulson's body, puncture wounds, and scratched soles, and foreign objects.

Stop. Stop. Stop. But this . . . this will never stop. This is all entangled in who I am. How was this the path I chose? One I knew would be littered with the fallout of the very worst that life has to offer? Things I was destined to pick up and examine and touch and smell and never sidestep. Maybe, if I'm lucky, to climb over. Or destroy with minimal collateral damage.

Jesus Christ.

She glanced over at Joe Lucchesi. He was far away.

Who are we? Were we born broken that we chose to exist in a world of broken things? Is that, really, the only place we can be comfortable?

Where is the comfort? Where is it? We were wrong. We are wrong.

Ren sensed a presence in front of her. She slammed on the brakes. She and Joe shot forward and back, striking nothing, holding tight. A woman glared at Ren through the windshield, slammed her hand on the hood of the car, pointed at the red light she was about to plow through.

'I'm so sorry,' said Ren, mouthing it, making it clear. 'I'm sorry.' *I'm so sorry. This isn't me. What* is *me?*

Joe reached out and put a hand on her forearm, squeezing it. 'Are you OK?'

'Yes. Sorry. I'm . . .' *a mess.* But she knew she didn't need to finish it. They knew what they both were.

Departures was busy with people who looked so different to them, who had no idea who these two people were, brought together by an evil that had triumphed on a grand scale before it had died.

'Well . . .' said Joe, 'I guess I'll see you around.'

'Yes.'

They hugged. When they pulled apart, they looked into each other's eyes.

Who are we now? To ourselves . . . to each other.

'Thank you for everything,' said Joe.

'Thank *you*,' said Ren. *I don't know if I can ever bear to see you again.*

'I'm so sorry about your friends,' said Joe. 'You lost good men.'

Tears welled in her eyes. *Don't cry. You might never stop.* She managed to nod.

'Joe . . .'

Maybe don't say it.

He looked at her, waited.

Don't. It won't be the right thing to say.

'What?' said Joe.

Biology is one thing. But Duke Rawlins is gone. He's dead. He lives on nowhere.

'Nothing,' said Ren.

'If you're ever in New York . . .' said Joe.

'Thanks,' said Ren. 'Safe trip.'

'Daddy!' they heard. They both turned to see Grace and Camille walking toward them. Grace started to run.

Her little bowed legs . . .

Ren gritted her teeth.

Tears, tears, threatening tears.

'Gracie!' He crouched down, holding out his arms. She jumped into them, burying her head into his neck, just like the first time Ren had seen her.

Tears spilled down Ren's face.

Not in front of Grace. No.

She wiped them swiftly away.

She could see the same from Joe as he kissed Grace's head.

'I missed you so much,' he said, so intensely Ren could barely stand to watch.

Joe blinked away his tears, pulled himself back from Grace and stared into her eyes.

Please find nothing there of Duke Rawlins. Please.

'Missed you too, Daddy!'

'What are you doing back in Denver?' said Joe.

'We're going on vacation!' said Grace.

Joe frowned. Camille was smiling.

'We're going to Disney World!' said Grace. 'You, me, Shaun, Camille, Granddad, Pam!'

'Did you get a job while you were gone?' said Joe. 'You're treating us all to a vacation.'

Grace laughed. 'Granddad got us tickets.'

And could never have imagined this weekend was going to end on anything but a graduation high.

Joe raised his eyebrows at Ren. The see-I-told-you-my-dad-has-to-play-the-bigshot look.

'Well, Granddad did a wonderful thing,' said Joe.

'She helped!' said Grace, pointing to Ren.

Well, of course.

'She told us your flight number, your flight time!' said Grace. 'Shaun is on the way!'

Joe was barely keeping it together.

Distract. Distract.

'You have fun,' said Ren. 'Lots of it. Extra for me.'

'Yay!' said Grace.

Joe smiled, hugged Grace tighter, kissed her sandy hair.

Ren walked away.

Love. Conquers. All.

73

Ren kept walking toward the exit.

I will tell Ben nothing to hurt him, and I will never hurt him again. I know my triggers. I will not place myself at the end of that barrel. I vow to be well, to be sober, to be in control.

You will never be in control.

Yes I will.

You won't.

I can try.

You will fail. You always do.

I will fight harder.

You've said that before.

I will not fail.

You are helpless.

I am not helpless.

You are. You are sick.

I'm not sick.

Look at the destruction you crave.

I don't crave destruction.

It always finds you. You find it. You are magnetized. You are dark, magnetic, black as Duke Rawlins.

I am white light.

You are delusional.

I'm a good person.

I am louder than your kindest thought. I win. I always win. You're a mess, you always will be, you'll always feel, in your soul, that everything is about to go wrong and it's all your fault. Because it is your fault. You're the bomb. You're about to blow up. Didn't that resonate with you? Ha. You and inside your head and Duke Rawlins and inside his. It's an adjoining hall of fucking mirrors. That's what this is. You can't escape it. There are only mirrors, no doors, no windows. Blinding reflection.

NO! NO! NO!

Ren stopped, stood still, took out her cell phone. She scrolled through her contacts.

Everett. Her heart sank. She kept scrolling until she saw Robbie's name.

Hurt yourself more. Go on. Hurt. Do it. Dial them. Hear their messages. Hear them tell you they'll return your call. But they never will. You will never hear their voices again, never laugh with them. Suffocating thought, isn't it? You're powerless. You can't change that. Ever. They're gone.

Ren started to cry. *I'm so tired. I'm just so tired.*

Kill yourself, then. What's the point? End it.

She struggled to breathe through the tears.

Call Ben. He'll help you. Even though you know you hurt him. And you're a liar. You selfish bitch.

I didn't mean to hurt him. I didn't want to. I don't know what happened.

You can't help it is what happened. You're weak and indulgent.

I love Ben. With all my heart.

No, you don't. You have no clue what love is. You're one of those people.

No, I'm not.

You are! All you do is ruin love. You wouldn't ruin something so beautiful if you truly knew what it was?

I . . . don't understand it myself. Stop it. Stop. Stop. Stop. Stop.

Ren slumped onto an empty bench, buried her head in her hands. Tears poured down her face.

I can't go any further. I can't move. Oh God. I can't breathe. Please no one see me. Security's going to come. What will I say? I've lost my mind. I'll be sedated and carried away and . . . breathe. Breathe.

I am louder than your kindest thought.

Get. Help.

She sat on the bench, breathed, thought of nice things, breathed, controlled it.

Just get to the Jeep. Get that far.

She sat into the Jeep and started the engine.

Regular things, aftermath, regular things.

She drove.

I'm going home to no real home.

Pack a bag, go to Janine's. You're going to Janine's.

She felt relief at this one small certainty.

Minutes from the apartment, the phone rang.

Gary. Don't get into it. He has problems of his own.

She picked up. 'How are you doing?'

'I'm home, I checked myself out. I'm good. Ren, where are you exactly? We need to talk. Could you stop by the house?'

But Ren had trailed off. She was looking ahead. 'Oh my God,' she said. 'I gotta go, Gary. There's . . . it's, it's . . . it's my brother! Outside my apartment!'

She ended the call. She parked the car, jumped up, ran to Matt, threw her arms around him. 'Oh, thank God, thank God, thank God.'

Tears were spilling down his face. He couldn't speak. He was just holding her as she cried.

'How did you know what happened?' she said. 'I mean
. . . how did you get here so soon?'

Oh, God. What's wrong with him? What's wrong with his face?

'What is it?' said Ren. 'What's wrong?'

'Oh, Ren . . . Wait 'til we get inside—'

'No!' said Ren, 'No! What is it? Is it mom? Dad? Ethan?'

'I don't know how to tell you this . . .'

'What is it?' said Ren.

Matt gripped her arms, looked her in the eyes. 'Gary called
me a few days ago. He . . . was worried you weren't taking
your meds. He said you kept denying it. He was . . . at a
loss what to do.'

'He called you?' said Ren. 'A few days ago? Oh my God.'
*Was I that bad? 'Showing signs of mania'. But why are we talking
about this?*

'Not just me,' said Matt. 'He called Ben too. He flew in
yesterday afternoon – my flight was delayed. We were
supposed to meet Gary and you and Janine and Robbie in
the office.'

Oh, no. Oh, no. Please don't let this be what I think it is. 'So
. . . was . . . was that meeting yesterday . . . that was
supposed to be an intervention?' Ren put her hand to her
mouth then took it away to let the words tumble out. 'What
the fuck? Oh no. Oh my God.' She paused. 'Hold on . . .
where's Ben? If he flew in yesterday? I've been trying to get
hold of him all night.'

Matt, wonderful, sensitive, kind Matt, managed to answer,
despite his quivering mouth, and the tears now pouring
down his face. 'I'm so sorry, Ren. I'm so sorry . . . he was
in Safe Streets when Duke Rawlins arrived.'

'What? Ben?'

'He arrived early . . . he . . . he . . . was shot instantly.
He died, Ren. I'm so sorry.'

'No,' said Ren. 'Someone would have heard. I went in that way. I saw—'

'Rawlins used a silencer—'

'No!' said Ren. 'I was in that lobby. There was no one there apart from that poor realtor, Valerie. Just Valerie's body . . . on the floor . . . no one else. I swear to God—'

'He's gone, Ren,' said Matt. 'Ben's gone, sweetheart. I'm so sorry.'

'But . . .' *He can't be!* She stared at Matt. Her heart plunged. *Oh no – the basement . . . the basement door was banging. Oh my God. Is that where he put him? Threw him down into the basement? That's what he did with him?*

She studied Matt's face.

'He died instantly,' said Matt. 'It was a single gunshot. He didn't suffer.'

Ren pressed her hands to her mouth, her voice muffled as she cried. 'No . . . no . . . no.' Tears poured down her face, spilling over her hands. 'No.'

Not Ben. Not my gorgeous Ben who wouldn't hurt a fly.

This is not my life. This is not my life. This is not my life.

'No,' she said, collapsing into Matt's arms. 'No. No. No. No.'

This is all my fault.

This is all my fault.

ACKNOWLEDGEMENTS

Thank you to my agent, Marianne Gunn O'Connor, who brings light wherever she goes. Thanks also to Vicki Satlow, and to Pat Lynch.

To Sarah Hodgson, my talented editor and novel enhancement specialist, thank you so much for all your thorough and thoughtful work.

Many thanks to Kate Elton and the entire team at HarperCollins.

To Charlie Redmayne, thank you for your dedication to authors and the stories they have to tell.

Big thanks and congratulations to Kate Stephenson.

Thank you, Lucy Dauman, for your organisational talents.

Thank you to supreme copy-editor, Anne O'Brien.

Thank you to Tony Purdue for making things happen.

To Darley Anderson, special thanks for your support, wisdom, and friendship.

To SA Phil Niedringhaus, I always appreciate your swift, enlightening responses, and entertaining one-liners. Thank you, again.

To Cheryl Moore, Investigator with the Jefferson County District Attorney's Office, thank you once more for being so generous with your time and knowledge.

To Ger McDonnell, thank you for your kickstarting serial killer counsel.

Thank you to Anam Cara's Sue Booth-Forbes, who, with heart, dedication and energy, powers limitless creative dreams.

To my lawful sister Lanes of the extraordinary brain, thank you so much for always being there to listen, read, support, and crack me up.

Thank you, Ian Fahey – I couldn't have done it without you, buuuhd. Thank you, also, for playing *House of Cards; "I love this game!"*

To Dick Tobin, thank you for your considered reading, and plot inspiration.

To Donagh Wiseman, thank you for coming to my rescue and making this book Airborne.

To Aaron Byrne at The Web CTB, thank you for your speedy proofs processing.

Thank you and huge love to my family.

To my friends, thank you for being the best in the world.

And the award for Best Supporting Role in a Crime Drama goes to Paul Kelly.